I0564533

AUGMENTATION BAY

The Harvesting Chronicles

Book 1

∞

Sarah & Sherree

The Sisters of Scream

Augmentation Bay is a work of fiction. Characters, names, places, and events are either a product of the author's imagination, or if they are real, they are used in a fictional context. All activities, descriptions, and information contained in Augmentation Bay is for entertainment purposes only and should not be relied upon for accuracy or be replicated in any way.

All opinions are for fictional purposes only and are in no way representative of the authors personally.

Augmentation Bay or any portion may not be reproduced or used in any manner whatsoever without the express written permission of the authors except for the use of a brief quotation for the purpose of a book review.

Authors: Sarah & Sherree, The Sisters of Scream

First Published 2023
ISBN: 978-0-6457865-0-7

Cover Art: Painted Dragon Studios
Mapwork: The Art of Caleb Peregrine
Author/Editor: The Sisters of Scream
www.facebook.com/thesistersofscream
Copyright © The Sisters of Scream 2023
All rights reserved

CONTENT WARNING

This novel contains mature themes and intense scenes that may be distressing to some readers. Please be advised the following content is present:

- Graphic violence, including torture, beatings, dismemberment, and scenes of bodily mutilation.
- Medical horror involving non-consensual surgeries, forced organ harvesting, and graphic descriptions of transplants and dissection.
- Sexual content and references, including power-play dynamics, coercion, and scenes of intimacy under high-stress situations.
- Abuse and trauma, including verbal, physical, and psychological abuse from authority figures, as well as parental abuse.
- Depictions of mental distress, including hallucinations, dissociation, trauma responses, and suicidal ideation.
- Homophobia and slurs, including homophobic language used by abusive characters.
- Death of characters, including on-page deaths and executions.
- Institutional cruelty and systemic dehumanization.

This book is intended for mature audiences. Reader discretion is strongly advised.

Dedicated to anyone who's ever felt like giving up.

The climb to greatness is steep for a reason.
Some days, it will hurt.
Some days, it will feel endless.
But you might be closer than you think.
If you give up now,
you'll never know how far you've come—
or how far you could go.

Prologue

∞

During the year 2700, a plague spread, endangering humanity. People with O- blood died, and doctors couldn't determine why.

Thirty-seven percent of the world's population perished, and any child born with O- blood died within days. The plague continued terrorizing humanity for the next hundred years. Toward the end of the century, a leaked report exposed the United Nations as the ones behind the attack. The Earth was dying, and all attempts to find another planet capable of sustaining life had failed. They had decided that humanity itself had become a plague and needed to be culled.

However, the biological weapon they created failed, causing the epidemic known during the Age of Disdain. In the years that followed, doctors worked on a cure. They believed understanding the plague's genetics would make it easier—but they were wrong.

Researchers rushed the treatment. Although people born with O- blood stopped dying, most of the population's organs began failing.

Now, a new plague terrorizes humanity.

Most of the world fell back in line, doing as the government commanded. Citizens continued receiving fresh doses of the "cure"—a cure that caused more harm than healing. Parts of the world, however, refused to continue being poisoned. Under the guidance of a rogue politician, a large island in the Pacific Ocean was purchased, and a new society was formed.

Power consumed the politician, driving him mad. He began calling himself "The Shepherd" and claimed to be doing the true creator's work. Her name was Zoti. The large island community became *The Nation*—an advanced society stuck in the Middle Ages, ruled by The Shepherd's descendants and Cypher Industries.

Although the creator is a woman, women have almost no rights. There are only two recognized genders: male and female. At birth, our genders are branded on our wrists—triple moons for women and double moons for men.

Zoti created man and woman to bind and breed. If you refuse to follow these laws, you're taken away. Sometimes, you never come back. And if you do… it's not really you anymore.

When you're given the death sentence, you're auctioned off like cattle. The highest bidder gets your organs, and you die on the operating table. The wealthy survive, and the poor—hungry and desperate—resort to crime. When they're caught, authorities lock them away in Augmentation Bay. Most of the time, only their organs make it out. The high demand for organs means higher penalties for petty crimes. Even if someone goes in for five years, you're unlikely to ever see them again.

No one knows all the atrocities The Nation has committed, but I can tell you the ones I know.

And it begins in the year 3031, with Jaysen Elliot Masters.

PART ONE

CHAPTER ONE

Jaysen Elliot Masters

∞

The door to Limbo slammed shut behind Lucian, locking Jaysen in the dark once more. The heavy echo rang through the stone corridor like the toll of a bell announcing a death sentence.

Jaysen watched Lucian's silhouette vanish into the flickering shadows. His gait was sharp and quick, a slight limp in his left step. Even that seemed rehearsed—controlled.

Would I really kill Kaylus if I had the chance? The question echoed in Jaysen's mind. He'd said it out loud. To Lucian. Which meant soon, The Nation would read it.

Maybe it doesn't matter anymore. Izzy's safe. She's home—with Mother and Father.

That was all that counted.

Time twisted around him in Limbo. Minutes bled into hours. The only thing certain was that he wouldn't be seeing the courtroom—not after what he'd done to Kaylus. The Enforcers said it was "in the Court's best interest" to keep him caged like a rabid dog.

"He's a ticking time bomb," they whispered.

They weren't wrong.

The lights overhead buzzed, barely hanging on to life. Thin bulbs suspended from the arched ceiling flickered weakly, casting shivering pools of cold light that barely touched the wet stone floor. The air stank of mildew and rusted chains. The scent soaked into his skin.

This place was wrong—too quiet, too still. Like a predator's den.

Jaysen sat in the dark, bound and waiting.

No tech. No comfort. No way to tell if it was day or night. Just the echo of water dripping and the ticking of an ancient clock mounted like a trophy above the corridor. He couldn't look away from it. Couldn't ignore the way each tick hit his skull like a hammer.

"Three seventy-six," he muttered, counting the minutes since Lucian had left.

I wonder when an Enforcer will come and take me.

Jaysen had learned to recognize them by color.

Not just the armor—but what it meant.

Back in the Blacklight District, before the arrest, it was the metallic purple that flashed through the haze of neon. The Blacklight District Patrol. Quick to crack down, but just as quick to vanish. They didn't bother with words. They had stun-rods—and a quota to fill.

Then, there was Midnight Blue.

City Patrol.

Brutal. Unforgiving. Their boots hit harder than their fists, and their fists hit like sledgehammers. They didn't need reasons. They were the reason.

Now, in Augmentation Bay, the colors had changed.

The Argentine Enforcers were everywhere here—gray and dull, their armor scratched and tired-looking. No need for polish in a place like this. Their silence spoke louder than sirens. They didn't run. They didn't shout. They just watched. And waited.

Every now and then, Jaysen caught a glimpse of black. The rookies. The Black Enforcers were still in training, still unassigned, drifting between factions like ghosts. It made them unpredictable—hungry for approval, desperate to prove themselves.

Worse than seasoned killers were the ones trying to earn their stripes.

He'd only ever seen the green ones once— A flash of Emerald on the screen during a rare newsfeed. Feltwood Mountain Patrol. Survivors said they were quiet. Efficient. The kind who made you vanish before you even knew they were near.

And then there were the golden ones.

The Shepherd's Guard.

They moved differently. Precise. Untouchable. Like they knew the rules didn't apply to them because they were the rules.

Crimson Red was harder to forget.

They didn't just march. They thundered. The Army, the Air Force, the Navy—everything rolled into one machine. When they moved, the ground shook. When they stopped, it was to destroy something.

And above them all, as if conjured from a different world entirely, were the Pearls.

Generals.

Their armor shimmered like light trapped beneath water. Soft. Beautiful. Terrifying. Everyone answered to them. Even the Golden. Even the Crimson. The Pearls didn't yell. They didn't need to.

One glance, and the others snapped into place.

Jaysen had only seen one up close. Once. They didn't speak. But their eyes locked onto his, and in that moment, he'd felt smaller than he ever had before.

The hierarchy was clear. It had always been clear.

Color-coded.

Enforced.

And inescapable.

Footsteps.

Not soft. Not rushed.

Deliberate.

Jaysen's pulse quickened as the figure emerged—armor, glinting. It wasn't the gray of an Argentine Enforcer.

It was pearl.

His breath caught.

The Enforcer said nothing. Didn't need to. The door to Jaysen's cell creaked open. Cold metal shrieked across stone.

Move.

Jaysen obeyed, rising slowly. The chains around his wrists clanked, tight and short—designed to keep him crawling if he tried to run. The shackles around his ankles were thick enough to break bone with a wrong step.

He moved as fast as he could. Which wasn't fast at all.

The stone floor was uneven, every step a gamble. He misjudged one and caught his foot on a jagged lip. The chain snapped taut. Jaysen's body pitched forward—arms trapped, unable to break his fall.

He hit the ground, face-first.

A white-hot burst of pain erupted across his face. The taste of blood hit his tongue—sharp, metallic, and hot. He could smell it too. Thick and coppery, mingling with the scent of moss and mold.

A hand seized the back of his shirt—lifting him with unexpected ease. Not cruel. Not kind. Just efficient. Like a mother wolf lifting her pup by the scruff—silent, instinctual.

Still dazed, Jaysen staggered forward, his feet dragging, the pain in his face pulsing in time with the lights that flickered above.

Something was torn open. He could feel it, but he couldn't see the damage. Not yet. There were no reflective surfaces in this dungeon—not even glass. Not unless you counted blood.

They walked for what felt like hours. The corridor grew narrower, darker. The smell of bleach fought with the rot. A lost battle.

The Harvesting, Jaysen thought. *That's where I'm going. Why else send a Pearl?*

The corridor opened into a room that chilled him to his bones.

The Warden's office.

He didn't need to be told to sit. He felt the firm pressure of the Enforcer's hand guiding him into the chair—cold fingers like iron clamps.

The Warden arrived a moment later, his boots clicking methodically as he crossed the room. He sat behind a steel desk, every movement rigid, mechanical. The fluorescent light buzzed overhead like a dying insect trapped in a jar.

The Warden didn't look up as he flipped open Jaysen's file. His face was a roadmap of old scars. The skin around them was stretched tight like parchment, sweat already beading along his forehead.

"Jaysen Elliot Masters," he muttered, more to the paper than to the man sitting across from him. "Charged with grievous bodily harm with intent. Extortion. Blackmail."

Tick.

Tick.

"The evidence is overwhelming. Multiple matching statements. You forfeit your right to a lawyer. No appeal."

Jaysen's throat closed. His pulse thudded louder than the ticking of The Warden's clock.

"You will serve thirty years in Augmentation Bay. No parole. The Pearl Enforcer will take you for processing. Any misconduct will extend your sentence." Finally, he looked up. His eyes were as dry as his voice. "Do your time, Mr. Masters, and we won't have any problems."

The Enforcer didn't speak. But the Warden caught the blood still trickling from Jaysen's face.

"Get that shit patched up. We can't have him dying before we run the tests."

The chair scraped against the floor as the Enforcer hauled Jaysen to his feet once more.

This time it didn't feel like a wolf rescuing its pup.

It felt like being removed from the litter altogether.

Discarded.

Unwanted.

The walk to the infirmary was a silent, grim procession.

The Pearl Enforcer's grip was firm—unyielding, but controlled. Not a word passed between them, only the echo of their footsteps, distorted by the damp corridor walls. Every so often, Jaysen's blood would drip from his face to the stone floor with a wet *plip*, like a countdown to something far worse.

The corridor bent into a shadow-drenched hallway lined with steel doors that hummed with old electricity and older secrets. At the end waited a single light—flickering, jaundiced. Beneath it, a door creaked open on its own, like it had been waiting for them.

The infirmary.

If Augmentation Bay was a prison, this room was the autopsy lab.

It was cold and smelled like antiseptic and fear. The kind of cold that sank past your skin, rooting itself in your bones. A rusted dental chair sat in the middle, surrounded by ancient medical trays, hospital beds, and empty vials with yellowed labels. A nurse—older, frazzled—jumped to her feet when she saw Jaysen.

Her eyes darted to the wound on his face. "You've got to be kidding me," she muttered, already moving toward the cabinets. "They said it was just evaluation and processing…"

She opened drawers, grabbed gauze, and slammed instruments onto a tray. The sound was loud in the quiet.

Jaysen's eyes stung. Blood was leaking into them again, thickening in the corners. He blinked it away, trying to focus. A cracked window in the door behind them caught his gaze. The reflection was warped, smeared—but enough.

He froze.

The face staring back at him was unrecognizable. His sandy-blonde hair was matted with dried blood. Fresh red pouring from a gash that ran from his brow, across the bridge of his nose, and down to the cheekbone. A brutal, raw diagonal. Like someone had tried to carve him open.

Another scar to add to the tally. But this one… this one would speak louder than the others.

Before he could process it, the Enforcer moved. They gripped him again and forced him down into the dental chair. The leather cracked under his weight. Straps hung loose on either side, used too often and never cleaned.

The nurse approached, wiping his face with cold antiseptic. The sting jolted through him.

"The adrenaline's wearing off, I see," she said quietly.

Jaysen didn't respond.

She pulled out a cloudy jar filled with a clear liquid. Dipped a thick-tipped syringe into it and drew the numbing agent. Jaysen's eyes widened when she angled the needle toward his face.

He flinched.

"To numb it," she explained. "You'll want it. Trust me."

He forced himself to stay still. The needle slid into his brow. A white-hot jolt of pain. His whole body tensed, hands gripping the arms of the chair until his knuckles ached.

Seconds later, the numbness set in. Cold, strange, not quite relief.

She began stitching.

Pop… pop… pop…

The sound of the hooked needle piercing his skin reminded him of the Warden's ticking clock. Precise. Unforgiving. Like his flesh was a piece of cloth being sewn shut.

Pop… pop… pop…

Thirty-two stitches.

By the time she finished, his pulse was erratic, his vision fuzzy. Blood loss. Shock. Maybe both. The nurse turned to the tray—three oversized needles gleamed under the sickly light.

Jaysen's stomach turned.

"Time for testing," she muttered, more to herself than anyone else.

She held each syringe with care, then plunged them into his arm, drawing vial after vial of blood. By the time the third one was filled, Jaysen's head lolled slightly. His breath shallow.

"Not yet," the nurse snapped.

She spun toward a cupboard and returned with a tall glass of cloudy yellow liquid. "Drink. All of it."

Jaysen hesitated. It looked like someone had scooped up runoff water from a gutter.

He brought it to his lips. The texture hit first—grainy, thick. The taste was worse. Like salt and metal and something sour, spoiled.

He gagged, nearly spit it out.

"Finish it," the nurse said. "It'll help you heal. And keep you conscious."

It took every ounce of willpower. He forced it down, sip by choking sip. The Enforcer stood unmoving, looming in the corner like a statue carved from steel and silence.

When the glass was empty, Jaysen felt it—an unnatural warmth spreading through his limbs. Not comforting. Just… *wrong*. Too fast. Too strong.

"Vitality Serum," he murmured under his breath.

He'd heard of it. Rumors. Whispers. A drug that revived the half-dead. Made the body feel better while the soul screamed underneath.

The nurse whispered to the Enforcer then, a voice barely audible over the buzz of the lights. "The media are outside. He's already bruised to hell. If he faints during transfer, they'll crucify us."

The Enforcer responded with a grunt—barely human. They moved forward, took Jaysen by the shoulder, and hauled him up again.

Back into the corridor.

He stumbled with every step, the serum surging through his system like wildfire. His wound throbbed with ghost-pain. His ears rang. The air felt thinner than before.

Then—

Flash.

Voices.

The door opened to the outside, and blinding light swallowed him whole.

Reporters shouted. Cameras flared. Jaysen squinted through the chaos, but every pop of a lens was a hammer to his skull. The Pearl Enforcer's grip tightened, dragging him forward.

They passed through the crowd in seconds, but it felt like hours.

The doors of the next building slammed shut behind them, sealing away the light—and the noise.

And just like that, the silence returned.

The corridor was darker than before. The lights above barely worked. The only sound was Jaysen's breath and the familiar dragging of the chain at his feet.

At the end of the hall, a heavy door loomed.

A message engraved into the metal glinted in the half-light.

The door loomed like a mouth ready to swallow him whole.

THE AVIARY was engraved across the top in cold, jagged lettering. The Pearl Enforcer said nothing. Just reached forward and shoved it open.

The sound—metal on metal—screeched like a beast in pain.

The stench hit him first.

Rot. Sweat. Desperation.

Jaysen's eyes adjusted slowly. Rows of cages stretched into the dark, stacked floor upon floor—twenty, maybe more. Thin metal walkways lined the tiers, with narrow staircases at either end. Each staircase was caged in, guarded by Argentine Enforcers—some with hounds, all with guns.

The noise came next.

Screaming.

Laughter.

Howling.

Voices from every direction, layered on top of each other until it was impossible to tell if they were human.

"Fresh meat," someone whispered.

"Fresh meat!" someone else screamed.

And then they all joined in.

"Fresh meat! Fresh meat! FRESH MEAT!"

Jaysen's pulse thundered.

The Pearl Enforcer shoved his head and shoulders down, forcing him into a bent position—his body locked at a ninety-degree angle. Their grip was tight, holding the chain around his waist with practiced strength.

He had no choice but to walk, crouched, humiliated, and bleeding through his stitches.

The pain screamed with each step. Blood dripped onto the cold stone floor—steady, rhythmic. Drip… drip… drip…

A crimson breadcrumb trail marking his arrival.

The cageys screamed louder.

He didn't look up. Couldn't. But he could feel them. Eyes. Teeth. Fingers gripping bars. Breaths rattling through rusted metal. This wasn't just prison.

This was a feeding ground.

The cages blurred together, one after another, until they stopped at a cell halfway up the row. The Pearl Enforcer unlocked the door with a clang that split the air. It swung open like the maw of a predator.

Without a word, they shoved Jaysen inside.

He hit the floor hard—knees slamming against cold, uneven concrete. He barely caught himself.

Not long now. Just stay upright. Just hold on…

The Enforcer yanked off his shackles.

Then they leaned in.

Their helmet was inches from his face—the strange gas mask hiding their identity, but amplifying their voice into a low, distorted growl.

"Keep your head down and your hands behind your back. Don't move until the door closes. If you move… I shoot."

Jaysen froze. The tone wasn't angry. It was worse—it was *certain*. Like they'd done it before. Like they'd enjoy doing it again.

He dropped his head.

He counted the seconds.

One.

Two.

Three.

SCREECH. THUD.

The cage door slammed shut behind him.

He waited—just a little longer—until the screaming outside the cage shifted. They were taunting someone else now.

Jaysen lifted his head and looked around.

The cell was barely wide enough for two beds, placed parallel with a rusted desk and bolted chair in between. The shelf above them held a few warped books coated in dust. To the right, near the cage door, was a sink and toilet—if you could call it that. The "toilet" looked more like a chamber pot with a drain. The faucet barely dripped, rust caked around the tap.

He rose to his feet slowly, stretching until his hand scraped the ceiling. The air was damp. Heavy. There was no breeze. No circulation. Just heat and stench and decay.

Jaysen turned to the bed on the left and collapsed onto it. His whole body ached. The mattress was thin, lumpy, and barely there—but it might as well have been a cloud.

He placed his hands over his ears, trying to drown out the chanting.

But the cageys didn't stop.

And neither did the noises in his head.

The tick of the Warden's clock.

The pop of the needle tearing through his skin.

The drip of blood on the floor.

Tick. Pop. Drip. Tick. Pop. Drip.

"Hell of a view, isn't it?"

The voice cut through the static in his mind.

Jaysen jolted upright, heart leaping into his throat.

He hadn't seen anyone.

But now—he did.

On the other bed, a man sat propped up, holding a battered book in one hand and cracked reading glasses in the other. His face was lined with age, but not weakened. His beard was streaked with silver, hiding a scar that peeked out just above his lip.

"Relax," the man said. "If I was going to kill you, I'd have done it before you got comfortable."

Jaysen's shoulders dropped a little. "Didn't see you."

"Most don't. Connor." He extended a hand, weathered and calloused.

"Jaysen," he replied, shaking it. It felt like shaking sandpaper wrapped around steel.

Connor leaned back. "Don't mind the noise. The screaming stops after the first day—*if* you don't react. But show them it gets to you…" He ran a finger along the scar hiding beneath his beard. "It only gets worse."

Jaysen nodded, swallowing hard.

He sat back down, every part of his body still on edge.

Connor stretched out and gave him a half-smile. "You'll pick up little tricks. Everyone does. Just don't die before you learn them."

Jaysen shifted on the bed, trying to find a position that didn't feel like lying on a slab of scrap metal. The mattress offered no comfort—thin, uneven, probably older than he was. His entire body felt like it was stitched together with pain.

He tried not to think about how long thirty years would feel in this place.

"How long've you been caged?" he asked, voice quiet.

Connor didn't look up from his book. "I'm a lifer."

Jaysen blinked. "No chance of getting out?"

Connor closed the book, setting it beside him. "Had a five-year sentence. That was twenty years ago."

"What happened?"

"They keep adding time. Petty infractions. Talking back. Contraband. Insubordination," he said with a bitter smile. "One day, you blink and realize they've stacked life on top of life. I'm only still here because I got lucky."

"Lucky?" Jaysen asked, not understanding.

"Didn't end up at The Harvesting. Yet."

The name chilled him.

Before he could ask more, a low grinding noise groaned through the Aviary. The screaming quieted almost immediately. The cageys above started chanting.

"Drop the covers! Drop the covers!"

Jaysen's brow furrowed. "What's happening?"

Connor sat up and nodded toward the ceiling. "Lights out. Get ready."

Thick, black fabric began to lower from the ceiling—heavy velvet curtains dropping tier by tier, layer by layer. As they descended, the overhead bulbs vanished one by one. The shadows deepened. The air grew still.

Jaysen stood, watching the light vanish like it was being swallowed whole.

The darkness was too much. Too complete. The covers sealed off everything—sound, sight, even breath.

"Connor," Jaysen whispered, tension creeping into his voice. "Does it always get this dark?"

Connor didn't answer.

Jaysen turned—and jumped.

Connor was lying back on his bed, already blended into the shadows. Eyes open, watching the ceiling like it might fall on them.

"You get used to it," Connor said finally, his voice low and far away. "Eventually."

The last layer of curtain dropped.

Blackness devoured the cage.

Jaysen felt it immediately. The pressure. The void. A blanket of silence thick enough to choke on.

His ears rang.

His thoughts raced.

He couldn't tell where he was in space anymore—like his body had dissolved into the dark.

Panic bloomed.

What if I'm still bleeding? What if I pass out? What if I disappear in here and no one even notices?

Tick. Pop. Drip. Tick. Pop. Drip.

He curled into himself, squeezing his eyes shut.

"Mate," Connor said softly. "You're not gonna drown in it. Breathe."

Jaysen focused on his voice. Let it tether him. Ground him.

He's here. I'm here. I'm not alone. Not yet.

He stretched back out.

Eventually, the silence didn't feel quite so loud. The panic settled into something else—heavier. Numb.

Sleep didn't come easy. But eventually, it came.

∞

A loud grinding noise split through the black.

Jaysen jolted upright, heart pounding, blinking through sticky eyes. The curtains were rising—light bleeding through the gaps. He squinted toward the upper tiers.

His pillow was stiff—dried blood soaking through the fabric. Both his own and Kaylus'.

The sting on his face came rushing back.

Connor was already sitting up, calm as ever. "Sleep well?"

"Define 'well,'" Jaysen rasped.

Connor chuckled. "Shower's soon. Don't enjoy it too much."

Jaysen smiled. "We get showers?"

"Kind of."

He followed Connor's gaze across the tiers. Men stood in their cages, stripping down without shame. Steam began to rise. Hoses were being dragged through by the Argentine Enforcers.

Connor pulled off his shirt. "Don't be shy, mate. We all get to know each other... real quick."

Jaysen hesitated, then stripped. His clothes were stiff with blood and sweat. He laid them on the bed.

Connor pulled a plastic sheet from beneath his mattress and covered his own clothes.

"Keep 'em dry," he said. "It's the only pair you've got."

"I'd cover your eyes!" Connor shouted.

Then. Soapy water.

Jaysen barely had time to react before it slammed into him. He staggered, shielding his face. The force felt like it could peel skin.

The second spray came—hot water this time. Scalding. Cleansing.

Jaysen exhaled. The steam wrapped around him like a ghost. For a moment, it felt like he was somewhere else. Somewhere safer.

And then it ended.

Abrupt.

The air turned cold again, and they stood dripping in silence.

A new Enforcer walked past their cage with a hose the size of a cannon.

Connor nodded. "Dryer."

Jaysen braced himself.

A rush of heated air blasted them, spinning their damp hair, drying them in seconds. Then, silence.

Connor walked over and pulled the plastic off his bed. "Told you. It's not much, but it's regular. Only thing in here that is."

Jaysen turned to his clothes—still soaked in dried blood.

Before he could grab them, Connor tossed him a clean shirt and trousers. "Can't have you walking around looking like fresh kill."

Jaysen blinked, holding the folded clothes like they might vanish. "Thanks."

"You'll owe me some dacks though," Connor said with a wink.

"Deal."

He pulled on the clothes. They smelled vaguely of rust and vinegar, but they were clean. Mostly.

"Why are you helping me?" Jaysen asked, still adjusting his shirt.

Connor shrugged. "We're cageys, mate. Roomies. Unless you die, or I die, or one of us gets harvested… we're in this together."

Jaysen was still toweling his face with a piece of his old trousers when the noise started—shouts, alarms, barking. The kind of chaos that has a rhythm to it. The kind you feel in your ribs before you understand what's happening.

Connor froze mid-motion, eyes snapping toward the top tiers.

"What's going on?" Jaysen asked.

Connor didn't answer.

The cageys above were yelling—words Jaysen couldn't make out at first. Then came a crackle of static from a radio.

"Suspect is traversing the cage roofs. Permission to fire?"

Gunshots followed. Sharp. Echoing. Merciless.

And then—

"THE HARVESTING WON'T TAKE ME!"

A voice from above. Raw and wild. Like it had ripped itself from the man's throat on its way out.

Another shot rang out.

"YOU'LL HAVE TO BE QUICKER THAN THAT! GOOD LUCK GETTING MY ORGANS NOW!"

Jaysen's blood ran cold.

The cageys below began chanting.

"JUMP! JUMP! JUMP!"

Jaysen pushed his face to the bars, craning his neck. At the very top—fifteen stories up—a figure darted across the metal rafters, shackles rattling. The man was barefoot, shirtless, barely more than a shadow against the light.

And then he jumped.

Jaysen saw the whole thing.

The man didn't flinch. Didn't hesitate.

He soared for a second—weightless.

Then hit the concrete.

THUD.

A sickening crack echoed through The Aviary.

Jaysen flinched, stumbling back, hand to his mouth.

The man's body twisted unnaturally, limbs bent the wrong way. Blood pooled quickly, seeping into the cracks of the floor.

"Shit," Connor muttered. He leaned against the bars, jaw tight. "Another one."

Jaysen couldn't look away. "Why did he do it?"

Connor didn't answer right away. He stared down at the mess of bone and blood. "Some of them would rather die on their terms than be harvested like livestock."

The Enforcers moved in, silent and methodical. They rolled the body onto a stretcher, but it was too late. The organs were ruined. The product was spoiled.

One of the Enforcers cursed and spat near the body.

Jaysen whispered, more to himself than to Connor, "I hope I don't end up like that…"

Connor looked over at him and sighed. "Then don't give them a reason to add more time."

The blood trail stretched across the floor as they dragged the man away. Even after the body was gone, the silence in The Aviary lingered. The cageys had stopped chanting.

No one cheered.

No one laughed.

Just the quiet hum of desperation settling back in like it never left.

The blood was still wet on the concrete.

Even as the Enforcers dragged the body away, Jaysen couldn't look away from the stain it left behind. Something about it clung to him. Not just the sight—but the *feeling*.

Then came the ringing.

A high, thin hum in his ears, like the air itself was holding its breath.

And in that moment, his mind… slipped.

He was somewhere else.

The mountain air was thin and cold.

He stood at the edge of a clearing in front of a small cottage—weather-worn, the roof sagging under snow. The trees loomed like sentinels, their branches stripped bare.

And hanging from the wooden beams of the porch…

Two figures.

Side by side.

Their faces were lost in shadow, necks stretched unnaturally. Rope creaked softly in the wind. There were no birds. No movement. Just silence—and that awful, suffocating stillness.

Jaysen took a step forward.

Snow crunched beneath his feet. Or maybe it wasn't snow. Maybe it was ash.

He tried to see their faces.

He *needed* to see their faces.

But the harder he stared, the more they blurred. Like smudged ink on wet paper. Familiar. Foreign. Gone.

And then—

"Jaysen."

Connor's voice snapped him back.

The Aviary returned in full force. The blood. The sweat. The cage bars pressing cold against his back.

Jaysen blinked.

The image of the cottage lingered at the edge of his vision like smoke.

He couldn't place it.

Didn't know when or where.

But something about the memory clawed at his gut.

The rope.

The silence.

The knowing.

Someone he'd lost? Or someone he hadn't met yet?

Jaysen shivered, suddenly colder than he had been all day.

Connor watched him carefully but said nothing.

The quiet between them stretched. Heavy. Haunted.

The body was gone.

The floor had been mopped, the blood smeared into cloudy pink streaks.

Like it could ever really be erased.

The Aviary quieted again.

The cageys retreated back into their shadows. The chanting stopped. The madness fell still—but not silent. Not really.

Jaysen sat on the edge of his bed, eyes unfocused. The flickering lights above buzzed in his ears, like a distant swarm that never landed.

Connor sat opposite him, elbows on knees, staring at the same stained floor.

For a while, neither of them spoke.

Then—Connor sighed. Not a dramatic one. A tired one. Like a breath he'd been holding too long.

"I was about your age when I first stepped into this place," he said.

Jaysen looked up, surprised. Connor's voice was softer than usual. Not casual. Not joking.

"I didn't think you could survive here and still sound like a person," Jaysen muttered.

Connor smiled faintly, but it didn't reach his eyes.

"Sometimes, you have to remember who you were. Even if it hurts."

He leaned back against the wall. Let his head rest there for a moment.

"And *I* was an Iron Hunter. Not a good one, but good enough to stay alive. My little brother, Sammy—he was all I had left after our parents passed. He was sick. Something rare. We couldn't afford treatment. Could barely afford to eat."

He paused. Let the silence settle again, like dust on an old story.

"I started stealing scraps from the edge of Feiron's claim. Tiny pieces of raw iron. Nothing anyone would miss. At least, that's what I told myself. Sold them for medicine. Just enough to keep Sammy breathing. And he started getting better."

Connor's eyes dimmed, his voice dropping lower.

"But I got greedy. Sloppy. Thought I could get away with more. Thought I had time."

A bitter laugh escaped his throat.

"They caught me coming back from a run. Dragged me in. Straight to Limbo. I never even made it home. Never got to say goodbye."

Another pause.

A colder one.

"I don't know what happened to him. Whether he thought I abandoned him. Whether he lived another week. Whether he died waiting at the window."

The silence wasn't awkward. It was *held*. Like a breath no one wanted to release.

Jaysen swallowed, his voice hoarse. "I'm sorry."

Connor waved it off. "No pity in here. It's just the way things went. I got five years for petty theft. Now I'm here for life."

He turned to Jaysen finally. Eyes tired, but steady.

"You asked why I'm helping you," he said. "It's not charity. I couldn't protect my brother. Maybe if I help you figure this place out, you won't end up like I did."

Jaysen nodded, the weight of Connor's story settling in his bones.

He didn't ask more about Sammy.

He didn't have to.

Some pain was shared simply by surviving.

CHAPTER

TWO

The Eyes Beyond The Cage

∞

The first rule of the Big Cage was simple:

Don't look lost.

Even if you are.

Especially if you are.

The Pearl Enforcer didn't speak as they led Jaysen and Connor through a rusted side door beneath the Aviary. Jaysen walked in silence, his body still sore, every step a reminder of the last twenty-four hours. His wrists itched where the shackles had rubbed raw.

Connor moved ahead, posture relaxed but alert. Like someone who knew exactly how far he could push the walls around him without getting crushed.

The corridor was different down here. Wider. Older. The lights flickered less frequently—not because they worked better, but because half of them had burned out completely. The ones that still glowed cast long, skeletal shadows across the walls.

At the end of the hall: a gate.

Tall. Reinforced. Streaked in rust that looked like dried blood.

The Pearl Enforcer unlocked it without a word.

As it groaned open, the smell hit Jaysen first—body odor, rot, cheap disinfectant. Underneath it all, the copper tang of blood.

Then came the sound.

Voices. Dozens of them. Maybe hundreds. Shouting. Laughing. Barking like animals. The clang of metal. The snap of bone.

Jaysen flinched as the door shut behind them.

This wasn't a holding space. It wasn't a cage.

This was *an ecosystem*—twisted and violent and alive.

The Big Cage.

It was one massive chamber, no divisions, no cells—just open space packed with the worst of what Augmentation Bay had to offer. Factions. Packs. Territory. Corners marked with piss and blood. The ground was cracked in places, stained in others. There was no privacy, no softness. Just concrete, sweat, and hunger.

And in the middle of it all, like a feeding trough dropped in the center of a kennel, was a long rusted rail lined with cracked bowls

"Trail mix. Lucky you." Connor said wryly.

"Trail mix?" Jaysen asked, confused.

But Connor was already walking.

Jaysen followed, careful not to make eye contact with anyone. He could feel them watching—eyes tracking his every step, waiting for a stumble.

They reached the trough.

An Argentine Enforcer stood at one end, scooping from a long metal rail filled with dried oats, hard nuts, and what might have once been fruit—shriveled bits of red and brown that stuck to the sides like old gum. It wasn't warm. Wasn't seasoned. Just dry, flavorless fuel.

Trail mix.

If you could call it that.

Jaysen watched as others stepped forward, scooping portions out with their bare hands, cupping it like treasure, and sliding it into their pockets. No bowls. No utensils. Just fingers and cloth and hunger.

Connor followed suit, collecting his ration.

"Keep it dry," he muttered. "Eat small. Store the rest."

Jaysen mimicked him, reaching into the trough. The oats scratched at his palm. The fruit was tacky. He stuffed the mix into his pants pocket and stepped back.

His stomach growled.

But instinct told him not to eat yet.

Not here.

Not with everyone watching.

Jaysen filled his pockets and followed Connor to a cracked bench near the cage wall. The concrete beneath them was stained and scored with carvings—names, warnings, final thoughts. He sat carefully, one hand still guarding the oats and nuts in his pocket.

"I'm understanding all these references to birds now," he muttered, eyeing the cage bars above.

Connor gave a dry smile. "The irony."

"The irony," Jaysen echoed, more to himself.

They ate in silence—pinching bits of dried fruit and oats, chewing slowly like they were still learning how.

A shadow passed near them.

Then, without a sound, someone sat on Connor's other side.

"Connor, son."

The voice was low and worn like river stone. Jaysen turned.

The man beside them was older—sixty, maybe older—but stood with the kind of quiet confidence that didn't come from strength. His silver hair was neatly pulled back, and his beard matched, trimmed clean. There were deep lines around his eyes, but they belonged to someone who smiled often. Or used to.

Jaysen didn't feel threatened.

He felt… steadied.

Connor sat up straighter. "Charlie."

Charlie nodded once, then turned to Jaysen. "You're the new one."

"Yes, sir," Jaysen said.

Charlie raised a silver brow and gave a soft laugh. "You're very polite. I like that about you already."

He reached out his hand.

Jaysen shook it. "Jaysen."

Charlie gave a gentle nod. "Good to meet you, son."

His gaze lingered for a beat—curious, but not invasive. He looked at Jaysen the way someone looks at a sealed box they already suspect holds something heavy.

"You've still got that look," Charlie said. "Like your body's here, but your head's still catching up."

Jaysen didn't answer.

"That's all right," Charlie went on. "Everyone wears that face their first few days. Some never take it off."

He pulled a small handful of trail mix from his coat pocket and ate slowly, savoring each bite. His hands were steady, worn, familiar with waiting.

"Most cageys panic their first time down here," he said. "Eat too fast. Talk too much. Pick a fight. Doesn't end well."

"I'm just watching," Jaysen said. "Trying to learn."

Charlie nodded. "Good instincts. This place doesn't reward bravery. It rewards quiet."

Connor added, "Charlie's been here longer than most of the walls."

Charlie chuckled. "And most of the rats, too."

He glanced around the Big Cage—not with paranoia, but with practiced awareness. He didn't scan for danger. He noticed it before it asked to be seen.

"You stick close to Connor," Charlie said. "He's got sense. Doesn't spend it where it won't matter."

He reached into his coat and pulled a small silver flask. Unscrewed the top. Took a long, thoughtful sip.

Then handed it to Connor.

Connor took a drink and passed it to Jaysen without a word.

Jaysen hesitated, then drank. The burn hit quick—sharp and bitter—but left behind a warmth that curled like smoke in his chest.

Charlie watched him. "Careful, son. That warmth'll lie to you."

Jaysen nodded, coughing once as he handed it back.

Charlie capped the flask and tucked it into his coat.

"Keep your food close. Keep your words closer. And don't meet eyes unless you mean it."

A silence settled between the three of them—not awkward, but heavy. Weighted by the place, the rules, the cost of staying alive.

Charlie broke it gently.

"So, son… what'd they put you in for?"

Jaysen hesitated.

Connor didn't press. Just waited.

Jaysen looked down at the trail mix in his hand. Rolled a piece of dried fruit between his fingers before he spoke.

"I beat someone half to death."

Charlie raised a brow but said nothing.

Jaysen went on, voice low. "It was the Governor's son. He tried to force himself on my little sister."

A pause.

"I didn't think. I just… did what I had to do."

Charlie nodded slowly, like he was adding up all the pieces of a story he already half-knew.

Connor let out a quiet breath. "And they sent you here for that?"

"Grievous bodily harm. Extortion. Blackmail." Jaysen shook his head. "They stacked the charges. Said I threatened the family or something. No lawyer. No appeal. Straight to Augmentation Bay."

Charlie leaned forward, elbows on his knees. His voice was calm, but steady. "You did the right thing, son."

Jaysen looked up.

"Izzy," he said softly. "My sister. She's safe now. That's what matters."

Charlie nodded. "It is. Don't ever forget it."

Jaysen tucked the trail mix back into his pocket. His hands were shaking, but only a little.

Connor clapped him once, lightly on the shoulder. "Well," he said, "you're in the right place for people who did the right thing at the wrong time."

Charlie smiled faintly. "Happens more than you'd think in here."

They sat together for a moment longer, the noise of the Big Cage humming around them like distant thunder—close enough to remind them where they were, but not close enough to touch.

Not yet.

Connor glanced at Jaysen, studying the split flesh along his brow, the bruises still blooming purple down one cheek.

"That how you got the wound?" he asked. "The fight with the Governor's son?"

Jaysen shook his head. "No. That came later."

He flexed his jaw, wincing slightly.

"I tripped. Chained up. Hit the floor face-first on the way to processing."

Charlie made a quiet sound—not quite a laugh, not quite sympathy. "This place takes its piece early."

Jaysen nodded. "Pearl Enforcer didn't even flinch. Just dragged me off again."

Connor's jaw tightened. "Sounds about right."

Charlie leaned forward slightly, resting his arms on his knees. "They don't see us, son. Just product moving down the line."

The lull didn't last long.

The subtle rhythm of the Big Cage—the murmur of voices, the crunch of footsteps—was disrupted by a deep mechanical groan.

Gates.

Heavy ones.

Jaysen looked toward the far end of the chamber where a set of reinforced doors—twice the size of the ones they'd entered through—were grinding open.

Connor shifted on the bench beside him. His posture stiffened.

"What is it?" Jaysen asked.

Charlie stood. "Top-level cageys," he said, voice quieter than before. "Don't move. Don't stare."

Jaysen followed their gaze as they came into view.

There were fifty of them—maybe more—all chained together at the wrists and ankles with thick industrial cuffs, linked by a central tether that snaked through their restraints like a steel spine.

They moved in perfect sync, their steps controlled by the chain—small, dragging, barely enough room to lift their feet. Their uniforms were darker than the others, stained with something more than time. Their hair was long, matted. Skin like paper. Eyes wild.

They weren't silent.

Some growled under their breath. Others laughed—quiet, breathy laughter like they were hearing something no one else could. One man chewed his own shoulder until a Pearl Enforcer slammed a fist against his helmet with a sharp *clang*, bringing him back in line.

"They look like they're barely human," Jaysen muttered.

"They are," Connor said. *"Barely."*

Each cagey was flanked by Enforcers—four Argentine, two Pearl—surrounding the chain like armor-clad wolves herding rabid dogs. The Enforcers never spoke. Never broke rhythm. Their armor was ghost-white, their visors blank and lightless.

Their eyes couldn't be seen—only the reflection of what they were willing to destroy.

"They get thirty minutes," Charlie said. "No more."

"Why are they chained?" Jaysen asked.

Connor kept his voice low. "To remind them what happens if they step out of line."

The procession moved through the cage, the chain clinking with each step. Conversations died as they passed. Cageys turned away. No one made a sound.

They were led to the troughs.

There was still food.

Not much—but *enough*.

The lower levels had made sure of it. A few handfuls of oats, some dried fruit, a scattering of nuts—just enough to keep the top-levels from going feral. Not generosity. Just strategy.

"They leave that on purpose," Connor said, watching the line. "So they don't riot."

One by one, the top-level cageys were unshackled and allowed to sit or kneel beside the troughs. Fingers twitching, they dug into the leftovers. Some crammed food into their mouths like animals. Others sniffed the fruit first, laughing at some private joke. One just held a piece in his palm, staring at it like it spoke.

Then one of them muttered.

Low and guttural. Directed at no one.

"Burned my sister for less," he said, giggling.

The cagey next to him nodded. "I burned three."

Neither of them looked at the food again.

Jaysen's skin crawled.

At the end of the line, one dropped to his knees—not from pain, but choice. He slammed both hands into the bottom of the trough, scattering the food, laughing like a child in water.

An Enforcer moved.

One quick, precise strike to the back—the butt of their gun driving down into the cagey's spine with a sickening thud. The man dropped. Froth pooled at the corner of his mouth. The others didn't blink.

"They don't scream anymore," Connor murmured.

"They're just holding it together," Charlie added, voice low. "So, they get their thirty minutes."

The cageys moved like they hadn't in days—stalking into the faded white-lined corner of the Big Cage, stretching muscles, throwing punches at the air.

A single basketball rolled from a wall hatch.

No teams. No instructions.

Just pressure.

Some shot baskets. Some muttered. One man circled the perimeter nonstop. Another began doing push-ups until his elbows collapsed. A few just sat, rocking.

The tension was electric.

Too much silence inside too many broken minds.

And then—

The ball bounced.

Hard.

One of the cageys picked it up and hurled it full force into another man's face. The impact echoed. The man staggered, wiped his mouth, looked up just in time for the attacker to rush him.

They went down hard—two bodies colliding in a blur of motion.

The attacker raised his hand.

Something glinted.

A jagged length of sharpened bed spring—twisted, rusted, meant for nothing but pain.

He drove it into the man's chest.

Once.

Twice.

Thrice.

Quick. Precise. Intentional.

The victim flailed beneath him, gasping wetly as blood soaked through his uniform and spread across the floor.

The top-levels went wild.

Several rushed the rec area, howling, fists clenched, brandishing sharpened bed springs and jagged lengths of broken bed poles— whatever they could wrench from the rusted bones of their cages. Others dove into the fray barehanded, biting and clawing, driven by instinct and madness.

The Enforcers reacted.

One Pearl raised a hand.

The hounds were released.

From a grated gate along the eastern wall came the sound of claws on concrete.

Then they came.

Fifteen, maybe twenty hounds, lean and black, fast and silent. Just raw muscle and instinct.

They surged into the riot like a living weapon—fur flashing, jaws open.

The first hound leapt and clamped onto a cagey's neck, shaking violently. The man gurgled once and fell still. The hound dropped him and moved on.

The second took down a runner from behind, dragging him back into the fray by the throat.

"They're trained for it," Connor said flatly. "Throat only. Organs intact."

The top-levels fought back.

One cagey slammed a hound against the concrete with a broken pole. Another grabbed one mid-leap and smashed it into a wall. Two stabbed at a snarling dog with twisted metal, howling with fury.

But the hounds didn't stop.

And neither did the riot.

Lower-level cageys joined in, drawn by instinct, chaos, or the sheer momentum of violence. Suddenly, the entire Big Cage was alive with shouting, fighting, screaming.

The Enforcers escalated.

Beanbag rounds were fired—deep, concussive thuds echoing across the chamber. Cageys dropped clutching ribs, faces, legs.

A smoke bomb hissed, spreading thick gray gas across the floor, swallowing the air.

"Gas!" someone shouted.

The hounds retreated on whistle cues. The Enforcers swept forward.

The overhead siren shrieked.

"DOWN ON THE GROUND!"

Charlie's hand clamped on Jaysen's shoulder.

"You'd better take this, son." He pressed the flask into Jaysen's hand. "You need it more than I do."

Jaysen blinked through the smoke and tucked it into his pocket.

Charlie's voice came again, steady as always: "Now lay down. Hands on your head. Don't move until you hear the bell."

Jaysen dropped flat, cheek to concrete. The sting of smoke clawed into his eyes and throat.

All around him—screams. Boots. Dogs whining. Bodies being dragged.

Beside him, Connor's voice, low and dry: "Think it'll be much longer?"

Charlie replied softly, "They're taking the last of them now."

Then it crept in.

The noise.

The one that wasn't part of the riot.

Ticking.

Soft at first. But it grew louder the longer Jaysen stayed still. Not mechanical—biological. Like it came from inside his skull.

Pop.

Sharp and wet. Like fingers snapping underwater. Followed by another. And another. The sound scattered across the floor, echoing where no sound should echo.

Drip.

Slow, steady. Not water. Thicker. He could hear it sliding down the back of his neck, though there was nothing there.

Tick.

Pop.

Drip.

The same sounds he'd heard in dreams he never remembered.

He pressed his forehead to the floor, gritting his teeth. Pulled at his own hair, just enough to remind himself what was real.

Then a hand touched his calf—firm, grounding.

Charlie's voice, low but solid: "It's okay, son. They're coming to get us now. It's almost over."

A bell rang.

The noise ceased.

The Enforcers stopped shouting.

The gas began to clear.

Jaysen, Connor, and Charlie rose together and joined the line heading back to the cages.

Jaysen slipped his hand into his pocket and wrapped his fingers around the flask. He stepped carefully, avoiding the blood-slick floor, the fallen cageys, and the slain hounds with their throats punctured by sharpened poles.

He said nothing.

He just kept walking.

The walk back through the Big Cage was silent.

No one spoke.

Not after what they'd seen.

Jaysen slipped his hand into his pocket and felt the cold flask. He counted his steps like it would slow the return—each one a beat of defiance against the chaos left behind.

The floor was littered with bodies—cageys with their throats torn out, eyes glassy and wide. A few hounds too. Some intact. Some not.

Jaysen moved carefully, eyes forward, until his foot caught on something soft, wrong.

He staggered and looked down.

It was a hound.

Still breathing.

Barely.

A jagged bedpost had been driven through its chest. Its limbs twitched. Its throat made a low, broken sound—not a growl, not a bark. A cry.

One eye locked with Jaysen's.

And in it, he saw himself.

Half-dead.

Unwanted.

Waiting in limbo for someone to finish what had been started.

The creature blinked slowly, as if it, too, was aware it wouldn't last much longer.

Then came the Pearl Enforcer.

Without hesitation, they gripped the broken post and wrenched it free from the hound's ribs.

The animal convulsed.

Then, with a single, brutal movement, the Enforcer slammed the post through its skull.

Silence.

They stood over the corpse for a long moment. Jaysen couldn't tell if they were staring with pride or regret. Maybe nothing at all.

He stepped back, bumping into Connor.

"Move forward," the Pearl Enforcer said.

Jaysen obeyed.

But he couldn't help looking down again as he passed. Not at the hound—

But at himself.

The Enforcer's command still echoed behind them, but Jaysen wasn't thinking about the order.

He was thinking about the man with the makeshift blade.

The one who'd thrown the ball. Who crossed the line first. Who stabbed another inmate in the chest, not once, but three times—calm, direct, like he'd been waiting for the chance.

And he wondered—

Why?

Was it personal?

Or was it just time?

Something about the precision of it, the speed, the silence—it didn't feel like chaos. It felt like *permission*. Like the man had held it in for weeks. Maybe months.

Then, when the gates opened, the chain fell away, and the Enforcers pretended not to look—he'd done what he came to do.

Maybe the dead man had taken something from him. Or said the wrong thing once in the dark.

Or maybe— Maybe that kind of violence didn't need a reason anymore. Maybe in a place like this, the need to kill just builds up. Like pressure behind your eyes.

And it only ever has one way out.

Jaysen's stomach tightened.

Not from fear. Not exactly. But from recognition.

He glanced sideways at Connor and Charlie walking beside him—quiet, familiar shapes against the corridor's harsh light. What would it take to push someone like Charlie to kill? Connor? Myself? Maybe nothing at all. Maybe that was the whole point.

∞

Back in their cage, the silence was thicker than usual.

The open space of the Big Cage swallowed sound differently—no walls to bounce things back, just concrete, steel mesh, and a sliver of daylight from windows too high to reach.

Jaysen sat on the edge of his mattress, elbows on his knees, watching the dust drift in the low light. His shirt clung to his back. His lungs still burned from the gas. His ears rang from the gunfire.

Connor leaned against the bars, knees drawn up, a worn paperback resting on his leg. He wasn't reading it. Just holding it like a shield.

"I keep seeing it," Jaysen said finally. His voice felt too loud in the hush. "The guy who got stabbed. The hound with the bedpost in its chest."

Connor didn't answer right away.

"The Enforcers used beanbag guns," Jaysen added. "Not real bullets. Why?"

Connor exhaled through his nose. "Because they can still kill you."

Jaysen looked over. "With beanbags?"

Connor nodded. "They aim for the skull. The spine. The lungs. Knock the wind out. Break ribs. But they won't ruin your insides. Not the important ones."

Jaysen frowned. "You mean the organs."

"They want the good parts intact," Connor said, his voice quiet. "Organs, muscles, anything clean and transplantable. A few broken bones won't stop the surgeons. But a punctured kidney? A bullet through the liver? That's wasted material, and less iron for the prison."

Jaysen rubbed both hands down his face. "Fuck."

Connor shifted slightly, still staring through the bars. "They don't keep us alive because they care. They keep us alive because we're more useful breathing."

Jaysen leaned back until he was flat on the mattress, eyes open to the darkening mesh above the cage.

"Feels like I understand this place a little less with every hour."

"Nah," Connor said. "You're starting to understand it perfectly."

Neither of them spoke for a long time after that.

There was nothing else to say.

The silence after their conversation stretched.

Jaysen lay back on the mattress, staring at the rusted mesh above, trying not to think about throats, beanbags, or how close death felt in this place.

Connor shifted.

Then: "You ever notice my dacks?"

Jaysen blinked, turning his head slightly. "…What?"

Connor tapped the fabric at his knee. "Cleaner than yours."

Jaysen frowned. "You saying I stink?"

"I'm saying you're wearing half the Big Cage on your legs," Connor said, a smirk tugging at his mouth. "You want clean dacks, you've got to trade for them."

Jaysen sat up slowly. "You trade… for pants?"

"Clean ones, yeah."

There was a pause.

Jaysen stared at him. "That's the stupidest thing I've ever heard."

Connor leaned back, folding his arms behind his head. "Stupid until you're not sitting in your own rot. Until the seams aren't rubbing you raw. Trust me, mate—clean dacks are worth more than soap in here."

"How?"

"I trade time," Connor said. "That's my thing."

Jaysen raised an eyebrow. "Time?"

"Yeah. People lose track in here. Days bleed. Nothing to mark it but noise and sleep and whatever's in the troughs. But I always know when the full moon's coming."

He said it like a secret.

Jaysen frowned. "So?"

Connor turned his head, looked at him fully. "That's when they harvest."

The cage went still.

"I've been right every full moon since I got here," Connor said, voice low. "Every time. No guesses. No slips. They ask me now. Even the ones who won't look at me any other day—they come when it's close."

Jaysen's expression darkened.

"That's why they trade with me. Clothes, food, soap—whatever they've got. They know I'll give them the right answer."

He let the words settle before adding, "It's just a trick. Learned it hunting iron. You watch long enough, you feel how the pressure changes. Even in here, with no windows and no clocks—the moon still pulls at everything."

Jaysen didn't laugh.

But he didn't scoff either.

He just nodded.

Once.

Slow.

Then after a pause: "Why are the top-level cageys like that?"

Connor looked up at the ceiling.

"The grinding sound. When they drop the covers."

Jaysen nodded again. "Yeah. It's awful."

Connor's voice dropped. "Now imagine that, but it's right above your head. Not once a day. Not on a schedule. Just… *random*. Could be three times in an hour. Could be nothing for days. And when it comes, it's like the ceiling's caving in."

He tapped a knuckle against the metal slats beside him.

"They're locked in those cages with no warning. No sense of time. Just sudden thunder right overhead, shaking the bars, making your bones vibrate. Wakes you up screaming. Makes you flinch at silence."

Jaysen didn't say anything.

Connor went on, quieter now. "They say it's not just the sound. It's the waiting. The not knowing when it'll hit. Some of them start twitching even before the real drop comes—phantom grinds. Some go days without sleeping."

Jaysen's voice was a whisper. "That's what sends them off?"

"Eventually, yeah. Noise like that—relentless, sharp, close? It *carves* you. Peels back the edges until you're just a raw thing, waiting for the next impact."

He looked back at Jaysen.

"That's what top level does to you. Doesn't just break your mind. It keeps *breaking it again*."

Jaysen lay back down slowly, staring up at the rusted mesh above.

Don't think about it. Don't picture it. Don't imagine the grinding right over your skull, the way it rattles your teeth and makes the dark feel alive.

Don't see yourself twitching in your sleep, mumbling, rocking like the ones you swore you'd never become. Just breathe. And hope—really fucking hope—you never end up on top level.

Then it came. Not loud. Not like up there. But sharp enough.

The grinding.

Metal shifting somewhere above, distant but clear—like teeth dragging across steel. He'd heard it before. But this time… this time, it crawled into his ears and set up camp behind his eyes.

It's in your head, he told himself. *It's always been in your head.*

But it wasn't alone.

Now it was joined by the tick of the Warden's clock, still echoing in memory.

The pop of skin when the needle sank in. The drip of blood. Somewhere. Always. Dripping.

Jaysen pressed his palms to his ears.

It didn't help.

The sound was inside him now.

Don't let it in. Don't let it take root.

Darkness swallowed the cage.

And Jaysen lay there, listening to the metal hum of madness whispering through the mesh.

The grinding faded.

But the light faded with it.

One by one, the overheads blinked out.

Not all at once—no mercy like that. Just slow. Deliberate. Like someone was dragging a blanket over the world, inch by inch.

Jaysen lay still as the cage darkened around him, as shapes disappeared, as Connor's silhouette melted into shadow. Until there was nothing.

Just the rustle of cloth. A cough from somewhere across the Aviary. Then silence.

And then—

The sounds came back.

Tick.

Pop.

Drip.

And beneath them, curling up like a memory—

The grinding.

It echoed from nowhere. From everywhere. Muffled, warped, like it had tunneled straight into his skull and started chewing.

The tick wasn't a clock anymore—it was his heartbeat. Fast. Ragged. Drumming against his skull like it wanted out. The pop, a gunshot echoing in his jaw. The drip—*the drip was his own blood,* slow and steady against concrete.

He couldn't see. Couldn't breathe.

The dark wasn't just around him now.

It was in him.

He squeezed his eyes shut, but it didn't make a difference. His thoughts were louder than the room. The room wasn't even there anymore.

Just sound. And black. And the threat of losing something he wasn't sure he could ever get back.

Get a grip.

Get a grip.

Get—

A bright light hit him.

Jaysen flinched, throwing an arm up against it.

The sharp white glare cut through the black, sudden and blinding.

Then it tilted, softened.

And behind it—Connor's face.

Half lit, half grin.

"I got it in trade," he said, lifting the small, smuggled torch in two fingers like it was a sacred relic.

Jaysen blinked up at him, chest still heaving.

Connor leaned back just enough to let the beam rest gently between them, glowing across the floor like a campfire.

"Figured you could use a little light, mate."

The torch's beam still flickered between them, warm and steady. Jaysen's breath had started to settle.

He reached into his pocket and pulled out the flask—worn, dented, warm from his body heat.

He unscrewed the cap slowly and took a sip. The burn lit his throat like a match struck too close, but it steadied his hands.

Without a word, he offered it to Connor.

Connor took it, raised it slightly in silent thanks, then drank. He hissed through his teeth. "Charlie reckons it's nail polish remover," he said, voice low. "Probably isn't far off."

"Burns like it," Jaysen muttered.

They passed it back and forth once more.

"Skol," Connor said. The word hung in the dark like a quiet ritual.

"Skol," Jaysen echoed, and they both drank.

Connor leaned back against the bars, the flask resting in his hand. "To Henry," he said quietly. "He didn't deserve what happened today."

Jaysen nodded. "To Henry."

Another swig. No words.

Connor stared off into the dark. "He reminded me of Sammy."

Jaysen turned slightly toward him.

"My little brother," Connor said. "Not the way he looked—just… the way he was. Always joking, always trying to make people laugh, even when things were falling apart."

He paused. "Right up until they sent him to top level."

He lifted the flask again. "To Sammy."

Jaysen raised his hand slightly. "To Sam."

They drank.

Connor cleared his throat. "Your sister… What's her name?"

"Izzy."

Connor nodded slowly. "To Izzy, then. May she be safe and far from here."

"To Izzy," Jaysen echoed.

They drank again. Slower this time.

Jaysen let the burn settle in his chest before he spoke. "I stopped Kaylus before he could hurt her. But… I don't know if she saw it that way. She looked so scared. Not of him. Of me."

Connor met his eyes. "You did what you could, mate."

Jaysen looked away, jaw tight.

The torch flickered once but held.

They sat in the hush that followed, two men bound by guilt, by grief, by the dark.

Jaysen whispered, "Do you think she hates me?"

Connor didn't look at him. Just answered. "I think she's waiting for you to come back."

They passed the flask one last time.

Jaysen took a final swig and tucked the flask under the edge of his mat.

For a moment, neither of them spoke.

Jaysen reached up and turned off the torch.

Darkness returned like it had been waiting.

Thick and slow and alive.

He lay there, trying to keep his breathing steady. But the silence didn't stay silent for long.

The sounds crawled back in.

Tick.

Pop.

Drip.

Grind.

He clenched his jaw.

Don't think. Just breathe.

But something shifted.

The dark stretched wider.

And then he saw them.

Eyes.

Watching from beyond the cage.

One of them had a split running straight down the center, torn like paper.

Unblinking.

Locked on him.

They didn't move.

Didn't blink.

Didn't need to.

Jaysen stared back, his body rigid, breath caught halfway.

They're still there. They've always been there.

He shut his eyes tight.

But the darkness behind his lids was no better.

∞

Jaysen was in the Feltwood Mountains.

The air sliced through him—cold, thin, relentless.

A little boy—five, maybe younger—sprinted through the trees, screaming.

Jaysen tried to run, to help, but he was stuck. Boots dragging through frozen dirt. The boy slipped further away, his cries sharp and distant.

Jaysen looked down.

A rusted chain was bolted to his ankle.

He followed it through leaf rot and frostbitten roots until it vanished under a wooden hatch.

He dropped, pulled it open, and climbed into the dark.

The hatch slammed shut behind him.

The cold wasn't around him anymore. It was inside.

He crouched low, chest tight, breathing ragged.

A door opened. Light spilled in—blinding and sharp.

Jaysen jumped, cracked his head on something above him— a benchtop?

A faceless man stood in the doorway.

He moved quickly—arms reaching, silent.

Jaysen tried to run, but his body locked.

His voice caught in his throat.

He clenched his eyes shut—

—and opened them at a funeral.

Two coffins. No flowers. Izzy stood beside them. Frozen. Eyes glazed and white. Skin around them bruised black.

"Izzy!" he called out. "What happened?"

She didn't answer.

Her mouth opened—far too wide—and she shrieked. The sound—part scream, part growl—rattled his spine.

Her skin flaked away like ash.

Jaysen turned and ran.

No more chain. Just flight.

He burst through doors—into the Warden's office.

The massive clock on the wall ticked backward, too fast, too loud.

The Warden appeared behind him, growing, distorting, until he towered like a twisted god.

Jaysen backed into the clock—and fell through.

Then he was in a dentist's chair.

A nurse above him threaded a hooked needle through his lips, stitching his mouth shut.

He thrashed. The Limbo shackles held him down.

A Pearl Enforcer stepped in, lifted him like a doll, and hurled him into a trough.

Trail mix. Dried oats. Fruit. He sank into it, choking, drowning—and dropped again.

Concrete hit him hard.

The Big Cage.

He looked up.

The faceless man stood in the middle of the court, holding a bloodstained basketball.

Jaysen scrambled to his feet. "WHAT DO YOU WANT!"

The man bounced the ball. Each thud spilled more blood across the floor.

Each thud made Jaysen feel smaller.

He stepped forward.

And from the pocket of his jacket—

a pocket watch swung.

Clicking.

The metal face glinted coldly.

Jaysen stared at it.

But it wasn't his reflection in the glass.

It was the little boy's.

The same boy from the trees—eyes wide, lips trembling, covered in dirt.

Frozen. Staring back.

Jaysen's breath hitched.

The man stepped closer.

Reached out.

Grabbed Jaysen by the shoulders.

And shook him.

His voice cracked through the air—distorted, low, and too familiar.

"Wake up, Jaysen!"

Jaysen struck out—punches, kicks—blind and wild.

"WAKE UP, JAYSEN!" the voice roared again, deeper now, the mouth stretching, tearing at the corners.

The faceless man's form blurred—for a flicker—Connor's voice inside it.

Jaysen screamed, the dream shattering like glass around him.

∞

"Wake up, mate. It's just a dream."

The distorted voice still echoed in Jaysen's skull as his eyes snapped open.

He was drenched in sweat, chest heaving. The world blurred, then sharpened—cage mesh above, steel bars beside.

Connor sat on the edge of his mattress, one hand steady on Jaysen's shoulder, the other holding the small flashlight between them. His face was pinched with concern, but his voice stayed level.

"You right, mate?"

Jaysen sat up slowly, wiping his face with the back of his hand. "Yeah… Just a bad dream. Nothing to worry about."

Connor didn't press. He gave a quiet nod and sat back, the torch still lit between them.

The boy's face from the dream still floated behind Jaysen's eyes. Izzy's mouth opening too wide. The blood on the basketball court. The eyes beyond the cage.

He swallowed hard.

The familiar sounds were already creeping back in—*tick… pop… drip… grind…*

The overhead grinding kicked in next—*real* this time—and Jaysen flinched instinctively.

But the rising covers brought a strange relief. That meant showers.

He stood and stretched the tension from his shoulders, taking a breath that felt thinner than it should've.

As the covers rolled back, Jaysen's eyes flicked upward, scanning the rooflines. No movement. No alarms. No madmen leaping to their deaths this time.

He turned back to the cage, methodically making his bed, tucking the flask safely into the folds of his sheets.

"Connor," he said quietly, "can you not mention last night to anyone?"

"No worries, mate." Connor was already halfway into his shirt. "My brother used to have nightmares. I've had 'em too. You'll probably get sick of hearing this, but you get used to it."

Jaysen gave a weak laugh. "Doubt that."

They stood in the middle of the cage as the enforcers approached. Jaysen closed his eyes for just a second, feeling the weight of sweat and nightmare grime clinging to him. The shower washed it all away—at least for a moment.

New briefs. Clean skin. A different man.

He turned to thank Connor—but the bell blared, cutting him off.

The cageys around them started yelling.

"RUN TO THE REAPER! RUN, RUN TO THE REAPER!"

Jaysen's head jerked toward the sound. Panic surged.

He looked to Connor, fear raw in his face.

Connor's voice was low, steady. "Full moon's tonight."

Jaysen's stomach dropped.

"It's time to show The Harvests."

He didn't need to ask what that meant.

"Just don't stare," Connor added. "Some of them don't get purchased. If one comes back and remembers your face…"

Jaysen nodded quickly, eyes lowering.

But when the line of Harvests passed—heads bowed, wrists bound, flanked by Enforcers and their hounds—Jaysen couldn't help but look.

And when he did, his breath caught.

"Connor!" he choked out. "It's… it's…"

He covered his mouth with both hands.

"Charlie," he whispered.

∞

Charlie

The curtains muffled most of it.

Just like the covers in the Aviary.

Muted sounds: the thrum of machinery, the hum of music, the occasional distant voice. But every time the velvet parted, it hit like a slap—screams, fanfare, the throb of applause.

And then the curtain would fall shut again.

Charlie stood in line, wrists clasped behind him, bare feet pressed to the cold concrete. His shoulders ached. His mouth was dry.

He tried not to think about Connor—but that only made the thoughts come harder.

He remembered the man's voice, cracking jokes just to fill the silence. The way he looked at people when he thought they weren't watching— *not with hate*, like most cageys, but with hope. Fragile, stubborn hope.

Charlie hoped he hadn't seen him in the line.

He didn't want that to be the last image burned into Connor's head.

Another prisoner was dragged forward.

"YOU CAN'T DO THIS!"

The scream punched through the curtain just before it parted again. For one brief second, everything was loud—blindingly loud—and then it vanished as the velvet fell shut.

Charlie blinked, heartbeat climbing.

And then it was his turn.

The Enforcer grabbed his arm.

The curtain opened.

Light. Sound. Heat.

The stage swallowed him.

The noise surged. Music—brash and frantic. Color spun in every direction. Reds, blues, strobes blinking like a warning. A carousel of madness.

Beyond the floodlights, a sea of buyers waited in the shadows. Dozens. Maybe hundreds. Hidden faces. Watching.

Must be to keep them anonymous, he thought grimly.

An Enforcer pushed him forward with a shove.

"Here we have Charles Ernest Harrington, a spritely sixty-five," the voice crackled through the speakers. "Blood type O+. All organs are viable. Convicted for conspiring with the terrorist organization known as The Renegades."

The crowd booed.

Charlie didn't flinch.

"They gave him a death sentence—and now he's ready for the highest bidder!"

A spotlight pinned him in place.

"Give us a spin, Charles!"

Charlie turned—because they wanted him to.

The stage felt like it dipped under his feet.

He caught himself, knees locking.

Bright white lights. Loud music. A scream in the crowd.

Then, suddenly—

everything dropped out.

Lights gone. Sound cut. Darkness closed in.

And Charlie's body hit the floor like a sack of meat.

∞

The blur of bright lights greeted Charlie when he opened his eyes. Beeping noises echoed in his ears. He caught the soft murmur of a man and woman talking just out of sight.

"He shouldn't be seeing all this," the woman whispered.

"Well, what did you want me to do?" the man replied sharply. "The infirmary's at capacity because of that shit show yesterday, and we can't have him dying yet."

Cabinet doors banged open and shut.

Charlie blinked and turned his head. His eyes swept across the room.

The Harvests were laid out like dolls. Some unconscious and tethered to life-support machines, others… already opened. Ice boxes beside the tables, organs packed and labeled. Those who hadn't been touched yet were marked in pen across the chest.

He closed his eyes. *Don't look. Don't see. You're still alive. You're still here.*

But the sting in his ankle reminded him he wasn't untouched.

A brace. Tight and thick, climbing halfway up his calf.

He opened his eyes again.

"Why did you fix it?" he croaked.

A hand settled gently on his forearm. "Don't try to sit up," the woman said softly. "The restraints won't allow it… and you gave your head a nasty bump in that fall."

Charlie turned to the voice. She was kind. Gentle. Auburn hair and eyes like spring leaves. Her name tag read *Jessica*.

"Be sure to keep those stitches clean," she added.

"Clean?" he echoed. *Why fix me at all?*

"Mr. Harring—"

"Please," he interrupted. "Call me Charlie."

She smiled faintly. "Charlie. No one bought your organs. Once you can walk, you'll be free to return to your cage. Until the next moon."

Her voice had honey in it, but the words still stung.

Another voice cut in like a scalpel.

"Only because no one wanted a feeble old man's organs."

Dr. Zygote stood nearby, peering over his glasses with a look of disdain. "How can they expect to be kept alive by organs from a man who can't even keep himself standing? Doesn't even have a rare blood type."

Jessica prepped the morphine shot as Zygote kept talking.

"They'd be back here in just a few moons for more. He's not worth the iron. Should've sent him to The Pits before he's leathered and worthless."

The morphine hit.

The edges of Charlie's vision softened.

He turned toward Jessica. "Thank you, Jessi…" he mumbled.

Then sleep took him.

∞

Jessica

The steady beep of the monitor was the only sound in the surgical bay. Jessica watched the green line pulse across the screen, steady now— no more erratic dips. The morphine had done its job, dulling the edge of pain in the man lying before her.

He was still. Pale under the harsh surgical light. His hands, weathered but strong, rested beside him like he'd just finished a long day's work instead of barely surviving The Harvest floor.

Jessica exhaled slowly and peeled off her gloves, tossing them into the waste bin with a quiet snap. Her fingers tingled from the adrenaline. It always buzzed through her like this after the close ones.

She didn't know much about him—Charles Harrington, the paperwork had said. Sixty-five. Unpurchased. Rejected from The Harvest like expired meat. But the moment he'd collapsed onstage, something in her shifted. It wasn't just sympathy. It wasn't just protocol.

It was a feeling.

A gut instinct she'd learned to trust in this place.

There was still something alive in him. Something unbroken.

She stepped closer and gently adjusted the blanket across his chest. The surgical light caught the edge of his silver hair—still thick, curling a little at the temples. He had that weathered, quietly handsome look. Like someone who'd once been strong enough to carry the world but had learned, over time, how to let it go in pieces.

She caught herself staring and quickly looked away.

Don't romanticize, she scolded herself. *You don't know him. He could be dangerous. Bitter. Just another cagey with a soft look and a dark core.*

But he hadn't looked dangerous when he tried to stand on his own. He'd looked proud. Tired. Like he didn't want to be seen as less than he was.

Her fingers brushed his wrist as she checked the I.V. line. His skin was rough with calluses. A laborer's hands.

There was something strangely reassuring about that.

She reached under her collar and retrieved a tiny plastic packet tucked in the lining of her bra. Small white pills. Just enough to dull the pain until the next moon. She crouched beside the table and scribbled a quick message on a piece of paper. Then folded the pills inside, and slipped them into his pocket.

Another quiet rebellion.

She wasn't doing it for recognition.

She did it because, sometimes, when someone like this man looked at you—with that brief flicker of confusion, of pain, then of thanks in their eyes—it reminded her why she hadn't walked away from this place.

Not yet.

He shifted slightly on the table, and she stilled, one hand on his blanket. His eyelids fluttered. For a breath, she thought he might wake.

Instead, he exhaled her name—barely more than a whisper.

She felt it in her chest like a wire pulled tight.

"Jessica." He breathed.

He didn't say it like he was afraid.

He said it like he'd dreamed it.

She lingered for a second too long, watching the rise and fall of his chest.

"You're going to be okay," she whispered, brushing a curl back from his brow.

Then she turned away, picked up the mop, and began cleaning the floor.

Because no matter how kind his voice had sounded, no matter how steady his heartbeat now rang in her ears—she was still in Augmentation Bay.

And in this place, hope was dangerous.

But she couldn't help it.

She hoped he would live.

And she hoped, somehow, he'd remember her face.

∞

Charlie

The beep of the monitor was steady again.

He didn't remember falling asleep.

The ache in his ankle was distant now—muted by whatever they'd pumped into him. His head felt clearer than before, though still wrapped in fog at the edges. Somewhere nearby, pages rustled and someone muttered under their breath.

"This is *my* surgery, Jessica… Don't forget your place…" the voice mocked with gentle sarcasm.

Charlie smiled faintly and cracked one eye open.

Jessica sat at the workbench with her back to him, shoulders rising and falling with a deep sigh. Her auburn hair spilled over her shoulder, catching the overhead light. She was muttering again, mimicking Zygote's drawl in a way that made Charlie bite back a chuckle.

He let the laugh escape anyway.

Jessica spun in her chair, startled, turning the shade of a ripe apple. "Mr. Harri— Charlie," she stammered, already rising from her stool and brushing her hair behind her ear.

His shackles had been removed.

He tried to sit up, slower this time.

"You're awake," she said, softer now. "How are you feeling?"

He groaned a little, lifting his hand to his head. "Like I got trampled by a mule and kissed by a brick wall."

She smiled. "That sounds about right."

Then she turned, grabbed something from the counter, and came back with a small white pill and a paper cup filled to the brim.

"Here. Painkiller. And…" She held the cup out to him. "Ice water. Fresh."

Charlie blinked at it like it was a ghost.

He took the cup and raised it to his lips.

The first sip hit him like a blessing. Cold. Clean. Sharp against the roof of his mouth. It trailed down his throat like memory, settling deep into his chest, waking something that had been asleep longer than the pain.

He closed his eyes and savored it.

He hadn't had cold water since they brought him here. Not once. Not during intake. Not after The Harvest. Not even in the cages.

He'd forgotten the simple luxury of it.

Shit, he thought. *I missed this.*

When he opened his eyes again, Jessica was still watching him.

Not like he was broken.

Not like he was inventory.

Just… watching.

"I almost forgot what cold water felt like," he said quietly, voice rough with truth.

She smiled again. "You looked like you needed a reminder."

The ache in his ribs flared as he shifted on the table. The ankle brace was tight, but not unbearable. He could move. That had to count for something.

Jessica stood nearby, holding a crooked wooden cane and wearing that gentle expression she hadn't dropped since he woke up.

"It's time to try to walk, Charlie," she said, stepping closer. "Hold on to my hand and take it slowly. It's been a few days now… you'll be unsteady."

He accepted the cane, but hesitated before taking her hand.

She offered it without pressure—just open and waiting.

He wanted to take it. Hell, he wanted to lean into it.

But that stubborn voice in his head—the one that had kept him alive this long—was louder.

"I may be sixty-five, but I'm tougher than I look," he said with a wink, mustering what charm he could manage. He released her hand gently and planted the cane. Then stepped forward.

The brace slipped.

His body pitched. Too fast to stop. His temple clipped the side of the surgical table, and everything went white for a second.

Jessica gasped, then dropped to her knees beside him.

"Don't try to be strong with me, Charlie," she breathed, already reaching for the alcohol wipes. "I'm here to help you."

He didn't protest when she helped him sit back on the table. His pride was bruised. His head was bleeding. But when she pressed the antiseptic to the cut on his brow, all he could think about was how close she was.

Her hands were soft but practiced, confident. Her perfume was subtle—vanilla and something else. Something warm. Pumpkin, maybe? It reminded him of the candy his mother used to sneak him on Hallows Eve, before The Nation banned the holiday altogether.

She began stitching, careful and precise.

Then—without meaning to—he leaned into her hand. Just for a second. Just to feel something kind.

"Charlie… sweetie," she said gently. "I need both hands for this. I don't want to hurt you."

He blinked, pulled back. His cheeks burned. "Right. Of course."

She finished stitching in silence.

Then he cleared his throat. "When do I get to go back to my cage? Before I embarrass myself any further."

Jessica looked up, her eyes catching his with something that almost looked like concern. Then she smiled—a little crooked, a little sad.

"Are you sick of me already, Charlie?" she asked lightly, teasing him just enough to break the tension.

That laugh. It was like the wings of a butterfly. Or the sound a flock of doves might make, taking flight in the distance—soft, impossible, and far too rare for a place like this.

She helped him down again—one hand on his back, the other guiding his elbow. He stood slower this time. Smarter. The pain was still there, but so was her presence, and somehow, that balanced the scale.

"Take it slowly, Charlie," she warned.

He gave her a sideways smile. "I'd say I've learned my lesson."

The brace wobbled once more—but this time, she was already there, sliding her arm around his waist.

"You cracked a rib, remember?" she whispered. "You don't have to prove anything to me."

His cheeks burned again. Not from pain. From the way she said *me*.

He let her hold him just a little longer than he needed to.

And for the first time in a long while, Charlie didn't feel like stock.

He felt seen.

He was still holding the cup when the door opened with a hiss.

"Ahh, Mr. Harrington, you're up, I see."

Dr. Zygote's voice always sounded like it had something sour behind it. The man moved like a crow picking through something already dead—tall, gaunt, balding on top with a curtain of graying hair circling his head. His glasses caught the sterile light, twin discs of judgment that never quite looked you in the eyes.

Charlie lowered the empty cup and gave a slight nod.

Zygote looked over the rims of his lenses. "Good to go then?" he asked, and continued immediately, not waiting for an answer. "Any numbness, Mr. Harrington?"

Charlie shook his head. "No, Doctor." He glanced at Jessica, managed a soft smile. "Feeling fine 'n' dandy."

He stood, gripping the cane, careful to mask the wince. Zygote stepped in close, studying the bandaged ankle without a word, then moved to his filing cabinet and scribbled on a form.

Jessica lingered beside Charlie, her presence steady. Reassuring.

Then the doors burst open.

A whip-thin woman stormed in, her voice cracking like glass across concrete. "WHERE'S MY HARVEST, ZAYNE? HE SHOULD BE HERE, WAITING!"

Dr. Lancet.

Charlie didn't need an introduction. Her name carried weight in whispers. Her frame was taut with rage, lips pulled tight across sharpened words.

"Oh, Evelyn," Zygote muttered without looking up. "Your Harvest is in The Farm being held for you. Everything's perfect for the precious Dr. Lancet."

"Have they put him under yet?" she snapped.

"No," Zygote sighed. "He's been kept awake for three days—just as you requested. I don't understand why. It will only strain Mr. Morgan's heart."

"*My* heart," she said, lips curling.

Zygote finally looked up. "Not yet, it isn't," he said dryly. "And mind how you speak to me. You still need me for the transplant."

Then his attention snapped to Jessica.

"Jessica. Escort Mr. Harrington back to The Aviary."

Charlie caught the subtle shift in Jessica's posture—tense, but not fearful. Controlled.

She turned to him with a quiet smile. "Let's get you back."

As Dr. Lancet's gaze swept toward him, her eyes narrowed.

"What the hell is he still doing here?" she barked. "He shouldn't be hearing any of this. Get him out of here now!"

"That's exactly what's happening, Evelyn," Zygote said through clenched teeth. "Now, for Zoti's sake, stop carrying on."

"Dr. Zygote, you should be—"

"Goodbye, Evelyn," he snapped, much more forcefully this time.

She stood still a moment longer, vibrating with fury, then turned and stormed out, muttering under her breath.

Jessica's fingers brushed Charlie's shoulder, a light touch before she moved ahead to open the door.

They stepped into the corridor.

The door hissed closed behind them, and the world outside the surgery rushed back in—bright, cold, humming with distant machinery.

Charlie squinted. His eyes hadn't adjusted to the hallway lights yet. Too much white. Too much silence. Too much memory.

Jessica was still beside him, walking slow to match his limp. Her hand hovered near his arm, not touching now, but close enough that he could feel the warmth of her presence.

The Light Mile.

He'd only seen it once before—on the way to The Harvest.

He never thought he'd see it again.

They passed the first set of reinforced doors.

"The Chute," read the one on the right. "The Cell," on the left.

He frowned. The words weren't labels. They felt like threats.

Then *The Cell* door cracked open.

A woman burst through—young, hair disheveled, eyes like shattered glass. She didn't stop. Didn't look at them. Just kept running down the hall until she vanished around a corner.

Charlie turned his head, couldn't stop himself.

Inside The Cell, sleek digital boards lined the walls. Each displayed a name, written in clinical block lettering, with a matching code beside it:

M. Kreed – D9

J. Seery – D10

H. Summers – D11

I. Masters – D12

L. Cerven – D13

T. Johnston – D14

Rows of them.

Inventory.

Jessica's voice pulled him back.

"Come on," she said gently. "We don't want the Enforcers thinking you're getting curious."

Charlie nodded. "It's just been a while since I've seen anything that isn't concrete or bars. Even walls with names are better than nothing."

They walked on.

"The Farm."

Another door.

Another weight in his gut.

Charlie didn't ask what happened inside. He didn't need to.

Behind them, the hallway creaked.

He turned and saw her—Dr. Lancet, emerging from *The Farm*, wheeling a gurney with a body strapped tight to the rails. His eyes darted, wild, lips moving without sound. Alive, but not really.

Charlie froze.

He recognized him. Michael. The same man who had killed Henry during the riot on the top level. The memories flashed—too fast, too brutal—the way Michael had stabbed Henry three times, the blade sinking deep into Henry's body. That had been the spark—the moment the riot had started, blood spattering across the floor. The chaos, the fighting. All of it kicked off by Michael's brutal act.

It had turned the prisoners into animals, scrambling for control, just to survive the madness that followed.

Michael had been one of them—a fellow prisoner. But not anymore. Now he was something else entirely.

Dr. Lancet's footsteps echoed as she wheeled the gurney away, the body shifting slightly with each motion. She was whistling—a soft, almost careless tune. It didn't fit the grim scene. The cheerful melody felt wrong, out of place, but she whistled along as though nothing in the world could disturb her rhythm. Her eyes were focused ahead, and the body on the gurney might as well have been an object, not a man.

Charlie turned away.

He didn't want to see it. Didn't want to think about what Michael had become or how the system had chewed him up and spit him back out like a monster.

He faced forward. Moved forward.

The end of the hallway rose like the edge of a blade. There was no label on the final door. Just steel. Cold. Waiting.

Jessica stopped a few feet from it.

"This is where I leave you," she said. Her voice had softened again. No sarcasm. Just quiet sorrow.

He turned to her.

"It's been an absolute pleasure, Jessica," he said. And he meant it.

She smiled—small, fragile.

Then the steel door hissed open.

The Enforcer was already waiting.

Charlie gave Jessica one last glance, then stepped through.

And just like that, she was gone.

∞

The door to his new cage slid open with a cold hiss, and the Enforcer motioned for him to move forward, shoving him slightly in the back.

"Cripples can't walk up stairs," the Enforcer muttered, a sneer in his voice. "So you've got a new cage, old man."

Charlie barely had time to react before the Enforcer gave him another shove, forcing him to take a step. His cane dug into the floor, helping him steady himself as his body protested the movement.

Charlie winced, grinding his teeth against the pain that shot up his leg. But there was no sympathy here. No patience.

The door slammed shut behind him with an echo that filled the small space. The lock clicked, final, cold, and unyielding.

The cage was identical to all the others—the same size, the same metal bars, the same thin mattress barely fitting the bedframe. The air was thick and stale, a mix of old sweat and lingering metal. He glanced around, noting the absence of any personal items. There was nothing here to remind him of who he was, of where he came from. Just the cold, hollow emptiness of the cage. The same as every other.

A low growl escaped from the back of his throat as he hobbled toward the bed. Nothing had changed. It was the same relentless isolation, the same feeling of being lost inside an endless system.

Charlie settled down on the bed, cane still in hand, and felt the small parcel tucked into his pocket. He hadn't noticed when Jessica had slipped it in there, but it was there now. Slowly, he pulled it out, hoping for some small comfort in the midst of everything.

Inside, there were eight small white pills, and a note, folded neatly:

C.- One now and then one per day. -J.

Charlie let out a small sigh of relief. At least this wouldn't be as hard to bear as he feared. He swallowed one of the pills dry, feeling it settle warmly in his chest. It wasn't much, but it dulled the pain—just enough for now.

He tucked the rest of the pills back into his pocket and lay back on the bed, staring up at the steel ceiling. His mind wandered back to Jessica—her quiet kindness, the way she had smiled at him, slipped the pills to him like it was nothing at all. It was the first time in what felt like forever that someone had shown him anything remotely close to care.

The sound of bells echoed down the hall, signaling the return of the other cageys from The Big Cage.

Charlie didn't move. He stayed still, listening as the noise of rattling cages and muffled voices grew louder. Some of the men had returned, exhausted and broken, others still strung out from the madness of the day. The noise of their struggles drifted in.

The Enforcers ushered the men into their cages, the rustling of their bodies, the sound of cuffs clicking, the low grunts of exhaustion. But as the men were moved past his cage, a familiar face caught his eye.

It was Jaysen.

The younger man looked at him with wide eyes, recognition dawning slowly as the covers were about to fall.

"Charlie?" Jaysen whispered, his voice hoarse with shock.

Charlie's eyes met Jaysen's. He smiled faintly.

Before he could speak, Connor—just as surprised—stood beside Jaysen, his mouth hanging open.

"Charlie, is that really you?" Connor's voice cracked with disbelief.

Charlie nodded, offering a soft chuckle despite himself. "Fancy seeing you boys here."

The covers slowly began to lower as the two men stood in shock, their eyes locked on him. The noise from the others continued to fill the air, but for a moment, everything fell silent between them.

Then the covers fully dropped, and he was left alone again, the curtain of darkness falling around him. The men had gone—leaving him in a quiet that was both a relief and a weight.

He closed his eyes, and for a moment, allowed himself to feel something that wasn't pain. The fleeting connection with Connor and Jaysen—those familiar faces—was enough to calm the storm in his chest.

CHAPTER THREE

The Harvet

∞

Michael

The cold metal straps dug into Michael's wrists, holding him down against the gurney with unrelenting force. He could feel the slickness of his sweat, the harsh rhythm of his breath, but his body wouldn't obey. His muscles trembled, his mind screamed, but he couldn't break free.

He had to get out of here. Had to get away before it was too late.

"Stop struggling, Michael," Dr. Lancet's voice cut through the haze in his mind, cold and clipped. "It's no use. You know how this ends."

Her words were a mockery, a distant whisper that grated on his nerves, sending an involuntary shudder through him.

His gaze flicked over her—her silhouette sharp against the sterile light, her movements as fluid as ever, as if this were routine. As if this was just another day at work.

She was whistling. A soft, airy tune, as though she were strolling through a garden instead of pushing him toward his end.

Michael's pulse raced, the blood pounding in his ears. He clenched his jaw against the panic clawing its way up his throat.

"Please, you don't have to do this," Michael growled, struggling against the restraints that seemed to tighten with each movement. "There's still time."

Dr. Lancet didn't flinch. She barely even acknowledged him, whistling her tune as she pushed him along. But then, her lips curved into a slow, mocking smile.

"Time?" she mused, her tone dripping with scorn. "You think you still have time? How adorable."

The sound of her footsteps was methodical, each step a reminder of how far he had fallen. How helpless he was now, strapped to this gurney, moving closer and closer to The Harvest.

His eyes scanned the walls of the Light Mile, the cold, sterile tiles flashing past. He tried to fix his gaze on something—anything—other than the inevitable fate awaiting him, but there was nothing to focus on. Just the endless stretch of white walls, the hum of distant machinery, and the silence that pressed in from every corner.

There was no escape. No one would save him. Not this time.

The door to The Harvest loomed ahead, its cold steel frame blocking the way to whatever awaited him inside. It felt like the gates of hell itself. His heart thundered in his chest as they neared, each second stretching into eternity.

"Please," Michael whispered, his voice low but filled with desperation. "Just let me go."

Dr. Lancet didn't respond immediately. She whistled a little louder, the tune twisted in its oddness, as if she were enjoying this, enjoying his suffering.

Then, with chilling calm, she said, "You don't want your last moments spent crying like a baby, do you, Michael?"

Her eyes flicked to his face, her smile widening slightly as she saw a tear escape from the corner of his eye.

"Pathetic," she muttered under her breath, then wryly added, "But I guess it's a little too late for pride now."

The gurney halted. The door to The Harvest was open.

Michael's eyes locked onto the bright, fluorescent lights of the room beyond, the sterile white walls, the tables, the sharp tools awaiting him.

Everything in him screamed to fight—to run—but his body wouldn't move. He was trapped. Like prey caught in a snare, too weak to escape, too broken to resist.

Dr. Lancet smiled, her eyes glinting coldly as she leaned over him. "Don't worry, Michael. It will all be over soon."

The door slid shut with a heavy thud, and the world seemed to narrow to that single, terrifying sound.

∞

Michael felt it pierce his skin, cold liquid sliding into his veins. It was sharp, sudden. For a split second, he thought he could still fight it. He tried, pushing against the weight of the drug that was already seeping into his system, willing his body to move, to resist.

But then it hit. A wave of something dark and heavy that crawled over him, suffocating his will, drowning his thoughts in a fog of paralysis. His muscles tensed, a final, desperate rebellion against the creeping numbness—but then… nothing.

His body, his own body, betrayed him.

No. No, no, no—this can't be happening. This isn't how it ends.

His limbs wouldn't move, his chest felt tight, but his mind—his mind was still wide awake. Every thought, every scream trapped inside his head, a silent cry for mercy. It was a nightmare, but it was real, and he couldn't wake up.

I can't move. I can't do anything. Zoti, please…

Dr. Lancet's voice sliced through his panic like a blade, cold and indifferent.

"You're going to feel everything, Michael," she said, her voice steady, almost soothing. "Every incision, every cut. But you won't be able to move. You won't be able to scream. And don't worry. Those machines are going to keep you alive as long as possible."

Her words slammed into his mind, each syllable adding weight to the suffocating terror that was building in his chest.

I won't be able to scream? His heart thudded harder, a raw pulse of panic that seemed to echo through his frozen body. *I won't be able to move. I'll just… lie here? Trapped?*

The panic started to spread, making his pulse quicken, his breath shallow. The cold, sterile air around him seemed to close in, pressing against his chest.

No. No, I can't do this. I won't just lie here. I have to fight. I have to escape.

But his body refused to listen. The sedative was too strong. He couldn't even twitch, couldn't even blink. The horror of it—the sheer helplessness—was suffocating.

And then there was that sound. The whistling. Dr. Lancet's soft, eerie tune that floated through the sterile air. It was so wrong. She was preparing for something, and it was all business to her. Every note, every breath, was a cruel mockery of his fear.

I'm nothing to her. Just a piece of meat. A body.

His heart raced, but his body didn't respond. His thoughts were screaming, fighting to make sense of it all, but the paralysis kept him locked in place.

Dr. Lancet moved closer, her hands delicate, calculating. His eyes stayed locked on her—unable to escape the sight of her, calm, focused, as though she were preparing a routine surgery. *This isn't routine. This isn't a fucking surgery. This is me, lying here, trapped, waiting for her to tear me apart.*

Her fingers grazed over the scalpel beside her, the cold steel gleaming in the light. The sound of metal against metal, the instruments clinking together, made his skin crawl. He knew what was coming. He could see it in her eyes, feel it in the air. Every inch of her calm was like a countdown to something horrific.

She's going to cut me open. She's going to take me apart, piece by piece, and I won't be able to stop it. I won't even be able to scream.

"Don't worry," she said wryly, her tone flat, as she positioned the scalpel at the top of his chest. "This is just business. You should feel honored."

Honored? She's going to cut me open like an animal. I'm not some specimen—I'm not some… thing.

Her words sank deep into his gut. The finality of it hit him hard, like a punch to the chest. His whole body screamed for release, for freedom, but his mind was the only part of him that was still alive—trapped, screaming, caged inside this paralyzed body.

Then she pressed the scalpel down. The sharp edge sliced into his skin, a clean, cold line just beneath his throat. At first, there was no sensation—just a cold pressure. But then, slowly, the pain began to register. The pressure of the incision. The tearing of tissue.

Michael wanted to jerk away, to scream, to fight—but he couldn't. The pain grew, an unbearable burn as she moved the scalpel deeper, his chest opening, his organs exposed, but he could do nothing to stop it.

This is it. This is really happening.

His breath hitched, and for a moment, he could see it all—the open wound in his chest, the blood pooling around him, the reflection of his own exposed body in the mirror above him. Every detail was visible, a grotesque reminder of how completely helpless he was.

"Good," Dr. Lancet murmured, almost pleased with herself. "You can feel that, can't you? It's all perfectly fine. No movement, no escape. But you'll feel everything. You'll feel your heart slowing. You'll feel your lungs collapsing."

Michael's chest tightened painfully as she went deeper, her hands tracing around his lungs. Every breath felt harder. Every beat of his heart sounded louder, more desperate. He was suffocating, drowning in his own awareness of his body being torn apart.

I can't breathe. I can't move. Zoti, please…

But she didn't stop. Dr. Lancet moved with surgical precision, her hands pulling his lungs free, inspecting them with the same detached interest as if she were holding a specimen jar.

"Beautiful," she whispered, almost lovingly, as she traced the tissue of his lungs. "My organs are just… beautiful."

It's not beautiful. It's not beautiful!

But Michael couldn't say a word. His body wouldn't respond. His thoughts felt like screams locked in a cage. His mind was alive with terror, but his body betrayed him.

The reflection in the mirror above him showed her hands inside him—his heart still beating, still pulsing weakly, but with each passing second, it was growing weaker. He could feel it, the slowing rhythm. The final countdown.

"This is the beauty of it all, Michael," Dr. Lancet said, her voice soft, almost affectionate, as she cradled his heart in her hands. "I get to feel the life ebbing out of you, and you get to feel every second of it. You get to witness your own demise."

The horror of her words cut through him. He wanted to scream. He wanted to fight—but there was nothing. His mind was alive, but his body was nothing more than an unwilling participant in her cruel ritual.

Dr. Lancet looked down at him with an expression that was almost amused, as if she had all the time in the world.

"You'll die, Michael. Slowly. But at least you'll know why."

Her hands moved again, deeper into his chest. The dark, numb wave of unconsciousness crept closer.

The world was narrowing, his breath becoming slower, his body slipping further away from him.

And with that, Michael's last thoughts were drowned in darkness.

∞

Dr. Lancet

Dr. Lancet's eyes narrowed as she glanced at the timer ticking beside her. It had been nearly thirty minutes since she'd summoned Dr. Zygote. Thirty minutes of waiting. Her fingers tapped restlessly against the edge of the table, the same impatient rhythm she had used countless times before, but this time it felt more pronounced.

She could feel her weakness setting in, her body faltering with every breath. Her lungs ached and her heart—her heart beat sluggishly, not as strong as it once was. She wasn't sure how much longer she could endure the decay of her organs before she collapsed entirely. But the organs she'd harvested from Michael, still cold in the iceboxes beside her, would fix that—if she could just get them transplanted.

Zygote, where the hell are you?

Her pulse quickened in frustration as she stared at the iceboxes. The organ transplant was her only chance. She needed it now. Her time was running out.

She flicked the ash off her cigarette, her eyes still fixed on the door. Thirty minutes. That was too long.

Why hasn't he come? The thought echoed in her mind. She needed to survive. These organs would keep her alive, and yet, here she was, waiting.

Her gaze flicked over to the iceboxes once more. The lungs, kidneys, liver, and heart were already stored, the key to her survival. But it felt like Zygote was dragging his feet again. *This delay is unacceptable.*

Another minute passed.

Finally, the door creaked open, and Dr. Zygote strolled in, looking unhurried. He didn't look remotely concerned about the time wasted, and it irritated her more than it should have.

"What took you so long?" Dr. Lancet snapped, her voice sharp. "You should have been here thirty minutes ago. You're just across the hall— don't tell me you're that decrepit to walk over here that slowly."

Dr. Zygote didn't respond right away, his eyes taking her in with that characteristic indifference. "I had other matters to attend to," he said, as though that should excuse his tardiness. He moved closer to the table without any real sense of urgency.

Dr. Lancet's frustration mounted, and she felt it curling inside her chest like a coil. The transplant needed to happen now. Her hands clenched the edge of the table as she glared at him.

"Don't make me wait any longer, Zygote," she demanded, voice tight with barely controlled anger. "I need it now."

Dr. Zygote raised an eyebrow, nonplussed by her urgency. "Patience, Evelyn. You're lucky you're getting this at all."

Her teeth clenched, and she forced a smile. "Yes, I'm lucky indeed. You know exactly what I need. Can we just get on with it?"

Finally, Dr. Zygote moved to the table, starting to gather his instruments. His slow pace only irritated her further. The sense of urgency was suffocating, and yet Zygote acted like he had all the time in the world.

The iceboxes stood at the ready, their contents perfectly preserved— her salvation. Dr. Lancet's body was failing, and if she didn't get the transplant now, she'd be too weak to continue. The cracks in her system were deepening. Her pulse was sluggish, and every breath felt like a labor. But once the organs were inside her, she'd be strong again.

Move faster, Zygote. Don't waste any more of my time.

Her breath hitched as she felt a new wave of weakness hit her. Every moment counted now. The cold numbness creeping in. The familiar ache in her chest, each beat of her heart a reminder of how much longer she had left before the life inside her would fade.

I need this transplant now.

∞

Dr. Zygote

Dr. Zygote stood quietly at the edge of the operating table, observing Dr. Lancet's still form. She had finally fallen unconscious after he administered the sedative, her body now limp, ready for the transplant. The faint hum of the sterile lights filled the room, and he felt the weight of his responsibility settle over him. The organ transplant was a delicate procedure, but it wasn't his first.

His movements were measured as he gathered the necessary instruments—scalpel, forceps, clamps. His eyes flicked toward the iceboxes where Michael's organs were carefully preserved. The lungs, heart, kidneys, and liver were in perfect condition, each one ready to be seamlessly integrated into Dr. Lancet's body. Dr. Lancet had been the one who had purchased Michael's organs at the bidding, not him.

Dr. Zygote had simply been tasked with the procedure—the work that had to be done to keep her alive. He was detached from the drama of the auction and the motivations behind it. For him, this was just another surgery.

If she survives, it will be because of me. Because of my work.

Dr. Zygote walked over to the table, pulling on his gloves with deliberate precision. The soft click of his gloves against the table was the only sound as he began to prepare. But then, with a slight smile, he reached into his lab coat pocket and pulled out his Walkman. He flipped it on, and the soft hum of music began to fill his ears, steady and soothing. It wasn't loud, but just enough to help him focus. The rhythm of the surgery needed to match the beat of the music. Calm, controlled.

Taking a deep breath, he moved toward Dr. Lancet's body, administering the final dose of sedative to ensure she remained unconscious throughout the transplant. The needle slid easily into her vein, the fluid traveling through her body quickly, ensuring she wouldn't wake until the work was done.

He watched her for a moment, noting the slow rise and fall of her chest as the sedative took full effect. Then, he focused his attention on the iceboxes at the side of the room, where Michael's organs waited, preserved and ready for implantation.

Dr. Lancet's lungs had been failing, her heart weak, her kidneys barely functioning. These organs—Michael's organs—were the key to her survival. She had paid for them, and now he would ensure they were properly integrated into her system.

Dr. Zygote began prepping the operating table, checking the sterile equipment laid out in front of him. His hands were steady, moving with a calm and practiced efficiency. There was no need to hurry. The procedure was straightforward. He was used to this.

He adjusted his gloves and carefully selected the scalpel, ensuring the blade was sharp and precise. This wasn't the first transplant he had performed, and it wouldn't be the last. Dr. Lancet would wake up with new organs, the ones she had desperately needed. For him, it was just another day in Augmentation Bay. Another procedure. Another set of body parts to be exchanged.

The sound of the Walkman was a quiet hum in the background, providing a steady rhythm to the procedure. He didn't find it necessary to speed up or slow down to the beat, but it kept him in the right mental space—focused, calm.

Once the final sutures were made and the organs securely in place, Dr. Zygote stepped back and admired his work. He leaned over, inspecting the now-stable form of Dr. Lancet, the lines of her body beginning to adjust to the new organs inside her. She would wake up soon, and the new organs would begin working, restoring her to full strength.

For now, at least. He allowed himself a small smile.

He left the room quietly, the music still playing softly in his ears as he walked out, leaving Dr. Lancet to recover, her life now intertwined with the organs of another.

But not without flipping her the bird.

∞

Dr. Lancet's eyes fluttered open, her senses slowly returning as the sedative's haze began to lift. The sterile scent of the room filled her nose, and she felt a faint twinge of soreness in her body. She was aware of the soft beeping of the monitors beside her, but what struck her most was the absence of pain in places where it had once been unbearable.

The transplant...

Her mind slowly pieced together the fragments of what had happened—Dr. Zygote's procedure, replacing her failing organs with the new ones she had bought from Michael. The new organs inside her felt strong, a surge of vitality rushing through her system, pushing away the lethargy that had plagued her body.

Her head spun slightly as she tried to sit up, the room slightly swaying as the sedative wore off. She took a deep breath, her chest rising and falling steadily, the new lungs taking in the air with ease.

I'm alive. The thought lingered in her mind, and she let out a breath of relief.

She shifted slightly in the bed, and that's when she heard it. The sound of footsteps approaching, the creak of the door opening.

A voice. The Warden's voice.

"Evelyn, you're awake." The Warden's tone was firm, but there was a hint of something softer, more reassuring, as he spoke.

Dr. Lancet turned her head toward the voice. Standing beside him was a young woman with dark brown curly hair and blue eyes, her expression hesitant, unsure. Shabina was looking at Dr. Lancet with an awkward, nervous smile, nodding slightly as she took in the sight of her.

The Warden stepped forward, standing beside the bed. "Evelyn," he said, his gaze flicking to the young woman, "meet your new assistant, Shabina."

Dr. Lancet blinked slowly, still processing everything. She didn't need an assistant. She had been running surgeries on her own for years.

"I don't need an assistant," Dr. Lancet sneered, her voice hoarse from the sedation. "I'm perfectly capable of doing my job alone."

The Warden's expression hardened, but his tone remained calm. "This is your third surgery, Evelyn… Shabina will be your assistant, and I won't hear more about it."

Dr. Lancet's jaw tightened as she tried to push herself up in the bed, the weakness of her body still very present despite the surge of energy she felt from the transplant.

Shabina shifted awkwardly, looking at the floor, then back at Dr. Lancet.

The Warden took a step back, his voice sharp. "I'll leave you two to it. Shabina will take care of whatever you need."

With that, The Warden turned and walked out, leaving Shabina standing there, unsure of what to do next. The silence between them was palpable.

Dr. Lancet sat up, her body aching from the incision, the healing process already underway but still tender. She pointed toward a tray on the workbench that contained a jar of yellow powder and a glass of water. "Get me that," she commanded, her voice still rough from the sedation. "Hurry."

Shabina rushed over to the tray, her hands shaking slightly as she mixed the powder into the water. She brought the glass back to Dr. Lancet, who drank it in three large mouthfuls.

"Well, what are you waiting for? Clean the surgery," Dr. Lancet snapped, setting the glass down with a sharp movement.

Shabina hurried to comply, moving to clean up the surgical area. She gathered the scattered tools, wiped down the counters, and locked away the equipment into the storage cupboard. She glanced up at Dr. Lancet, hesitant.

"Is there anything else you need?" Shabina asked.

Dr. Lancet glanced at her briefly, a flicker of annoyance crossing her face. "I need you to go get Zayne. Then I need you to stay out of my way."

Shabina nodded quickly and left the room, her awkward footsteps fading into the corridor as Dr. Lancet's eyes followed her.

The doors clicked shut behind Shabina.

Silence. Sterile and momentary.

Dr. Lancet moved like a shadow toward her workbench. She pulled open a slim drawer, revealing a hidden compartment: a nearly spent pack of cigarettes, a matchbook, and a single glass vial labeled in her own handwriting. She lit one with a flick of her thumb, the tip flaring to life. The first drag hit like a sedative.

Smoke curled upward in slow spirals. The faint burn of ash mingled with the smell of bleach.

Then—

"All that iron…"

The voice slithered into the room before the man did.

"…straight down the drain."

Dr. Zygote entered without fanfare, but there was nothing quiet about his presence.

His lab coat was stained—less like he hadn't cleaned it and more like he wore the blood as proof of his genius. His gray hair was unkempt, tufts sticking out at odd angles like static held them in place. His eyes, glassy and manic, glinted behind smudged lenses. He was younger than he looked, and older than he acted.

Dr. Lancet didn't flinch. She blew a stream of smoke toward him and said nothing.

Zygote's smile stretched too wide.

"Why do you even bother, Evelyn?" he asked, walking with a disjointed bounce, like each step came at a different speed than the last. His fingers twitched at his sides, itching for something to hold—or dissect.

Lancet tapped ash into the tray beside her. "Working with you, Zayne?" she muttered. "I need these."

He tilted his head, eyes fixated on the glowing cigarette. His grin widened, lips cracked at the corners.

"Ahh. Still so dramatic."

"Was the insemination a success?" she asked.

Zygote's expression lit up—manic glee flaring like a spark to dry kindling.

He reached into the inner pocket of his coat and pulled out a wrinkled photograph. It was an ultrasound, already smudged from overhandling. He slapped it down onto the surgical tray with a flourish.

"More than successful." His voice dropped into something reverent. "Twins."

Dr. Lancet blinked.

Twins.

Her cigarette paused halfway to her lips. "You're certain?"

"Perfectly." He leaned in close, lowering his voice as if the walls might lean in to hear. "Viable. Stable. Miraculous."

He was pacing now, practically vibrating, his hands gesturing wildly in the air.

Dr. Lancet set her cigarette down, mouth dry. "The Shepherd will want to know."

"We'll tell The Warden first," he said with a sharp jerk of his head. "Then the parents. Eventually." He spun toward her, gleeful. "They only wanted one, remember?"

She scowled. "They made it very clear."

"And yet," Zygote said, lifting the ultrasound again and cradling it with something that bordered on reverence, "here they are."

"What do we do with the other?"

Zygote's fingers tapped against the metal tray, twitching rhythmically.

"Cypher wants a pair. The Shepherd's been foaming at the mouth for twins since the last failed clutch."

Lancet scoffed. "They'll want both."

"And they'll pay for both," Zygote said, still smiling.

The door swung open.

"Who wants what set of twins now?"

The Warden entered, Shabina right behind him, awkward as ever.

"I found her wandering," he said flatly, gesturing to Shabina. "She said you dismissed her." He fixed his gaze on Dr. Lancet. "Care to explain?"

"I don't need an assistant," she replied without missing a beat.

"And I don't care," he growled. "You have one. Use her. Now—twins?"

Zygote stepped forward like a magician revealing the final card in a trick. "Confirmed. Our first set."

The Warden went still.

When he spoke, his tone dropped into something darker.

"The Brennans don't need to know. Tell them the insemination failed."

Zygote blinked. Dr. Lancet turned toward him.

"Failed?"

"Tell them the incubator was not viable. Offer a retry. Free of charge." The Warden's voice was a razor. "They only wanted one. They'll get it. Later."

Both doctors turned to look at Shabina.

"What about her?" Lancet asked.

"I trust Shabina," the Warden said simply. "I chose her myself."

Shabina nodded. "I won't breathe a word."

Dr. Lancet didn't blink. But her jaw tensed.

"Fine," she snapped. "But what do we do with the twins?"

"Zygote, handle the call to the Brennans. Say the procedure failed. I'll speak with Donovan." The Warden's eyes narrowed. "He'll pay more than iron for a matched set."

Zygote gave a sharp nod, already halfway out the door, muttering to himself and clutching the ultrasound like a relic.

The Warden turned back to Dr. Lancet.

"Don't think I can't smell that," he said, his voice cool.

She raised an eyebrow. "It's my lungs. My iron."

"And my risk." His voice sharpened. "You get a discount I could lose everything for."

She looked at the stubbed-out cigarette.

"Fine. I'll quit." Then, quieter: "But I want something from you in return."

His gaze didn't soften.

She looked over at Shabina. "Fetch more Vitality Serum."

The girl vanished.

Dr. Lancet stepped closer to the Warden. Her voice dropped. "My daughter is missing. I think the Renegades took her."

"Then you should go to the authorities."

She hesitated.

"…I think she might've joined them." Her throat clenched. "I need proof before I make it worse."

The Warden was quiet.

Then he placed a firm hand on her shoulder.

"It's not your fault, Evelyn. They poison minds. Twist truth into heresy."

She nodded.

"Thank you."

His hand moved to her cheek. "You smile too little. You should fix that."

She allowed herself a faint smile.

Then—

CLACK.

Shabina returned with the serum. "Uh, sorry."

The Warden let go of her, face hardening again.

"Nothing to apologize for," Dr. Lancet snapped. "We were just talking… about the twins."

The Warden straightened his coat. "You'll be back to your old self in no time."

He exited without another word.

Shabina lingered.

"He likes you," she said, almost shyly.

Dr. Lancet shot her a glare sharp enough to cut glass. "Keep the conversation professional. This is a work environment."

Shabina dropped her gaze. "Yes, Doctor."

∞

Dr. Zygote

Dr. Zygote stood behind his desk, phone pressed to his ear, his fingers absently tapping a cracked pen against a stack of folders.

"Yes, Mr. Brennan, I understand your concern," he said, voice smooth, practiced. "But unfortunately, these outcomes aren't unusual."

He flipped through the top page without looking at it.

"Sometimes the process doesn't take. Internal factors vary. Not every incubator proves viable."

The client's voice crackled through the speaker—tight, annoyed, demanding.

"No, your contribution wasn't the issue." A pause. "The incubator is to blame. It's been pulled from rotation."

He pulled the ultrasound photo from beneath the paperwork and slid it to the side, careful not to crease it.

"You'll be offered a retry at no additional cost. First access to the new round of candidates. All aligned to your original specifications."

Zygote kept his tone steady, even as his jaw tightened.

"Yes, Mr. Brennan. You'll get what you paid for."

He ended the call before the man could launch into another tirade.

The phone hit the desk with a dull thud. For a moment, Zygote just stood there.

Then he sat down slowly, hands dragging down his face.

His eyes fell on the ultrasound again—two small shapes suspended in shadow.

"This isn't going to end well."

∞

Dr. Lancet

She stood outside The Warden's office, barely breathing, one eye fixed on the narrow crack in the door.

Inside, The Warden's voice was low but firm. Authoritative.

"I need you to get this message to our friend," he said as Dr. Zygote took a seat, hunched and twitchy as ever. "They must keep it confidential."

He handed Zygote a small scroll, sealed with wax. Something important. Something hidden.

Dr. Zygote scoffed. "I'm a doctor… not a messenger."

Idiot. She rolled her eyes.

The Warden's glare shut him up instantly. His voice dropped a notch darker.

"You will do this, Zayne. And I won't hear another word about it. Be sure to speak to him about the twins." His right eyebrow lifted—a subtle threat.

Zygote snatched the scroll like a spoiled child denied dessert. As he stormed out, muttering nonsense, Dr. Lancet adjusted her posture and stepped forward—composed, calm, calculating.

Timing was everything.

She swung the door open just as he passed, pretending surprise.

"Zayne," she said with a sharp nod, brushing past him as though he were nothing more than a gust of foul-smelling wind.

Inside, The Warden jolted to his feet, startled, then quickly composed himself. His eyes softened as he moved toward her, reaching out.

"You should rest, Evelyn."

She hated how he said her name—like it meant something to him.

She pulled her arm away from his grasp. "Oh, don't fuss. The Vitality Serum did its job just fine… I'm fine."

Truthfully, she wasn't. Her body ached. The wounds from the Harvest were still tender. The skin behind her ribs felt raw, as if it hadn't settled back into place. But pain had its uses—it sharpened her focus.

"What are you doing here?" he asked, clearly caught off guard.

She offered him a small, knowing smile. "I hoped to talk to you. If you're not busy."

He leaned against the edge of his desk, trying to look relaxed. She sat beside him, letting her smirk linger a little longer than necessary.

"I have some… tests I'd like to perform on the incubator and the twins," she said slowly, curling her words like smoke. "Zayne can't know about them."

He tensed. *Good.*

He looked at her cautiously, expecting more. She gave him nothing.

"What tests?" he asked finally. "You surely can't expect me to say yes when I don't know what they are."

She smiled wider, just enough to unnerve him. "I just want to take a few DNA samples." She leaned in, lowering her voice. "I'd be extremely grateful if you could help me."

Her hand found his knee, gentle at first.

"You've been wanting this for a while. Haven't you, Wyatt?" She grinned and bit her lip. "I've wanted you, too."

His breath caught.

Got you.

"Evelyn…" he said, voice dipping into that gravelly tone she'd heard too many times. As her hand slid up his thigh, his body stiffened. Her gaze met his, unwavering.

He grabbed the back of her hair—rough. Predictable. He stared into her eyes for a heartbeat, then yanked her head back and pressed his mouth against her throat, kissing and biting like a starving beast.

She groaned, both from pain and pleasure. She liked pain, in more ways than one. His hands found her thighs, lifting her onto the table. Pain flared in her abdomen.

Not here. Not yet.

"Wait," she gasped. "Not here."

He froze, still holding her hair, then let go and stepped back. He adjusted his jacket, straightening himself out like nothing had happened.

"Of course. Let's get these DNA samples. Dr. Zygote is out of the office for the rest of the day. We have time now."

That was easier than I expected, she thought as she followed him down the corridor toward The Cell. *I thought I would have had to fuck him a few times first.*

She smirked to herself.

Men are so fucking stupid.

The Warden strode ahead, authoritative again.

"Go. Patrol Detachment." He motioned toward the Argentine Enforcer stationed outside The Cell. "Come back in two hours."

The Enforcer froze a moment—processing—then turned and walked away in silence.

"That should be enough time, right?"

Dr. Lancet nodded, already stepping past him. She moved toward the door on the other side of the room.

"Quick. In case Jessica shows up."

∞

Dr. Zygote

Dr. Zygote sat in the back of the black armored limo, the world outside hidden behind tinted windows. He looked down at the scroll The Warden had handed him, still sealed with wax, still warm with secrecy.

"I'm risking everything for him," he muttered. "And yet he still keeps me in the dark."

The limo slowed at an intersection. Outside, the city pressed in — people packed on sidewalks, gray buildings stacked like storage units. The air reeked of wet iron and desperation.

Zygote sneered at the sight.

"Look at them… sheep. Packed into a pen, waiting for the wolves to pick which ones they want for dinner."

The light changed, and the limo turned sharply, heading out of the central district and onto a long stretch of cracked highway. Towering metal fences lined the road, scarred with decades of graffiti and protest. The city slowly thinned. Rain began to dot the windows.

Zygote looked down at the scroll again, curiosity finally winning.

He tilted it, peeking through the center.

Lancet's daughter is missing. Please locate, start with The—

The roll blocked the rest.

His eyes narrowed.

"Evelyn has a daughter?" he whispered. "She's never mentioned her before."

A sudden knock startled him.

He looked up as a young man opened the door and slid into the seat across from him. Lean, tense, and soaked from the rain—long black hair, dark eyes like wet stone, and the sun-kissed skin of someone who spent a lot of time outdoors.

"Valentino."

Zygote gave him a curt nod. "Get comfortable. It's going to be a long drive today."

Valentino said nothing. Just leaned back, eyes out the window.

The limo passed through a security gate at the city's edge and began climbing the winding roads toward Feltwood Mountains.

Once the last checkpoint disappeared behind them, Zygote leaned forward.

"I have a message that needs to be delivered to The Architect. Immediately."

Valentino didn't look away from the window. "And what do I get for delivering it?"

Arrogant little bastard, Zygote thought.

He pulled a heavy pouch of iron from under the seat and tossed it into Valentino's lap.

Valentino caught it, tested the weight, and slipped it into his coat without a word.

Then Zygote handed him the scroll.

"The Architect's eyes only."

Valentino held it delicately between two fingers, like something that might stain him.

"You know my fee includes information… Doctor," he said, voice flat but sharp.

Zygote bristled. "Patience is not a skill all can master," he said. Then, after a tense pause: "The Cell's latest insemination was… productive. Twins."

Valentino turned his head slowly. His expression cracked — just slightly.

"Twins? There hasn't been any since…"

Zygote smiled, all teeth and no warmth. "Since your brothers."

The temperature in the limo dropped.

"Any luck finding them?" Zygote asked casually.

Valentino stared out the window again.

Zygote pressed on. "I'm telling you, The Renegades have them. Probably locked away, wasting time and iron. If I could meet The Architect myself, we could work together. Find them. Don't you want to help your poor baby brothers?"

That did it.

Valentino snapped around.

"They all left me!" he shouted, his voice cutting through the car like a blade. "I don't want to help them— I want to kill them! They vanished. My whole family disappeared into the sunset and left me behind!"

His breath came fast and shallow. A vein pulsed in his forehead.

"The Architect raised me. He is my family. My only family. And I will not betray him by bringing you to him."

His voice dropped. Cold. Final.

"Make sure Jaysen Masters gets the death sentence. He's counting on it."

Zygote didn't speak.

Valentino shoved open the door as the limo pulled over to the side of the road near a weather-beaten trailhead.

Rain tapped against the roof.

He turned back, eyes burning.

"You'd better watch your mouth, old man. One day, it's going to get you into a lot of trouble."

He slammed the door.

The limo didn't move right away. Zygote sat in the stillness, fingers tightening on his coat lapel.

"So sensitive," he muttered, his voice quieter now. Shakier.

Outside, Valentino walked into the rising mist of Feltwood Mountains as the rain fell harder, hiding him in gray.

∞

Valentino

Valentino moved through the trees in silence, the branches clawing at his coat like fingers that didn't want him to pass.

The mountain loomed ahead, distant but familiar.

"Why did you let him get to you?" he muttered. "He's just a crazy old man."

But the words didn't help. Zygote had gotten under his skin. Again.

Three hours into the trek, the terrain thickened. Old roots twisted underfoot, and thorny vines clung to his legs like they meant to pull him back. He ducked beneath a low limb when voices cut through the trees — harsh and urgent.

"TURN AROUND, MARCUS! LET ME GET MY CLOTHES, AND I'LL LEAVE!"

A woman. Angry. Scared.

Valentino crouched and moved toward the sound, quiet as breath. He slipped between a curtain of brush and froze at the edge of a clearing.

A small spring sat in the middle, dark and glassy. A young woman stood waist-deep in the water, trying to shield herself with crossed arms. Her hair was soaked, curling around her face.

She was shouting at a man pacing the edge of the spring.

"JUST TURN AROUND, MARCUS!"

The man—Marcus—grinned with a twisted sort of pleasure, but finally turned away with a scoff.

The woman—who Valentino didn't recognize—scrambled out of the spring and rushed toward a bundle of clothes on a mossy rock. Her movements were quick, frantic.

Marcus turned before she could even grab a shirt.

He crossed the clearing in a few long strides.

"Don't," she warned, backing up.

He ignored her.

He grabbed her arm and yanked her toward him.

"I said don't!" she hissed, trying to twist free.

His grip only tightened.

"I will have you," he growled. "One way or another."

His other hand groped her. She cried out, struggling harder.

"You think you're better than me?" he spat. "You act pure, but you're not. You're nothing special. You'll give in—like the rest."

He tried to kiss her.

Valentino rose. His body was tense, every muscle coiled. He reached for the branch above him, ready to step in—

But then she acted.

Her knee shot up and cracked Marcus square between the legs.

He dropped like a stone, howling and curling into the dirt.

She snatched her clothes, tears streaming down her cheeks, and ran into the forest without looking back.

"I'LL GET YOU FOR THAT… FREAK!" Marcus roared after her, still on the ground, breath ragged.

Valentino stepped into the clearing.

106

"She handled herself," he said, voice cold. "But if she hadn't, you'd be dead right now."

Marcus groaned, dragging himself upright.

"I'm not here for lectures, Val. I want the info. That's the deal."

Valentino didn't answer right away. Then: "The Cell is expecting twins."

Marcus froze, brushing off his muddy pants.

"Twins?" His tone shifted. "And the incubator?"

"Don't know," Valentino replied. "That's all I was told."

Marcus swore under his breath.

"Fine," he said. "The Council claims they've found The Hidden Heir. But there's a catch."

Valentino arched a brow.

"They sent him to Augmentation Bay."

His blood ran colder.

"Who is he?"

"I don't know," Marcus said. "Not yet."

Valentino let the silence stretch, then narrowed his eyes. "Heard anything about my brothers?"

Marcus smirked. "Nope. Probably dead."

Valentino's jaw tightened.

"When you stop being useful," he said calmly, "I'll kill you myself."

Marcus's smirk faltered.

He turned and stormed off into the trees, following the same trail the woman had disappeared down.

Valentino watched him vanish. Alone now, he glanced at the sky. Clouds broke open to reveal the dim burn of fading daylight.

"Guess I'm sleeping out here," he muttered.

He found a dry patch beneath a thick pine and settled into the dirt. No fire. No shelter. Just leaves and cold and the memory of her scream.

He looked up through the canopy. The stars were starting to show.

"I'll find them one day," he whispered.

Then he closed his eyes and let the wind pull him into sleep.

∞

Dr. Lancet

"You said nothing about giving it something, Evelyn!" The Warden's voice cracked like a whip as they emerged from The Cell. His grip on her arm was tight, urgent.

"What was it?"

Dr. Lancet didn't flinch. She let him lead her — for now.

She smirked as they reached his office. He ushered her inside, slammed the door shut, and locked it.

"Calm down," she said smoothly, pulling her arm away once the lock clicked. "We have to keep the twins safe. This is how we do that."

She reached into her bag and pulled out a small laptop, opening it with practiced precision. The screen cast a faint glow across her face.

"We will not lose these ones," she said. "Not like that fool who calls himself The Architect."

She felt his eyes on her before she heard his footsteps.

"Why didn't you want Zayne to know?" The Warden asked.

She let out a low scoff, still typing.

"Something's off about him. He mutters to himself constantly. Talks like someone's always listening. We can't risk him slipping. Not now. Not with this."

She showed him a small screen on her phone. On it, a map, with a small flashing light over Augmentation Bay. A tracker.

The Warden stepped closer, his voice softer now. "And this is why I hired you, Evelyn."

He placed a hand on hers.

She pulled away, eyes narrowing. "Then why are you phasing me out?"

A beat of silence passed between them.

"I'm not stupid, Wyatt," she said, standing to face him. "I know why you hired Shabina. She's there to take over the surgery… isn't she?"

The Warden didn't answer at first. Then, he grabbed her hand.

Clenched it.

"Only when you're ready to leave." His voice had a new edge now.

The pressure on her hand increased. Sharp. Intentional.

"But if you don't stop with these hysterical outbursts... if you don't stop dismissing Shabina..."

He pulled her in close.

"If you don't do as you're ordered..."

His mouth brushed her ear.

"Then I'll make sure you're ready." His breath was hot. "I'll make sure you never get another organ from The Harvest again. And I'll stop looking for your daughter."

Her blood ran cold at that. A threat more intimate than violence.

To be cut off from The Harvest is a death sentence.

He knew that.

He bit her neck.

Again.

"We're as alone as we're ever going to be in this place," he growled.

Then he shoved her against the wall.

She hissed, her back slamming into the cold panel. He grabbed both her wrists and pinned them above her head with one hand, the other pulling at his belt.

He pressed his chest against hers—right where the fresh wound still throbbed from the last transplant.

She let out a moan, unfiltered, a strange blend of pain and something else.

The sound seemed to drive him further.

He bit down harder on her neck, then released her. Unbuttoned his slacks.

"Time for you to give me what you promised."

He didn't wait for her answer.

The Warden shoved her against the wall again, harder this time, enough to knock the air from her lungs. She gasped, but it wasn't fear. It was need.

His hand wrapped around her throat, pressing just hard enough to blur the edges of her vision.

"You like this," he growled.

She couldn't speak. Didn't need to.

She looked him in the eye and smiled.

His mouth crashed into hers—biting, claiming, consuming. His other hand was at her waist, yanking fabric, tearing where it didn't give fast enough. She clawed at his back.

He pulled her arm behind her back, twisting until her shoulder strained. She moaned into his mouth, half pain, half pleasure.

He pressed her harder against the wall, his hips locking hers in place. She felt the sharp sting of his belt buckle scraping her skin as he pushed her skirt up and yanked her underwear down.

"Say it," he hissed in her ear.

"I like this. More."

His grip tightened.

He didn't ask again.

Their bodies collided in rhythm, violent and hungry. The tile was cold against her back, but she didn't care. She wanted the bruises. She wanted the burn. Every slam of his hips, every dig of his nails into her thighs, every ragged breath between clenched teeth—it was all power, all control, all pain.

And she loved it.

She bit his neck. Hard. Enough to draw blood. He answered with a slap across her face that sent her head reeling—but she didn't look away. She didn't flinch.

She smiled.

He didn't last long.

When it was over, she slid to the floor with him, both of them panting, scratched, and shaking.

And then the sun disappeared from the window.

∞

The sun had long since vanished beyond the concrete skyline.

Shadows crept through the office. Cold tile pressed against Dr. Lancet's bare back. She reached for her clothes in silence.

She wasn't staying.

"No," The Warden said behind her, already recovering, already in control again. "You will stay here tonight."

She didn't bother looking at him. Just pulled her shirt back on, still damp with sweat and her own blood.

"I'm not sleeping on the floor," she snapped.

He crossed to the desk, pressed a hidden switch.

A wall slid open, smooth and silent.

Behind it: a room concealed in soft light, walls padded, a bed massive and clean, sheets ironed into rigid precision. It smelled like secrets.

"You won't be sleeping on the floor." He winked.

Of course. Of course he has a room like this.

Dr. Lancet walked slowly toward the bed, eyeing the space like a surgical theater.

"So that's why your office always seemed bigger from the outside," she muttered. "I knew you were hiding something."

The Warden laughed and moved to the bar tucked in the corner.

He poured himself a glass of scotch, tilted it back without a word, then looked at her over the rim.

"There's a lot you don't know about me, Evelyn. This is only the beginning."

He said it with a smile, but something in his voice made her skin crawl.

She sat on the edge of the bed, near the nightstand. There, waiting: a full glass of Vitality Serum.

"There's another glass of Vitality Serum on the bar," he said, casually. "With some sleeping pills. Have them. Get some rest. I'll be needing you again in a few hours."

He left the room without waiting for a response.

The wall hissed closed behind him.

Click.

The lock slid into place.

Dr. Lancet didn't move at first.

She stared at the wall where he'd vanished. Then she stood and crossed the room, palms pressing flat against the surface.

No movement.

No seam.

"What the fuck is he doing?" she muttered. "Why did he lock me in?"

This wasn't part of the game.

She pressed harder, searching for a button, a release, anything. Her fingers scraped along the molding, behind furniture, inside the drawers.

He wouldn't risk locking himself in. There has to be a way out.

Her thoughts grew scattered. Her limbs heavier.

The glass on the table was empty.

She hadn't realized she'd drunk the whole thing.

She grabbed the one from the bar, and downed it in three slow gulps.

As she sat the glass down, she knocked it over.

Her breathing slowed. Vision blurred.

The world around her spun.

There's another glass of Vitality Serum on the bar… with some sleeping pills…

The Warden's voice replayed in her skull like a looping recording.

She swayed and caught the edge of the bed.

"They were in the serum," she whispered, blinking hard.

Her body was shutting down. Not from exhaustion.

From something else.

"I'll get him for that," she slurred.

Her legs gave out. She sank into the mattress, eyes fluttering closed against her will.

"This wasn't supposed to happen…"

Her words were soft. Fading. Muffled into the pillow.

And then she was still.

∞

She was back in the operating theater. But this time, she wasn't standing over the table.

She was on it. Strapped down. Metal dug into her wrists and ankles. Her head was pinned tight, immobilized. She tried to move, but her body didn't listen.

The room smelled like bleach, copper, and something older. Decay under gloss.

Then came the sound.

Whistling.

Her whistling.

Only… it wasn't coming from her lips.

A silhouette stepped out from the dark.

Wearing her coat. Her gloves. Her face.

But the eyes—

Michael's.

Cold. Amused.

"Don't worry, Evelyn," the voice said, dripping with calm contempt. "You're going to feel everything."

The scalpel gleamed in the figure's hand—steady, practiced, precise. Her hand. His intent.

She tried to scream.

Nothing.

No voice. No breath. Just the crushing weight of helplessness.

"I've waited a long time for this," the doppelgänger whispered.

The scalpel touched her skin, right below her sternum. She didn't feel pressure.

She felt invasion.

Pain bloomed—sharp, slicing, cold.

Blood pooled at her side, trickling over the table's edge in thin, steady streams.

The lights above flickered, dimming. In the surgical mirror overhead, her chest was open. Spread wide. Her lungs pulsed erratically in the fluorescent hum. Her heart still beat—but it was exposed, vulnerable, watching.

She couldn't look away.

"You always wanted to be the one holding the knife," Michael's voice mocked. "Now you'll see how it feels."

Another cut. Deeper.

She tried to move. Scream. Something.

Nothing.

Her reflection in the mirror began to twitch—uncontrollably. But she wasn't moving.

It was. It looked at her, eyes wide with terror. It mouthed her name— Evelyn—over and over, like a child begging to wake up.

Then, the reflection morphed, and Michael was there.

Still.

Silent.

Smiling.

∞

Dr. Lancet woke drenched in sweat. Her lungs ached like they'd been screaming. Her hands trembled as she dragged them across the sheets, clutching at fabric—not restraints. She was in a bed. Her bed.

Sort of.

114

The room was dim—lit by wall sconces that buzzed faintly as they flickered. The darkness didn't stay long enough to settle, but it kept trying, pressing in at the edges every time the lights dipped.

A chill crept through her bones as a breeze kissed the back of her neck. She pulled the covers up reflexively. That's when she saw it.

The mirror above the bed.

And in it—Michael.

Lying on her operating table. Chest cracked open. Organs missing. That same unblinking stare. That same smile.

Her breath caught. She didn't look away.

The wall behind her hissed open.

She shot up from the bed.

"What's wrong?" The Warden asked, stepping into the room like he owned her panic.

"What's wrong?" she snapped, voice sharp with disbelief. "*WHAT'S WRONG?* You drugged me and locked me in your room, Wyatt!"

He chuckled. "I never locked you in, Evelyn." He walked to the bedside table and casually picked up a remote sitting next to the lamp. "The control was right here."

Her cheeks flushed with heat. "That… that wasn't there before."

"You must've been tired." His voice softened. Faux-concerned. "I'm sorry you misunderstood me earlier. I only put the sleeping pills in your drink to make them easier to take."

He held out the remote.

"Please… don't leave." He smiled. "I need you."

She stared at the remote. Then at him. Then the wall. Her fingers flexed slightly, but not enough to be considered resistance.

I need to make sure I stay on the Harvest list. I need to stay here with him and make sure he doesn't take me off… and I do like the way he fucks me.

"I suppose I could stay tonight," she shrugged.

She handed the control back to him.

He took it with one hand. Grabbed her wrist with the other.

"Good girl," he growled in her ear—then shoved her back onto the bed.

He climbed on top of her, tearing at her clothes with eager, calloused fingers. Pain lanced through her freshly stitched chest, and she gasped.

He grinned. "Still healing?"

She didn't answer. Just arched against him.

He shoved her legs apart with his knee, one hand in her hair, the other ripping the fabric down her center until it gave way with a sharp *rrrip*. The cold air bit her skin. Then he was inside her—no buildup, no preamble. Just a single, brutal thrust that drove the breath from her lungs.

She cried out. The pain was sharp. Raw. And she welcomed it.

His rhythm was punishing—fast, hard, relentless. He didn't slow. Didn't speak. Just gripped and took. The bed rocked beneath them, the frame shuddering against the wall.

He bit her shoulder, deep enough to bruise. Her moan was a gasp and a growl, pain bleeding into pleasure. She didn't flinch—she leaned into it.

"You like that?" he hissed. "Of course you do. You like it when I hurt you."

He grabbed her wrists and pinned them above her head with one hand, the other pressing between her legs with brutal precision. Her hips bucked instinctively, trying to keep up with his rhythm. Her body burned—everywhere. Her chest, her wrists, the bruises forming beneath his touch.

She was close.

Too close.

The pain in her chest sharpened, and that only pushed her over the edge. She came with a violent shudder, back arched, gasping against his shoulder.

He finished a moment later, spilling into her with a grunt, his teeth grazing her neck one final time before he collapsed beside her.

Silence.

Then breath.

116

Shaky, shared, raw.

She opened her eyes.

The mirror stared back.

Michael hadn't moved.

Still watching.

Still smiling.

She lifted her hand slowly and traced her fingers across her chest, right along the line of the healing incision. The pain was faint now. A dull throb beneath her fingertips.

In the reflection, Michael mirrored her—dragging phantom fingers across the hollow of his own open chest.

"What are you doing, Evelyn?" The Warden asked from beside her. "Is it causing you pain?"

She froze.

"…Uh. Yes," she said quickly, pulling her hand away.

He rolled over and grabbed a small gel tube from the nightstand.

"This will speed up the healing process," he said. "Lie down."

She obeyed.

He squeezed the gel into his palm and rubbed it gently across the wound. The sting faded almost instantly. The warmth was strange—tingling, cool at first, then blooming with a chemical kind of relief.

"What is this stuff, Wyatt?" she asked, staring at her chest. "I've never seen anything like it. It's… amazing."

He smiled. "I like when you use my name. You're the only one in here who does. I almost forgot I had one."

He kissed her shoulder as he worked.

"This is a new serum Donovan's been working on. Not available to the public yet, but he'll release it soon."

She watched the skin around the incision calm and pale. The redness faded before her eyes. The wound was already tighter, more closed.

"Astonishing…" she murmured. "I'll need a stockpile when it's released. Make sure you get it for me, Wyatt."

"Of course," he said, smoothing the last of the serum across her skin.

The wall hissed open again.

A Pearl Enforcer stepped inside.

"Sorry, sir," they said quickly when they caught sight of Dr. Lancet under the sheets.

"What is it?" The Warden snapped.

"There's an urgent matter that requires your attention."

He stood without hesitation, already re-fastening his shirt and belt.

"Get some rest," he said to her. "I'll be back soon."

He started toward the exit. Paused.

"There's water on the table," he added. "If you're thirsty."

The wall closed behind him.

Dr. Lancet sat up slowly.

Her gaze drifted to the table.

The glass of water sat perfectly still.

Untouched.

Waiting.

"I don't think so," she muttered under her breath. "I'm not falling for that again."

She leaned toward the bedside table, reaching for the remote.

The tabletop was empty.

No remote. No control.

Her fingers stilled.

She checked the floor. The blankets. The drawers.

Nothing.

She looked toward the sealed wall.

"Wyatt," she whispered. "What the fuck are you doing?"

She got up, pressed her palms to the wall, searching for a seam, a switch—anything.

There was none.

No way out.

She was locked in again.

Trapped.

With Michael still watching her from the mirror.

Still smiling.

CHA▽TER
FOUR

The Detachment Gibbets

Jaysen

"Jaysen… Jayse."

Connor's voice cracked like something inside him had finally given way. "It was Charlie. I swear it was. You saw him too… right?"

"I saw him," Jaysen said.

He pulled the flashlight out from under his bedroll, flicked it on, and aimed the beam toward the stack across from them. Toward the cage beyond the thick black velvet. Like that would help. Like light could do anything here.

He knew damn well he wouldn't see Charlie through it. But still… he looked.

"No one bid on him. He's okay." He muttered, more for himself than Connor.

Connor didn't respond right away. His stare stayed fixed on the spot above, breathing shallow and uneven.

"Until the next full moon," he finally whispered. "What happened to him, Jaysen? He looked… old. Like something chewed him up and spat him back down here."

Jaysen didn't answer at first. He reached down, pulled the flasks from the crevice behind his bed, and handed one to Connor.

"Here."

They both took long swigs. The stuff burned going down—cheap, acidic, full of bite. Just the way they liked it.

"Jaysen… he's hurt."

"I know." Jaysen's voice was flat, but not without care. "But he's strong."

He looked over at Connor's face—bruises spreading like shadows across his cheekbone, a thin scab beneath his eye. Blood still crusted near his ear where the skin had split days ago.

"He'll be all right," Jaysen added, quieter now. "I wonder what he'll think of all this."

He nodded at Connor's face. The mess of it. The state they were all in. Just a few days ago, Charlie wouldn't have recognized them—hell, Jaysen barely recognized himself.

"Let's rest," he said finally. "We can't do anything standing here."

He dropped onto his bed, hard. No ceremony.

Connor hesitated, then followed suit, slumping onto his mattress. The flask stayed in his hand, fingers curled tight around it like it was a lifeline.

They sat in silence for a while, staring at the black-draped cage.

Finally, Jaysen raised his flask.

"To Charlie."

Connor met his gaze. Lifted his own.

"To Charlie."

Jaysen smirked. "It's gonna take a lot more than The Harvest to kill that old bastard."

Connor let out a dry laugh. "That it is… that it is."

They drained what was left of the vodka. Bitter. Warm. Gone.

Jaysen stashed the flasks behind the frame and leaned back. He pulled his book from under the mattress, flipped it open without really looking at the words. Connor did the same—two men pretending not to be haunted by what they'd just seen.

Eventually, the pages blurred.

The weight behind their eyes took over.

Books closed.

The flashlight clicked off.

Then, darkness returned.

Jaysen lay flat, arms over his chest, heart still pacing like something was about to happen.

He turned his head.

Looked toward Charlie's cage.

Nothing. Just black.

He knew he wouldn't see him. But he pictured him up there—sitting on the edge of his bed, hunched forward, cane across his lap, face sunken. Older than before. So much older. And quiet in a way that made Jaysen's gut twist.

And then he saw them again.

The eyes.

Staring at him from the dark.

Beyond the cage.

Watching.

They didn't blink.

Didn't move.

Jaysen didn't reach for the light. He didn't flinch. He just watched back, until the black pulled him under.

∞

Jaysen was back in Feltwood Mountains.

The air was cold—too cold for the season. The sky above was bruised, thick with smoke. The old cabin loomed behind him, sagging into the hill like it was trying to disappear.

He was screaming.

Running.

The front door slammed open behind him, and he sprinted down the path, lungs burning. He didn't need to look back.

But he did.

And he saw them.

A man and woman—strung up from the rafters like butchered stock. The Emerald Enforcers stood beneath them, armor gleaming under the cabin's flickering lights. Blank. Unfeeling.

The man twitched once. Then went still.

Jaysen ran harder.

The faceless young man burst through the doorway after him, feet silent over the soil. But Jaysen was too fast. He veered off the path, weaving through trees like he knew the forest's every secret.

He didn't stop until he found the dead tree.

The same one.

Blackened and hollowed, like a wound in the earth.

He crawled inside.

And when he emerged, he was somewhere else.

The barn.

Same as before.

The light filtering through the cracked boards painted long shadows across the hay-strewn floor. Jaysen was in the corner, knees to chest. Breathing shallow. Eyes wide.

Footsteps approached.

The faceless man.

Still walking like he had all the time in the world.

Jaysen tried to scream but only choked on the silence. Tears blurred his vision—but he refused to shut his eyes.

Not again.

The man knelt down. Close now.

And in the polished face of the pocket watch he always carried, Jaysen saw it.

The boy.

That same little boy. Staring out at him with hollow eyes.

"WHAT DO YOU WANT?" Jaysen screamed.

The faceless man's shape twisted. Warped. Shifted—

Suddenly, he looked like Connor.

But wrong.

His mouth didn't move when he spoke—his voice came from somewhere deeper, warped and echoing.

"WAKE UP, JAYSEN!"

It lunged forward, grabbing him by the shoulders and shaking him.

Jaysen fought back. Kicking. Punching. Thrashing.

"WAKE UP, JAYSEN!" the distorted growl came again, louder now.

The mouth on Connor's face started to tear, splitting at the corners like something too wide was trying to get out.

It kept tearing.

And still it shouted—

"WAKE UP!"

∞

Jaysen sat up fast as cold water slammed into him.

He gasped, coughing, heart still racing from whatever hell he'd just been pulled from.

"I'm sorry, mate," Connor said, already backing away. "I had no other choice."

Jaysen blinked against the drip running down his face. The world was still half-shadow, half-nightmare. Then he saw Connor—flashlight in one hand, a dented bucket in the other. His face looked worse than it had earlier. His left eye was nearly swollen shut, with a fresh gash just beneath.

And he was keeping his distance.

Jaysen wiped at his face with the heel of his palm. "No, Connor. I'm the one who should be sorry…" His voice was raw. "I was the one who gave you the bucket, remember? Told you to use it if it happened again."

He paused, looked down at his trembling hands.

"We might need to tie me down next time. I can't keep bruising you up like this."

Connor shrugged like it was nothing. "Nah, mate. It'll take more than a few knocks to do me in." He gave a crooked grin. "Besides, have you seen how scared the other cageys are of you now? A loose cannon on the bottom floor scares the absolute shit out of them. We get all the good trades lately."

Jaysen glanced at the bucket—half-full with rinse water from the showers. "It does come in handy," he admitted quietly.

He stood, muscles sore, shirt clinging to him, soaked and sticking cold to his back. He peeled it off, wiped the worst of the water from his face and chest, then handed it to Connor.

Connor wrung it out and hung it on the makeshift clothesline— salvaged from wire, a snapped shoelace, and one of the less moldy bandages another cagey had passed along.

"I never thought I'd appreciate a clothesline so much," Jaysen muttered, shaking his head. "Let alone a dodgy one like this."

Connor handed him a dry shirt. Jaysen pulled it on in silence, then reached into a fold in the mattress and offered Connor a small packet of alcohol wipes—creased, half-used, probably lifted from the infirmary.

"You're bleeding," he said. "Here. Use these."

Connor took them without a word. Dabbed at the split skin under his eye, wincing once. Then handed the packet back just as the velvet shroud over the cages began to rise.

That sound—the grinding steel cables, the mechanical groan—made them both turn.

Jaysen clicked off the flashlight, tucked it and the wipes into his pocket, and stepped beside Connor as the cage beside them was revealed.

Charlie sat there, just as they'd left him in the dark.

Still. Upright. That same tired warmth in his eyes.

"Fancy seeing you boys here," he said with a soft chuckle.

They all laughed, quiet and low, like it hurt a little to do it.

Jaysen and Connor took each other in—then looked at Charlie again. There was something in his posture that hadn't been there before. Something heavier.

Charlie stood slowly, leaning hard into his cane.

And that's when they saw it.

The brace on his ankle.

Neither of them said a word, but the concern hit them both like a punch to the chest.

Charlie saw it. Gave a small shake of his head.

"Don't worry, boys. No one wants to bid on a decrepit old man."

His smile didn't quite reach his eyes.

Then he looked at Connor—really looked. The swelling. The bruises. His expression shifted.

"And what exactly happened to *you*?" he asked, voice colder now. "Who do I need to deal with?"

Just then, the bell rang.

It was time for The Big Cage.

∞

Charlie

The three of them sat together on the benches, pockets stuffed with trail mix. The Aviary thrummed around them, metal groaning somewhere overhead, the scent of sterilized sweat and rust hanging low in the air.

It almost felt normal.

Almost.

Jaysen glanced sideways at him, chewing slowly.

"What happened to you, Charlie? We thought you were dead. Especially when you didn't come back from The Harvest."

Charlie shrugged, picking a cashew from his hand and flicking it away.

"Well," he said, grinning, "I survived my first Harvest. Walked the stage like a damn champion. And then—right at the finish line—I tripped."

He gave a little laugh. Light. Easy.

"Wasn't even a proper fall. Just lost my footing and took a bit of a tumble. Somehow, messed up my ankle. Think I scared the hell out of one of the Enforcers."

Connor raised an eyebrow. "You fell?"

"Like a sack of potatoes," Charlie said with a smirk. "Woke up in some sterile room, body aching, pride a little bruised."

"And someone just patched you up?" Jaysen asked.

Charlie smiled—softer now. "I was lying in an operating theater with an angel watching over me."

Both men looked at him.

"An angel?" they echoed in unison.

"I heard the surgeon was mental," Connor added.

Charlie shook his head quickly. "Not Dr. Lancet. No, she didn't even perform the Harvest this time—she was one of the bidders."

"Wait… *Dr. Lancet* bought someone?" Jaysen asked, frowning.

"She bought Michael," Charlie said. "Needed the organs. Zygote's the one who handled the slicing."

Connor looked even more confused now. "So Dr. Zygote's the angel?"

Charlie rolled his eyes. "No. Let me finish."

He glanced between them, then down at the floor, the memory of her still vivid—Jessica's gentle voice, her kind eyes, the way she'd called him *Charlie* with real care.

"Jessica," he said, voice lower. "Zygote's assistant. She looked after me. Gave me something that actually worked."

He reached into his waistband and, after a quick glance to make sure no Enforcers were looking, slipped a single pill into Connor's hand.

"You might need one of these, son."

Connor popped it without hesitation.

Charlie nodded at the bruises. "Now, what the hell happened to your face?"

Connor smirked. "Jaysen's been having night terrors. Hard to wake him sometimes. He swings before he opens his eyes."

He nudged Jaysen with an elbow. "Hell of a right hook."

"Enough about that," Jaysen muttered. "I already said sorry."

He pulled a small, wrinkled packet from his pocket and passed it to Charlie with a nod.

"Keep those stitches clean."

Charlie stared at the alcohol wipes.

"What the fuck is going on here?"

Connor grinned. "Ever since Jaysen started throwing punches in his sleep, the lower levels treat him like a damn landmine. They keep offering him supplies—just in case."

"The first one's free," Jaysen added with a crooked smile. "You'll have to pay next time."

They all laughed, the sound low but real.

Then someone approached.

A tall, thin young man with long black hair, a bold white streak running through one side, and mismatched eyes—the right green, and the left blue. His presence didn't feel like it belonged, and yet he looked right at home.

"I hear I need to talk to you if I want protection on the ground level," the young man said, extending a hand to Jaysen.

"The name's Xavier," he said smoothly.

Jaysen shook Xavier's hand.

Without asking, Xavier slid onto the bench between Connor and Jaysen, casual as anything, like he'd known them for years. As he sat, he pressed a crinkled packet of alcohol wipes into Jaysen's hand.

"I also heard you're going through these like toilet paper," he said with a crooked grin. "I see why now."

Jaysen lifted an eyebrow.

The wound across his face was healing well, but it still needed care. Alcohol wipes had become something of a social bribe—handed to him by cageys who wanted to stay on his good side.

"I just happened to have run out," Jaysen said, giving Charlie a wink. "Thanks, Xavier. I'm Jaysen. That's Connor, and the old man's Charlie."

He tucked the wipes into his empty trouser pocket.

"Don't recognize you though."

"Fresh drop," Xavier said, stretching his arms like he'd just woken up from a nap. "Got here maybe ten minutes ago. Barry over there said you were the guy to talk to."

He jerked his chin toward Barry, who gave the group a nod and went back to gnawing on something suspiciously gray.

Jaysen narrowed his eyes. "How the fuck did you get alcohol wipes in ten minutes?"

Xavier smirked. "Timing, mostly. Hit the infirmary just before some psycho started throwing fists. Belted the nurse to hell. While the Enforcer was dealing with that mess, I helped myself. Argentine unit brought me down here—barely looked at me. No search."

He puffed out his chest like it was a badge of honor. "Cleanest entry in history."

Then, with zero caution, he reached into his pockets and pulled out a scalpel, a couple of pill packets, and a few capped syringes.

Connor nearly choked. "Fuck, mate! Put that shit away before we all get shipped to top-level!"

Xavier looked mildly amused. "Relax. Nobody's looking at me yet."

Connor was already helping him stuff the items back in his coat.

"You'd better help him," he said, looking at Charlie. "Enforcers don't even know he exists yet. Show him how not to get gutted in his sleep."

Charlie sighed, deadpan. "He clearly needs it."

Xavier shot him a grin. "I'll take notes, grandpa."

Just as they were tucking away the last syringe, Lincoln dropped onto the bench next to Charlie. He didn't say a word at first—just stared.

Short blond hair. Stiff as concrete. Muscles packed into his sleeves like someone had vacuum-sealed him into his shirt.

Then came the low, deliberate growl.

"Don't think I didn't see that… fresh meat."

Xavier stood up instantly, grinning like he'd been waiting for this exact moment.

"And what do you think you're gonna do, Ken?" he said. "Go cry to Barbie?"

Lincoln stood without a word.

Chest to chest now. Lincoln, towering over Xavier. Tension thick enough to cut.

Jaysen stepped between them before the first punch could land.

"Don't start this shit, Lincoln. I'll sort him out." His voice was flat. Cold. "What do you want?"

Lincoln didn't look away from Xavier.

"I want the scalpel. And one syringe. From him. For my silence."

Jaysen turned to Xavier.

"You want my protection?" he asked. "Pay the man."

Xavier exhaled, clearly unimpressed. "Seriously? You're running a toll booth already?"

But he handed over both items without further argument. Smooth. Calm. Like it didn't cost him a thing.

Lincoln snatched them, shoved them in his pocket, and walked off without another word.

The four of them sat in silence for a moment as the buzz of the Aviary returned.

The top-levels would be arriving soon.

The day's haul had been impressive—five flasks of vodka, twenty pairs of briefs, a spare scalpel, two more packets of alcohol wipes, and an extra flashlight.

They split it clean between them, hiding the goods deep in their clothes and pockets.

Xavier, now included.

The last thirty minutes in the Big Cage passed without incident.

That, in itself, felt unnatural.

There were murmurs, some tense stares, and a few sharp whispers exchanged in corners, but no blows thrown. No sudden screams. No blood on the floor. Even the Enforcers' hounds seemed bored.

Charlie kept his voice low as they were funneled back toward their cages, his shoulder brushing lightly against Connor's.

"I still can't believe Jaysen's the go-to guy now," he said, just above a whisper. "Feels like it's been years. Not days."

Connor didn't answer right away. He kept his pace even, his eyes trained ahead where Jaysen walked a few steps in front of them, shadows folding across his shoulders like a second uniform.

"I mean… I *know* how it happened," Charlie continued, lowering his head slightly, like he was just commenting on the weather. "But still… how the fuck did it happen *so fast?*"

Connor gave the smallest nod.

"There's more to him than he lets on," he murmured. "And I'm gonna find out what it is."

His voice was calm. Measured. Almost friendly. The kind of tone that didn't carry.

Then he gave a quiet chuckle.

"He's just good at it. That's all, Charlie."

Charlie walked in silence for a few more steps. Then he slowed.

"I'm proud of you, Connor."

Connor glanced at him, brow furrowing slightly.

"You've become a good man," Charlie said, his tone thickening at the edges. "And I'm sorry I didn't tell you about my sentence. Thought it'd be easier for you if I didn't."

He swallowed hard. "But then I saw the look on your face…"

He stopped walking. Just for a moment.

"I'll never deceive you again. I'm sorry."

Connor rested a hand gently on Charlie's back, his touch quick but genuine.

"Don't stress about it," he said quietly. "I get it."

They reached their cages—new neighbors now. Metal stacked like tombs.

One after the other, they stepped inside.

The doors slid shut behind them with a sound that never got easier

∞

"What the bloody hell are you thinking, kid? You're going to get yourself harvested," Charlie said in a low hiss as Xavier reached into his pocket.

The kid was about to pull out the flask Jaysen had given him, right there in plain sight.

Charlie leaned forward slightly. "Wait until they drop the covers. It won't be long."

Just then, an Enforcer passed by their cage. Helmet angled their way.

Charlie stilled.

The Enforcer lingered for a second too long—like they'd caught a scent.

But nothing was out. Nothing obvious.

They moved on.

Charlie turned his head slowly, and shot Xavier a look. One raised eyebrow. A quiet, heavy *are you trying to die?*

If I hadn't said something, he'd be halfway to the top-level by now. This one's going to be a tough one.

The familiar grind of cables overhead began. The covers descended, slow and steady, swallowing the Aviary in creeping shadow.

Xavier didn't look up. Didn't even twitch.

He sat like he'd seen it all before. Like none of it surprised him.

Charlie watched him.

Too calm. Too sure. Like he already knows the rules—and doesn't care.

When the velvet hit the floor, Charlie flicked on his flashlight, the soft beam casting a dull glow through the dark.

Xavier had already cracked the flask and was mid-swig. A big one.

"Woah. Take it easy, kid."

Xavier lowered the flask with a sharp look. "Stop calling me *kid*. I'm not a kid."

Charlie didn't flinch. "Okay... *son*," he said gently. Measured. "Take it easy. That stuff's strong. Not like the garbage you find outside."

Xavier rolled his eyes and took another swig anyway. "I'll manage," he muttered. "If I go blind, I'll consider that a win."

Charlie raised an eyebrow but said nothing.

"I'm fine," Xavier added. "Just leave me be. I'm sure I'll be out of your hair soon enough."

Charlie sipped from his own flask, slower, quieter.

"Now what exactly do you mean by that, son?"

Xavier didn't answer. Just leaned back against the bars and stared at the ceiling like it might give him better company.

Charlie exhaled slowly, voice low but firm.

"Look... if you want Jaysen's protection—and you're planning on surviving down here—you need to talk. Especially if I'm going to risk my neck for you."

He nodded at the pocket. "Stealing from the infirmary. Almost drinking while the covers were still up. That's the kind of stuff that gets people *seen*."

He held Xavier's gaze. Steady. Calm.

No threat. No judgment.

Just experience talking.

Xavier didn't break eye contact, but his smirk faded, just a fraction.

"Not used to people giving a shit," he muttered, more to himself than to Charlie.

Charlie took another sip from his flask, eyes never leaving the young man beside him.

"Now what exactly do you mean by that, son?"

Xavier didn't answer at first. His shoulders stiffened slightly, like he was bracing for something. For once, no smartass comeback.

Charlie kept watching him, calm and steady.

Xavier shifted. The smartass smirk that had been plastered across his face since the moment they met began to fade.

"I heard…" he started, voice hoarse. "I heard you can get a chance to volunteer."

Charlie blinked.

Just like that, the act cracked.

And there he was—Xavier, not the swaggering kid who'd mouthed off to Lincoln, not the one smuggling scalpel blades like it was a joke. Just a scared, determined young man.

"My family's about to lose the farm," Xavier continued. "They're starving. I mean really starving. And when I found out about the volunteer program…"

He trailed off, his voice catching.

He looked up at Charlie—and his eyes were glassy. Brimming.

Charlie didn't speak. Just listened.

"I thought if I got in here, I might get the chance," Xavier said. "If you're young enough, and in for life, they ask. And if you volunteer… your family gets a cut."

Charlie furrowed his brow. He'd been in Augmentation Bay for years. Heard a hundred stories. A thousand lies. But this?

"What volunteer program are you talking about, son?"

Xavier wiped at his eyes roughly with the back of his hand.

"Your family gets twenty percent of what you're sold for."

Charlie's hand came up to his forehead. His fingers ran through his silver-streaked hair.

"You want to be harvested?" he said slowly, like he was trying to convince himself he'd misheard.

"Well, no… not really," Xavier said. "But I thought it was worth it."

His voice was cracking now.

"So I stole ten pieces of iron. Thought that'd get me a life sentence. But I only got fifty years. Fifty."

He shook his head, laughing bitterly.

"I need a life sentence so I can, one day, maybe… volunteer."

When he finished, he dropped his head into his hands and let out a long breath—less like a sigh and more like he was deflating.

Charlie stared at him.

All that flippant, cocky swagger—it had been armor. Smoke and mirrors. A show put on by a boy desperate to make sure his family didn't vanish with the dirt.

"Where'd you hear about this volunteer program?" Charlie asked after a long moment. His voice had gone quiet. Careful.

"I had a friend. His family was in the same situation. His older brother—Henry—he was here. A few days ago, a Pearl Enforcer and The Warden showed up at their house."

Xavier's voice dropped.

"They gave his mum a cheque. It was signed by The Architect."

Charlie's jaw clenched.

"They told her Henry volunteered for The Harvest," Xavier continued. "Said the cheque was their cut—for his redemption."

He looked up again, his face raw.

"Some bastard killed him though. During the riot. So he didn't bring in as much as he would've alive. But the family's comfortable now. Comfortable enough to live. And I'm going to do the same."

Charlie struggled with his decision.

Everything in him wanted to talk Xavier out of it—this reckless, tragic plan. But he could already see it in the boy's eyes: the steel beneath the swagger, the kind of resolve you couldn't bend, only delay.

There was no changing his mind.

So maybe Charlie couldn't stop it.

But he could slow it down.

Buy the kid time.

Time to grow out of the desperation. Time to see the truth of this place for what it was. Time to *survive* long enough to change his own damn mind.

And maybe, in the meantime, Charlie could dig up more about this so-called volunteer program—because something about it still stank.

He sighed and leaned forward.

"Acting the way you are, son…" he said quietly, "it won't get you a life sentence. It'll get you killed. By Lincoln. Or some other cagey who doesn't like the way you breathe."

Xavier looked up, but Charlie didn't give him a chance to argue.

"And if you get caught with all that shit in your coat?" he continued. "That's not a path to volunteering. That's a red tag. Straight to The Harvest. No questions. No choices. No cut for your family. Just silence and a slab."

He paused, voice dropping to a grim murmur.

"You won't be worth a single ounce of iron. Not to anyone but this place."

The words hung heavy between them.

"You may think you've got this place figured out," Charlie added, softer now. "But trust me—you don't. Not yet."

Xavier's mouth twitched, like he wanted to fire back, but nothing came. For once, he held his tongue.

Charlie leaned in closer.

"So cut the flippant act. And maybe I can help you." He hesitated. "I'm not exactly thrilled about helping someone get harvested… but I know a lost cause when I see one."

He turned the flashlight Jaysen had given him in his hand, and held it out.

"So if you're set on doing this… you better do it smart."

Xavier blinked.

"Next time we're in the Big Cage, make sure an Enforcer sees you with this," Charlie said. "But never—and I mean never—tell them where it came from."

Xavier took the flashlight with both hands, handling it like it was heavier than it was.

"I'll get another," Charlie added with a faint smile. "That'll buy you five years, if you're lucky. But don't get greedy. Don't get caught too often. Or too close together. They'll catch on, and when they do, you'll be fucked."

He leaned back, voice falling quiet again.

"This'll take time. Good thing we've got a lot of that in here."

Xavier stared at the flashlight. His grip tightened around it.

"Thank you," he said.

Charlie nodded once. "They'll search your cage when they catch you, so we'll need to move our stuff before that happens. Jaysen and Connor can hold it. They know how to keep things buried."

He let go of the flashlight.

"I knew Henry," Charlie said after a beat. "Good man. Connor's old cagey, actually."

Xavier blinked. He hadn't expected that.

"One day, they just… moved him to the top-level. Never told us why. Never heard from him again. It nearly broke Connor."

Charlie's voice turned low, heavy with memory.

"And I knew the bastard who killed him, too. Don't worry, son. He got what was coming. Michael. He ended up on the Harvesting floor. Dr. Lancet bought him."

Xavier's eyes darkened.

Charlie nodded. "She's not right in the head. If he suffered, and I bet he did… it was her doing."

"*Good*," Xavier growled. "I just wish I'd been the one to make him pay."

"And then what?" Charlie snapped, sharper than he meant to. "You'd be rotting on the top-level right now. Or worse."

He softened again.

"Don't do something stupid because of your feelings. That's not how we stay alive in here. That's how we get killed."

I hope this is enough, Charlie thought. *Enough to keep him from jumping headfirst into this nightmare before I can talk to Jaysen and Connor.*

He raised his flask.

"We drink together in here," he said.

Xavier raised his in response.

They clinked. Drank.

"Now go piss before we turn off the flashlight," Charlie muttered. "I need my beauty sleep."

He tucked the flask beside his bed and eased down onto his back with a quiet groan.

Xavier, now definitely drunk, stumbled to the corner and missed the chamber pot entirely.

"Fucking hell," Charlie muttered.

Xavier wobbled back, collapsed onto his bed, and passed out—leaving the flashlight still glowing beside him.

Charlie sighed, pushed himself up with a grunt, grabbed his cane, and hobbled over.

He pulled the thin blanket over the boy's shoulders, took the flashlight, and turned it off.

"I hope I'm doing the right thing helping this poor kid," he mumbled.

Then he shuffled back, lowered himself into his bed, and finally closed his eyes.

∞

Xavier

Xavier woke to the sound of the covers being lifted.

The grinding of steel cables overhead pulled him from sleep, and for a moment—just a moment—he swore he saw something in the corner of the cage.

A cat.

Tortoiseshell colored. Thin. Its face pinched like a gargoyle.

The kind of cat that used to roam his parents' farm, half-feral and always vanishing before you could get too close.

But before his eyes could focus, it was gone.

Like it had never been there.

I guess I'm homesick already, he thought as he sat up, rubbing the sleep from his eyes.

He reached immediately for his pockets. Started stashing everything he had—pills, scraps, wrappers, anything small enough to hide—ready to hand it off to Jaysen and Connor before the Enforcers saw him with the flashlight.

His heart jumped. "The flashlight, Charlie!" he breathed, yanking his sheets back. "It's not here."

"Calm down, son," came Charlie's voice.

Xavier turned.

Charlie pulled the flashlight from his coat pocket. "You gotta be more careful with your drink," he said, shaking his head. "You passed out holding it. I figured you might fumble again."

Xavier let out a shaky breath.

"But you're getting ahead of yourself," Charlie continued. "We've got to shower first. Empty those pockets."

Right. The showers.

The daily humiliation of it.

He started pulling everything out, tucking items under the cot and behind loose stones until he was empty-handed.

The Enforcers arrived not long after, armed with their hoses. The blast of water stung. The cold bit deeper than usual today. Then came the drying mist—hot, chemical, leaving his skin tight and raw.

When they were clean and dressed again, Xavier couldn't stop moving.

He paced from wall to wall, biting at the skin around his nails.

I wish they'd hurry up.

"I thought I told you to calm down, son," Charlie muttered after a while. "It won't do you any good pacing like that. You're making me nervous. I don't like being nervous."

Xavier forced himself to sit on the edge of the cot, but his fingers kept moving, teeth worrying the edges of the skin near his knuckles.

An Argentine Enforcer passed their cage.

They didn't say anything.

But they stopped.

Paused.

Looked in.

And for a breath too long, stared directly at Xavier.

Then they moved on, boots clicking along the steel.

Charlie turned toward him. "Maybe they *did* notice you weren't placed in here properly, son," he said. "You'd best be ready for a new cage when we come back."

Xavier swallowed.

"Charlie," he said quietly, "you don't have to help me. I can see you're torn up about it."

Before Charlie could answer, a voice came from the next stack over.

"What's Charlie helping you with, then?"

Connor.

Xavier stiffened.

Charlie opened his mouth—then shut it again.

The bell rang before either of them could say more, sharp and final, echoing off the concrete.

Time for The Big Cage.

Xavier stood. Started pacing again, short and sharp across the narrow floor.

"If the Enforcers see you doing that," Charlie said, "they'll make sure we go *last*."

He stepped in front of Xavier and placed a hand on his shoulder, steady.

"Stand here," he said.

Charlie moved him into position—center of the cage, beside him.

Still, Xavier kept biting the skin from the edges of his fingers.

Eventually, the lock released on Jaysen and Connor's cage. They stepped out first.

Then it was Charlie and Xavier's turn.

The Enforcer led them down the row, slow and methodical, pausing to release others, one cage at a time.

Xavier didn't look back.

He just tried to keep his hands still.

After collecting their trail mix, the four men found a spot to sit.

Charlie and Xavier only had enough room in their pockets for one handful each. The rest had to be left behind—risk was heavier than hunger today.

As they sat, Connor didn't waste time.

"Okay, Charlie," he said, reaching into his pocket and popping a handful of raisins into his mouth. "What exactly are you helping Xavier with?"

Charlie hesitated.

Just enough to be noticeable.

Xavier caught it and stepped in before Charlie could decide.

"How about I start?" he said. He didn't wait for approval.

"The cageys don't know this," Xavier began, keeping his voice just above a whisper, "but apparently… if you're here for life—and you're young, healthy—The Warden might allow you to volunteer for The Harvest."

Jaysen and Connor both froze mid-chew.

"Volunteer?" they said in unison—far too loud.

All four men tensed.

They glanced around quickly, making sure no Enforcers were in earshot. When it seemed safe, Xavier continued.

"If you volunteer, your family gets twenty percent of the iron they sell you for," he said. "That's what I'm trying to do. I want to volunteer—so my family can survive."

His voice had lost its flippant edge.

"Charlie's helping me… make sure I do it properly."

The silence that followed was heavy.

Jaysen and Connor exchanged a long, unreadable look.

Finally, Connor spoke.

"How do you even know this is real?"

Before Xavier could answer, Charlie cut in—quiet, but firm.

"Connor… Xavier knew someone who did it. Their family got a cheque. From The Warden. Signed by The Architect."

He paused.

Then said it.

"It was Henry."

Connor's breath caught.

His head dropped.

He didn't speak.

Didn't move.

Jaysen broke the silence. "So what exactly is the plan?"

"Xavier's got fifty years," Charlie said. "He needs life. We're going to help him get seen—by Enforcers—with contraband. Little things. Small infractions. Just enough to stack time without sending him to the top-level."

Charlie reached into his coat and began pulling items from his pockets—quietly passing them to Jaysen.

"Today it's the flashlight," he added. "We need you to hold the rest of our shit in case they search our cage."

Jaysen hesitated.

Connor didn't lift his head.

"This isn't what I meant when I said help him," Connor muttered.

Charlie's voice tightened. "He's going to do it anyway. It's better if I help him—and make sure he lives long enough to *try*."

Jaysen looked at Connor, then back at Xavier, who was already handing him a small roll of gauze and a blister pack of pills.

Eventually, both Jaysen and Connor took the items—silent, grim—and stashed them in their pockets.

That was when Lincoln sat down.

Again.

His shadow fell across the group as he took his usual place nearby, eyes sharp and too aware.

No one said a word.

But everyone noticed.

"You don't learn your lesson, do you… *fresh meat?*" Lincoln said as he approached.

His voice was low, but it cut through the noise around them like a blade.

He stood in front of Xavier, broad and unmoving.

"I think I'll have something from that never-ending pocket of yours," he added, smiling without warmth. "You know… for my silence."

Xavier didn't flinch.

He pulled his hand from his pocket and held out a small, open palm of trail mix.

"Sorry, Ken," he said. "That's all I've got. I gave everything else to Jaysen here."

Lincoln stared at the nuts and dried fruit like Xavier had spit in his face.

Then he smacked Xavier's hand hard, scattering the trail mix across the floor. Before Xavier could move, Lincoln grabbed a fistful of his shirt.

But he didn't get any further.

Jaysen stepped between them.

Fast.

"Lincoln," he said, voice flat, calm. Dangerous. "Xavier's with us now. Find someone else to fuck with."

A beat.

"Now—do you *need* something?"

Lincoln's jaw clenched. His shoulders rolled.

"I need more vodka," he said through gritted teeth.

Jaysen didn't blink. "It's going to be a few days. And you owe me plenty already. Don't forget that."

Lincoln pulled a dented flask from his pocket and shoved it into Jaysen's hand.

"I know," he sneered. "I'll pay you. Don't worry."

He turned to leave, muttering over his shoulder, "Control that mutt… or I'll put it down."

Xavier didn't miss a beat.

"I don't think Barbie approves of animal cruelty, *Ken!*" he called after him.

Lincoln didn't turn around—but his fists curled tighter as he walked away.

Charlie, Connor, and Jaysen all turned to Xavier.

Glared.

Xavier shrugged. "What? He started it."

Charlie shook his head, rubbing at his temple.

"C'mon, son," he muttered. "I know you've got a death wish, but don't kill yourself before you get it *right*."

Jaysen remained silent.

"The top-level will be in soon," Connor said after a beat, picking up on what Charlie hadn't said aloud. "You'd better get going. If they see you with that flashlight… there'll be a riot. You'll get killed."

He gave Charlie a quiet, sympathetic smile.

Xavier stood, wiping his palms on his pants. He glanced at each of them, then plastered on a grin.

Without a word, he pulled the flashlight from his pocket and began tossing it into the air, catching it lazily as he strutted toward the center of The Big Cage.

His other hand slipped into his pocket and curled around the flask he'd kept hidden.

I know Charlie said to take it slow, he thought, *but my family needs that money now.*

Behind him, he could hear Connor murmuring to Charlie.

"Are you sure this is the right thing to do?" he asked. "I know you want to help him, but this just seems mad."

"I don't think it seems mad," Jaysen said.

Connor turned, surprised. "You're not thinking of doing this too, are you, mate?"

"No," Jaysen said with a reassuring nod. "I've still got a chance to go home. I'm not doing anything that stupid."

He glanced at Connor, grinning faintly. "Besides… I couldn't do that to you. You might end up with Lincoln as your cagey."

Connor scoffed. "Yeah, we can't have that."

Charlie didn't laugh.

He kept his eyes on Xavier.

"I'm making sure it happens as slowly as possible," he said, almost to himself. "He doesn't know that part. Five years, maybe once every couple months. If he changes his mind… he won't be too deep."

Across the yard, Xavier smirked.

I've got more figured out than he knows. And I won't change my mind. As long as my family needs me… this is what I'm doing.

An Argentine Enforcer entered the Big Cage, moving fast, boots heavy, helmet scanning the crowd.

They'd seen the flashlight.

Charlie, Connor, and Jaysen watched as the Enforcer closed in.

Xavier stood his ground.

Just before the Enforcer reached him, he threw the flashlight in the air again.

It spun once.

Then the butt of the Enforcer's gun slammed into his gut.

Xavier folded, gasping as the flashlight slipped through his fingers and clattered to the ground beside him.

They didn't wait.

The Enforcer snatched the light, grabbed Xavier by the scruff of his shirt, and hauled him to his feet.

They shoved him forward, toward the doors at the edge of the cage.

As he stumbled, Xavier caught Charlie's eye.

Charlie dropped his head into his hands.

"I hope I've done the right thing," he muttered.

The top-level cageys were being brought in now—herded in lines, watched from every angle. The noise level rose, more boots and breathing than words.

Then Lincoln appeared again.

He loomed over the three men, arms folded.

"Looks like the mutt's gonna take care of itself for me," he sneered.

"That's enough, Lincoln," Jaysen snapped, rising to his feet in one fluid motion.

He stepped directly into Lincoln's path, eyes sharp.

"You keep pushing, I'll cut you off. You owe me too much already."

A pause.

"Try me. One more time… I dare you."

Lincoln held his stare for a second longer than necessary.

Then he stepped back.

And the Enforcer shoved Xavier through the doors.

Xavier tried to catch his breath as they marched him down the corridor. His ribs ached from the blow. His legs struggled to keep pace. He hadn't had a second to recover.

His heart was pounding.

His shirt clung to him with sweat.

But he didn't look back.

The Argentine Enforcer shoved Xavier through the door of The Warden's office and forced him down into a chair across from the desk. The wood creaked under him, but The Warden didn't look up.

He was already at his drawer, one finger delicately trailing across a row of files like he was choosing wine.

"Mr. Wheeler," he said, plucking a folder free. "What an unfortunate interruption."

He glanced at the Argentine Enforcer, then at the flashlight on his desk, now scuffed and dented from the scuffle. "This is what I was called away for?"

He sighed and set the folder down with exaggerated care.

"I was in the middle of a very… *delicate* discussion with Dr. Lancet," he said, adjusting his cufflinks. "And now here we are, dealing with a boy who hasn't even been properly processed."

He opened the file.

A thin smirk curled across his lips.

"Interesting. You're not even officially registered in my system yet," he said, raising a single eyebrow as he looked up. "Technically, Mr. Wheeler, you're not a prisoner here. Not yet."

Xavier met his eyes but said nothing.

"Which makes your little stunt today even more impressive," The Warden continued. "Smuggling in contraband. Flaunting it, no less. Right in the middle of The Big Cage. Bold."

He tapped the flashlight once with a manicured nail.

"If you're going to break the rules in *my* prison," he said, voice cooling, "you're going to pay the price."

Xavier shifted in his seat.

Just hurry up and give me my years.

But The Warden wasn't done.

He shut the file, folded his hands, and stared at Xavier for a long moment, studying him like a puzzle that had already given away its edge pieces.

"You strike me as clever," he said. "Naive. But clever. There's intent behind the idiocy. And that makes you dangerous."

He stood from his chair, slow and deliberate.

"I think a little time in The Detachment Gibbets will remind you where you are."

He turned toward the Argentine Enforcer.

"Seventy-two hours," he said. "Let's see what that does to his cleverness."

The Enforcer nodded and moved in.

Xavier's legs were barely under him when the Enforcer grabbed his arm and started dragging him toward the door.

"Detachment?" Xavier choked. "No…"

He twisted, tried to break free.

The Warden adjusted his glasses with one finger and didn't raise his voice.

"Struggle, Mr. Wheeler," he said coolly. "And I'll add another twenty-four."

Xavier froze.

I can't… I can't let him get to me…

He went still, his heart pounding in his chest like it wanted to punch its way out.

The Enforcer hauled him forward without another word.

As the door swung open, The Warden called after them, voice light and venomous.

"Welcome to *my* prison, Mr. Wheeler."

Xavier didn't respond.

Didn't look back.

He just let them take him.

When they reached the door to The Aviary, Xavier braced himself, expecting to be shoved through.

But instead, the Argentine Enforcer yanked him to the right.

A narrow stairwell waited.

Stone. Worn. Spiraling upward in a tight coil that felt far too ancient to exist.

They pushed him forward.

Up the stairs.

Step after grinding step.

No windows. No handrails. Just cold stone and echoing breath.

As Xavier climbed, the motion made his head spin. Each turn blurred into the next, the walls folding in like a snake tightening around him.

I hope this ends soon.

He stumbled once. The Argentine Enforcer caught him with one hand—briefly steadying him—then shoved him harder.

At the top, a heavy metal door waited.

Painted black.

Labeled in white stencil:

THE DETACHMENT GIBBETS.

The Enforcer reached forward and unlocked the latch. The door creaked open.

And darkness spilled out like smoke.

It wasn't just dark—it was *hungry*. A thick, pressing absence that dulled the light from the stairwell behind them. Swallowed it whole.

Xavier's heart kicked in his chest.

He heard a soft *click*, then a low mechanical *buzz*.

He turned to the Enforcer.

A faint red light blinked once across their mask—scanning, glowing like eyes.

"Sweet mask," Xavier said, trying to keep his voice even. "Can I have one? Always wanted night vision."

His voice cracked on the last word.

The Enforcer didn't respond.

Just gripped his arm again and led him in.

The floor beneath them was metal, cold and shifting. The room smelled like rust and oil. Their path weaved—left, then right, then left again—an echo of The Aviary's maze, but quieter. Heavier.

And then—

The voices.

Whimpers.

Soft. High-pitched. Human, but barely.

Xavier froze as the sound rose in the dark around him.

Most of the words were lost to the air. Choked sobs. Muffled pleas.

But one voice stood out.

One word, over and over:

"*Quiet.*"

The Enforcer shoved him forward.

Xavier staggered into something that gave under his weight—then swung back violently on metal hinges.

The whole structure screeched.

"Get in," the Enforcer growled.

The whimpering voices flinched.

Xavier reached forward blindly, hands feeling metal bars. A circle. Thin. Just wide enough to sit curled, tall enough to hunch.

He climbed onto the swinging platform, the metal swaying beneath his weight. It groaned loudly—announcing him like a bell.

The bars surrounded him. A cage within the dark.

The Enforcer shut the gibbet behind him.

It screamed as it closed.

The other voices whimpered again.

And then the Enforcer walked away, boots echoing until they vanished.

Xavier was alone.

Alone in the dark. Suspended in a swaying cage. Surrounded by whispers and fear.

Well… this backfired.

He sat, trying to fold his legs into a comfortable shape. The metal floor was cold. The bars pressed against his shoulders.

I should've gotten processed first. What a waste of a good flashlight and—

He stopped.

The vodka.

His heart skipped.

They didn't search me.

His hand slid slowly into his pocket and wrapped around the flask.

But then he remembered the flicker of red light across the Enforcer's mask.

What if they're still in here? Watching me.

He stared into the dark.

Waited.

Nothing.

No sound but the others. The whimpers. The distant groan of metal.

It's either going to get me more time in here… or more years. I suppose… fuck it.

Xavier unscrewed the flask, took a fast swig, then let it sit in his lap.

Waited.

Nothing.

No boots. No voices. No punishment.

Just the dark.

He took another sip. Then shook the flask.

It sloshed—barely.

Seventy-two hours… better make it last.

He tightened the lid, returned it to his pocket.

A low grinding sound filled the air suddenly—brutal and mechanical, boring into his skull like a drill. It surrounded him, vibrated through the bars, crawled into his teeth.

He clamped his hands over his ears, but it didn't help.

The sound felt *inside* him.

When it stopped, the silence was even worse.

The whimpering had returned.

Xavier raised his head, breathing hard.

I'm not going to let this get to me.

I must be inside the roof above The Aviary. That grinding... that was the covers being dropped. So I've got time before it happens again... hopefully.

I can do this.

He shifted again, trying to sit more comfortably—but there was no comfort here. Just pressure and steel.

He pulled the flask out again, took one more swig—longer this time—then tucked it back in his pocket.

Then, he closed his eyes.

And tried to sleep.

∞

Jaysen

As the covers began to lower, the grinding above drowned out most thought.

But even beneath the shriek of metal and the press of shadow, Jaysen could feel the shift in the cage.

Charlie's face had gone still.

His eyes were locked on the doors across the yard—on the same path they'd once escorted Jaysen through. But tonight, they remained closed.

Xavier hadn't come back.

Before the velvet dropped fully and darkness took hold, Charlie turned toward them.

The worry was written all over him.

"He'll be okay, Charlie," Connor said, trying to speak above the last of the grinding. "He's probably just in a new cage... like you said."

Charlie didn't answer right away.

He stared at the door a moment longer.

"We haven't seen an Enforcer bring him through," he muttered.

His voice wasn't loud, but Jaysen heard the edge in it. The doubt.

Charlie wasn't just worried. He was bracing for something worse.

Jaysen glanced toward the far wall, toward the corners of the Aviary they couldn't see.

"Maybe he came through another entrance," Jaysen offered. "One we don't have a view of. It's possible, right?"

Charlie looked at him.

Then gave a slow nod.

"Maybe."

That was all he said.

"Night, boys," he added a moment later, and without waiting for a reply, he rolled over, facing the wall. As the thick velvet separated them.

Jaysen lay back against his cot, hands folded across his chest, staring into the black above them.

The air was heavy. Still.

Too quiet for comfort.

∞

The next day in The Big Cage, the air felt thinner.

Jaysen couldn't tell if it was the light or the silence, but something was wrong. Off. Like the entire room was holding its breath.

Charlie was already pacing when they arrived. His eyes scanned every face, every cagey, every shadow that moved. He checked every corner of the yard—twice. He even watched the Enforcers longer than was wise.

But Xavier wasn't there.

Finally, Charlie sat down beside Jaysen and Connor, his knees stiff, jaw clenched.

He didn't say anything right away.

Neither did they.

But all three felt it—the hollow space where Xavier should've been.

"This was a terrible idea," Charlie muttered, voice low. He dropped his head into his hands. "I thought I could slow him down… give him room to change his mind. But I handed him right over."

Jaysen didn't know what to say.

Connor rubbed the back of his neck, quiet for once.

Then—

"What's the matter, old man?"

Lincoln.

His voice was sharp, smug.

He stood over them again like he owned the ground beneath their feet, arms folded, boots planted.

"Did you lose your little pet?"

Jaysen felt something snap.

He didn't even think about it.

Didn't weigh the odds.

He just stood, fast.

Lincoln started to smirk.

Jaysen hit him.

A clean punch, straight to the jaw.

Lincoln reeled backward, his smile gone mid-sentence. His heel caught the edge of the bench behind him, and he stumbled. Arms flailed once—too late.

He went down hard.

His head cracked against the concrete with a sharp *thud* that silenced half the yard.

Then he was still.

Flat on his back.

Unconscious.

Jaysen stood over him, chest heaving. His fist throbbed, but he didn't care. He didn't even blink.

Around them, cageys stared—some in awe, some in alarm, most in disbelief.

Charlie looked up slowly.

"Bloody hell," he whispered.

Connor's eyes darted between Jaysen and the Enforcers across the yard. "That's gonna get attention," he muttered. "Real fast."

Jaysen didn't look away from Lincoln's motionless form.

"Let it."

The last thing Jaysen remembered was the flash of movement—the butt of an Argentine Enforcer's rifle swinging toward his face.

Then—

Darkness.

∞

When he came to, he was lying on a stiff cot in the infirmary, a pounding ache in his head and dried blood crusted near his temple.

And The Warden was standing over him.

"Mr. Masters," he said, voice cool and composed, but with a sharp edge. "It seems you still haven't learned how to keep your head down."

He didn't raise his voice. He didn't need to.

He stared at Jaysen for a long moment, then clicked open the file in his hands. "Fighting. Disrupting order. Assaulting another inmate in front of witnesses. Tsk."

The Warden stepped in closer, lowering the file.

"I was pulled away from an important meeting for this. Do you understand the gravity of that, Mr. Masters?" he asked, adjusting his glasses. "Dr. Zygote and I were in the middle of something critical. And now… here I am. Babysitting a cagey with too much pride and too little sense."

Jaysen didn't move. He just watched him. Breathing slow.

"Another fifteen years should do the trick," The Warden said with finality, snapping the file shut. "You clearly need more time to reflect."

He turned, walking toward the exit, then paused and looked over his shoulder.

"And… since you like throwing punches so much—forty-eight hours in The Detachment Gibbets. See if the dark helps you think."

He walked out without waiting for a response.

Didn't look back.

Across the room, Lincoln sat smugly as a nurse finished stitching up the gash on his temple—the one he'd earned falling on his own damn ego.

He grinned at Jaysen.

"Have fun in The Detachment Gibbets," he said with a sneer. "Most people go mad up there."

Jaysen didn't respond.

The nurse finished her work and waved over an Enforcer to take Lincoln away.

The moment he was gone, the room shifted.

Quieter.

Softer.

The nurse returned to Jaysen's side.

She crouched beside him and opened a fresh packet of alcohol wipes.

"This'll sting, sweetie," she whispered.

Then she dabbed gently at the cut on his face.

Jaysen flinched, but she didn't pull back. Her presence grounded him in a way nothing else here did.

Not safety.

But not cruelty either.

Just something human.

The room had emptied.

Only the hum of medical equipment and the faint echo of Enforcer boots remained somewhere outside.

The nurse glanced around, then pulled a small white pill from her pocket and handed it to Jaysen with a paper cup of cold water.

"Quickly," she whispered, urgency in her tone. "You'll be glad to have had it once you're up there."

Jaysen didn't hesitate.

He tossed the pill into his mouth and drank the water down in one long gulp. The cold bit sharply at the back of his throat.

He handed the empty cup back. "Thank you, ma'am."

She smiled softly.

"Please… call me Jessica."

He blinked.

"You're the angel Charlie was talking about," he blurted, the words tumbling out before he could stop them.

Jessica giggled, then gently dabbed the alcohol wipe across his wound again.

"I'm an angel, am I?" she teased. "Charlie is such a sweetheart. I hope he's doing well?"

"He is," Jaysen said, quieter now. "Thanks to you."

She didn't respond right away, just kept working—careful, precise, like she wanted to make the moment last.

And for a moment, Jaysen forgot where he was.

Forgot the weight of the years just added to his sentence.

He looked at her—*really* looked—and understood why Charlie had called her that. There was something unshaken in her. Kindness that hadn't been scrubbed out.

And it didn't make sense.

What was someone like her doing in a place like this?

Before he could ask, the door creaked open.

A Pearl Enforcer stepped into the infirmary—armor gleaming, posture rigid.

Time was up.

Jessica gave Jaysen one last pat on the shoulder.

"You'll be okay," she said softly. "Just… keep your head. You'll need it."

Jaysen nodded once.

Then the Enforcer was beside him, taking him by the arm, leading him out.

As he stepped toward the door, Jaysen caught a glimpse of his reflection in a nearby glass cabinet—brief, distorted, but clear enough.

The new wound cut diagonally across the older scar he'd earned on his first day in Augmentation Bay.

Together, they formed a jagged, imperfect X over his eye.

He looked away.

And walked out.

The Pearl Enforcer said nothing as they led Jaysen up the winding stone staircase.

Each step echoed—hollow and cold—coiling upward like it could go on forever.

Jaysen's ribs ached with every breath. His head still throbbed. But he didn't ask questions. He just climbed.

When they reached the top, the Enforcer unlocked the heavy metal door marked THE DETACHMENT GIBBETS and pulled it open.

Darkness rolled out like smoke.

Jaysen squinted—eyes still adjusting—but then froze.

Staring back at him from just beyond the threshold were *eyes*.

But not just any eyes.

Those eyes.

The same pair he'd seen watching him in the night from beyond the bars of his own cage.

Pale. Unblinking.

And one of them—split straight through the iris.

He flinched, stumbling back into the Pearl Enforcer. They reached up, flicked on their night vision, and a thin red light passed over their mask.

Jaysen's skin crawled.

The Enforcer grabbed his arm without a word and pushed him forward into the dark.

No sound now but the soft clang of boots on metal and the low drone of moving air.

"Where are we?" Jaysen asked loudly, trying to anchor himself with the sound of his own voice.

The whimpering began instantly—soft, fragile sounds from all directions, rising like a wave.

"Quiet," the Enforcer growled.

But then a familiar voice rang out above the noise:

"OH SHUT IT, YA NONGS!"

Jaysen blinked.

I know that voice… It's Xavier!

The Enforcer stopped beside a swinging metal platform, shoving Jaysen forward.

"Get in."

The metal groaned beneath him as he stepped onto the platform, its hinges screeching. It rocked gently as he found his place inside.

More whimpering.

"I SAID SHUT IT, DICKHEADS—OR I'LL START SINGING AGAIN. I'LL DO IT*!*"

Silence.

"Xavier?" Jaysen whispered once the Enforcer's boots had faded.

"Jaysen?" came the loud reply, followed by another wave of whimpers.

"WHAT'D I TELL YOU, DICKHEADS? ONE MORE NOISE AND I SING—LOUD!"

Silence again.

"Shit, mate," Xavier called more quietly. "What are you doing up here?"

"I'm here because I knocked out Lincoln," Jaysen muttered, adjusting inside the too-small cage. "Charlie's worried sick about you. Lincoln was being Lincoln—giving him shit."

"You knocked out Ken?" Xavier's voice was lit with awe. "What a bloody *legend!*"

"Fifteen extra years for being a legend," Jaysen sighed. "Not my finest move."

"So if I knock out Ken, *I* get fifteen years?"

"Don't be stupid. He'd kill you."

Xavier chuckled. "I'm taller than you. If you can do it, I can."

"I got lucky," Jaysen muttered. "Where *are* we?"

"We're in the roof above The Aviary," Xavier explained. "Right next to the gears for the covers."

"Why here?"

"You'll find out."

As if on cue, the gears activated.

The hellish grinding sound rose up around them, deep and metallic, shaking the entire structure.

It ripped through the bars, vibrating in their bones.

Jaysen pressed his palms against his ears, but it didn't help.

And through it all, he saw them again—those eyes, still lingering just beyond the edge of the dark, watching.

Always watching.

When the grinding finally stopped, the silence that followed wasn't really silence.

The whimpering returned—low and fragile, a broken chorus from the surrounding cages.

Then, cutting through it with unearned confidence, came Xavier's voice. Singing.

Off-key. Too loud. Absolutely made up.

Swingin' in my fancy cage,
Can't remember the time or age,
Still got vodka, not all bad,
Could be worse—I've not gone mad!

Jaysen laughed.

Not because it was funny—though it kind of was—but because it was Xavier. And somehow, despite the metal, the dark, and the smell of rust and fear, he was still singing.

Still being Xavier.

Then the meaning caught up with him.

"Wait... did you say *vodka*?"

"Yeah, mate," Xavier said with a grin in his voice. "They didn't search me before they tossed me in here."

Jaysen blinked, reaching slowly into his pocket.

Felt it.

Cool metal. Solid weight.

He pulled out his own flask, popped the cap, and took a swig.

The familiar burn grounded him.

"They didn't search me either," he muttered. "Guess being unconscious has perks."

"At least we've got something to toast with," Xavier said. "Cheers to creative sentencing."

Jaysen let the flask rest in his lap and leaned his head back.

"I don't do so well in the dark," he admitted. "I keep seeing these eyes. They're always there. Watching."

A beat.

Then Xavier, a little quieter now, said:

"You mean *those* eyes?"

Jaysen turned his head slowly.

And saw them.

Just beyond the bars—barely there, but unmistakable.

A single pair of pale eyes.

One of them split through the iris like a scar.

Staring.

Unblinking.

Always.

"THEY'RE REAL!" he shouted, his voice echoing louder than he meant it to.

The whimpering started immediately—soft at first, then rippling out through the darkness like a wave of panic.

But the eyes vanished.

Gone in a blink.

As if they'd never been there.

Jaysen and Xavier sat in stunned silence, both staring into the dark where the eyes had been just moments before.

Neither said anything.

For a long while.

Then, Jaysen spoke—quieter now, breath shaky.

"I thought I was going crazy. I've been seeing them since I got here. I was scared to tell Connor or Charlie… I figured they'd think I was losing it."

He rubbed his face with both hands. "I need a drink."

"Me too," Xavier muttered. Then, louder: "And I need these dickheads to *SHUT THE FUCK UP!*"

Xavier took a long swig from his flask, cleared his throat dramatically, and said, "Let's sing, shall we?"

Without waiting for an answer, he launched into it:

Swingin' in my fancy cage,
Can't remember the time or age,
Still got vodka, not all bad,
Could be worse—I've not gone mad!

Jaysen let out a dry laugh, then took a swig of his own. When Xavier rolled into the next line, he laughed:

Swingin' in my tiny cage,
I haven't seen the light for days!
Those eyes that watch us in the dark…
They almost made poor Jaysen shart!

The two of them laughed—too hard, too loud.

The sound echoed, breaking the tension like a hammer.

They raised their flasks and toasted across the darkness neither of them could see through.

And then—together—they started the song over again.

When they finished their last swig for the night, the vodka did its job.

The metal cages creaked beneath them, but Jaysen's limbs felt weightless, his mind finally quiet.

And when he drifted into sleep, the *eyes* didn't follow him.

For the first time since arriving at Augmentation Bay, Jaysen slept without nightmares. No panic. No gasping awake. No invisible watchers beyond the bars.

Just silence.

Just sleep.

Cramped and hunched in a swaying cage suspended above hell, it was—somehow—the best rest he'd had in weeks.

But before long, the peace ended.

The hellish grinding began again.

The gears overhead screamed to life, sending vibrations down the bars and into their bones. Jaysen groaned, hands clamped over his ears.

It didn't help.

It never would.

But they tried anyway—because hope was stubborn that way.

"*Fuck,* I need to piss," Xavier muttered from the cage beside him when the gears stopped.

Jaysen chuckled. "Well… this is gonna be awkward."

He could hear Xavier shuffling, hunched over, trying to angle himself out through the bars.

There was a pause. Then a splash.

"Shit—*most* of it got out," Xavier grumbled, followed by the clink of his cage rocking with the effort.

Jaysen laughed.

"You're gonna need a shower after this, mate."

"Shower? Nah. Just let it age like wine," Xavier grunted.

Jaysen grinned, then started singing again, half-slurred, half-inspired:

> *Xavier tried to take a piss,*
> *Instead, he covered himself in it!*
> *Lucky he didn't need to shit!*

Their laughter burst out, bouncing through the metal and dark.

But this time, they weren't the only ones.

A chorus of laughter joined them—hoarse, cracked, and real—from other prisoners locked away in the Gibbets.

It was short-lived.

But it was loud.

And for a moment, it felt like they'd taken something back from the place that tried to take *everything*.

∞

Connor

When Jaysen hadn't returned to their cage for two days, Connor started to worry.

He tried not to show it—tried to keep calm, to stay rational—but Charlie had already stopped pretending. They hadn't seen Xavier either. No whispers. No movement in the shadows. Just silence.

Now, they sat in The Big Cage, trail mix in their hands, barely touching it. Picking at raisins like they might reveal answers if they looked long enough.

Neither of them spoke.

Not until—

"Fancy seeing you here."

The voice came from above.

Connor looked up.

Jaysen stood there, grinning, arm slung around Xavier's shoulder like they hadn't been missing for two full days. Both looked like hell— bruised, sleep-starved, and barely clean—but alive. And proud of it.

Connor shot to his feet, grinning from ear to ear. "Where the hell have you two been?"

"Didn't Lincoln tell you?" Jaysen asked, just as Lincoln stepped up behind them.

"I'm not your messenger," Lincoln growled. "I see you found your mutt up in The Detachment Gibbets."

"Well, that's fine, Lincoln," Jaysen said, glancing back. "But I would've considered it a favor if you had."

Xavier snorted with laughter.

Lincoln didn't.

He clenched a fist and took a step toward Xavier—but Jaysen moved before anyone else could.

Quick. Calm.

He stepped between them with that same stillness he'd used last time.

And Lincoln flinched.

Just enough.

Jaysen raised his good eyebrow and gave him a look that said all it needed to.

Lincoln turned and stormed off, lips tight, fists tighter.

"You look terrifying, mate," Connor said, shaking his head.

"Gee, thanks," Jaysen muttered. "Maybe that's why Lincoln's finally listening."

Charlie chuckled. "Or maybe it's the belting you gave him. Either way… it's good to have you boys back."

Jaysen and Xavier dropped onto the bench across from them.

"It's good to be back," they said in unison.

Connor raised an eyebrow. "Well, it looks like a new friendship's been forged."

"Sure has," Jaysen said. "And a longer one at that. I got an extra fifteen years."

"You got fifteen years and two days in Detachment—for punching Lincoln?" Connor said, his voice full of disbelief.

"Yup," Jaysen said, with the tone of someone who'd already processed the absurdity and filed it away.

"Then I get three days in the Gibbets and no extra years?" Xavier blinked. "This place is fucked."

"I'm so sorry, son," Charlie said, his tone heavy with guilt. "That was my mistake. We should've waited until you were processed properly."

Xavier shrugged, smiling. "It's okay," he said, throwing an arm around Jaysen's shoulder. "Jaysen and I had a blast."

Then, without warning, Xavier began to sing—loud and off-key—and Jaysen joined in. Their voices carrying across the yard with an absurd kind of joy:

Swingin' in my fancy cage,
Can't remember the time or age,

Still got vodka, not all bad,
Could be worse—I've not gone mad!
Swingin' in my tiny cage,
I haven't seen the light for days,
Those eyes that watch us in the dark…
They almost made poor Jaysen shart!
Xavier tried to take a piss,
Instead, he covered himself in it!
Lucky he didn't need to shit!

Charlie and Connor both burst into laughter. Connor nearly dropped his trail mix.

The other cageys looked on with confusion, but for once, no one said a word.

The men all laughed—really laughed, shoulders shaking and mouths wide—until Charlie and Connor said in perfect unison:

"That fucking prison cat."

"What?" Jaysen asked, blinking.

"Prison cat?" Xavier echoed immediately, leaning forward.

Connor grinned. "The eyes that watch you in the dark—one of them looks split, doesn't it?"

Jaysen let out an exasperated breath. "You've seen them too?"

"Yeah, mate," Connor said. "Most of us have. It's this cat. Lives somewhere in the prison. No one knows where exactly, but she's always popping up. Scares the shit out of people. Looks like a gargoyle."

"Probably *is* a gargoyle," Charlie added. "I reckon one of the hounds bit her. That's why her eye's split."

"I *saw* that cat!" Xavier said, his voice lighting up. "The other morning—when the covers were rising. Just for a second. But it was her. Tortoiseshell, right?"

"That's the one," Charlie chuckled. "Has she been scaring you, son?"

"More than you know," Jaysen muttered. "She's the one who started my night terrors."

The table erupted with laughter again, louder than before.

Connor, wiping a tear from the corner of his eye, suddenly paused. "Wait a tick. You had *vodka* up there?"

"Haven't you noticed, Connor?" Xavier said, smirking. "They don't search us before throwing us into The Detachment Gibbets."

"I've never been sent there."

"You're lucky," Jaysen said. "I'd have gone mad up there if it weren't for Xavier."

Xavier grinned, nudging Jaysen with his elbow. "Well, *shucks*. You helped me too, you know."

The four of them sat together in The Big Cage, eating, laughing. Everything felt… normal again. Or at least as normal as life in Augmentation Bay could get.

During their time in the yard, cageys continued sneaking Jaysen contraband—quietly, like before—but now, it was more.

More offerings. More deference.

He received a new flashlight, which he handed to Charlie and Xavier. He passed off alcohol wipes, and a bundle of clean clothes he immediately gave to Xavier.

"Save those for after your shower," Jaysen said, chuckling. "You stink. Hopefully it's soon."

Xavier sniffed himself and groaned. "It *better* be soon."

"Tomorrow, actually," said Connor casually, munching on his trail mix.

Jaysen blinked. "Thank fuck for your internal calendar."

"I can't wait to get clean," Xavier muttered dramatically. "And piss in peace."

They all laughed again.

And for the first time in days, the Big Cage felt lighter.

∞

Xavier

"What was it like up there?" Connor asked, his voice carrying softly through the Aviary.

"It was dark… and loud," Jaysen replied from the next stack over. "Xavier made it easier, though. He's a pretty good kid."

"I'm not a *kid*," Xavier shot back from his own cage. "I can't be much younger than you. How old are you, anyway?"

"I'm twenty-six," Jaysen called. "How old are *you*?"

"*Twenty-five,*" Xavier said with pride. "So stop calling me kid."

"Okay… baby-face it is," Jaysen said, laughing.

Xavier grinned and shook his head.

Then came the familiar chant.

"DROP THE COVERS!"

Voices rose across the Aviary like a wave.

Xavier hadn't even noticed the gears begin to grind, but now the vibration filled the space—metal groaning as velvet began its slow descent.

But it wasn't so jarring this time. After the Gibbets, the noise felt distant. Tame.

"It's not so bad anymore," Jaysen said—just loud enough to be heard.

"I was thinking the same thing," Xavier replied.

They both fell quiet as the covers continued to fall.

The dim overhead lights vanished, one by one, until the last sliver of glow disappeared entirely with a soft, final *thud*.

Darkness.

Silence.

Complete.

The covers had sealed them in.

No more talking between cages. No more shared jokes. Just the dark and the low hum of settling steel.

But Xavier didn't flinch.

The Gibbets had changed something in him.

Xavier let the silence settle over him. The kind that used to make his heart race now felt… familiar. Manageable.

A soft *click* cut through the dark.

Charlie's new flashlight flicked on in the cage next to him, casting a pale beam into the space.

Xavier flinched, raising a hand to shield his eyes. "Shit, that's *bright*," he muttered, mostly to himself.

But he was smiling.

Because even here, surrounded by metal and shadow, things didn't feel so dark, either.

Charlie chuckled as he handed Xavier a book. "Made the place homier while you were gone."

Xavier looked around and noticed it for the first time—the books lined up on the makeshift shelf, the clothesline strung at the back of the cage, a few neatly folded shirts hanging from it.

"I can see that you're a natural homemaker," he grinned, taking the book from Charlie. "Does this mean you're my cage wife now?"

Charlie shot him a flat look and dangled a flask in front of his face. "If you want another one of these, you'd best not call me that again."

"Sorry, boss. Won't happen again," Xavier said quickly, holding up his hands in surrender. He laughed, and Charlie passed him the flask.

"I'm glad you're back," Charlie said as he settled into his bed. "I missed your flippant attitude."

"I missed you too," Xavier replied. He lay back on his bed, flipping the book open, but his eyes didn't move across the page. His thoughts were loud.

Charlie noticed. "You're not gonna have a drink with me?" he asked.

Xavier sat up, put the book aside, and pulled out his flask. "Of course I am," he said with a smile that didn't quite reach his eyes. "Was just waiting for you. After all, we drink together in here, remember?"

Charlie raised his flask. "Skol."

"Skol," Xavier echoed, and they both took a swig.

The silence that followed was comfortable. For Charlie.

For Xavier, it was suffocating.

His fingers clenched around the flask. He opened his mouth once—then closed it.

Charlie glanced over at him.

"Hey, Charlie…" Xavier's voice cracked slightly. "I wanted to ask you something."

Charlie turned. "Of course, son. What's on your mind?"

Xavier hesitated again. He stared down at the floor, then at the book in his lap, then back to Charlie. His breath caught in his throat.

"You can tell me anything," Charlie said gently.

Xavier swallowed hard.

"Charlie… do you follow Zoti?"

Charlie's posture shifted, just slightly. The question was dangerous. Risky. Something you didn't ask—not even here.

"You know we're not supposed to talk about that, son," he said softly, his eyes scanning the shadows as if expecting an Enforcer to step through the wall.

"I know," Xavier said quickly, voice low. "I know, it's just…"

He looked away. His hands trembled slightly as he gripped the flask.

"Charlie, I'm… I'm gay."

He said it fast, like ripping off a bandage. Then braced for the blow that might come after.

Nothing.

He continued quickly. "I haven't told anyone in here. Only a few friends from back home ever knew. Most of them are gone now. I've been too scared. Scared that if I said it, I'd be taken. Labeled. Used. But I needed someone to know. Before I…"

He trailed off.

Charlie was quiet.

Xavier stared at the floor, breathing fast, as though the air had turned thinner.

"I needed *you* to know," he finished, barely a whisper.

Charlie didn't speak right away.

He stood from his bed, walked over, and sat down beside Xavier.

No judgment. No hesitation.

Just presence.

Charlie put an arm around his shoulders and gave a gentle squeeze.

"It's okay, son," he said. "I don't follow Zoti. And I don't care who you are—except that you're *you*. That's what matters. You can trust me… and you can trust Jaysen and Connor too."

Xavier's breath hitched.

His head dropped into his hands.

"They don't follow her either?" he asked, voice cracking again.

"Few people do in here," Charlie replied. "Most just keep quiet about it. You talk too loud, you end up in a box. Or worse."

Xavier wiped his face with the back of his sleeve. "Thank you, Charlie," he said hoarsely. "And don't worry. You're not my type."

Charlie let out a laugh. "There's that flippant attitude I missed."

They both chuckled, the heaviness lifting just enough for Xavier to breathe again.

"Will you help me tell Jaysen and Connor?"

Charlie nodded. "Of course, son. They'll be okay with it, but we'll have to be careful. Some cageys would sell that kind of info in a heartbeat."

"Lincoln," Xavier said, the name bitter on his tongue.

Charlie's expression darkened. "Exactly. I don't know what he believes, but I *do* think he'd use it against you if he thought it'd buy him anything."

"I figured as much," Xavier said, leaning back. "People like that… you can spot 'em."

"I think it's time for some sleep," Charlie said, standing again and returning to his bed. "It's going to be nice to stretch out tonight, I'm sure."

"You're not wrong," Xavier said, following suit. "Thanks again, Charlie. For everything."

Charlie just smiled and nodded.

Xavier rolled onto his side, reached up, and flicked off the flashlight.

The cage fell into darkness.

But, it didn't feel lonely.

∞

As the covers rose and dim light bled into the cage, Xavier stirred beneath the thin blanket.

He stretched, groaned, and sat up.

The first thing he noticed was the smell.

"Zoti's dick, I can't wait to get rid of this stale piss stench," he muttered, already tugging at his shirt. "Today's the day."

Charlie glanced over, already prepping for the showers, folding what he didn't want soaked beneath the corner of a plastic sheet.

"How are you feeling today, son?" he asked. "You ready for this?"

"I've never been more ready," Xavier said, unbuttoning his pants with a sense of ceremony. "I'm nervous, I guess… but I know I'll be okay. You being here helps."

The two men stepped into the middle of the cage and waited side by side.

When the Enforcers came around with their hoses, the blast of cold water hit hard—but this time, it felt like relief. The filth, the sweat, the stink of the Gibbets—all of it washed away, if only for a moment.

Afterward, wrapped in clean clothes, Xavier stood straighter. Lighter.

He ran a hand through his damp hair and exhaled.

New day.

They waited quietly for the escort to The Big Cage.

That's when Xavier saw it.

A flick of movement.

Tortoiseshell. Small. Right at the edge of a pillar.

"That's her!" Xavier said, eyes wide. "That's Prison Cat's tail!"

But as soon as he spoke, the tail vanished.

Charlie chuckled. "I think you're seeing things, son. She doesn't come down here when the covers are up."

"It *was* her," Xavier insisted. "I swear."

Of course, she was gone.

The bell rang before he could argue more.

Xavier and Charlie stepped into line, joining the slow shuffle of cageys moving through the Aviary.

Then—

A streak of fur shot out from the row Xavier had pointed to.

"*IT WAS PRISON CAT!*" he shouted.

The tortoiseshell darted between the cageys, weaving through legs like a shadow with claws. She darted right behind Xavier—then straight between Connor's legs.

Connor stumbled forward, knocking into Jaysen, who didn't have time to brace.

Both men went down hard.

Connor's right knee slammed into the concrete with a crunch. He rolled onto his side with a grimace, already grabbing at it as the swelling began.

Jaysen hit face-first—again—but at least this time, he got his hands down. Even so, a line of red bloomed along his jaw where a stitch had given way.

"That fucking Prison Cat," Connor groaned.

The surrounding cageys burst into laughter—some mocking, others genuinely amused.

An Argentine Enforcer stepped in, hauled both men to their feet, and turned them toward the infirmary without a word.

As they limped away, Xavier grinned after them.

"Told you it was her."

Charlie shook his head, barely hiding his own smile.

∞

After two hours in The Big Cage, Charlie and Xavier started to worry.

174

They hadn't seen Connor or Jaysen since the fall—and the longer the wait stretched, the more Xavier's nerves buzzed.

"Surely they wouldn't get sent to the Detachment Gibbets just for *falling…* would they?" he asked, voice tight as he took a swig from his flask.

The metal was cold against his lips as he tipped his head back, desperate for the burn to distract him.

When he opened his eyes, they were standing right in front of him.

Connor, limping, his knee strapped tight with thick gauze.

Jaysen, face freshly stitched, but still smirking like he'd walked away from worse.

"Nah, mate," Connor said with a grin, struggling to sit. "Still haven't been to the Detachment Gibbets. Twenty years and counting."

"Here." Jaysen reached out, helped Connor ease down onto the bench, then dropped onto it beside him.

"Jessica sends her best," Connor added, smug. "And now we *definitely* understand why you took your sweet time getting back from the infirmary. She's *gorgeous.* Xav, you gotta meet her."

Xavier let out a laugh—but it was forced, tight.

His chest squeezed as the words swirled in his throat.

"Yeah… about that…"

He glanced sideways at Charlie.

Charlie met his eyes and gave a subtle nod, his hand resting lightly on Xavier's back. "It's okay, son."

Xavier stared down at his flask. His fingers curled around it so tightly it creaked.

His voice barely came out.

"I… I've been meaning to tell you both something. Something big."

He swallowed, throat dry despite the drink.

"I've only ever told a handful of people before. People who are mostly gone now. And I haven't said it here—well once to Charlie—but, I had to wait, because I didn't know if it was safe. I didn't know if you'd…"

He hesitated. His hand was shaking now.

Charlie didn't say anything, but he didn't move away either.

Xavier took a breath. Then another.

"I'm gay."

The words dropped like lead.

"I've hidden it my whole life," he said quickly, eyes still on the ground. "Not because I was ashamed—but because I knew what The Shepherd would do. What they'd do *here*. I've watched people disappear for less."

His voice broke.

"But I didn't want to lie to you anymore. Not if I'm going to volunteer. Not if… if it's going to be soon."

Silence.

Xavier held his breath.

He couldn't bring himself to look at them. Not yet.

Then—Jaysen's voice, calm and sure:

"Xav… I'm glad you trusted us."

Xavier looked up slowly.

Connor was smiling.

"You're our mate," he said, quiet but firm.

"That's not gonna change."

Xavier's eyes stung. He blinked, hard.

And then he laughed—a single, breathless sound—more relief than humor.

Charlie patted his back again, steady and warm.

For the first time in what felt like forever, Xavier wasn't holding anything back.

He was just… himself.

And they were still here.

Still with him.

He could've stayed in that moment forever—until Lincoln sat down.

Right at their table.

The warmth drained like a bucket with a hole in the bottom.

Jaysen stood immediately.

His tone was flat. Cold.

"We don't want any of your shit, Lincoln. What do you want?"

Lincoln raised both hands in mock submission.

"I'm not here to start shit," he said. "I just need to talk for a few minutes."

Xavier eyed him with suspicion. "What's the matter?" he asked with a smirk. "You need Jaysen's protection now?"

Lincoln's eyes snapped to Xavier, rage flickering just beneath the surface.

He held himself back.

"Shut it, mutt," he growled through clenched teeth. Then, turning back to Jaysen: "Barry's not too happy with me right now. Think you or Charlie could talk to him for me?"

"What'd you do this time?" Charlie asked, not looking up from his trail mix.

Lincoln picked at a hangnail. "He heard what I said to you the other day. And now, unless you and I are good, he won't give me any more smokes."

Charlie raised an eyebrow. "So you're coming to make peace?"

Lincoln shifted. "More or less."

"I'll talk to him," Charlie said after a pause. "But you need to stop fucking with Xavier."

He looked up, eyes sharp. "And don't worry. He will stop fucking with you."

Lincoln's jaw flexed.

"Fine," he muttered.

Charlie stood and walked off toward Barry, leaving Lincoln with the rest of them. He didn't say anything. Just waited.

Xavier studied him in silence.

The sandy blonde hair in a messy crewcut. The beard—dark, but streaked with white. Broad shoulders. Tall. And those piercing blue eyes that, if they didn't belong to such an ugly soul, might have been considered beautiful.

If only you didn't have an ugly heart, Xavier thought.

Lincoln noticed the stare.

"What are you looking at, mu—" he stopped himself, corrected with a forced sneer, "Xavier?"

"Oh, nothing," Xavier replied casually, shrugging.

Then he turned to Jaysen. "I think it's time for a drink."

Knowing Lincoln didn't have any, he pulled out his flask and tipped it back with dramatic flair.

Lincoln snatched it mid-swig and emptied it in one go.

Xavier stared, half-stunned, half-impressed. "Wow. No shame left at all."

But the show wasn't over.

An Argentine Enforcer across the yard had seen the exchange—and they were already marching over, purposeful and silent.

Connor, Jaysen, and Xavier froze, watching the Enforcer close in.

Lincoln noticed the stares and turned—just in time for the butt of a rifle to connect squarely with his left eye.

The blow dropped him instantly.

His body hit the floor of The Big Cage with a dull *thud*, limbs limp, flask clattering to the side.

Blood pooled beneath his cheek, seeping from a split through his eyelid.

As the Enforcer hauled him off the ground and dragged him away, Xavier stared down at the unconscious man.

That one piercing blue eye—now ringed in red—peered through the gash, half-lidded, staring up at him.

Xavier exhaled and muttered, just loud enough for himself:

"I suppose your face will match your heart now."

Charlie sat back down, a fresh packet of cigarettes in his hand.

He looked at them like they were a problem.

"Well," he muttered, "what am I supposed to do with these?"

"I'll take them, boss," Xavier offered, holding out a hand. "If you're cool with me smoking in the cage?"

Charlie raised an eyebrow. "It's your body," he said, passing over the packet. "But you owe Lincoln a pack when he gets back."

His tone didn't leave room for interpretation.

Xavier nodded, more serious now. "Understood," he said, and slid the packet into his pocket.

"Did you see Ken's eye?" he added, a grin curling at the edge of his mouth.

Charlie's look turned into a glare.

"Sorry—*Lincoln's* eye," Xavier corrected quickly, hands up. "That's not gonna be pretty."

Charlie didn't respond. Just leaned back and stretched his legs like the conversation was done.

∞

When it was time to return to their cages, Xavier walked in silence beside him. He'd picked up a lighter from Barry—a quiet trade, no words, just a glance and a nod. The kind that didn't need attention.

Back in his cage, Xavier sat on his bed, the clean clothes from earlier still carrying the faint scent of soap.

It had been five days since his last cigarette.

His craving was growing like a storm cloud in his chest.

He reached into his pocket, fingers closing around the loose cigarette he'd already taken from the packet. It rested against his palm like something sacred.

He didn't light it yet.

Not until the covers dropped.

He lay back, one hand behind his head, the other loosely holding the unlit cigarette.

His ears were tuned—waiting.

For the faint grinding of gears.

For the rising chorus of cageys chanting *drop the covers* like a hymn of routine and rebellion.

The countdown to darkness.

The countdown to his first drag.

"How are you feeling, son?" Charlie asked, glancing over with that fatherly intuition of his.

Xavier sat up on his bed, fingers tapping against his thigh, eyes flicking toward the ceiling.

"I'm feeling perfect, thanks to you, boss," he said with a grin. "I appreciate everything you've done for me." He leaned back against the wall. "I just wish I could have a cigarette already."

As if summoned by the craving, the hum of the gears began overhead.

Xavier looked up, smile stretching wider.

"Looks like it won't be long," Charlie chuckled.

The velvet covers dropped, blotting out the light with that familiar *thud*.

In the dark, a small flame sparked to life—Xavier's lighter. It lit up the cage for a moment before Charlie switched on the flashlight, casting a steady glow.

Xavier took a long, deep drag from the cigarette he'd been holding onto all day.

It didn't taste right.

Not bad… just different.

He pulled it from his mouth and looked at it in the new light.

It wasn't a tailor-made. It was hand-rolled.

"Charlie…" he said slowly, voice slightly hoarse. "Does Barry sell anything other than cigarettes?"

Charlie turned toward him, caught sight of the rolled paper in Xavier's hand—and laughed.

"Shit. I didn't think Lincoln smoked weed!"

Xavier blinked, then took another drag. His head spun in a slow, pleasant spiral.

"Holy shit. This is hard enough to find outside—and old mate's got it *in here!*"

"You still cool, Charlie?"

"Only if you share," Charlie said with a wink.

Xavier slid over beside him, and the two passed the joint back and forth in easy silence.

"I suppose I'll have to owe Barry more than I thought," Xavier muttered.

"Don't worry, son," said Charlie. "I'll sort it out."

They stretched out on the floor, lying side by side, staring up at the steel roof like it was a starless night sky.

"The person who designed this place must've been seriously messed up," Xavier said.

Charlie was quiet a moment.

"Maybe," he replied. "But I suppose I can see how this place could've been good. It's just The Shepherd that fucked it up."

"Yeah… I guess."

They fell quiet again.

Xavier let his gaze soften, his breathing slow. The buzz from the joint curled around his thoughts like fog.

Then he heard something.

A low, familiar hum—but not from the gears.

He sat up, blinking against the flashlight beam—and saw them.

Two eyes.

Just outside the cage.

Wide, pale.

One split down the iris.

"Hey… kitty?" he whispered.

He raised his hand, coaxing gently.

Charlie sat up as the small tortoiseshell figure pushed her head through the bars. She hesitated… then backed up—squeezed under the dropped velvet cover—and vanished into the mess of shadow and cages.

"Tell me you saw that, Charlie!"

Charlie yawned, stretching his arms. "Saw what?"

"THE FUCKING PRISON CAT!" Xavier blurted.

Charlie just laughed. "You're high, son. Time we get some sleep."

He padded back to his bed.

Xavier shook his head and followed, eyes still darting to where the cat had been.

"I suppose I am," he muttered as he lay down. "There's no way she could've squeezed her head through there anyway…"

He clicked off the flashlight.

Darkness returned.

And with it, the slow spin of the world as Xavier drifted into sleep.

∞

When the covers rose and the first sliver of dim light crept beneath the edge of the cage, Xavier stirred from a deep, dreamless sleep.

Charlie was already up.

He sat cross-legged near the back of the cage, quietly reading by the soft flame of the lighter—keeping the flashlight off so as not to wake him.

"You were snoring like a fucking donkey last night, son," Charlie said, snapping the book shut with a soft *thump*.

Xavier yawned, stretched, and rubbed his face. "Sorry, boss. That shit knocked me out. Might have to get some more from Bazza."

"So it's *Bazza* now, is it?" Charlie chuckled as he stood and crossed to the shelf to put the book away. "He'll like that one."

He turned back to Xavier, more serious now. "Just don't expect you'll be getting it as easy as everything else, son. *Bazza* may be able to get weed, but it won't be much—and it won't be free."

Xavier nodded as he sat up fully, reaching for his flask out of habit.

Charlie continued, "You should look after yourself. Healthier organs go for more."

He said it casually as he walked to the back of the cage to piss.

Xavier leaned back on his elbows. "I guess so. But I've been smoking for ten years. If there's any damage, it's already done."

He exhaled slowly, grinning to himself.

"Might as well enjoy myself before some rich cunt's enjoying my organs."

Charlie laughed as he zipped up. "Good way to look at it, I suppose."

$$\infty$$

When Xavier saw Barry take his usual seat across the yard, he stood and made his way over.

Charlie had offered to handle it—but Xavier didn't want him to.

He's done enough for me already.

He dropped onto the bench beside Barry, casual but focused.

"Hey, Bazza," Xavier said, flashing a quick smile. "Was wondering if you could help me out?"

Barry looked up from his game of dice. He was older than Charlie— by at least a decade. If Xavier had to guess, he'd put him somewhere between seventy-five and eighty, though something in his posture made him feel younger. Like he wasn't done yet.

"What can I do ya for?" Barry asked.

"That pack of smokes Charlie picked up from you yesterday. The ones meant for Lincoln."

"Yes. What about it?"

"Well… Lincoln got flattened right before he could take 'em. So… I sort of took them. And I was hoping," Xavier said, lowering his voice slightly, "you could get me another pack—for him. And maybe… a few more joints? For me?"

Barry raised one snowy eyebrow. "You and Lincoln are good now?"

Xavier shrugged. "Wouldn't say we're good. But we've got an agreement."

Barry looked at him a beat longer, then nodded.

He reached into his coat and handed over a sealed cigarette packet and a small, dented aluminum container.

"Everything you need for yourself is in here," he said, tapping the tin with one knuckle.

Xavier took it and pocketed both.

"You owe me," Barry said, raising that eyebrow again. Then he smirked. "And I know where you live. With Charlie."

The smirk disappeared as quickly as it came, replaced by a much more serious look.

Xavier laughed nervously and stood, extending his hand.

"Thanks, Bazza."

Barry took it, his grip surprisingly strong. "If you get caught, you didn't get it from me."

Xavier nodded once and made his way back to where Charlie, Connor, and Jaysen were sitting, halfway through their trail mix.

"I said I'd take care of it, son," Charlie said, finishing his mouthful without looking up.

"You've helped me enough, Charlie," Xavier said as he sat down. "I can sort this one out myself."

He smiled, tapping his pocket.

"When do you think we could try again, boss?" he added. "They've processed me now, so we shouldn't have any problems."

Charlie took a slow swig from his flask before answering.

"We'll have to wait a while, son. If you get caught again so soon, they'll throw you back in The Detachment Gibbets. Minimum."

He frowned, glancing at Jaysen and Connor, who both nodded in agreement.

"Give it a month. Maybe two."

Xavier sighed but didn't push. "Okay, boss…"

A beat passed.

"What do you reckon Lincoln's gonna get for yesterday?"

Charlie scratched at his jaw. "Probably another ten years and a cage on a higher level. He's getting close to life. I think he's sitting at eighty years now."

Xavier winced. "Guess I'd better be a bit more friendly."

Charlie side-eyed him. "That'd be wise."

"I'll try. It's just hard when he's such a jerk…" Xavier smirked. "But so fucking hot."

Charlie barked a laugh. "Ahh, so *Lincoln's* your type?"

"Only when it comes to his *looks*," Xavier said. "That's where it ends."

CHAPTER IVE

Control

Dr. Lancet

The door opened.

The Warden stepped inside, eyes flicking from her pale face to the crushed cigarette on the floor.

"What did I tell you about that?" he asked, voice cool.

She said nothing.

He stepped closer.

"You're slipping, Evelyn. That mirror, this mess... maybe I should lock you in here. For your own good."

She swallowed hard. Then shifted.

"It's harder than you think," she whispered. "I... I'm worried about my daughter. The stress... It got to me."

She stepped forward, tracing her fingers down his chest. "It was my only vice. But now, you're here."

Her voice dropped.

"Now you can be my vice."

His eyes gleamed. He pulled her close, lifted her onto the counter. The cold tile pressed against the backs of her thighs, grounding her in the now, as his body pressed in.

"I know what you're doing, Evelyn," he growled.

"Good," she whispered. "So do I."

The belt slid from his waist. The leather hissed, slow and deliberate, like a serpent drawn to heat. He looped it around her neck, pulling it snug—not enough to choke, not yet. Just enough to own.

Her breath hitched.

He stepped back for a moment, eyes locked on hers as he unfastened his pants. The sound of the zipper sliding down was deliberate—taunting.

His cock sprang free—thick, flushed, and already pulsing with arousal. He stroked himself once, slow and possessive, the tip glistening.

Dr. Lancet moaned softly at the sight, her thighs parting further in invitation. Her voice was barely above a whisper. "Don't make me wait."

He didn't.

He thrust into her without warning.

She gasped, a sharp intake that broke into a moan. Her body rocked against the mirror behind her, its cool surface kissing her back, the pressure a perfect contrast to the fire blooming in her abdomen.

The scar across her chest—still fresh, still tender—pulled with each motion. It ached.

And the ache *thrilled* her.

She arched into the rhythm, her legs wrapping around him as she whispered, "Don't stop. Not until I scream."

He bit down on her shoulder—hard. Her cry echoed off the tile walls, cut short by the belt tightening around her throat. Her vision shimmered at the edges.

"Harder," she groaned, voice strangled with pleasure.

He obliged.

His hips slammed into hers, each thrust deliberate, punishing. One hand gripped her waist. The other fisted her hair, yanking her head back so her throat stretched taut against the leather.

Pain flared.

It was bright. Raw. *Delicious.*

She wanted to crawl inside it, let it swallow her whole.

She moaned louder, her nails clawing at his back. "I want to feel it tomorrow," she breathed. "Make me remember you."

He growled in response—feral, lost in control. He was always composed, always collected—but not with her. She stripped him down to instinct. Dominance. Ownership.

The belt tightened again.

She gasped.

And in the flicker of her vision—just behind her eyelids—Michael's eyes watched.

Cold. Patient. Splitting at the seams.

Watching her take pleasure from the body that housed his stolen organs.

Her release came hard—sharp, unrelenting. She choked on it, jaw clenched, spine bowed as her body trembled around him. The scar across her chest pulsed like it had its own heartbeat.

The Warden followed with a low grunt, thrusting once more as he spilled inside her.

For a moment, everything was still.

Their bodies pressed together, breath ragged, slick with sweat.

Then he stepped back, re-buckling his belt, his composure sliding neatly back into place.

Dr. Lancet stayed where she was, legs spread, trembling, the ghost of pain still singing in her bones.

She touched the mirror behind her. It was cool.

Whole.

But she could feel him.

Michael was still inside her.

"I have to get to work, Wyatt," said Dr. Lancet as she rubbed the red ring around her neck.

"No… you don't. Shabina is doing the menial tasks. You're having a few days off… to recover."

She glared at The Warden, and he smirked.

"Have a bath," he commanded her. "You should clean yourself up."

He looked her up and down.

Is that a look of disgust? she thought, watching his smirk fade into a scowl. *Why does it make me want him more?*

Dr. Lancet grabbed her torn clothes. They slipped through her fingers and dropped to the floor.

"I'll lay something out on the bed for you to wear," The Warden said, collecting the scraps. "These are no good."

He turned the tap on and tested the water with his hand.

"The towels are in there," he said, gesturing toward the cupboard. Then he left the room.

Dr. Lancet turned to the mirror again. Her reflection met her eyes this time.

Just her.

She sighed with relief.

Then she stepped into the bath.

The warmth welcomed her.

And for a while, she let it hold her.

The Warden stepped back into the room without knocking, holding a small white tube between two fingers. He approached the edge of the tub and set it gently on the rim, within her reach.

"Vitality Gel," he said. "Use it on your chest. The scar's inflamed."

Dr. Lancet didn't answer. She reached for the tube with wet fingers, inspecting the label before unscrewing the cap. The Warden left.

The gel inside shimmered faintly, tinged with an iridescent green. She squeezed a generous line onto her palm, then slowly began to rub it into her skin—from the base of her throat, down the full length of her scar.

It tingled. Not unpleasantly. Just enough to make her nerves stand on end.

She let her head fall back against the edge of the tub, eyes closed.

Michael's voice echoed from memory: *Let me in.*

Her fingers stilled over her abdomen.

"I already did," she whispered.

$$\infty$$

Valentino

When Valentino awoke, the sun was bleeding through the forest canopy in golden streaks. It burned into his eyelids until a shadow moved across it, blocking the light.

"Who are you?" a mousey voice asked, barely above a whisper.

He scrambled upright, disoriented, heart pounding.

"I'm sorry," the voice came again. "Please don't be scared… Do you need help?"

His vision sharpened. Standing in front of him was the woman from the night before—the one who had vanished like mist. Pandora.

"Uh… hi," he mumbled, rubbing the back of his neck. He was still groggy, sleep clinging to him like fog. "I'm fine… Thanks. I'll just be on my way now."

He turned, but her voice stopped him again.

"Are you sure? You look a little low on water. I have a bottle… if you'd like it?"

He hesitated, then glanced over his shoulder.

"You don't know me," he said flatly. "Why would you help me?"

Pandora stepped forward, her expression soft. "Because it's the right thing to do." She held the water out to him without flinching.

"I have nothing to give you in return."

"That's okay. I just want to help."

Something shifted in his chest. An ache. How could Marcus have ever treated her like she was less than this?

She's so… sweet.

He took the bottle gently. "Thank you." He turned toward her and offered the smallest of smiles. "I'm Val. Nice to meet you."

"Pandora," she said. Her voice was soft, but sure.

"What brings you out to the mountains?" she asked.

Valentino hesitated, watching her carefully.

Be careful, he told himself. *You don't know her.*

"I… uh… hunting," he replied, rubbing the back of his neck again.

Pandora giggled. "One of my friends does that too—rubs his neck when he's stressed… or lying," she said playfully. "It's okay. You don't have to tell me."

She reached into her bag. "Would you like some strawberries?"

His eyes widened. "Strawberries? You have strawberries?"

She sat on his makeshift bed and pulled out a small cloth sack. He sat down beside her, watching with quiet awe as she drew out a plump, red berry.

"Here," she said, holding it out. "They're delicious."

Valentino stared at it, then at her, before finally taking it. He bit into the fruit and groaned.

"Holy fuck," he murmured, eyes fluttering shut. "I never thought they'd be so sweet. They're… fucking amazing."

Pandora tilted her head. "You've never had strawberries before?"

He shook his head. "My father… he's allergic. Never let them in the house."

"Well, if you'd like…" She played with a strand of her hair, shy and sincere. "I can leave you a bushel once a month. Just here. That way, you can enjoy them without your father being hurt."

He blinked at her. "Why would you do that?"

"You seem like you need it," she said simply. "And if I can help… I will."

He inhaled sharply.

She placed her hand on his knee.

"It's okay," she said gently. "I'm one of the good guys."

He looked down at her hand, then placed his over it.

"That's easy to see," he said. "But I'm not. I'm not one of the good guys."

His voice dropped to a whisper. "You shouldn't be helping me. You probably shouldn't even tell anyone you met me."

The air between them thickened. Her lips parted slightly. His gaze dropped to her mouth, then returned to her eyes.

"Do you always help strangers like this?" he asked, voice low.

"Only the ones who look like they've forgotten what kindness feels like."

That did it.

Before he could think, before he could talk himself out of it, he stepped forward, slid his arms around her waist, and pulled her in. Their bodies aligned, heat passing between them like a secret. He kissed her— deeply, hungrily. A kiss born from hunger and disbelief that someone like her could exist in a world like his.

For a heartbeat, she kissed him back.

Then—

"PANDORA!" a voice bellowed.

They tore apart as Marcus's scream cut through the trees.

"GET THE FUCK AWAY FROM HIM, PANDORA!"

Marcus stormed toward them, eyes wild, fists clenched.

Valentino stepped in front of her—but Marcus didn't stop.

He grabbed Pandora by the hair and yanked her sideways, dragging her with brutal force.

She cried out, stumbling.

Valentino saw red.

He launched forward, slamming into Marcus and taking him down hard. They hit the earth with a sickening thud as Pandora scrambled back, clutching the side of her head.

She cried out and screamed names Valentino couldn't make out—his heartbeat thundering too loud to hear—as she ran toward the overgrown path Marcus had come from.

He wrapped his fingers around Marcus's throat and lifted him off the ground like dead weight.

Marcus coughed and gasped, dropping a tangled fistful of Pandora's black curls.

As the hair fell between them, something in Valentino snapped.

"You're lucky The Architect wants you alive," he growled, voice low and seething. "He said nothing about hurting you."

He hurled Marcus into the trunk of a tree. The crack of impact echoed.

Marcus grunted, struggling to his feet.

Valentino grabbed him by the collar and drove his fist into Marcus's stomach—once, twice, again. Brutal, punishing.

Marcus dropped to the dirt, wheezing.

Valentino stood over him, eyes burning.

"Touch her again," he spat, "and I *will* kill you."

He drove his boot into Marcus's gut.

"I'm not the weak boy you once knew, Marcus. I won't let you hurt another woman."

He leaned closer, voice like steel.

"You should remember that."

Valentino gathered what strawberries he could from the grass, his hands trembling not from fear—but fury.

Then he disappeared into the trees, swallowed by the forest's shadows.

∞

Marcus

Marcus staggered to his feet, one hand clutching his bruised ribs. Blood filled his mouth, the taste metallic and bitter. His face twisted into a snarl, eyes blazing with humiliation and hate. Rage rolled through him hotter than pain, scorching what little patience he had left.

"I'll rip them apart for this," he snarled, spitting into the dirt. "That freak and that whore won't get away with it. Now, where did she go?"

He limped toward the overgrown pathway, but before he could take three steps, a figure emerged from the shadows ahead—a young man with long dark hair, brown eyes, and tanned skin.

"Marcus," the man snarled.

Marcus sneered. "DJ."

"Stay away from Pandora," DJ snapped. "You don't want me getting The Council involved, do you?"

Marcus scoffed and pushed past him.

"Stay away from Pandora," another voice commanded from deeper in the path.

A second young man stepped forward—nearly identical to DJ, except his long hair was tied back. He blocked Marcus's path.

"We mean it, Marcus," they said in eerie unison.

Marcus glanced over his shoulder toward the brush where Valentino had vanished, his jaw tightening with fresh hatred. He turned back to the twins with a crooked, venomous smirk.

"Stay out of my way, Nick, DJ," he growled. "Pandora isn't worth my time anyway. Tell that freak she can enjoy the messed-up thing she has going on with you two... After all, twins share the same toys... right?"

He tried to push past Nick, but Nick grabbed his wrist and yanked him close, their faces inches apart.

"We aren't kidding, Marcus," Nick said through clenched teeth. "Stay away from her, or you're going to regret it."

Marcus jerked his wrist free, smirking defiantly as he straightened his shirt and dusted off his pants. He limped away without looking back.

"Why is he limping?" DJ asked quietly.

Nick's eyes narrowed.

"I don't know."

Once Marcus had vanished into the trees, the twins exchanged a glance, then turned down the path together.

"Let's go see Pandora," Nick said. "She's probably heading for the waterfall. She's going to need us."

∞

Valentino

Valentino made his way up the mountain, still mumbling about Marcus. His fists clenched at his sides as he stomped through the underbrush.

"That smug bastard," he muttered. "Always acting like he's better than everyone—like he's untouchable."

His breath came fast, each word heating his chest. "At least Fred and Vince are tolerable. Marcus is just… just… FUCK!" He yelled in frustration, his voice echoing through the trees.

"Watch your language, boy," a deep voice came from the shadows.

Valentino froze.

"I… I…" Fear shot across his face. "Father… I'm sorry," he finally said. "What are you doing out here? Someone might see you!"

An Emerald Enforcer stepped out of the shadows.

"Unlikely," he said confidently.

Valentino jumped back at first.

The Architect laughed.

"Take it easy, boy. I don't even have the voice distorter… Now tell me what you've discovered." He stepped closer.

"The Hidden Heir," said Valentino. "He's been found."

"Who is he?" asked The Architect.

"I don't know," Valentino said nervously. "All Marcus could tell me is that The Council found him… and he's in Augmentation Bay."

The Architect nodded slowly.

"See what the others know," he said flatly. "And in the meantime, I have a name… I need him… taken care of. Considering The Council think they've found the Heir in Augmentation Bay, they will attempt to break him out… An assassination during… Well… that will make it quite thrilling."

The Architect handed a torn piece of paper to Valentino.

"Xavier Wheeler… What did he do?"

"He knows too much," The Architect said bluntly. "Names, locations, timelines. Things only someone on the inside could know. If he talks to the wrong person, it could unravel everything. Now, is that all your information?"

Valentino shook his head.

"The Cell… they're expecting twins."

The Architect stayed silent momentarily, then tilted his head.

"And how do you feel about that, Valentino?"

Valentino shrugged.

"I don't feel anything about it."

The Architect nodded again.

"Now go… We're running out of time."

"Wait… I have a message for you." Valentino handed the scroll to The Architect. He took it and disappeared into the shadows.

Then Valentino hurried up the mountain.

The trail was long, winding, and far more treacherous than he remembered. Loose rocks shifted under his feet, forcing him to catch himself on gnarled roots and moss-slick stones. Tree branches clawed at his arms and snagged his sleeves, leaving faint scratches across his forearms. The air grew thinner with each step, his breaths turning sharp as the incline grew steeper.

He slipped once, catching himself hard on his hands, the paper from The Architect nearly tumbling from his grip. He clenched it tighter, jaw set.

No shortcuts. No time to rest.

The Architect's orders buzzed in his skull louder than the wind tearing through the trees.

He pressed on, sweat slicking his back, the burn in his legs matching the churn in his stomach. It wasn't just the climb—it was what waited at the summit. The part of the job he hated most. Sentencing someone to death.

"Finally!" a man's voice came from just above him.

"Fred, Vince… Sorry… I got turned around."

Two men were waiting near a lookout, and Valentino approached them.

"What have you got for us?" asked Vince with a smirk. "Let me guess—another baby goat to kick over? A lizard to intimidate? A rogue garden gnome?" He cackled and nudged Fred. "I mean seriously, Val. Last time was a kid. A kid."

Fred snorted.

"I almost didn't take that one. I thought it was a prank assignment."

"A warm-up exercise at best," Vince added.

Valentino looked down at the paper in his hand. *The last one was a kid?*

The words hit harder now, slicing through his thoughts. Dread prickled beneath his skin. *No… Father wouldn't…* He told himself that like a prayer—but there was a crack in his voice even thinking it.

He hadn't pulled the trigger. He hadn't been there. But the name? The name had come from him.

He tried to picture the child. Tried to recall any detail—hair, eyes, age. Nothing. Just a hollow in his memory, like his mind had refused to hold onto it.

Killing a kid… that's something I wouldn't do. Couldn't.

But he didn't stop the order. He hadn't even questioned it.

Was that still the same thing?

"Earth to Val…" Vince pointed at the paper. "Is that the name?"

Valentino looked up at the men.

"Uh… yeah, it is," he said sheepishly.

198

He handed the piece of paper to Fred.

"It's a name. That's all I've got. He's in Augmentation Bay… you'll have to figure the rest out yourselves. Will that be a problem?"

Fred and Vince exchanged a glance, then looked back at him.

"Not at all," said Fred.

"It will be double the fee though… That won't be a problem… will it?" asked Vince.

∞

Dr. Zygote

As Dr. Zygote returned to Augmentation Bay, he gazed at the city lights off in the distance. The rain across the windows streaked them, and he smiled wickedly.

"Soon they're all going to see… They need me… Society would crumble without me and my precious incubators," he mumbled as the gates closed behind the limo. "They don't understand it yet—none of them do. They look at me and see a man in a lab coat. But I am genesis. I am womb and flame and evolution. Every advancement, every miracle they cling to comes from me. And one day, when their systems collapse and their order falters, they'll crawl to me, begging for salvation. And I will choose who gets to be reborn… and who gets to rot."

∞

When he entered The Warden's office, the man was barking orders at the Pearl Enforcer.

"We will need another batch of Enforcers. The Warden paced like a caged animal, his boots echoing through the corridor. "Double the patrols. I want Command informed within the hour. I want eyes on every level, every exit. We've lost too much in the past."

He turned sharply to face a Pearl Enforcer.

"The twins are our top priority. We aren't losing these ones. Not to sabotage. Not to luck. Not to incompetence."

His jaw was tight. His voice, steel. "Not this time."

The Pearl Enforcer nodded.

"Right away, sir." They turned and marched down the corridor and out of sight.

Dr. Zygote walked in and The Warden stopped.

"Zayne... did you get the message to him?"

Dr. Zygote nodded.

"The Architect wants you to give Jaysen Masters the death sentence," he said bluntly, then stormed away.

∞

"You're meant for greater things than this, Zayne. You should work for Cypher, not that joke," Dr. Zygote muttered as he stormed into his surgery.

"I'll get there one day... Then everyone will see just what I'm capable of."

He heard Jessica clear her throat from the doorway and spun around.

"Jessica," he blurted. "Go get me the files for IM-1."

She nodded and rushed out.

When Jessica returned, Dr. Zygote was elbow-deep in a fridge full of small glass jars, muttering to himself.

"I know... I know... It's here somewhere."

Jessica cleared her throat again.

"The files you asked for, sir," she said.

Dr. Zygote bumped his head on the shelf above him as he shot up and glared at her.

"Announce yourself next time!" he snapped. "Now go make yourself useful. The incubators need cleaning, and maintenance."

Jessica nodded once more, then left the surgery.

"She can't know," Dr. Zygote muttered, holding the ultrasound between two fingers like it was something filthy. "None of them can. Not yet. Not until it's perfect. Not until I'm ready."

He flicked a lighter and brought it to the edge of the ultrasound. The flame danced hungrily as he fed it into the flame.

"Secrets and science, Zygote. That's all this place is. Flesh and formulas. You give them a little heat… and they show you their true composition."

He watched the image blacken and curl.

"They think I'm just some cog in The Warden's machine. They think I'm beneath Cypher's radar."

A dry laugh escaped him.

"Fools. I'm not beneath it—I'm always watching it. Always two steps ahead. They'll all know soon enough. When the twins emerge, flawless and pure… who do they think they'll thank?"

He turned back to the fridge, eyes gleaming.

"Not The Warden. Not The Council. No… They'll beg for my wisdom. For my mercy."

He went back over to the refrigerator and continued searching. "Aha, here it is," he said triumphantly, pulling out a batch of jars filled with a bright blue liquid.

He picked up the file, left the surgery, and approached The Cell.

∞

Dr. Lancet

Dr. Lancet pulled out the plug and dried herself off, the soft towel rubbing against her skin. The chill of the bathroom seeped in as she wrapped it around herself, the fabric barely clinging to her damp body. She walked toward the mirror. Her hands trembled slightly as she wiped the condensation from the glass.

And there he was.

Michael.

His grin deepened, twisting into something far more sinister. His eyes gleamed with malice as he tilted his head, his expression shifting from playful to something darker, filled with wicked satisfaction. The air in the bathroom thickened, freezing her skin as his presence seemed to consume the space. He moved closer, slowly, deliberately, his smile widening as he closed the gap between them.

Dr. Lancet took a sharp breath, stepping back from the mirror. Her heart pounded in her chest. She couldn't shake the feeling that something had shifted within her—the hallucinations were becoming more persistent.

"What do you want from me?" she whispered, her voice breaking with fear she couldn't suppress.

Michael's smile grew even wider, crueler. "I don't want you fucking up my organs, Evelyn," he purred, his voice a low, venomous hiss that sent a chill through her chest. The words twisted, taunting her as if he could feel her fear seep from her skin. "You think this is over? You think you can just move on?"

Dr. Lancet's eyes narrowed, her fists clenching. She took a step forward, but her body was trembling—fear now taking root deep inside her. Her reflection twisted into something unrecognizable—Michael's grinning face stared back at her, his eyes mocking. Her own image seemed to fade, swallowed by his sinister presence.

"They're *my* organs," she spat, the words thick with anger and panic. She wanted to scream at him—wanted to strike him—but fear held her back. She stepped closer, forcing herself to meet his gaze, though it felt like her body was betraying her.

Michael extended his arm, the motion slow and deliberate. His fingers brushed the mirror's surface, and the temperature in the room dropped, her breath turning to mist. The bath stopped draining, the water pooling in the sink, and the tap suddenly turned on, its stream harsh and mocking in the silence. The mirror seemed to pulse, as if alive with his malice.

Dr. Lancet whipped around, her heart hammering in her chest. The tap ran freely, the water splashing into the sink as she glanced over her shoulder, only to find the room eerily still. She turned back to the mirror, and Michael was gone, but the malice lingered, thick and suffocating in the air.

The tap turned off with a sharp click, leaving only the deafening silence. The air felt heavier now, as if the space itself was suffocating her.

Her face stared back at her in the mirror—hollow, tired, and lost. No Michael. No reflection of what he had been. Just her, standing there, her heart racing, her skin cold with dread.

Dr. Lancet took a deep breath, trying to steady herself. Her stomach churned as the dread gnawed at her insides. She needed to move on. She needed to be strong. But there was a crack in her composure that she couldn't seal.

She walked out of the bathroom, her footsteps unsteady as the weight of the hallucination clung to her. The silence pressed in, too loud. On the bed, neatly laid out, was a red lace nightdress and gown, a stark contrast to the chaos in her mind. The Warden had arranged them, perfect and pristine, their delicate stitching gleaming under the soft light above her head.

Dr. Lancet's fingers brushed over the stitching, tracing the fine design, almost as if she were trying to anchor herself in something real. "It's so… intricate," she murmured to herself, her voice barely above a whisper, a ghost of awe lingering on the words.

She picked up the nightdress, inspecting it. The fabric felt soft, almost impossibly delicate beneath her fingers.

"How much iron does Wyatt have?" she mused aloud, though the question was more rhetorical than anything. She was lost in the delicate beauty of the piece—the silk stitching that resembled cherry blossoms in full bloom. The design entranced her, a kind of strange, hypnotic beauty that she couldn't tear her eyes from.

She dressed quickly, the fabric falling flawlessly over her aging body, molding to her curves like a second skin. The weight of it felt luxurious, almost decadent. For the first time in decades, she felt—sexy.

She stood in front of the body-length mirror on the far side of the bedroom, watching herself. The nightdress fit her perfectly, clinging to her in all the right places. She traced the edges of the dress over her chest, watching herself closely, her breath coming in shallow pulls.

But then, as she inched closer to the mirror, something shifted again.

A high-pitched sound—sharp, jarring—began to reverberate in the air, cutting through her thoughts like a blade. It was the same tune Dr. Lancet had whistled while pushing Michael down the Light Mile. It felt wrong. It felt like an intrusion.

She covered her ears, trying to block it out, but the sound only intensified, growing louder and more insistent.

"WHAT DO YOU WANT?" Dr. Lancet screamed at the mirror, her voice cracking. The mirror splintered once again.

"I… Don't… Want you… Fucking up… MY ORGANS!" Michael's voice came again, louder and clearer, as his smile grew unnaturally wide. "Do we have to do this the hard way?"

Dr. Lancet's heart pounded in her chest as the mirror shattered, the glass splintering across the floor. His hand protruded through the jagged edges, blood pouring down the mirror and spilling over the floor.

She stepped closer, drawn to him, despite the fear that clawed at her throat.

What am I doing? she thought, her breath shallow.

Her fingertips brushed Michael's hand. She felt a strange heat—a pull toward him, an odd mix of terror and desire.

For a moment, she felt like she was drowning in it. The image of Michael, his wicked smile, the haunting echo of the whistling tune. She couldn't look away.

∞

Dr. Lancet ran, her breath ragged, the sound of Crimson Enforcers pounding behind her. She weaved in and out of the chaos—the bombs falling from the sky like deadly confetti, each explosion shaking the ground beneath her.

"You're almost there," she muttered to herself, though the words felt distant, like a mantra.

But the armored car ahead, the thing that promised escape, grew smaller and smaller, slipping away from her grasp as though mocking her. She tried to scream, but the sound never left her throat. Her legs burned with fatigue, muscles trembling with the effort to keep moving, to keep running toward safety.

But her body betrayed her. She stumbled, falling forward onto the ground, scraping her palms against the pavement. The pain felt distant, like she was watching it happen to someone else.

And then they were there. The Crimson Enforcers surrounded her, their armored bodies closing in like a cage.

"TRAITOR!" they shouted, their voices a guttural chant that drilled into her mind. "TRAITOR!"

Dr. Lancet covered her face, curling into herself, trying to block them out. But their voices—their rage—was too loud, too suffocating.

She rolled onto her back, and she was suddenly on a medical table, strapped down, the sterile smell of the room mixing with the metallic scent of blood. Michael's face appeared above her, his grin as cold as ice, his hands steady as he pushed her down the Light Mile.

No, this isn't real, she thought, trying to shake herself free from the haze. I'm awake. This is a hallucination. This isn't me.

But it didn't stop. His whistle filled the air—the same tune she had whistled the day she harvested his organs, the very sound that had haunted her since.

She struggled, trying to move, but her body wouldn't respond. She was trapped in the memory—his memory—of him pushing her into the surgery room.

The pressure of the wheels beneath her, the coldness of the metal surrounding her, it all felt too real.

She kicked against the restraints with all her strength. Her leg broke free—then her arm. But before she could push herself up, the Argentine Enforcers appeared from nowhere, their hands like iron as they forced her back down.

This can't be happening.

Michael loomed above her, a twisted smile spreading across his face, a needle in his hand, large and terrifying.

"I'm going to enjoy this," he purred, his voice low and dark, filled with sick anticipation.

Dr. Lancet's breath quickened. Her chest tightened in fear, but the restraints made it impossible to move. She could only watch as Michael leaned down, the needle plunging into her skin.

The moment the needle pierced her skin, a wave of numbness washed over her, and her body went slack. She was sinking, drowning in the feeling, her pulse thumping in her ears.

Michael's face hovered above hers, his grin widening again as he pulled the scalpel from his side. The cold gleam of the blade burned into her vision.

He pressed it to her chest, the metal cutting into her skin, slicing with precision she couldn't escape. The pain was blinding, overwhelming—like a wave crashing over her—but it was muted, distant, just as it had been when she cut into Michael. Her own scream had been swallowed, locked in her chest, but she felt the echoes of it. The agony. The violation.

Blood—black and thick—began to ooze from the wound, and she could feel it, hear it, the rush of it dripping, soaking into her body, coating her like it had done to him.

And then, as she lay there, the tune continued, looping in her mind, until it was all she could hear. Michael's voice, his smile, and the sickeningly sweet melody all twisted together, drowning her in the horror of the memory she couldn't escape.

But there was something else—a flicker. Just a moment. Her body tensed, almost welcoming the pain. Could it be? she thought. Could she... enjoy it again? A tiny voice from somewhere deep inside whispered her old self, the one that didn't care, the one that felt something different when she was with Wyatt.

She remembered the heat, the satisfaction, that rush of pleasure brought by the pain. The way it had felt when he touched her, when he'd taken control.

The darkness she'd buried so deeply in herself for so long began to stir. For a moment, it felt almost intoxicating—the control, the power over someone else's body, someone else's suffering. But there was also guilt. That gnawing feeling of something wrong mixing with the pleasure.

Michael's smile flashed in her mind, his mocking expression—as if he could sense that tiny pleasure stirring within her. He had been the one to suffer under her hands, and now she was feeling what he'd felt.

She closed her eyes, trying to push it away, but the image of Michael lingered, like a shadow she couldn't outrun. The way he looked at her, the way he had suffered, and the way she had relished it—the painful realization hit her harder than any needle or scalpel ever could.

∞

"EVELYN!"

The Warden's voice snapped her from the trance.

She blinked. Her hands were slick with blood.

At her feet, a jagged shard of mirror glinted red under the low light.

"What have you done?" His voice trembled—not with fear, but something closer to disbelief.

She looked down again, only just noticing the pain. The sting. The mess. Both palms were slashed clean open, red blooming across the floor beneath her.

"I... it slipped," she muttered.

Don't tell him about Michael. He'll think I've gone mad. Have I?... Gone mad?

Her gaze flicked to the mirror once more.

Michael stood there, his wicked grin unchanged. He raised the shard in his hand like a toast—and then pressed his index finger to his lips.

"Shush," he whispered.

Then he dropped the shard and vanished into her reflection.

The Warden lunged forward, tearing his shirt off and wrapping it tightly around her hands.

"Evelyn, for Zoti's sake, you need to be more careful. You *need* your hands. They're your most valuable tool." He tightened the knot. "Let's get you to Dr. Zygote."

"No," she said sharply, pulling away. "He doesn't need to know about this."

The Warden's face darkened. "You can't treat wounds like these yourself. Especially not when you're like this."

"I'm fine."

"You're *not* fine." His voice rose. "Stop being so bloody stubborn and come with me. *Now.*"

"Wyatt..." Her voice dropped to a whisper. "Zayne can't see me. Not like this."

He hesitated. His eyes traced the blood on her hands... then her nightdress. The silk. The red lace beneath her robe.

A pause.

"I suppose you're right," he muttered. "I'll get Shabina."

She wanted to protest again—*I don't want her to see either*—but she bit it back.

She's better than Zayne, she reasoned. *Easier to manipulate.*

She nodded wordlessly as The Warden grabbed a fresh shirt and stormed from the room.

Dr. Lancet sat still, the warmth of the blood on her palms cooling too quickly. She could feel her pulse there now—sluggish and traitorous.

The Warden's shirt was wrapped tightly around both hands, but it wasn't enough. Not to stop the pain. Not to quiet her thoughts.

You're losing control, Evelyn.

She stared down at the shard on the floor. It glinted faintly, catching just enough light to remind her of Michael's grin.

That damn smile. That mocking hush.

You used to be composed. Measured. Feared. Now look at you—slicing your own hands open like some trembling initiate in The Cell.

She exhaled through her teeth, nostrils flaring.

It had started with the hallucinations. First in sleep. Then in mirrors. Then... all the time. Michael's voice echoing behind her thoughts, smooth and slow like a scalpel across skin.

He haunted her. Not just the memory of him—the way he'd looked at her before the cut, the way his organs had responded to her touch—but the sense that part of him had never truly left her table. That some flicker of him had slipped into her, through her, during the transplant. A phantom cell that whispered.

She thought about the bed. The mirrored ceiling. The reflection of Michael, always watching from behind her own eyes. That same grin, that same "Shush."

He sees everything now. Because I let him in.

She closed her eyes.

Zygote would call it stress-induced psychosis.

The Warden would call it weakness.

But Michael—Michael would call it home.

A shiver crawled up her spine.

Play it smart. Play it small. Let them think you're still in control.

The doorknob turned.

Shabina entered first—stiff-spined, composed, but visibly unsure. Her eyes flicked across the office, landing briefly on the blood-soaked shirt wrapped around Dr. Lancet's hands. The Warden followed behind her, now dressed in a clean shirt.

No one spoke.

Dr. Lancet sat in one of the high-backed chairs in The Warden's office, her fingers twitching beneath the cloth. The air felt close, and thick—like it hadn't been moved in hours.

Shabina hesitated at the threshold. She clutched her kit tightly, then stepped forward with hesitant grace. Her gaze lingered on Dr. Lancet's wounds, but she kept her expression unreadable.

The Warden shifted, giving her a nod. That was all the instruction she needed.

Shabina crossed the room and knelt by Dr. Lancet's side, laying out her kit. Her hands trembled faintly as she peeled back the bloody fabric—but she forced them still, swallowing her nerves.

Then, gently, she began to dab the blood from Dr. Lancet's palms.

"I'm not hurting you, am I?" she asked, voice soft and almost rehearsed.

Dr. Lancet didn't answer—just a grunt, low and distracted, her eyes fixed on the floor.

"Evelyn," The Warden growled. "Shabina is helping you…"

Dr. Lancet's eyes flicked upward—toward the mirror above the bookshelf.

And there he was.

Michael.

Smiling.

That grin. That whisper behind her teeth.

"No, you're not hurting me," she said flatly. "I'm fine. Thank you."

Shabina exhaled subtly. A twitch of a smirk tugged at the corner of her mouth—more habit than confidence—and she continued her work in silence.

When she finished, she stood and packed the kit. "It may take some time to heal," she said. "I'm not sure if you'll be all right for the next moon's harvest."

Dr. Lancet's head snapped up. "You underestimate me, my dear," she hissed. "Don't think you'll get my job so easily. I was here long before you… and I'll be here long after you're gone. You're nothing but a… but a…"

She trailed off. The words were there. But they refused to come.

Shabina's smirk widened, though her voice remained polite. "Get some rest, Evelyn," she said. "You look like you need it."

She turned and exited the office without another word.

The Warden moved to his desk, his expression unreadable. His hand slipped beneath the edge—fingers brushing against something unseen.

Click.

The sound was subtle but final. Behind them, the hidden panel slid open, revealing the warm, low-lit space beyond.

"Shall we?" he asked, his voice smooth. Too smooth. Expectant.

Dr. Lancet didn't move.

She stared at the opening, into the dim room where the light seemed to bleed rather than shine. The air from within was warmer—cloying, scented faintly with something sweet and synthetic. It clung to her skin like a promise.

Her hands ached. Her mind throbbed.

"Evelyn," he said again, gentler this time. Almost coaxing. "It's late. Come inside."

She hesitated for a breath. Then another.

And then she stepped.

The sound of her bare feet brushing the floor seemed louder than it should have. She crossed the threshold slowly, like she was entering a place she no longer recognized—even though she had been here before. Even though she still hadn't left.

The light inside was low, golden, flickering from the sconces along the curved walls. The bed sat in the center, too large, too soft, covered in sheets that looked untouched but weren't. And on the nightstand, beside the folded edge of the blanket, sat the control switch.

Her breath hitched.

"See?" The Warden said from behind her, voice low and calm. "It's still there."

No… it wasn't there before… was it?

She stared at it, the way it rested so casually in plain view. As if it had always been there. As if *she* had simply missed it.

The thought pulsed once—then fell away.

Replaced with: *Maybe he'll fuck me again. Hurt me just the way I like it…*

She nodded. Eyes glinting.

She nodded.

The Warden stepped past her and sank onto the bed, patting the mattress softly beside him.

"Come here," he said.

She sat, her hands stiff in her lap.

He turned to her, took one hand gently in his own. "Show me," he said.

"I should keep them wrapped tonight," she murmured.

He raised a brow. "You don't want any of this?" His hand slipped into his pocket, retrieving a small silver tube.

She reached for it instinctively.

He pulled it back.

"Let me."

He began to unwrap her bandages, careful and precise. The cloth peeled away, and with it, the dried remnants of blood. Her skin was raw, inflamed—but the stitches held.

"She did a good job," he said. His tone had shifted—lower, thicker—as he squeezed a generous line of gel onto his fingers.

Then he touched her.

She moaned softly. The sting that had anchored her all evening melted beneath the cooling balm.

The Warden smirked. "Does that feel good?"

She nodded, breath shallow. Another soft sound escaped her lips.

He lowered her hands and massaged the gel deeper into her skin, slow and deliberate.

"Lay back," he said.

Her eyes fluttered closed. She obeyed.

He pulled out the gel again. "A bit more won't hurt."

The second application was slower. Lingering. Intentional.

Then, as he smoothed the gel into her palms, she heard the sound—quiet, familiar.

The click of a zipper.

Her eyes snapped open.

The Warden was leaning over her, his face unreadable, breath hitching slightly as he guided her hands downward.

"The stitches don't hurt anymore?"

"No," she breathed. "They don't."

He smiled. Wide. Controlled.

"Good."

Then he moaned, low and deep, as he wrapped her hands around his thick, throbbing cock..

He began to move her hands, slow at first, guiding her through the motion with practiced confidence. His breathing deepened, every sound purposeful. With each stroke, he pushed her palms tighter around him, pressing into the sting of her stitches.

She winced—but she didn't pull away.

The pain was sharp. Raw. Alive.

Her breath hitched. Her thighs clenched.

"You like that, don't you," he murmured. "The sting. The way it burns."

She didn't answer. She didn't have to.

He adjusted her grip, not too tight—never tight enough to tear. "Easy," he warned, almost sweet. "You tear open, you're no good to me."

Her fingers trembled, then tightened again.

She was soaking wet now, her body practically pulsing with tension.

"You're dripping, aren't you?" he whispered. "Pain and pleasure. My perfect little contradiction."

She shuddered.

He used her slowly, rhythmically, pumping into her palms without pushing her too far. She felt everything—the stretch, the heat, the ache. It was disgusting. It was exquisite.

And he *knew* it.

He grunted again, closer now, holding her wrists steady.

"You're so fucking useful like this," he growled. "So perfect when you don't break."

Then he came.

With a guttural groan, he spilled into her slick palms, jerking forward one last time before slumping against her, chest heaving.

He slumped against her, exhaling hard.

"Still in one piece," he murmured against her ear. "Good, good girl."

Evelyn didn't speak.

She just went to the bathroom, and cleaned her hands.

∞

Dr. Zygote

"Never you mind, Jessica. Just do your job," Dr. Zygote snapped as he slipped the emptied specimen jars into the pocket of his coat and stepped out from the back room of The Cell.

Jessica lowered her head immediately. "Yes, doctor. Sorry, doctor." She turned and hurried back through the archway, fumbling the sponges and linens cradled in her arms.

The door clicked shut behind her.

Dr. Zygote stood still for a moment. Then he exhaled—slow and quiet—and whispered, "It's going to work this time."

He adjusted his glasses, the gesture slow and precise.

"I corrected the instability in the last compound… This batch will hold. I know it." He paced the floor, muttering low. "They'll be stronger. Cleaner. The next stage in human evolution."

His voice dropped.

"Cypher will beg for them. The world will kneel."

He reached down, retrieved a cardboard box of files at his feet, and cradled it like something sacred.

"And Evelyn… Wyatt…" He smiled to himself. "They'll regret what they did. They'll beg me to take them with me, when the old world starts to rot."

He let out a dry, amused sound. Not quite a laugh. Not quite sane.

"And the twins…" he whispered. "The twins will be the final piece."

He carried the box into the surgery and set it carefully on his worktable. On top sat a single file. He opened it.

"I remember you," he murmured to the page. "You were so small. So weak. I didn't think you'd make it."

He thumbed through the notes, then paused at the name on the first page. He scoffed.

"This name doesn't suit you at all. They should've kept the one I gave you. The name of your mother. *Maya.*"

He slipped a photograph from the folder. Studied it.

"Our daughter," he whispered. "She looks just like you."

The voice came from behind him.

"Who are you talking to?"

He turned.

Shabina stood in the doorway.

"Shabina," he said smoothly, tucking the photograph back into the folder. "No one. I talk to myself, now and then. The only intelligent conversation I get these days."

He waved her in.

"Close the door."

She stepped inside, turned, and locked it without being asked.

"How is it going?" he asked.

"Good," she said. "They don't suspect anything."

They shared a glance. A quiet smile.

"Do you have anything for me?"

She stepped forward and relayed what she'd seen—Dr. Lancet's wounded hands, her silence, her distant eyes.

Zygote listened without interrupting. When she finished, he chuckled under his breath.

"She's unraveling. Finally. Maybe we won't have to remove her after all. She might handle it for us."

"There's something else," Shabina said. "She was wearing a nightdress. Silk. Red lace."

That caught him.

He blinked once. Then again.

"Where?"

"In his office," she said. "I didn't see them leave. I went back later and… they were gone. Like the room swallowed them."

Dr. Zygote said nothing for a long moment.

Then: "You've done well, Shabina."

Her eyes dropped. "Would Mother be proud?"

He stepped toward her and rested a hand lightly on her shoulder.

"I imagine she would."

She nodded.

"And you?"

"I'm proud of all my children," he said.

He returned to the worktable and withdrew the photo he'd hidden moments earlier. He held it out to her.

"I have something for you."

She took the photograph carefully. Looked down at the image.

"Why are you giving me this?"

He smiled.

"Because that's your sister," he said. "That's Maya. She's finally home."

Shabina stared at the picture.

"Can I see her?"

"Not yet," he said. "She's still… fragile."

Shabina nodded, but her voice softened again.

"What about Mother? Can I see her?"

Zygote's smile thinned.

"You know the answer to that."

"I know. I just thought—"

"You *can't* get sentimental in here," he cut in. "If anyone finds out who you are—who we are—we don't survive it. Understood?"

She nodded again. "Sorry. I understand."

"Good." He stepped back. "Now go find them. Lancet. The Warden. They've gone somewhere. Somewhere they don't want us seeing."

He adjusted his glasses again.

"And I want to know *why*."

∞

Dr. Lancet

Dr. Lancet woke to the pale crawl of sunlight slipping through the narrow window above the bed.

The light cast a faint glow across the sheets. Dust floated in the air like ash. The silence pressed in, heavy and still.

She turned her head to the nightstand.

Only the lamp remained.

She exhaled softly.

Her gaze drifted upward.

To the mirror.

She froze.

She wasn't there.

Michael was.

Laid out beneath the sheets, staring back at her from the glass above with that same wicked grin. The one that used to make her skin crawl. Now it looked… familiar.

Too familiar.

He tilted his head, just slightly.

She didn't.

But the image moved anyway—perfectly in sync, as if it *were* her. As if she no longer existed.

The grin stretched wider.

She sat up.

And in the mirror, Michael fell.

Straight down—like he'd been lying on the ceiling all along. He struck the glass with a sickening, silent force. The mirror fractured beneath him, a spiderweb of cracks blooming outward. Blood seeped from his chest and spread across the broken surface in slow, deliberate threads.

He kept smiling.

The red reached the edges.

The cracks deepened.

He stared straight into her.

Unblinking.

"EVELYN!"

The Warden's voice sliced through the room.

She flinched, breath catching in her throat.

He was at the foot of the bed now, eyes blazing.

"WHAT'S WRONG WITH YOU?"

She blinked.

Her hands.

One held a glass of scotch.

The other, clutched tightly: the full contents of a pill bottle.

Her voice stumbled out before he could speak again.

"I was tired. I must've tipped the bottle too far—"

The Warden's eyes shifted, slow and deliberate.

Toward the bar.

The bottle still sat there.

Empty.

He turned back to her, eyes colder now.

Harder.

"Do you think you can lie to me, Evelyn?"

His voice was calm. Measured.

But it landed like a threat.

Do as he says, you have to do as he says until you're sure you place in the Harvest is safe.

Her lips parted. "No," she whispered. "No, Wyatt… I don't."

The pills spilled from her palm, rolling across the blanket in dull silence.

He stepped forward.

Picked them up slowly, methodically, slipping them back into their container without a word.

Click.

He snapped the lid shut.

"What am I going to do with you?"

He set the bottle back on the bar.

Then crossed to the nightstand.

The control was there again. Neat. Waiting.

He picked it up. Weighed it in his palm.

"I gave you sanctuary," he said. "A private escape. A place no one else gets."

He turned to her.

"And this is what I get in return?"

Her chest tightened.

She didn't speak.

He stepped closer. Quiet. Steady.

Then he placed the control back on the nightstand beside her.

"I'm going to have to wash those lies out of your mouth," he said softly.

His hand closed around her jaw—slow but firm.

She inhaled sharply.

Then came the rasp of a zipper.

She didn't look at him.

She looked up—past him—into the mirror above.

Where Michael still smiled.

And she was nowhere to be seen.

His fingers tightened around her jaw, forcing her chin upward.

She didn't resist.

Couldn't.

Not now.

Not with the mirror still bleeding above her. Not with Michael watching.

"Open your mouth," The Warden ordered, his voice flat. Measured. Like a doctor checking vitals.

Dr. Lancet hesitated. Just for a moment.

But he didn't wait.

His grip shifted, forcing her lips apart as he stepped forward and unzipped his jeans.

His cock was already hard. Slick. Waiting.

And then—he thrust into her mouth.

Her breath choked in her throat.

The Warden's hand moved to the back of her head, fisting her hair as he began to use her. Not gently. Not slowly. Just enough control to keep her breathing. Just enough rhythm to keep her from passing out.

She grunted, the burn in her throat mixing with the pulse between her legs. The pain was dizzying. Her eyes watered, but she didn't close them.

She couldn't.

Because in the mirror above the bed, Michael smiled wider.

She could see herself now. Just barely.

But only in fragments—shattered pieces of glass, reflecting lips stretched wide, mascara running, her throat bulging with every thrust.

She moaned around him, and The Warden groaned low in his chest.

"Good girl," he murmured, driving deeper, watching her eyes roll back. "You like this, don't you?"

Yes, she thought. But she couldn't answer.

Didn't need to.

He slammed into her again—hard enough to make her gag. Her body jerked, but his grip held firm. Twisting in her hair.

Another thrust.

Another.

He was panting now, nearly shaking. His rhythm broke, then surged forward again—brutal, breathless, possessive.

Spit ran down her chin.

Her thighs clenched, heartbeat frantic.

She could taste him.

Salt. Heat. Control.

He hissed through his teeth as his body stiffened.

Then with a deep, guttural moan, he came—forcing himself as far into her mouth as her body would allow, shuddering as he released down her throat.

Dr. Lancet didn't move.

Didn't breathe.

Not until he pulled out with a final, wet sound, panting.

She coughed once, softly. Wiped her mouth with the back of her wrist. Her eyes didn't leave the mirror.

The reflection was still fractured.

But Michael's grin was whole.

The Warden tucked himself back into his jeans, breathing heavy.

He reached for her chin again, tilting her face to meet his.

"Still in one piece," he whispered.

And Dr. Lancet smiled.

Just a little.

∞

Valentino

The night wind cut through the forest like a warning. Cold. Sharp. It howled above the canopy, dragging the rain sideways.

Each drop hit like a needle.

Valentino kept moving, jacket pulled tight over his head, the fabric already soaked through. His boots sank into wet moss with every step. The branches clawed at his arms.

I hope she's okay.

Pandora's hair—dark, tangled, falling—flashed in his mind.

I hope she found shelter.

A flash of lightning split the sky. Thunder rolled after it, low and long, echoing through the trees like a distant roar.

Then another strike—closer this time.

I need to find shelter.

He pressed forward, deeper into the overgrown terrain, pushing aside vines and brush. The rain grew heavier. The howling wind grew louder, swirling around him like voices he couldn't understand.

Then he saw it.

A clearing up ahead.

Faint, flickering light danced between the trees.

He froze.

A fire?

A lantern?

Someone's out there.

His fingers slipped into his pocket and curled tightly around the hilt of the small blade he kept hidden there.

Be ready.

He moved forward—slow, deliberate. Each step muffled by the storm, his breath drowned by the thunder. The flickering light grew larger with each pace. Warmer. Closer.

He didn't see the moss-covered boulder until it was too late.

His foot slid.

He tried to catch himself—one hand shooting toward a low-hanging branch—but it snapped beneath his grip.

He hit the tree.

Hard.

Pain sparked across his skull. The world tilted.

His vision tunneled. The flickering light blurred. Everything tilted sideways.

And then—movement.

A shadow stepped into view, distorted by the rain.

He blinked, trying to focus.

The figure came closer.

Then the darkness swallowed him whole.

∞

When Valentino woke, the storm was still raging outside.

Wind howled through the trees. Rain lashed the mountains. Thunder rolled overhead like distant drums.

He was lying on damp stone.

A cave.

Narrow, cold, and dimly lit. Shadows danced across the walls, cast by a flickering light near the entrance.

His belongings were stacked neatly beside him.

His jacket. His bag. Even his boots.

He blinked, trying to remember.

What happened?

His head throbbed. He pushed himself upright, but the world tilted. A wave of dizziness hit him hard, and he staggered back, steadying himself against the rough wall.

Why didn't they tie me up?

Why didn't they kill me?

He moved slowly toward the mouth of the cave, careful not to make a sound. The wind outside was wild, the trees thrashing like they were alive. Flashes of lightning lit up the sky in bursts.

For a moment, he saw nothing.

Then—movement.

A figure stepped out from the tree line, just beyond the clearing.

Valentino's breath caught.

He stepped back into the cave, hand instinctively reaching for the blade in his pocket.

Gone.

His heart spiked.

He turned to lunge for his things—slipped on the mossy floor—and fell hard.

His head struck the stone wall.

The world flickered.

Faded.

And the dark took him once again.

∞

"Don't freak out this time… okay?" a voice squeaked as Valentino stirred.

His eyes fluttered open.

"Pandora?"

She was crouched near the cave entrance, holding a small wooden bowl out into the rain. Light from the fire behind her shimmered against the downpour.

"What… how are you up here now? Why?"

She giggled softly. "I came to watch the storm," she said sweetly. "It's so… magical."

Lightning flashed in the distance. Her smile didn't waver.

Valentino sat up, groaning. The room spun around him.

"Careful," Pandora said, suddenly beside him. "You hit your head pretty hard… *twice*."

She knelt beside him, tore a strip from the bottom of her skirt, soaked it in the rainwater, and gently dabbed the side of his face.

"You're lucky it's not worse," she murmured.

Valentino looked up at her, his eyes lingering on her hair.

"How are you?"

His fingers moved instinctively to the side of her head—where Marcus had dragged her.

Her long black curls were broken, uneven, pulled out at the root. He ran his hand through the tangled strands, and Pandora winced. A tear slid down her cheek.

He wiped it away with his thumb.

"Hey now," he said gently. "Don't cry… I think I can help."

Valentino stood slowly. Waited for the world to steady.

Then he crossed to his bag and rummaged through it.

When he returned, he held up a pair of scissors.

"I do my father's hair all the time," he said with a faint smile. "Come. Sit down."

Pandora sat on the log near the fire, eyes on the storm.

Tears still fell.

Valentino moved behind her, brushing her hair gently with his fingers before trimming the mess Marcus had left behind. The fire crackled beside them. Thunder rolled overhead.

Pandora's sobs were quiet beneath the sound of the storm.

But Valentino felt every single one.

And he cried silently with her.

When he finished, he ran his thumb under his eyes and exhaled slowly.

"There. You look just as beautiful as before."

Pandora turned red.

"Sorry," he blurted, dropping his gaze. "I… uh—"

"Thank you," she said softly, and kissed his cheek.

Valentino stilled.

Then smiled.

He ran his fingers along the undercut he'd shaped, then through the soft curls on the other side.

"You are… you know… beautiful," he said, voice barely above a whisper as he leaned in closer.

Pandora looked up at him—and another tear slipped free.

Valentino pulled back slightly. "Oh no… do you not like it?"

Pandora sniffled, then giggled. "That's not it."

She dropped her head.

"I was just remembering what you said to me earlier… about not being good."

Her voice softened.

"Well… Marcus is supposed to be one of the good guys. And I think you're better than him."

She looked up again, eyes shining.

"Why don't you stay?"

Valentino lowered his arms and sank back down beside the fire.

"I can't," he said quietly. "My father…"

Pandora didn't hesitate. "You can bring him too."

Valentino shook his head, eyes fixed on the flames. "No… I can't. He won't leave the house." He rubbed the back of his neck. "He's not… well."

Pandora placed her hand gently on his back.

"I'm sorry," she whispered. "I shouldn't have said anything."

He sat up straighter.

"Don't apologize," he breathed. "You didn't do anything wrong. It's just… we'd only bring destruction to you and your friends."

"I only have two friends here," Pandora said softly. "It would've been nice to have a third."

Her voice cracked, just a little.

Valentino reached for her hand and held it.

"I don't think I could," he said, voice barely audible. "Even if I stayed."

"Could what?" she asked.

He looked at her, eyes dark with something heavier than fear.

"I don't think I could be your friend."

Pandora's breath caught. Her eyes dropped.

But he wasn't done.

"Because I'd want to be so much more."

He lifted her chin gently.

And kissed her.

Soft. Careful. Certain.

Her breath trembled against his lips—but she didn't pull away.

When she leaned into him, he wrapped his arms around her like something sacred. The kiss deepened slowly—no urgency, no rush. Just the quiet rhythm of two people afraid to move too fast, but needing the closeness more than either of them could admit.

Valentino's hands slid to her shoulders, his fingers brushing her collarbone, her neck. He traced the curve of her spine, the swell of her hips, memorizing her shape like it was something he was never meant to touch.

"You're beautiful," he whispered, not as a compliment—but as a confession.

He slid the straps of her dress from her shoulders, and she let it fall, her breath shivering in the cold air.

But Valentino didn't rush.

He touched her like he was afraid she'd vanish—like every inch of her skin was sacred.

He kissed the bruises Marcus left behind. The curve of her neck. The hollow of her shoulder. The newly cut section of her hair.

She reached for his shirt, and he let her pull it over his head. Her fingers trembled against his chest, her eyes flickering with something that wasn't fear—but wasn't certainty either.

"Are you sure?" he asked, voice a breath against her cheek.

She nodded, slow. Soft.

"Yes."

He lowered her to the mossy floor beside the fire, his body hovering over hers, hands braced on either side of her.

She reached for him again—this time with no hesitation—and he kissed her as if she were the only thing left in the world that made sense.

Their bodies pressed together, skin against skin, slow and warm. He was gentle at first—almost too gentle—like he wasn't sure she'd let him stay. But when Pandora arched into him, her hands sliding down his back, Valentino's restraint gave way to something deeper.

He kissed her again. Slower now. Lips trailing from her mouth to her jaw to the base of her throat.

She shivered beneath him, not from cold—but from the weight of being seen. Touched. Wanted.

Valentino moved down her body, pausing to worship each inch of her. His lips grazed the swell of her chest. The curve of her ribs. Her stomach, soft and trembling beneath him.

Pandora gasped when he kissed the inside of her thigh—lightly, reverently—before looking up at her, waiting.

She nodded, her breath shallow. Trusting him.

He guided her knees apart, and when he lowered his mouth to her, it was with the kind of hunger reserved for miracles. He kissed her there like it was sacred. Like he could learn her with his tongue alone. Pandora's hands curled in his hair, her head tilting back as a sound escaped her lips—quiet, broken, desperate.

Valentino didn't stop.

He took his time, letting her fall apart on his tongue, one slow circle after another, until she was arching off the floor and whispering his name like a prayer.

Only then did he crawl back up her body, kissing her collarbone, her neck, her cheek—pressing his forehead to hers as she came down.

"Okay?" he whispered.

She nodded, lips trembling. "Yes."

He reached between them and guided himself to her entrance, pausing once more.

Pandora slid her arms around his neck and pulled him in.

The first push was slow. Careful.

Her body tensed around him—tight, slick, welcoming. Valentino groaned against her throat as he sank into her, one inch at a time, every movement measured.

She clung to him, her breath shallow, her hands gripping his shoulders like she didn't want to let go.

Valentino moved slowly, rocking into her with aching tenderness. Every thrust was deliberate. Intimate. A rhythm born of caution and care—and then, as her body adjusted around him, of need.

Their hips moved together. Skin sliding against skin. Mouths finding each other between gasps.

Pandora whispered his name again, and Valentino buried his face in her neck.

"You're perfect," he breathed.

She shook beneath him.

He didn't stop.

He held her close, his hands firm on her waist, as he moved inside her—worshipping every moan, every shudder, every broken sound she gave him.

They built slowly. Together.

And when she came—shaking, silent, eyes wide—Valentino followed her over the edge, muffling his groan in her hair as he spilled into her, pulse after pulse of something deeper than pleasure.

Afterward, they lay tangled in silence, the storm still raging just beyond the cave walls.

Valentino ran his hand down the curve of her back, kissing her temple.

Pandora pressed her face into his chest, her breath slowing.

He didn't speak.

He just held her.

And for the first time in years, he didn't feel ashamed of needing someone.

∞

Valentino held Pandora in his arms as she slept.

Her breath warmed the space beneath his chin. One hand rested lightly on his chest, her fingers curled in the fabric of his shirt like she was holding on without knowing it.

He didn't move.

He didn't want to.

The fire crackled low, and rain whispered beyond the cave. Her curls had fallen across her face again. Gently, carefully, Valentino brushed them away with the back of his hand.

Then lightning split the sky—white and sudden.

And in the flash of light, he saw a figure standing at the edge of the forest.

Still.

Watching.

Valentino's blood turned cold.

He eased Pandora off of him with painstaking care, trying not to disturb her. She shifted, murmured something in her sleep, but didn't wake. He pulled the blanket from where it had fallen behind the log and draped it over her shoulders.

He took one last look at her—peaceful, safe.

Then he stepped into the rain.

The figure hadn't moved.

"Father," Valentino said as he approached. His voice was steady, but his chest burned. "I thought you went home."

The Architect turned. Emerald armor glinted in the stormlight, rain streaking down the curves of the helmet. The rifle across his back gleamed under the flash of another lightning strike.

He didn't speak right away.

Then, slowly, he pulled the rifle into his hands and raised it—pointing it toward the mouth of the cave.

Toward her.

"What's going on here?"

Valentino stepped into the line of fire.

His pulse was a hammer behind his ribs.

"Nothing," he said. "She's just some fun for the night."

The words tasted like rust in his mouth.

"She means nothing."

The Architect didn't lower the rifle.

Valentino kept going. "She won't remember my name by morning. I barely remember hers."

His chest ached.

But his voice didn't shake.

The Architect's visor shifted slightly, scanning the cave entrance behind him. Then back to his son.

"That's all she'd better be," he said at last. "I don't want a repeat of the last one."

Valentino's gaze dropped to the mud between them.

"No, Father," he said. "Neither do I."

The Architect slung the rifle over his shoulder again and gestured with a sharp tilt of his head.

"Get your things. We leave now."

Then a pause.

"Don't wake her."

Valentino turned toward the cave, the glow of the fire, the silhouette of her curled beneath the blanket.

"If she means nothing," The Architect added, "she'll be easy to leave behind."

Valentino stood there a moment longer.

Then nodded, once.

This is to keep her safe.

He stepped back inside the cave, barely breathing. The fire had burned low, casting golden light across her sleeping form. The curve of her shoulder. Her steady breath.

He didn't say goodbye.

Didn't brush her hair back again.

He just picked up his bag.

And left.

The storm swallowed the sound of his footsteps.

A few breaths later, the fire crackled.

Pandora stirred.

Her eyes opened.

She looked around—then down at the empty space beside her.

And she knew.

Tears spilled silently down her cheeks as she sat up, pulling the blanket tighter around herself.

She had heard everything.

∞

They had walked in silence for nearly an hour, the only sounds the squelch of boots in the mud and the fading rumble of the storm behind them.

Valentino hadn't spoken—not since the cave.

But the weight in his chest hadn't eased.

Finally, he broke the silence. "What's going on, Father?"

The Architect didn't stop walking.

"I need you to get a message to someone," he said. His voice was low, taut with strain. "Someone in Augmentation Bay."

Valentino blinked.

The Architect never sounded like this.

Not rattled. Not uncertain.

Something's wrong.

"Alright," he said carefully. "Who's the message for?"

The Architect scanned the trees around them, as if they were being watched. Then he leaned in close and whispered into Valentino's ear.

Valentino froze.

"What?"

The Architect's expression didn't change. "You heard me."

Valentino exhaled, slow and tight. "You're serious."

The Architect nodded.

"This message goes to Mr. Matthews. If he understands it, if he wants more... he'll come for me. He'll bring Mr. Masters. And when that happens—" he looked directly at Valentino, "you help them escape."

Valentino hesitated.

Then nodded once.

"I'll bring in Fred and Vince."

The Architect didn't blink. "Can you trust them?"

"They've done worse for less."

The Architect gave a single, clipped nod. "Good. Get it done."

He handed Valentino a new backpack—canvas, worn, heavy with supplies.

"This should last you long enough. There's a clean entrance through the base of the shaft. You'll know it when you see it."

They reached the tree line.

A horse stood tethered in the clearing beyond—calm, quiet, waiting.

The Architect's voice dropped as he checked the straps on Valentino's gear. "This is delicate. You cannot fail."

Valentino mounted the horse and tightened his grip on the reins.

"I won't."

He looked once over his shoulder—back toward the mountains.

Toward the cave.

Then turned away.

"Fred and Vince are loyal to you," he said. "You can trust them. You can trust me."

Lightning cracked overhead as he rode off into the trees.

CHAPTER SIX

The Shepherd

∞

Lincoln

When Lincoln woke, he was back in the infirmary.

Again.

The lights were too bright. The air smelled like disinfectant and something burnt. He blinked, trying to clear the haze from his vision, and rubbed at his eyes—

Only to grunt in pain as his fingers hit the bandage over his left one.

"Don't touch it, sweetie."

Jessica's voice drifted over from a bench at the far wall. She was seated, paperwork scattered across her lap.

"It's going to hurt. Those stitches were hard to do, and they won't let me put you under again."

She stood and walked over, holding out a cup of water and a small white pill.

"Here. This will help."

Lincoln took them without question, swallowing the pill dry. "Where's the other nurse that used to work here?"

Jessica paused.

"Oh, sweetie… she passed away. I'm sorry."

"Fuck." The word punched out of him before he could stop it.

Jessica tilted her head. "You cared about her?"

Lincoln shifted uncomfortably. "Uh… yeah. She reminded me of my nan. Gave me extra painkillers when I was hurt."

He blinked hard. "My head's still pounding… and now my eye's fucked too."

He looked up at her, and something flickered in his face—desperation he didn't know how to hide.

Jessica's gaze softened, but she turned back to the bench.

"I'm sorry, sweetie. I'm not allowed to do that," she said as she opened a cupboard to her left, rifling through the shelves. "And you really shouldn't be asking."

"I'm sorry, Miss," Lincoln muttered.

She returned to his side.

And slipped her hand into his.

Lincoln froze.

Is she coming onto me?

But then he felt it—something small pressed into his palm. Jessica pulled her hand away, and his fingers instinctively closed around the object.

He glanced down.

A parcel.

When he looked up, Jessica winked.

"Put it away," she whispered.

Lincoln slid the parcel into his pocket just as Jessica pressed the white button on the wall beside them.

Moments later, the door opened.

The Warden entered, followed by an Argentine Enforcer in full armor. The room seemed to shrink around them.

"Mr. Jones," The Warden said flatly. "Ten years have been added to your sentence."

Lincoln stiffened.

"You will no longer reside on the ground floor. Enjoy the seventeenth level."

And just like that, The Warden turned and left.

The Argentine Enforcer strode forward without a word, seized Lincoln by the arm, and pulled him from the infirmary.

No time for questions. No time for anything.

They passed through corridors and reached the long metal gates at the edge of the pillars. Another Argentine Enforcer waited on the other side—with a hound.

The gates opened. The exchange was silent.

The hound padded up the stairs first.

Lincoln followed, flanked by the Enforcer.

Up.

Up.

Up.

Each step pulsed in his temple.

By the time they reached his new cage on the seventeenth level, the bell rang—echoing through the chamber like a siren.

Time for the cageys to return from The Big Cage.

Great. Time for a new cagey.

He rubbed the back of his neck.

The bell had just finished ringing when the sound of boots on steel grates echoed through the Aviary.

Lincoln stood near the back of the cage, one hand grazing the bars, trying to push the throb behind his left eye into the background.

From this height, the walkways twisted like veins. Below, The Big Cage emptied out as Enforcers herded the cageys upward, their movements sharp and efficient.

The seventeenth was next.

He rolled his shoulders, still aching from the infirmary.

The cage gate clanked open.

Lincoln turned—and froze.

The Argentine Enforcer stepped aside, gun slung across their chest.

And a man stepped in.

Broad-shouldered. Hair like dripping rain. A scar along his cheekbone. His jaw was set, his expression hard.

Their eyes locked.

The gate slammed shut behind him.

"You," the man said, teeth clenched.

Lincoln straightened. "Oh, for fuck's sake…"

They stepped toward each other, tension coiled tight.

Two seconds.

Three.

They squared up, inches apart, both fists clenched. The Enforcer raised their gun, the barrel glinting in the overhead light.

Silence stretched—taut and dangerous.

Then, at the same time—

"Shane, you ugly fuck!" Lincoln barked.

Shane's face cracked wide open. "Lincoln, you dumb bastard!"

They threw their arms around each other in a rough, back-slapping hug, both laughing like idiots.

The Enforcer held position for a moment, then slowly lowered the gun and moved on down the walkway.

Shane stepped back, shaking his head. "You in my cage now?"

Lincoln smirked. "Guess so. You always keep it this miserable?"

Shane scoffed. "Welcome to luxury living. Hope you like sleeping on half a mattress and steel springs."

Lincoln glanced around. One narrow bed against the far wall. The same as the others—thin, stiff, better than the floor, but only just.

Shane dropped onto it with a grunt and wiped his face with both hands. "Zoti… I really thought you were done for."

Lincoln leaned against the bars. "Honestly? Me too."

They shared a long look.

Then both men settled into the familiar silence of survival.

And for a moment, it almost felt like the walls weren't closing in.

When the Argentine Enforcers had returned to their posts, the grinding started.

The covers began to lower.

Lincoln flinched at the sound—metal scraping against metal, echoing through every bar, bolt, and bone. The cageys up and down the Aviary shouted and cursed, their voices rising in protest or panic. Lincoln covered his ears, but it didn't help.

The gears were everywhere. Inside him.

As the metal sheets passed their level, the world outside their bars vanished into shadow. The Aviary sank into mechanical dusk—cage by cage, floor by floor.

Then came darkness.

Shane reached under the bed, retrieved a small flashlight, and flicked it on. The beam cut through the gloom in a tight cone of pale gold.

He sat beside Lincoln and handed him a pair of noise-canceling earmuffs.

Lincoln took them without hesitation. He slid them over his ears. The grinding didn't disappear—but it dulled. On the ground floor, it had been a background hum.

Now it was the same here.

He looked over.

"Thank you," Lincoln mouthed.

Shane couldn't hear him, but gave a thumbs up and passed him a cigarette.

They smoked in silence, heads low, eyes forward. When the grinding stopped and the final cover locked into place, Lincoln peeled off the earmuffs and handed them back.

"Keep them," Shane said, flicking the last of his cigarette against the underside of the table, then carefully stashing it in a small container tucked behind one of the bars.

Lincoln finished his and handed it over. Shane nodded and added it to the stash.

"What'd you do to get up here?" Shane asked.

Lincoln scratched at his bandage. "Took Xavier's vodka. Got caught drinking it. You know Charlie's new friend? The one with the white streak. Looks kinda like a vampire"

Shane chuckled. "You're a dumb fuck."

Lincoln smirked.

Shane rolled his eyes. "You know you need Charlie. Probably best not to piss off his mates. After all, you hated me when I first got here, remember?"

He pulled a joint from his stash, lit it, took a hit, and passed it over.

"But there's always a way to bond."

Lincoln took the joint. "Maybe if you weren't such a cunt, I wouldn't have hated you when I first met you."

Shane grinned. "Maybe if *you* weren't such a cunt, more people would like you."

He leaned back.

"I mean, I like you. But I'm special."

Lincoln took a long drag, then exhaled.

"I'm fine," he said. "You're the only friend I need here."

Shane stared ahead for a beat.

Then leaned forward, elbows on his knees.

"But Lincoln…" he said quietly. "I won't be here forever."

Lincoln laughed. "You're here for life."

Shane didn't laugh.

Shane stood and started pacing.

"No, Lincoln… don't tell anyone, alright? If they find out, they'll kill me."

He didn't look up.

"I'm volunteering. For The Harvest."

Lincoln froze. His mind went blank.

"What?"

240

"I went to The Warden," Shane continued. "After Henry told me about this volunteer program. Said if you agreed to be harvested, they'd give twenty percent of your sale to your family."

Shane's voice stayed quiet. Measured. Too calm.

"I asked for the same deal," he said. "The Warden agreed."

He hesitated.

"The next day, Michael killed Henry."

Lincoln stared at him.

"I think The Warden had it done. Didn't want anyone else knowing about the program."

Shane's eyes finally met his.

"You know how bad things are at home, Link. This could change everything. I've got O negative blood. My organs will sell for a fortune."

Lincoln's jaw tightened.

He dropped the joint.

Then his fist slammed into the bars with a loud metallic crack.

"WHAT THE FUCK IS WRONG WITH YOU!?"

He crossed the cage in three steps and grabbed Shane by the front of his shirt, shoving him back against the bars.

Shane didn't fight back.

"I have to help my family," he said, calm but firm. "That's all this is."

"IT'S ABOUT *US!*" Lincoln snapped. "*WE'RE* SUPPOSED TO BE FAMILY!"

His voice cracked—but just for a moment.

Then he shoved Shane back and dropped onto the bed, elbows on his knees, fists clenched.

Shane stood still, letting the silence stretch. Then he picked up the joint from the floor, relit it with steady hands, and held it out.

"I'm sorry, Link. I really am. But I didn't have a choice. Not after I found out. You have to understand."

Lincoln didn't move.

Didn't speak.

Shane held the joint out a little longer.

Eventually, Lincoln took it.

He smoked without tasting it. Without looking at Shane. Just stared at the bars like they might offer some kind of answer.

"I can't understand," he said finally. "You're giving them what they want."

He turned, his voice low and bitter.

"You never even deserved to be here."

"I broke the law," Shane replied. "I knew what the penalty was. At least this way... I give my kids a chance."

He took a breath.

"Please forgive me. Dying with you hating me... I couldn't—"

"I don't hate you," Lincoln cut in, too fast. "I just... I don't want to lose you. You're all I've got."

He stood up again and started pacing, arms tense, movements sharp.

Shane watched him for a moment.

"That's why you should try being nicer to people," he said. "You push everyone away. Even Charlie's new friend—Xavier. I know you hate him. But maybe don't. Charlie doesn't keep bad people close."

Lincoln spun. "That little creep? He was staring at me today like he wanted to suck my blood—or suck me off."

"With that attitude," Shane said, smirking, "I doubt it's the latter."

He pulled another joint from his stash and lit it with a small laugh.

Lincoln gave a breath of something like a laugh—but it didn't reach his eyes.

Then he dug into his pocket and pulled out the parcel Jessica had given him.

Inside: five white pills.

He handed two to Shane.

"I didn't mean to lose it," he muttered. "You just caught me off guard."

Shane took the pills, nodded. "Thanks, mate."

"I don't get it," Lincoln said. "But I forgive you."

He looked at him—eyes hard, but steady.

"You're the closest thing I've ever had to a brother. I just need time. Alright?"

He turned and lay down on the bed, facing the bars.

"I think I'm gonna sleep."

Shane placed a hand on his shoulder. "I understand, brother."

Then he crossed to his own bed and lay down. The flashlight clicked off, and the cage went dark.

Lincoln stared into the darkness.

His throat was tight. His chest felt cracked open.

But he didn't cry.

He just lay there.

Holding it in.

Like always.

∞

Lincoln stood in his childhood bedroom.

The wallpaper was peeling at the corners. His old toybox sat in the corner, untouched for years. The overhead light flickered like a dying pulse.

His father was at the window, punching the wall.

"You hear me now!?" he bellowed between hits. "I told you this would happen!"

His mother sat curled in the corner, sobbing so hard her whole body shook.

Lincoln turned.

A boy was lying on his bed.

Still. Pale.

Blood dripped from his nose and ears, soaking into the mattress. His chest looked wrong—sunken, like it had caved in under something heavy. Lincoln looked down at his own hands.

They were covered in blood.

Sticky. Fresh.

He took a step toward the bed, but the boy shifted.

Morphed.

And became Shane.

Only this time, Shane's chest was split wide open. His ribcage stretched apart like broken branches. His organs pulsed, exposed, steaming.

Shane smiled up at him—too calm, too sharp.

"People will pay a lot of iron for my organs," he said.

His voice was sweet.

Wicked.

"I told you this would happen!" his father roared, spinning around. His face was red. Then it was bleeding. Then it was pouring.

Blood spilled from his mouth, his nose, his eyes.

It sprayed against the walls.

It surged across the floor.

Lincoln's mother screamed once before the wave reached her—and swallowed her whole.

Lincoln turned and ripped the door open.

But the blood followed, rushing past him and down the hallway in a roaring flood.

At the end of the hall stood the boy again—the one with the crushed chest.

Naked. Skin pale and stretched too tight. His eyes were wide. Black.

He wailed.

A sound so sharp it pierced Lincoln's skull.

Lincoln tried to run.

But his legs wouldn't move.

He tried to scream.

Nothing came out.

The boy rushed him.

Grabbed him by the shoulders.

Lincoln was frozen.

The boy's mouth opened wide—too wide—and mimicked Lincoln's silent scream.

Then Lincoln found his voice.

A broken, strangled sound escaped his throat.

But it was too late.

The boy leaned in and closed his bloody mouth over Lincoln's—slow, deliberate.

And pulled.

It was like his breath, his voice, his self was being sucked out of him. His knees buckled. His body went limp.

He was fading.

Then—

The boy's face twisted into something else.

Someone else.

Xavier.

Then, his face twisted once more.

Shane.

His eyes rolled.

His grip tightened.

And he began to shake Lincoln.

"WAKE UP, LINCOLN!" the boy growled.

Not pleading.

Commanding.

Malevolent.

∞

Lincoln jolted upright with a shout—body tense, breath shallow, the scream from the dream still caught in his throat.

His head crashed forward.

Hard.

Crack.

Shane reeled back, hands flying to his face.

"Zoti-fucking-hell!" he gasped, stumbling, blood gushing from his nose.

Lincoln blinked, disoriented. Sweat coated his chest. He couldn't tell what was real yet. The cage, the cold air, the weight on his chest—everything felt like it was lagging behind the sound of his pulse.

Shane grabbed a spare shirt and pressed it to his face, tilting his head back.

"Fuck me! You all right?" he asked, voice muffled by cotton.

His nose was already crooked. After so many breaks, it barely registered anymore—like stubbing a toe you forgot you had.

He reached into his stash with blood still running between his fingers, pulled out a cigarette, and handed it to Lincoln, along with the lighter.

"You look like you need this," he muttered with a half-laugh, blood leaking past his lip.

Lincoln took the cigarette with a shaking hand. His other hand was still clenched in a fist. He didn't say anything. Just sat there—chest heaving, sweat dripping from his brow, the scream still echoing inside his skull.

Then—

Shane curled in on himself, coughing. His body buckled at the waist. He wheezed once, twice—then collapsed to his knees.

"SHANE!"

Lincoln dropped to the floor beside him in an instant.

Shane was clawing toward the bed, one arm clutching at his chest. He couldn't speak. Just gasped and reached blindly.

Lincoln caught him under the arm, pulled his weight up, slung Shane's arm over his shoulder, and half-carried, half-dragged him to the bed.

Shane reached into his pillowcase with trembling fingers, pulled out a small grey inhaler, and pressed it to his lips.

He took two sharp puffs.

Then a third.

Lincoln hovered, his hand on Shane's back, bracing him.

When the wheezing began to ease, Shane slumped against the wall. His face was pale and soaked with sweat. His chest still rose and fell in short, stuttering breaths.

"They let you volunteer… and you have asthma?" Lincoln asked, voice low. Disbelieving.

Shane didn't answer right away. Just kept breathing.

Then, finally, he pulled the inhaler from his lips and slipped it back under his pillow.

"It's not asthma," he said softly. "Link… it's hypoxia. Brought on by emphysema."

He looked up at Lincoln—really looked at him.

"I'm dying."

The words landed like stones in a shallow pond. No drama. Just truth.

"My lungs are fucked," Shane said. "But the rest of me? My organs? Perfect. They gave me the spray to keep me going until the next moon."

He paused.

His voice cracked.

"But without it… I won't make it through the week."

Tears slipped from the corners of his eyes, silent and stubborn. Sweat glistened at his temples.

"That's why I volunteered," he said. "I'm going to die anyway. This way, I get to make sure my family's taken care of."

Lincoln said nothing.

Just stared at the floor.

The cigarette still burned in his hand, unsmoked.

Finally, he looked at it. The embers glowing. Flickering.

"I probably shouldn't be smoking these around you then," he said, his voice thin and wrecked.

Shane gave a weak smile.

"It's all right, brother. I've only got a few weeks left anyway. Not like quitting's gonna save me now."

He reached into his stash again, pulled out a flask, took a long swig, and handed it to Lincoln.

"I'm going to enjoy what time I've got."

Lincoln stared at the flask for a long moment.

Then he took it.

And drank.

"I'm sorry I yelled at you earlier," Lincoln said, voice softer now. "If I'd known…"

Shane held up a hand. "Please don't start treating me different just 'cause I'm sick."

He leaned back, shaking his head. "Let's enjoy the fact that we're cageys. I mean, how lucky am I? My last few weeks—and I get to live with my best mate. My brother."

Tears welled in Lincoln's eye, but he blinked them back.

Shane reached into his stash again and pulled out another joint, lit it, took a long drag, then exhaled with a cough.

"Share this time, won't ya?" he said, grinning as he handed it over.

Lincoln took it. "Sorry."

"Stop apologizing, ya nong." Shane nudged him in the ribs. "I'm going out my way. What could be better?"

"Uh, living?" Lincoln said flatly, taking a hit.

"That was a rhetorical question, Link."

They both laughed as Lincoln passed it back.

Shane took a drag, eyes squinting through the smoke. "Where would you be if you weren't here?"

Lincoln thought for a second. "I'd be living it up somewhere like Australia. Beaches… but close to the rainforest."

He smiled, the kind that came from a place deeper than memory.

"I'd lie right in the middle of the trees and stare up through the canopy. Watch the sky peeking through the leaves. I miss the sky."

"I miss pizza," Shane muttered. "All food, actually. I'm sick of fucking trail mix."

"Well, maybe you should stop fucking trail mix," Lincoln said, snorting.

They both cracked up.

When the laughter died down, Shane handed the joint back.

"I'd be on a beach," he said. "Sipping something fruity. Reading a good book."

Lincoln chuckled.

"What's wrong with that?" Shane raised an eyebrow.

"Nothing—'cept for the name."

"What?"

"Cocktail."

Lincoln stared.

Then lost it.

"COCK…" he wheezed through laughter. "…TAIL!"

Shane joined him, laughing so hard he nearly dropped the joint.

"Who decided that was the name?" Shane asked. "Like—'Yeah, let's put cock in the name. That'll go down smooth.'"

Lincoln took a drag and coughed from laughing. "If you think about it… a cock is just a front tail."

They both fell apart again, shoulders shaking, heads tilted back against the bars.

They passed the joint back and forth until it was nearly ash.

Shane stretched and groaned. "Time for sleep."

"Yeah," Lincoln said, already lying back on the bed.

They lay in silence.

And for the first time in a long while, both men fell asleep with a small smile still on their faces.

∞

The grinding started.

Low at first—then louder. Metal against metal. Relentless.

Lincoln stirred beneath his thin blanket, head pounding. Shane groaned beside him.

The covers were being raised.

Lincoln sat up, reached toward the bedframe for his earmuffs—only to pause when Shane shook his head.

"Not this time," he said, his voice groggy but firm.

Instead, they both grabbed their pillows and pressed them hard against their ears.

The grinding built—deep and mechanical, like the Aviary itself was waking up.

When it finally stopped, Shane let out a long breath and pulled the pillow from his face.

"We can't wear them when the covers come up," he muttered, sitting upright. "The Enforcers might see."

Lincoln nodded, rubbing the side of his head. "Right."

He stood and stretched, joints popping, then pulled a fresh shirt from his stash and started getting ready for The Big Cage.

"Hopefully, they let us out there soon," he said, pulling it over his head. "I found this little spot... If we time it right, I can catch the moonlight. Maybe a few minutes of sun."

Shane raised an eyebrow. "You chasing the moon now?"

"What else is left to chase?"

The bell sounded.

Both men froze.

But the Argentine Enforcers didn't move.

They remained still—then, without a word, dropped to one knee.

Right knee bent, left leg angled behind. Right shoulder pressed to their knee. Head lowered. Right fist braced against the floor. Left arm folded across their foreheads like a shield.

Motionless.

Silent.

"What the fuck..." Lincoln muttered.

He stepped to the bars and looked down.

Across the Aviary, other cageys had begun to do the same.

From the bottom levels up, they moved in unison—toward the center of their cages, bowing like the Enforcers. One by one. Cage by cage.

Shane stood beside him now, watching too.

"Well, shit," he said under his breath.

"The Shepherd's here."

"Link, you need to bow," Shane whispered, his voice muffled by the angle of his head.

Lincoln turned.

Shane was already in position—head down, right fist planted on the floor, left arm folded across his forehead.

"Hurry," he urged.

Lincoln hesitated only a second longer before moving to the center of the cage. He dropped to one knee and tried to copy Shane's posture as best he could.

The cold metal dug into his skin. His back curved awkwardly. His fists ached almost immediately. His injured eye throbbed under the strain.

Then came the silence.

Minutes passed.

Five. Ten.

Time bled out, slow and thick.

The Aviary, always alive with shouting and movement, was now completely still. Hundreds of bodies in synchronized reverence—Enforcers and cageys alike. No one moved. No one breathed too loudly. Even the hounds were silent.

Lincoln's knees began to burn. His shoulders cramped. Sweat collected at the base of his neck and slid down his spine. His bandage itched. The hum of the overhead lights became a roar in his ears.

"How much longer do we have to do this?" he whispered.

His voice sounded small—like it didn't belong in the space.

"Not much longer, Link," Shane murmured. "They should be close."

Another stretch of silence passed.

Then—

A sound.

Clink… screeeeech…

It echoed faintly—far away. Somewhere below. The distinct screech of stairway gates being unlocked.

Then footsteps.

Measured.

Slow.

Voices followed—soft, indistinct. Not angry. Not urgent.

Just… *controlled.*

The kind of voices people listened to without question.

Lincoln clenched his jaw and tried not to shift.

Every inch of his body was screaming.

But he stayed still.

And waited.

Because The Shepherd—

They were not someone you stood for.

"Mr. Jones. Mr. Kelly… heads up."

The Warden's voice cut through the silence like a blade.

Lincoln and Shane lifted their heads in unison.

Lincoln blinked, adjusting to the light with his good eye. The other was still swollen and useless beneath the bandage. He tilted slightly, compensating, trying to take in what stood before them.

A procession.

Three Golden Enforcers. The Pearl Enforcer at the rear. Five hounds—silent, watchful. The Warden, polished and unreadable. A striking woman. And behind her… The Shepherd.

The woman stepped forward.

She was tall. Powerfully built. Her blonde hair was cropped close to her head, her posture straight as steel. Even without speaking, she commanded the air around her. Her blue-grey eyes scanned them with clinical precision—unblinking, unreadable.

Lincoln's chest tightened.

She was beautiful, but not in a way that invited admiration. Her beauty came with weight. With danger. With control.

She raised a notepad in one gloved hand.

"The Shepherd wishes to know," she said, her voice clear and even. "If he were to make any changes here… what would you request?"

Lincoln stared, jaw half-agape.

The Shepherd cares about what's happening here?

"I…" he started, then stopped. His voice slipped out before he meant it to.

"I want to go outside," he said. Too fast, and too honest. "Not just see the sky through that tiny slit in The Big Cage. I want to really see it."

The woman nodded and scribbled something into her notepad.

"And you?" she asked, turning her gaze to Shane.

"A change in the menu would be nice," he said without missing a beat.

Another note.

"That will be all," she said, and turned with fluid efficiency.

The group began to move again—boots on steel, silent hounds close behind.

Lincoln shifted, craning to catch what he could with the eye that still worked.

The Shepherd trailed behind them—quiet, deliberate, unbothered.

Too young to be leading anything. Seventeen, maybe eighteen—but already carved hollow.

His face had no softness to it. No hesitation. His features were sharp, lips drawn into a flat, unsmiling line. His eyes—pale and pitiless—swept the Aviary without interest. Without care. The kind of gaze that didn't see people, only pieces. Assets.

He wore a golden cloak with matte-black trim, the shoulders armored and ceremonial, sitting too wide for his narrow frame. His long white hair fell in immaculate waves down his back, swaying slightly with each step.

He didn't speak.

Didn't acknowledge.

Just moved past like judgment wrapped in silk.

Lincoln stared after him, lips parted slightly.

"His father must have died," Shane muttered beside him.

Lincoln didn't reply.

Shane shifted closer. "Don't get your hopes up about the sky, Link. They do this every time there's a new Shepherd. It's a performance. That's all."

Lincoln kept watching until The Shepherd disappeared from view—until even his cloak was gone.

He hadn't realized the Pearl Enforcer was still standing nearby.

"Get back down," they ordered, voice low and cold.

Lincoln and Shane dropped their heads again, returning to the kneel that made their backs ache and their knees burn.

And they waited.

Until the bell finally rang, signaling that The Shepherd had left the Aviary.

∞

All anyone could talk about in The Big Cage was what they had asked for.

An outdoor cage seemed to be the popular choice. Even though Shane had told him not to get his hopes up, Lincoln couldn't help it.

He glanced over as he and Shane sat down with the others.

"What did you ask for?" he asked Charlie.

Charlie leaned back, arms resting on his knees. "Better food," he said with a small shrug. "Same as every other time. Won't happen. Never does."

"But it's still fun to talk about," Connor cut in with a crooked grin. "I asked for smokes." He held up a hand like he was giving a royal wave. "Did you see the look The Warden gave me?"

Jaysen chuckled.

Connor pointed at him. "This princess asked for private showers."

They all cracked up—except Jaysen, who rolled his eyes with practiced patience. "Considering the state of you lot, I stand by it."

"And you?" Jaysen asked, turning to Lincoln.

Lincoln shifted. "Outdoor cage."

Across the bench, Xavier laughed. Not cruelly—more like he was surprised.

Lincoln scowled. "What's so funny?"

"I asked for the same thing," Xavier said, brushing a lock of hair behind his ear. "Maybe we're not so different after all. How's your eye?"

Lincoln's jaw tightened. "Fine," he muttered. "No thanks to you."

Xavier sat up straighter, some of the softness leaving his voice. "Hey. I didn't make you take my vodka."

He reached into his coat and tossed a packet of smokes into Lincoln's lap.

"Here. Consider it a peace offering."

Lincoln looked down at the packet, then up at Xavier, brow furrowed.

Jaysen raised an eyebrow. "Huh. That's… unexpected."

Charlie just smiled faintly, watching the exchange. He didn't speak—just let the silence settle for a second.

Then Connor leaned forward, breaking it. "Guess The Shepherd's little parade really did something."

"For now," Charlie murmured. "Talk's cheap in here. It's action that matters."

Lincoln tapped the smokes against his knee, then tucked them away.

"I'm not apologizing," he said.

Xavier shrugged. "Wasn't expecting you to."

The air between them held—sharp, but no longer barbed.

Lincoln grunted as he stood. "Let's go."

Shane didn't move.

"I think I'll stay here, Link. I'm tired."

He patted the bench beside him and gestured for Lincoln to sit back down. His smile was gentle, but it didn't reach his eyes.

Lincoln hesitated, then dropped onto the seat again.

Shane turned toward Charlie. "How are you, old man? Thought you'd gone to The Harvest."

Charlie gave a tired shrug. "I did."

Lincoln frowned. "What do you mean? You're still here."

"No one wanted me," Charlie said simply. "Hopefully it's the same next time."

Shane gave a quiet nod. "Well… I guess we'll find out together."

He straightened his back slightly, as if standing taller might make the words easier.

"There's no point hiding it anymore. I'm headed there on the next moon too."

Charlie reached over and slung an arm around Shane's shoulder.

"Then do what I did. Hurt yourself on stage," he said, knocking lightly on the brace around his ankle. "Worked for me."

"On stage?" Lincoln asked, confused.

Charlie glanced at him, then leaned forward, lowering his voice and telling them everything he saw.

"They don't harvest us and then sell the parts," he said. "They auction us whole. Alive. We only get harvested after."

Lincoln went still.

Shane's brows drew in tight.

Charlie exhaled through his nose. "After the showcase, the infirmary was full, so they took me to surgery. I saw it."

He looked down at his hands for a long second.

"Rows of people. Prepped. Labeled. Still breathing."

Shane swallowed hard.

"And Dr. Lancet?" he asked. "She… she was bidding?"

Charlie nodded. "I saw her take Michael into another room. He was still alive. And he'd been in The Farm for three days."

He looked up, eyes dull but certain. "They don't just judge us on health. It's age. Crimes. Value. Like livestock."

"Zoti…" Shane whispered.

"It's fucked," Charlie said. "All of it."

There was a long pause.

Then Xavier, trying too hard to lighten the mood, gave a half-laugh. "So when I volunteer, I should do a little dance for them?"

He immediately froze—eyes wide, hands flying to his mouth.

Shane and Lincoln both snapped upright, their expressions shifting like lightning.

They looked at each other.

Then at Xavier.

"Shut it, son," Charlie muttered, rubbing his forehead.

No one laughed.

And for the first time in a while, even Connor didn't have something to say.

"It's okay, Charlie," Shane whispered. "I know about the program… Henry told me. The day before he—" Shane's voice caught, and he dropped his head.

"I think Michael killed Henry on The Warden's orders," he said quietly. "Right after I asked if I could volunteer… Henry was dead."

Xavier dropped his head into his hands.

"You weren't here for any of this. You didn't know Henry," Lincoln growled. "Why are you so upset?"

Charlie turned sharply. "Shut it."

Lincoln blinked, startled by the edge in Charlie's voice.

"Xav knew Henry outside," Charlie said. "He was there when Henry's family got their cheque."

"It's okay, Charlie," Xavier said softly, lifting his head as he stood. His eyes were red. "He doesn't care anyway."

Lincoln looked away as Xavier turned and walked off toward the bubbler.

Shane turned to Lincoln. "You need to stop this."

Lincoln frowned.

"I'm not gonna be here much longer," Shane added, coughing mid-sentence. "You need friends."

Lincoln was already moving. He pulled the inhaler from his pocket, uncapped it, and held it steady while Shane inhaled.

Charlie watched, brow narrowing.

"What's this then?"

"Just a bit of asthma. Nothing to worry about," Shane said quickly, before Lincoln could speak. "The Warden gave it to me after I volunteered."

Charlie raised an eyebrow.

"Don't lie to me, Shane. I know you better than that."

Shane sighed, the mask slipping.

"Nothing gets past you, huh?"

He sat back and rubbed his face.

"I've got hypoxia. From emphysema. This—" he held up the inhaler, "—this is The Warden's way of keeping me breathing until The Harvest. I've got O-negative blood. Buyers want my organs fresh."

He looked up at Charlie.

"Now I know how fresh."

Xavier returned, quietly taking his seat. He didn't look at Lincoln.

Lincoln grunted, eyes still on him. "Why did you volunteer?"

Xavier didn't answer.

The silence stretched.

His fingers twisted around one another.

"I said—why?" Lincoln pressed, voice low, but firm.

Xavier's jaw ticked.

He didn't look at Lincoln.

"Not that it's any of your business," he said finally, his voice tight. "But I can't yet. I need a life sentence first."

Lincoln didn't back off. "That's not what I asked."

Xavier's shoulders stiffened.

"You still didn't tell me *why*."

Xavier stood fast, the legs of the bench scraping harshly against the floor.

He looked down at Lincoln, eyes hard.

"I'm done with this conversation," he snapped, each word clipped and sharp.

Then he turned and walked away—his steps fast, shoulders rigid, like he needed to move before something inside him shattered.

Charlie shook his head. "Those two are like cats and dogs."

"If only they were as easy to train," Shane chuckled.

Connor leaned in, voice lowering. "Be careful, Lincoln. Don't you think Xav bears a striking resemblance to The Shepherd?"

"Oh yeah," Jaysen snorted, barely hiding a laugh. "He's probably the real Shepherd undercover. Making sure we follow all the rules. The one we saw today? Total decoy."

"My theory?" Connor said, grinning. "Illegitimate son of the Late Shepherd."

He and Jaysen cracked up, shoulders bumping. Joking about it until Xavier returned.

Xavier, now sitting again, rolled his eyes as he slid a new packet of smokes into his pocket. "Not this shit again."

"Just because I've got a white streak doesn't mean I look like that tyrant," he muttered. "It's called poliosis. He has white hair. Big difference."

He pulled out his flask from Barry, took a sip.

Connor nearly fell off the bench laughing. "The more you defend it, the funnier it gets."

Trying to be nice, Lincoln spoke up, his voice a little rough.

"I don't think you look like him."

Xavier turned, slow and wary. His eyes searched Lincoln's face—not with suspicion exactly, but with that familiar trace of hesitation. Like he wasn't used to people meaning what they said.

Zoti, this is harder than it should be, Lincoln thought. *But Shane's right. I've gotta try.*

"Well… that's nice of you," Xavier said finally, holding Lincoln's gaze.

There was a quiet beat between them.

Then Lincoln added, "Would you mind if I sipped that flask, Xav?"

The words came out steadier than he expected. His chest still felt tight.

Xavier raised an eyebrow, cautious.

"Only a sip this time," Lincoln said, lifting a hand.

Don't fuck this up.

"One sip," Xavier replied, handing over the flask.

The moment slowed.

Charlie's hand froze mid-shuffle in his trail mix. Shane leaned forward, elbows on his knees. Connor and Jaysen said nothing—they just watched.

Lincoln could feel all their eyes on him.

Zoti, you'd think I was holding a fucking grenade.

He took the flask carefully, raised it, drank—just enough—and handed it back.

"Thanks," he said, quieter than before.

Xavier took it, expression unreadable.

"No worries."

The tension cracked. The others exhaled.

Connor leaned back, hand over his chest. "That was fucking intense."

You're telling me, Lincoln thought, dragging a hand through his hair.

"You know what else is fucking intense?" Xavier asked, a smirk pulling at the edge of his mouth. "Sex while camping."

A beat—

Then Charlie chuffed.

Shane let out a quick, raspy laugh.

And then the others followed.

Lincoln laughed too—tired, but real.

Maybe this could work. Maybe I don't have to be at war with everyone.

Time passed.

Five hours in, and The Big Cage was still open. The sun had shifted, but the Enforcers hadn't moved to bring the top-level in.

The court was full. The food was running low. There was something stretched in the air—like a rubber band pulled too tight.

"I wonder what's going on," Charlie murmured, watching the far end of the walkway. "This isn't the usual Shepherd routine."

Shane nodded, frowning. "Yeah. There's something off."

"Maybe," Xavier said, hope creeping into his voice, "maybe they're actually going to give us some of what we asked for."

Lincoln didn't say anything. But something fluttered in his chest.

Don't get your hopes up, he warned himself. *That's not how this place works.*

Then—

The Argentine Enforcers moved.

Like clockwork. Each step timed. Each stance perfect.

Laughter stopped mid-breath.

Games ground to a halt.

Cageys took their places without needing to be told. Lincoln felt the weight drop back into the room. He sat up straighter, watching the shift ripple through the cage.

Then the top-level cageys came through.

One by one.

Silent. Hollow-eyed.

Two minutes at the troughs.

Two at the bubbler.

When the second row of top-level cageys reached the troughs, they found them empty.

A beat.

Then—

"WHERE THE FUCK IS MY FOOD!" one man roared, his voice cracking with hunger and rage.

Others took it up, fists banging the metal rails.

"YOU GREEDY FUCKERS!" another screamed, pointing at the lower levels.

And then they surged.

No order. No warning.

They charged.

Feet pounded the floor as the top-level cageys lunged toward the others like animals. Rage tore through them—wild and primal.

The first blow struck with a sickening crack.

Then blood.

It sprayed like someone had split a pipe.

Lincoln spun as screams erupted all around him. Men were being torn apart. Claws. Teeth. Bare hands soaked in red.

Some of them didn't even use weapons.

They ripped throats out with their teeth.

Argentine Enforcers rushed in, shouting orders, trying to hold the line—but it was already too late. Hounds barked and snapped, pulling people down. The air was full of panic, fists, and steel.

Then the alarm blared.

And the violence only escalated.

Lincoln fought through the chaos, shoving and elbowing his way through the riot. His heart slammed in his chest, his eye scanning for Shane.

They'd been separated.

Someone shoved Xavier forward—he hit the ground hard in front of Lincoln.

"SHANE!" Lincoln yelled, trying to push past.

"LINK!" Xavier shouted from the floor, voice cracking. "HELP!"

Lincoln turned, saw him reaching out, pinned beneath a rush of feet.

But he kept going.

I have to find Shane.

Then—

He saw him.

Shane, barely conscious, being dragged toward the basketball court by one of the top-level cageys.

Lincoln shoved a man aside. "SHANE!" he roared, lunging forward.

The court floor felt miles away.

The man dragging Shane slowed and leaned down close, his lips near Shane's ear.

"You shouldn't have told anyone," the man growled.

Then he brought the bedspring across Shane's throat.

The sound it made—wet and sharp—cut through everything.

Blood poured from Shane's neck, splashing down his chest, pooling beneath him as his body twitched.

Then stilled.

Lincoln stopped mid-step.

Everything else disappeared—the alarms, the screams, the walls.

All he could see was Shane's face.

His eyes open.

Unmoving.

Gone.

A scream built inside Lincoln's chest.

And then he charged.

He slammed into the man who'd killed Shane, wrapped both arms around his neck and squeezed.

The man thrashed, feet kicking.

Lincoln didn't let go.

His thumbs dug deep into the soft skin of the man's throat, pressing harder and harder until he felt the trachea start to give.

The man's eyes turned red, then purple. Blood bubbled from his lips.

He coughed—once—into Lincoln's face.

Then nothing.

His body sagged.

Lincoln dropped him without ceremony, chest heaving, hands soaked in blood that wasn't his.

He turned, wiping his face with a shaking hand. Only smearing more blood.

Shane lay still on the court.

Lincoln's breath hitched.

He turned back toward where Xavier had been.

Bodies piled there now—twisted, bloody limbs crushed under boots.

And in his mind, clear as a whisper through the noise:

I'm not going to be here much longer. You need friends.

∞

Xavier

Xavier's vision was blurring. Panic gripped his chest like a vice.

"JAYSEN!" he screamed, coughing through the blood in his throat. "CONNOR!"

The air was chaos—screams, alarms, the thundering of boots and fists and bodies.

Then something heavy slammed down on top of him.

A man—bleeding from the neck. His body convulsed once, then went still.

Xavier's lungs seized as blood poured from the man's mouth, warm and metallic, spilling across his face, soaking his hair, turning the white streak red.

It filled his mouth, ran down his throat.

He couldn't scream anymore.

His limbs flailed, then slowed.

Is this it? Is this how I go? Alone. Trampled. Suffocating in someone else's blood?

The pressure on his chest grew heavier.

He felt himself slipping—pulled into the darkness around the edges of his vision.

Please... please, someone...

Then—

The weight lifted.

He gasped.

A hand reached down, grasped his own—firm, strong—and hauled him upright.

Another arm wrapped around his waist, steadying him.

He could barely keep his legs under him. His feet slipped on the blood-slick floor.

When he looked up through blurred, bloodied lashes—

It was Lincoln.

His face was pale and streaked with something—tears, blood, maybe both.

"You… you came back," Xavier breathed.

His voice cracked.

Lincoln didn't answer at first. Just tightened his grip around Xavier's middle.

"It may not seem like it… but I do care," he said, barely louder than a whisper.

His eyes were locked on Shane's body across the court—what was left of it.

Xavier tried to speak. "Lincoln, I… I…"

But before he could finish, a body slammed into them, jarring them sideways. Lincoln grunted, then hoisted Xavier off the ground and began carrying him.

Xavier's arms clung to his shoulders, dizzy and stunned.

Why did he help me? After everything?

He looked at Lincoln's face—gritted teeth, bloody brow, locked forward—and felt something shift.

Lincoln fought toward the others—toward Jaysen, Connor, Charlie.

As Xavier's gaze drifted back over Lincoln's shoulder, it landed on Shane's body.

Stained. Still.

Something in Xavier's chest tightened. Not panic. Not grief.

Something quieter.

Something like understanding.

I should try to give him a chance.

∞

Jaysen

When Jaysen and Connor could finally stand again, they staggered toward Charlie and helped lift him to the bench.

The air was thick with blood, smoke, and screams.

Then came the click—sharp and metallic.

Smoke bombs hissed as Argentine Enforcers rolled them into the space.

Within seconds, gas filled the room, stinging Jaysen's eyes and burning his lungs.

He dropped to the floor, coughing violently as his vision blurred. Around him, others were choking, crawling, collapsing in the haze.

Jaysen squeezed his eyes shut and pressed his sleeve to his face, but it did little to help. He could barely breathe.

Everything slowed.

Then—silence.

The alarm stopped.

The gas fans roared to life overhead, blowing the thick clouds away. Slowly, shapes emerged again through the lifting fog.

Jaysen wiped his eyes, blinking through the tears.

The Pearl Enforcer stood at the center of the room.

"All inmates who can walk, return to your cages immediately!" they commanded.

The room stirred, cageys rising shakily to their feet. Some slipped on blood, others tripped over bodies. The floor was a battlefield—red, wet, scattered with limbs and crushed possessions.

Jaysen spotted Lincoln.

Covered in blood.

Not his own.

Lincoln dropped to his knees halfway to The Aviary, his shoulders shaking, hands trembling.

Xavier appeared behind him. "Lincoln," he said gently, crouching beside him, placing a hand on his back. "I'm so sorry… but you need to keep going."

Lincoln didn't look at him. "Fuck off, mutt," he growled through ragged breaths.

"Link, let me help you."

"I said fuck off."

"Keep moving, rat," barked an Argentine Enforcer towering above them.

Lincoln stood without a word, turned to the Enforcer, and punched them straight in the throat—right where the armor left a gap.

"I KNOW THE WARDEN ORDERED THIS!" Lincoln roared. "BECAUSE HE DOESN'T WANT ANYONE KNOWING YOU CAN VOLUNTEER FOR THE HARVEST!"

The room froze.

Every cagey stopped in place, eyes locked on Lincoln.

"Volunteer?" they whispered.

The Pearl Enforcer appeared behind Lincoln, swift and silent. They cracked their baton against the back of his knee, dropping him like a ragdoll.

Jaysen winced as Lincoln hit the ground.

He kept screaming even as they dragged him away, his voice hoarse and breaking.

"HE DOESN'T WANT YOU TO KNOW! YOUR FAMILY WILL GET IRON IF YOU VOLUNTEER!"

The door slammed behind them.

Silence fractured into whispers.

Dozens of cageys now muttering, eyes wide, voices rising.

"The cat's out of the bag now," Charlie murmured, glancing at Xavier.

"I wonder what The Warden's going to do to Lincoln," Xavier said softly.

When the men entered The Aviary, it looked different.

There were more beds now—welded onto the old ones, stacked into bunks. The metal still glowed faintly with fresh weld lines.

"Shit," Connor muttered. "Life in here's about to get much more crowded."

"Fuck the crowding," Xavier snapped. "I hope no one touched my bed!"

They exchanged worried glances, realizing all at once—they'd stashed things in their beds.

"Mr. Masters. Mr. Mathews. You will join Mr. Harrington and Mr. Wheeler," an Argentine Enforcer said.

The door to Charlie and Xavier's cage slid open.

All four men stepped inside.

"Well, isn't this just cozy," Connor said with a dry laugh, throwing his arms over Xavier and Jaysen's shoulders.

Jaysen didn't smile.

He caught Charlie watching him—hard.

"Charlie?" Connor asked, sensing the shift.

Charlie didn't answer right away.

His eyes were on Jaysen. Haunted.

"Your last name," he asked. "It's… Masters?"

Jaysen tilted his head, confused. "Yeah. Why?"

Charlie sat heavily on the bottom bunk, hit his head on the one above, and rubbed it.

"Son…" he said gently. "You'd better sit down."

Jaysen sat beside him, heart already pounding.

"What's going on?"

Charlie took a deep breath, then reached into his pocket, pulling the edge of an envelope just far enough to show a black-ink stamp.

"When I was walking back after The Harvest, I saw a door marked *The Cell*. I couldn't see much, but… I saw a list. Names. Numbers."

He placed a hand on Jaysen's shoulder.

"One name, Jaysen. Just one."

He hesitated.

"I. Masters."

Jaysen froze.

The breath left his lungs in a rush. His hands dropped into his lap.

"No," he whispered, voice breaking.

His head fell into his hands.

"She was supposed to be safe," he muttered, rocking slightly, shaking his head. "She was supposed to be *safe*."

"I'm so sorry," Connor said, falling to his knees in front of him. "Jaysen…"

"I have to help her."

His voice was quiet—but steady.

"What even is *The Cell*?" Xavier asked.

Charlie tucked the envelope back into his pocket. "That's what I've been trying to figure out. Along with the other rooms."

He glanced around.

"Lucky we all share a cage now," he said under his breath. "We'll know more once the covers are down."

∞

Lincoln

The Pearl Enforcer dragged Lincoln into the overcrowded infirmary.

The air was thick with blood and antiseptic, groans rising from every cot. Cageys lined the floor, some with torn shirts pressed to open wounds, others shivering and dazed.

Jessica moved alone between them—her uniform soaked through, her hands trembling from constant motion. She didn't look up when Lincoln entered. She couldn't. There were too many.

In the corner, The Warden stood tall, untouched by the blood and wreckage. He was speaking to the injured, one by one—each word clipped and condescending, as if the violence were beneath his notice.

Then his eyes landed on Lincoln.

"Mr. Jones," he said, shaking his head slowly. "Your consistency for causing problems in my prison is getting out of hand. These slanders against me are outrageous."

He paused, lips curling faintly.

"Seventy-two hours in The Detachment Gibbets will suffice."

Lincoln's heart stuttered.

The Warden turned to leave.

"But sir," Lincoln croaked, "I can't bend my knee. I won't fit."

"Ninety-six hours," The Warden snapped without turning. "And the Argentine Enforcer will make you fit."

Then he left the infirmary like he'd just swatted a fly.

The Argentine Enforcer grabbed Lincoln's arm.

"The nurse hasn't treated me yet," Lincoln muttered.

"Move," the Enforcer growled.

He was marched—no, limped—down the corridor, every step a sharp bolt up his thigh. Next, the stairs. They wound like a spine. He gritted his teeth, sweat slicking his brow as they climbed higher and higher, until the lights dimmed.

The Detachment Gibbets loomed ahead.

Steel cages no bigger than a man's body. Twisted angles. Rusted bolts. Screws bent inward like teeth.

The Enforcer shoved Lincoln into one, gripping his bad leg.

"Don't—wait—"

But it was too late.

The Enforcer forced Lincoln's knee into place with both hands. The joint bent unnaturally—and Lincoln screamed.

A sound ripped from his throat, ragged and deep, echoing through the long chamber.

Other cageys moaned for silence from the surrounding gibbets, their voices fractured and weak.

"SHUT UP, CUNTS!" Lincoln yelled, his voice hoarse, trying to find a position—any position—that didn't feel like fire crawling up his spine.

Then—

A hiss.

Low. Nearby.

"I need you to pass on a message when you return."

Lincoln froze.

"Who's there!" he barked.

The other cageys groaned again.

"Who I am doesn't matter," the voice whispered. "What I have to say does."

Lincoln strained against the bars, trying to see.

"I need to get a message to Connor. The Architect will pay you for it."

Lincoln stilled.

The Architect?

That name wasn't thrown around lightly.

The voice continued: "He knows where his brother is. He'll need to see me up here if he wants to know more. Tell no one else. And tell *him* the same."

Lincoln's breath caught.

"The Architect?" he repeated.

Silence.

"Hello?" Lincoln whispered.

Nothing.

"HELLO!" he shouted.

More groaning.

More protest.

"SHUT THE FUCK UP, CUNTS!"

Then—

The grinding.

That unbearable, soul-scraping sound.

The covers were coming down.

Lincoln clamped his hands over his ears, wishing—aching—for the noise-canceling earmuffs Shane had given him.

"Shane," he whispered.

His voice broke.

He was crying now. Full sobs. Raw, ugly, uncontained.

But the grinding masked it.

Thank Zoti for the grinding.

No one could hear him.

Maybe not even himself.

He rocked slightly, eyes clenched shut, fists balled into his hair.

"REAL MEN DON'T CRY," he roared.

Again.

"REAL MEN DON'T CRY!"

He repeated it like a lifeline. A curse. A prayer.

Words drilled into him by his father. A man who had never allowed softness.

By the time the grinding stopped, his sobbing had dulled into a quiet, broken whimper.

And his fists were still tangled in the hair he had torn from his scalp.

∞

Jaysen

As the covers lowered and swallowed the last of the dim overhead light, the cage fell into hush.

Then—a soft *click*.

Charlie switched on the flashlight and pulled the envelope from his pocket. The narrow beam caught the corners of a stained, folded sheet.

"It took a lot to get this," he said, voice low. "But it's worth it… if we can help your sister."

He unfolded the paper.

Blueprints.

Augmentation Bay—mapped in thin, curling lines. Tunnels. Sealed halls. Hidden service routes. It looked like a nervous system. Fragile. Complicated. Alive.

Jaysen leaned in.

Connor and Xavier followed, crowding close.

Jaysen's pulse thudded in his ears.

The longer he stared, the harder it was to breathe.

Izzy's in here. Somewhere in this fucking maze.

"How did you even get this, Charlie?" he asked quietly.

Charlie didn't answer right away. His eyes were on the map, tracing memory.

"How I got them doesn't matter," he said. "I've been planning this for a while… with help. People on the outside."

He tapped the corner of the paper with one finger.

"I don't think my chances are great. But you boys? Maybe you can make it. Maybe you can save her."

"I'm not leaving," Xavier said flatly.

Connor said nothing. His jaw was tight, eyes still locked on the page.

Charlie kept going. Calm. Measured.

"All that matters is we have them. This is more than we've ever had before. And we're not alone. We *can* find a way out."

"I'm not leaving," Xavier repeated, louder this time.

Connor looked up. His tone snapped like a wire. "Would you stop saying that?"

Xavier flinched. "I just—"

"Well, you just what?" Connor cut in. "This isn't about *you*, Xav. It's about Jaysen. It's about *his sister*."

Xavier stared at the floor, his shoulders hunched. "I didn't mean to." He stopped when Jaysen placed a steady hand on his back.

"It's all right, mate," Jaysen said gently. "You're not trying to be selfish. I get it."

Then, to Connor, he raised an eyebrow. "And *you* didn't mean to snap, right?"

Connor's jaw twitched.

He exhaled and looked at Xavier. "I'm sorry, Xav. I really am. We know you don't want to leave. We won't force it. But please... don't make this about volunteering. This is about helping Jaysen. Helping Izzy."

There was a pause.

Then Xavier's expression shifted.

His voice came small. "Wait—Izzy?" His eyes widened. "Izzy *M?*"

He sat straighter, color draining from his face. "That's your sister?"

Jaysen blinked. "What?"

Xavier leaned forward. "Long blonde hair. Blue eyes. Scar on the back of her neck?"

Jaysen's heart thudded in his chest. "You... you *know* her?"

Xavier nodded slowly, eyes glistening. "Yeah. I knew Reggie—one of her best friends. Before... before the Enforcers took them."

Connor's face twisted with confusion. "How do you know her friend?"

"There was an underground bar. People like me... we had our places," Xavier said. "Reggie was a regular. They introduced me to Izzy."

Jaysen stared at the floor. His mind was racing. Guilt pressed in from all sides.

Why didn't she tell me? Fuck, I would've protected her. I would've done anything.

"I would never have turned her in," he whispered, voice breaking.

Xavier wrapped an arm around his shoulders. "She didn't think you would. But... sometimes hiding feels safer than hope."

Then he smiled—just a little.

"She's not gay, by the way," he added. "She was just our mate. A bloody good one."

Then his head dropped too.

"I'm so sorry she's in here."

Jaysen's eyes burned. He didn't let the tears fall.

Not yet.

Instead, he curled his fingers into fists.

"She won't be for long," he said.

He looked up at each of them—Charlie. Connor. Xavier.

"I'm going to get her out of here," he said.

His voice didn't shake.

"If it's the last thing I do."

∞

Lincoln

Lincoln's knee felt like it was on fire.

Time had stopped meaning anything. There were no clocks in the dark. Only the sound of his own ragged breathing, the creak of the metal, and the echo of things he couldn't be sure he heard.

That voice…

Was it real?

Maybe I've been losing my mind since the moment they locked me in here.

His thoughts came slow and strange now, drifting like smoke.

Then—

Footsteps.

A soft *whirrrrr* of servo-motors. Night vision mask. Argentine Enforcer.

Lincoln blinked hard just as the gibbet door clanked open.

He didn't step out.

He fell.

A collapsed heap of bone and blood and ruined muscle.

"Get up," the Argentine Enforcer growled, as if he'd just tripped on a piece of garbage.

Lincoln grunted, blinking up at the light. Everything felt too loud. Too bright. His limbs didn't belong to him anymore.

I must've turned around in the gibbet, he thought vaguely as he staggered upright. *How the fuck did I even fit in there?*

He tried to walk.

His leg wouldn't respond.

So he dragged it.

The Enforcer didn't slow to match him. Just kept moving, one hand hovering near their baton.

∞

Lincoln clung to the wall as they descended the winding stairs. Each step a jolt of agony through his knee and hip. His fingers scraped against the stone, bloody and raw, but he needed the leverage just to stay upright.

He couldn't tell how far they'd gone. Every level looked the same.

"I need to see the nurse," he rasped.

"Shut up and keep walking," the Enforcer snapped.

Lincoln's head throbbed. His skin felt too hot, like he was burning from the inside out.

Keep going. Don't stop. You're almost—

His ears rang.

His balance gave out.

The last thing he saw was the door to The Aviary just ahead—blurry and swinging open.

Then the world tilted sideways.

And everything went black.

∞

"I'm so sorry, sweetie," a soft voice said, drifting into Lincoln's fog.

He stirred.

Every nerve felt wrong. His limbs were heavy. His mouth was dry.

"I did my best," the voice continued, "but I couldn't save your eye."

His head turned slowly. He tried to sit, but the weight of his body pulled him back down.

"What… what are you talking about?" he mumbled, his throat rough, his mind still tangled in anesthesia.

Jessica's voice came closer. Calmer now.

"The wound got infected. That, along with the trauma, caused phthisis bulbi. It put pressure on your optic nerve, then…"

She hesitated.

"Your eye globe shrank. I'm sorry. There was nothing I could do."

Her hand settled gently on his forearm. Warm. Real.

"You need rest," she said. "You've been out a couple of days now. Your body's been through a lot. I did what I could with your knee too, but…"

She looked down.

"I'm still learning. I'm sorry."

She handed him a cane.

"I'm not using that," he muttered, voice rasping from dryness and pride.

Jessica smiled softly, the kind that said she expected that response. "I understand."

She tucked it away and pulled something else from the cupboard.

"But you'll need this," she said, holding up a black eyepatch. "Don't worry—it makes you look rugged. Distinctive."

She reached for gauze and medical tape next. "I need to change the dressing before you go. That okay?"

Lincoln nodded slowly.

"Can I see it?"

Jessica blinked. "Of course. I'll get a mirror."

She rummaged again, then placed the mirror gently into his hand.

"As I said, sweetie… I did my best. But it doesn't look pretty."

Her voice carried something heavier this time.

Regret.

Shame.

She peeled the gauze back slowly, and Lincoln lifted the mirror to his face.

The socket was sunken, stitched, angry red around the edge. A mess of sutures and puckered skin. What was once his left eye was now a memory carved into his face.

He stared at it for a long time.

Then turned to Jessica.

"I do look more rugged," he said, managing a half-smile.

Jessica let out a breath that was almost a laugh. "More distinctive," she echoed.

She cleaned the wound gently, replaced the gauze, and secured the patch.

"You'll need regular checkups," she said when she was done. "Just keep it clean, okay, sweetie?"

She handed him a pair of small bottles—painkillers, and a few unfamiliar tablets.

"One of each every day. You know the painkillers. The others are antibiotics. It's important—you need to keep the infection from spreading."

He nodded. Said nothing.

Stored them in his pocket.

Jessica pressed a button on the wall, summoning the Argentine Enforcer.

Moments later, Lincoln was being marched back up the winding stairs.

Every step was pain.

By the time he reached The Aviary, he was trembling with exhaustion.

Inside the cage, it felt smaller than ever.

Four bunks now.

Three occupied.

Shane's was empty.

Lincoln stood in the doorway for a moment, just staring.

The absence was louder than the crowd.

He walked to Shane's bed.

Dropped onto it.

Didn't look at the others. Didn't speak.

Didn't even notice who the new cageys were.

The images came flooding back.

Shane on the court.

The bedspring slicing his throat.

Blood everywhere.

The screaming.

The chaos.

"Shane," Lincoln whispered.

He lay there for hours. Staring at the bunk above. Still.

When the grinding began, he didn't flinch.

Didn't cover his ears.

Didn't reach for the earmuffs.

Didn't ask for the flashlight.

He just closed his eye.

And pictured Shane on that first night—smiling, giving him a thumbs up.

As darkness swallowed the cage.

∞

As Lincoln was led down the stairs, he grunted with every step, dragging his leg like dead weight.

Each stair was a jolt of pain through his hip and knee. He leaned heavily on the cages for support, jaw clenched tight, trying not to show how close he was to collapsing.

When he entered The Big Cage, he didn't even bother with trail mix.

He went straight to the benches and dropped onto the edge of one, shoulders stiff, breathing hard.

"I can't believe The Shepherd actually listened to us," Xavier said as he, Jaysen, Connor, and Charlie came to sit with him.

Lincoln narrowed his eye, watching them as they approached.

Xavier held out a massive corn cob. "I'm so sorry, Lincoln. Shane was a good man."

Lincoln stared at him for a long moment.

Then he snatched the corn.

"Thanks," he muttered, eye not leaving Xavier's. "He was."

He took a bite, chewing aggressively, jaw working like it was angry too.

"I have some news for you," Charlie started, voice tentative.

"You're gonna see the sky," Xavier interrupted, grinning.

Lincoln choked.

Corn sprayed everywhere—mostly on Xavier.

"Zoti's balls," Xavier groaned, wiping at his shirt.

Jaysen patted Lincoln's back as he coughed. "Xav, take it easy."

He turned to Lincoln. "Look—The Shepherd's making changes. See that door?" He pointed to the far end of The Aviary. "They're calling it Free Range. Like we're a flock of fucking chickens."

Jaysen rolled his eyes.

"Still… it means we'll get to go outside."

Charlie smiled faintly but didn't look up.

"You will get to go outside," he said. "I'm not sure I'll still be around in six months. That's a lot of Harvests to survive."

His voice was light, but the weight behind it was heavy.

"No one's ever made it past two."

Lincoln finished the corn and looked around at the group.

"Why are you all sitting with me?" he asked flatly. "I don't need your sympathy."

He turned to Charlie. "And you won't get mine." He waved a hand. "Now fuck off. All of you."

Jaysen raised an eyebrow. "You're sitting where *we* sit, Link. We're just trying to be nice."

"It's what Shane would've wanted," Xavier said gently. He placed a hand on Lincoln's knee.

"Don't touch me," Lincoln growled.

Xavier pulled back. "Sorry. I was just… trying to comfort you. I can't imagine how much you must be hurting."

He looked down at his half-eaten corn, then held it out.

"Here. You look hungry."

Lincoln took it without hesitation. "I am. Thanks."

He chewed a few bites, then looked up at Connor.

"Hey… can I talk to you? Alone."

Connor blinked, surprised. "Uh… sure."

Charlie stood immediately. "Let's get some water, boys."

He guided Jaysen and Xavier away without another word.

Connor shifted on the bench. "What's up?"

Lincoln chewed off the las of the corn, and swallowed hard.

"When I was in The Detachment Gibbets… someone else was up there."

Connor frowned. "There are usually other cageys locked up—"

"It wasn't a cagey," Lincoln interrupted. "And it sure as shit wasn't an Enforcer."

He lowered his voice.

"They wanted me to pass on a message to you. But you can't tell anyone. No one. Got it?"

Connor's posture changed—his back straightened, his eyes narrowed.

"I'm listening."

Lincoln leaned in.

"They said The Architect knows where your brother is. And if you want to know more… you'll have to get sent to The Detachment Gibbets. There's someone waiting up there for you."

Connor's mouth opened.

But no words came.

He blinked. Once. Twice.

"My brother is dead," he finally whispered.

"Fine. Don't go," Lincoln said, shrugging like it didn't matter. "I don't give a fuck. I passed on the message. My job's done."

He stood up, still dragging his bad leg.

"Now you owe me."

Then he walked away.

Without another word.

CHAPTER SEVEN

Finding Dr. Lancet

Valentino

Valentino shook his head, rubbing his temples as his interaction with Lincoln echoed in his head.

What the fuck was that voice? What was I even trying to sound like—some kind of snake?

He winced and slid back into the tight, claustrophobic space he'd built in the room that housed the Detachment Gibbets. Sheet metal, fractured cage bars, and torn bits of blackout cloth surrounded him like a nest of secrets.

Another day in paradise. Or is it night?

Sealing off the crawlspace, he clicked on his lamp.

It was dim and fading, but enough.

From the folds of his backpack, he retrieved a small, weather-worn sketchbook. He flipped past pages of old faces, guard towers, and vents—until he reached hers.

Pandora.

He stared at the unfinished lines for a long time before lifting his pencil. The curve of her rose cheeks, the slope of her button nose—his hand moved slowly, carefully.

He closed his eyes for a moment.

The memory came easily. Strawberries. The way she'd offered one like it was treasure. The way her eyes had softened when he finally took it.

Valentino reached into his pack.

One left.

His last strawberry.

He cradled it in his fingers, breathed it in. The scent was fading, but still sweet—still real. He bit into it slowly, letting the juice linger on his tongue.

They are beautiful, he thought. *Just like her.*

Another bite.

I hope she's not upset that I left without saying goodbye.

The last bite vanished too quickly. He let the flavor dissolve in his mouth before setting the nub that was left of his pencil down next to the sketchbook.

Then it came—the grinding.

It started low, like it always did—but this time it felt closer, angrier. A monster made of steel and teeth, tearing its way through the walls.

The gears shrieked.

They scraped like metal bones twisting inside a dying beast, echoing off every surface of the rafters.

Valentino flinched.

It was louder up here—amplified in the metal crawlspace like it was screaming straight into his skull.

He curled his arms around his ears, pressing hard.

But it didn't help.

It never helped.

The sound reminded him where he was. What he was hiding from.

He waited for it to finish.

Then turned off the lamp.

Darkness rushed in like a wave.

I don't want a repeat of the last one.

The Architect's voice echoed in his mind—sharp, cold, full of implication.

Valentino lay down on the thin mat, curled around his pack like it could protect him from the weight of it all.

"No, Father," he whispered, the words barely audible even to himself. "Neither do I."

A single tear slid down his cheek.

He didn't stop it.

As the last echoes of the grinding finally died, Valentino let the silence fold in around him—

—and let the dark take him.

∞

Valentino was at the beach.

The sun hung low on the horizon, painting the sky in hues of rose and gold. The waves rolled in, slow and rhythmic, like the world had finally exhaled.

A woman swam in the surf—dipping beneath the waves, rising again with effortless grace. Her laughter drifted across the water, light and free.

Rachel.

He smiled as he watched her, knees drawn up, bare feet buried in the sand.

For a moment, everything was still.

Then—

"What did I tell you?" came a voice behind him.

Cold. Sharp. Familiar.

The Architect.

Valentino's smile vanished. He looked up at the figure looming above him, then back to the water—

Where Marcus was already dragging Rachel from the waves by her hair.

"No—RACHEL!"

She screamed as she hit the sand, limbs flailing.

"VAL!" she cried, trying to rise.

Valentino scrambled to his feet, heart slamming against his ribs.

"Please, Father!" he shouted. "I haven't told her anything!"

The Architect tilted his head, expression unreadable.

"You haven't told her anything..." he said softly—then his mouth curled. "Yet."

"You've grown attached," he added, stepping closer. "You've grown weak. You've forgotten the rules."

He gestured, and Marcus shoved Rachel back to the ground.

"This ends now."

"NO!" Valentino broke into a sprint, sand flying behind him. "MARCUS—PLEASE!"

But Marcus just grinned.

Then leaned close to Rachel's ear and whispered something Valentino couldn't hear.

Rachel's head snapped up. Her eyes locked with his.

"VAL!" she screamed, panicked. "Valentino—!"

The Architect nodded once.

And Marcus slit her throat.

Rachel crumpled to the sand just as Valentino reached her.

He dropped to his knees, catching her in his arms as her blood soaked the earth beneath them.

"Val..." she choked, eyes wide with terror. "Your... your br—"

Her words gurgled into silence.

Then she was still.

Valentino wailed, rocking her body. He pressed his forehead to hers, breath hitching as the grief tore through him.

Her hair was damp and short, streaked with blood.
He ran a shaking hand through it—
And it changed.
Blonde gave way to black.
Strands lengthened, curling into waves beneath his fingers.
Her face shifted too—jawline softening, brows narrowing.
Her lifeless features began to move.
To breathe.
To become Pandora.
Valentino jerked back, eyes wide in horror.
But he couldn't let go.
He couldn't stop the change.
The Architect's voice boomed again, now directly above him—
"THIS IS YOUR FINAL WARNING—NO ATTACHMENTS!"

∞

Valentino woke with a jolt.

He was panting—drenched in sweat, his heart still galloping from the dream. The scream had died in his throat, but its echo lingered in his chest.

He reached blindly for the lamp and clicked it on.

Dim, amber light pushed back the shadows.

He blinked down at the tight space around him—sheet metal, blackout cloth, fractured bars—and let out a slow breath.

Just another dream.

He sat up, pulled the new backpack close, and unzipped the top flap. His fingers rummaged quickly—searching.

Then—plastic.

He pulled out a small white bottle and grinned.

"Yes," he whispered. "At least he remembered this time."

He shook the pills in his hand, then glanced around his crawlspace.

He grabbed a bottle of water, popped the lid on the pills, and downed three with a long gulp. The bitterness burned briefly at the back of his throat—but then the tightness in his chest began to fade. His breathing evened out. The trembling in his hands dulled.

He leaned back against the wall, exhaling hard.

His fingers returned to the backpack.

One by one, he pulled out bags of jerky.

Two. Four. Seven. Ten.

"How long does he think I'm going to be here?" Valentino muttered. He stared at the growing pile, then shook his head.

"No… Father wouldn't do that to me. Not in this place…"

A pause.

He looked down at the packs again.

"This is just in case," he said firmly, like saying it aloud might make it true.

He tore open one of the bags and pulled out a piece. Bit into it.

Chewed.

"Not bad," he said with his mouth full. "Much better than the last batch."

He kept chewing, the taste grounding him. Familiar. Salty. Safe.

For now.

∞

Dr. Lancet

Dr. Lancet brushed her teeth for the fifth time.

The mint was sharp, almost burning. She welcomed it. Let it bite the inside of her cheeks. Let it drown out the thoughts she didn't want to follow.

She spat, rinsed, stared at her reflection.

Just her.

No one else in the mirror.

She smiled faintly. Relief, maybe.

But somewhere—deep in her gut—a small knot twisted. Tight and unspoken.

She ignored it.

She brushed her hair slowly. Wrapped the towel tighter around herself. Took a deep breath.

And stepped out of the bathroom.

"You took longer than usual," The Warden said, his voice coated in suspicion.

Dr. Lancet didn't answer.

"Take off your towel," he said.

She blinked. "What?"

"Take it off," he repeated, firmer. "I need to make sure you're not hiding anything. Anything you could… hurt yourself with."

His voice dipped into something darker. A low growl that prickled her skin.

Dr. Lancet dropped the towel without a word.

He circled her slowly.

His eyes didn't blink.

One hand rubbed the front of his jeans as he took her in.

"Against the wall," he said.

She walked to it immediately.

Like muscle memory.

He moved in behind her, grabbing her wrists, guiding her hands to the wall.

"Stay."

She nodded.

He leaned in. Bit the back of her neck.

A moan slipped from her lips before she could catch it.

"Quiet," he snapped.

Another nod.

His hands roamed—deliberate, thorough. Mapping every inch of her like he owned the terrain.

When he reached her waist, he used his foot to shove her legs further apart.

"Wyatt... I..." she tried to speak.

He grabbed a fistful of her hair, yanking her head back.

"I said *be quiet*."

Her breath hitched.

Her eyes flicked to the mirror across the room.

Michael was there.

Smiling.

Holding the control.

She looked away.

Pressed her cheek to the wall.

The Warden unzipped his jeans.

Do as he says... She told herself as she smirked. *You know you love this...*

He entered her roughly—without pause, without tenderness.

Dr. Lancet gasped at the sharp, familiar stretch. Pain first.

Then heat.

She didn't move. Didn't speak.

Not yet.

His grip on her hips was bruising, anchoring her to him as he set a punishing rhythm. The slap of flesh filled the room, harsh and relentless. Her palms flattened harder against the wall, her breath catching with each thrust.

"Don't move," he growled.

She obeyed.

But her body trembled.

With need.

With restraint.

Every inch of him pressed into her—his hands, his breath, his heat. He leaned forward and bit her shoulder, dragging his teeth slowly over her skin until she whimpered.

"Quiet," he hissed, voice like a blade against silk.

She bit her lip, her moan stifled.

The pain fed the pleasure. It always did. It twisted together—heat and hurt, control and hunger.

He reached around and pinched her nipple, hard enough to make her jerk.

"Don't test me."

She didn't answer.

But she smiled against the wall.

He rammed into her deeper. Harder. Her body opened to him, soaking with need. Every strike sent shockwaves up her spine—and still she didn't move, didn't beg, didn't break.

She loved this too.

His voice dropped, low and feral in her ear. "You feel that?"

She moaned softly. A nod.

"Say it."

"You," she breathed. "I feel you."

His hand slid down between her legs—slick, sensitive, desperate.

She gasped when his fingers found her, and she tried to shift her body.

He slapped her ass in warning.

"I said don't move."

She whimpered. Nodded. Obeyed.

And when she finally came—silent, shaking—he wasn't far behind.

He groaned, his release hot inside her, his hands never loosening from her waist until it was done.

Only then did he let go.

Only then did he whisper, low and pleased:

"You can move now."

Dr. Lancet stepped away from the wall, breathing hard, legs shaky, a grin ghosting the corner of her mouth.

She didn't look at him.

She just picked up her towel and walked back into the bathroom, every inch of her aching and satisfied.

∞

Shabina

Shabina wandered the corridors of Augmentation Bay for hours, footsteps echoing through dimly lit halls.

They have to be here somewhere, she told herself for the hundredth time. *Father is right. They can't have just disappeared.*

She turned down a narrower corridor, the air colder here, heavier. As she neared the stairs leading to the Detachment Gibbets, a shiver crept up her spine.

This place gives me the creeps.

She paused at the base of the staircase, eyeing the stone steps that twisted upward like a spine carved into the wall.

"You there," she said, addressing the Black Enforcer standing guard at the bottom. "Accompany me upstairs."

The Enforcer nodded silently and fell in line beside her.

They began the climb.

Shabina cleared her throat, trying to distract herself from the rising chill. "I bet you had big dreams," she said. "Of being a Crimson Enforcer. Or perhaps a Pearl? Instead, you're stuck here. In this... tomb."

The Black Enforcer didn't respond at first.

Then they stopped on the landing and turned slightly toward her.

"Just like you."

Shabina blinked.

That stung more than it should have.

"Just like me," she echoed, trying to make light of it. Her smile didn't quite land. "When did you start?"

"A week ago," the Enforcer said as they began the final flight.

Shabina's fingers tightened around the small device in her pocket.

She swallowed hard. "Just like me," she said again, more to herself this time.

"Just like you."

They reached the top. The door to the Gibbets stood before them—metal, bolted, and slightly ajar.

Shabina pulled a small pair of glasses from her coat and pressed the button hidden beneath one of the arms. A faint light flickered in the lens.

The Enforcer pushed the door open.

She stepped inside.

And the cold swallowed her whole.

Shabina's heartbeat quickened, her breath coming in short, shallow bursts.

I can't do this.

The thought struck hard, uninvited—and unwelcome.

Then a hand landed gently on her shoulder.

She flinched with a small squeak, her whole body locking up.

From the darkness around her, the voices stirred.

"Quiet…"

"Keep still…"

"Shut… up…"

The cageys moaned from their gibbets—hoarse, broken voices dragging through the dark like ghosts being stirred.

Shabina staggered back and bumped into the Black Enforcer's chest. They didn't push her away. They didn't bark at her.

They simply said, with surprising calm, "Your glasses."

The steadiness in their voice made her pause. She looked up, expecting cold detachment—but there was something softer behind the visor. Something careful.

She nodded. She could feel the warmth of them, even through the armor. It startled her.

She slipped the glasses on.

And the world changed.

Green and yellow outlines flickered to life—bars, frames, low-hung gibbets. Movement. Heatless silhouettes curled or shifting inside their metal prisons. The darkness became visible, but not less threatening.

In fact, it made everything worse.

The faces. The twitching hands. The too-long stares from sunken eyes.

Shabina drew a slow breath and took her first step forward.

The sound of her boots echoed more than it should've. The Black Enforcer followed silently, never falling more than a pace behind her.

She glanced back once—they weren't looking around like she was.

They were watching her.

Not like the others would.

Not with hunger.

With... something else.

Something she couldn't name.

It wasn't unpleasant.

She blinked and turned back around.

Focus.

"Cold in here," she muttered, trying to shake the shiver from her neck.

"It's always like this," they replied. "You get used to it."

Their voice was deeper than most Enforcers'. Slower. Not sharp like the others.

She didn't know why, but it helped.

She walked on—past the first row, then the second—heart pounding like a drum.

"I bet you wanted to be a Crimson," she said suddenly, trying to fill the silence. "Or a Pearl. Not... this."

There was a pause.

"Maybe," they said. "But some of us were meant for quieter things."

Their words sat strangely in her ears.

Not menacing. Not cruel. Just... present.

Then they added, softer, "That doesn't mean we don't see what happens here."

Shabina turned her head slightly, glancing at them again over her shoulder.

They were closer than before.

Watching her.

She felt her stomach twist—not with fear.

With something else.

It made her throat tighten. She turned back quickly, face warm, glad the glasses covered most of her expression.

What's wrong with me?

The gibbets creaked softly ahead. Somewhere in the dark, a cagey whispered:

"Still looking… still watching…"

The Enforcer's steps followed behind her—silent, steady.

And she kept moving.

Even if she didn't understand why her pulse had changed.

"How old are you?" Shabina asked, her voice quieter than before.

The Black Enforcer didn't answer.

She looked ahead again, watching the eerie glow of her glasses light the rows of gibbets like skeletons in stasis.

She reached the halfway point, then stopped.

"You're not very talkative, are you?" she asked, turning back toward them.

The Enforcer shrugged. "There's not much to talk about."

Shabina smirked faintly. There was something in the way they said it—soft, even-tempered. Not sharp like the others.

"Are you scared?" she asked, teasing them now, trying to lighten the tension curling in her chest.

A loud clanging rang out from deeper in the chamber. Metal on metal. Sudden. Unnerving.

The cageys stirred.

"Quiet…"

"Silence…"

"Don't speak…"

The voices hissed like a wind coming through rusted teeth.

Shabina squeaked and leapt forward—straight into the Black Enforcer's chest.

They chuckled—just once. It wasn't mocking.

"Are you scared?" they asked.

Shabina looked up and gave the smallest nod, cheeks warming instantly. She didn't know why they made her feel this way. Or why standing this close to them suddenly felt safe.

"Not like me," the Enforcer said gently, resting a hand on her shoulder. "It's okay… I've got you."

The words weren't said like orders. They were soft. Reassuring.

They guided her gently behind them with one hand.

Another clang echoed through the space—closer now.

Shabina instinctively pressed up against the Enforcer's back. The armor was cold, rough, and impersonal—but she stayed there. Their presence made the air feel more solid, more breathable.

Her fingers brushed lightly against the back seam of their armor. She told herself it was just for balance.

The groaning of the cageys grew louder, more chaotic. A muttering wall of broken sound.

Another crash.

Just ahead of them.

The Enforcer shifted, stepping forward slightly, and the movement jostled Shabina. She peeked around their shoulder—

And then it happened.

The gibbet to their right shook violently, chains clattering.

A blur of fur launched from the shadows.

Prison Cat.

The animal hissed and pounced, swiping at Shabina's face before she could duck. Her glasses flew off. Pain bloomed across her cheek in three deep gashes.

"Zoti—!" she cried, stumbling backward.

The Black Enforcer lunged, trying to grab the creature—but it was too fast. The cat vanished between the gibbets before their hand even closed.

When they turned around, Shabina was on the floor, crumpled.

One hand clutched the side of her face, blood already soaking through her fingers.

The other scraped desperately across the floor, searching for the glasses. Her breathing was rapid, nearly hyperventilating. Silent tears tracked down her face.

The Enforcer crouched immediately, scanning the ground. They found the glasses, lifted them—careful, deliberate.

The small whirring motor had gone quiet.

They looked down at her—not as a soldier.

As something else.

And Shabina, still clutching her face, looked up at them.

Something passed between them. Something trembling.

And not all of it was fear.

"They're broken," they said, holding up the glasses.

Shabina's heart lurched. "No, no, no…" she whispered, panic flooding back in.

She was on the ground, one hand clutching her cheek, the other pressed tight to her chest. She couldn't seem to catch her breath.

The Black Enforcer kneeled beside her and gently took the hand trembling at her chest.

She yelped in surprise.

The cageys moaned in response—low, guttural echoes rising from the gibbets.

"Listen to me," they said, their voice steady—but still distorted by the Enforcer's modulator.

"That voice distorter doesn't help," Shabina gasped. "You all sound like a creepy hive mind."

The Black Enforcer chuckled. Then came a soft click.

"Is this better?" he asked.

The distortion vanished.

Their real voice came through—low, warm, male.

Shabina blinked. "Much," she breathed. "Much better."

"Close your eyes," he said.

"What?"

"Trust me."

Hesitantly, she closed them.

"Do you remember the way we walked?" he asked.

Her breathing quickened again. She didn't answer.

He gently laid his gun on the ground and kept his other hand wrapped around hers.

"What's your name?"

"Shabina," she said through uneven, panicked breaths.

"Shabina…" His voice softened. She liked the sound of his voice. "I need you to breathe for me. Just breathe."

He inhaled deeply, exaggerated. Slowly. Then again.

Shabina mirrored him. Tentatively at first. Then deeper.

In… out. In… out.

The tremble in her fingers began to fade.

When her breathing steadied, he asked again, "Do you remember the way we walked?"

"I… I think so," she whispered.

"Good. I'm going to help you stand now. Okay?"

She nodded, eyes still shut.

He helped her to her feet with gentle strength. She clung to his hand. He retrieved his gun, slinging it behind his back.

"I'm going to lead you back the exact same way," he said. "Same steps. Same rhythm. You just follow me. I've got you."

Shabina nodded again.

Her hand was still shaking.

But as they walked, his grip stayed steady.

And eventually, hers did too.

"Please don't mention this to anyone," she said quietly. Embarrassed. Vulnerable.

"I won't," the Black Enforcer said. And she believed him.

"What's your name?" she asked after a moment.

He hesitated. "I'm… not supposed to tell anyone."

But not rushed.

His mouth was warm, steady, and she sank into it like she'd been waiting for it without knowing.

A blissful eternity.

A single breath that stretched too long.

Then—

Voices.

Footsteps just outside the door.

Mather broke the kiss and stepped back quickly. He reattached the mouthpiece of his helmet with a soft click—just in time.

The door swung open.

"Sir," Mather said, nodding curtly.

The Warden stepped in, flanked by a Pearl Enforcer and a dozen Black Enforcers. His eyes swept the room before landing on Shabina.

He tilted his head, feigning surprise.

"My goodness, child," he said smoothly. "What have you done to your face?"

"A cat, sir," Mather answered. "Lurking somewhere in the roof."

The Warden's mouth curved into a smirk.

"Ah yes… my Tortie girl. She's a mischievous one. Watch out for her."

Shabina turned, blinking up at Mather, then back at The Warden.

"She's *your* cat?" she asked through clenched teeth.

"Yes," The Warden replied, his tone sharpening as he straightened his stance. "Is that a problem?"

Shabina shook her head. "No, sir… sorry."

Without another word, she rushed past the others and into the stairwell, still holding her cheek.

The door shut behind her.

"Shabina… are you okay?" Mather's voice came through the modulator now—distorted, mechanical again.

The change startled her. She flinched.

"Sorry," Mather added, with a small shrug. "I have to wear it out here."

∞

Dr. Zygote

Dr. Zygote sat alone in his surgery, flipping through the thick stack of files he'd taken from The Cell. His fingers trembled slightly as he lifted the next dossier from the pile.

"You're all perfect," he murmured. "Especially you."

He traced the label on the folder with a twisted smile. IM-1.

"They're going to be everything I ever dreamed of... everything Shabina and Maya weren't."

The door hissed open behind him.

"Doctor," came Shabina's voice.

Zygote turned, the expression on his face flattening into disinterest.

"I... I need your help," she said.

A Black Enforcer stepped in behind her. Helmet sealed. Visor blank. Silent.

Zygote's eyes lingered on them for a beat too long before he moved.

"What happened?" he asked, noting the blood slicking through Shabina's fingers.

"The cat," she muttered.

He didn't need more detail.

"Ah," he said, opening a drawer and retrieving antiseptic and gauze. "She's gotten me too."

He angled his neck, exposing a thin white scar trailing beneath his collarbone. "Right here. Nasty little thing."

Shabina dropped her hand. Three fresh gashes slashed across her cheek—red and raw.

"Will it scar?" she asked quietly.

"Most likely," Zygote replied, already dabbing at the wound. "But don't worry. Looks don't matter in your line of work."

He gave a faint, humorless smirk. "I mean... look at Evelyn."

Shabina flinched but didn't speak.

The Enforcer behind her remained still. Watching. Waiting.

Zygote finished with a strip of bandage and stepped back.

"There," he said. "Done."

Shabina nodded and turned away without another word. The Enforcer fell into step behind her, silent as a shadow.

Zygote watched them leave, expression unreadable.

He didn't know who that Enforcer was.

He didn't like not knowing.

As the door sealed shut behind them, he murmured, "What's going on there?"

His gaze dropped to the bloodied gauze in the bin.

Then, slowly, back to the IM-1 file.

And he frowned.

∞

Shabina

Shabina walked the corridors once more, her steps measured, searching. The sterile air pressed in around her, humming with quiet menace.

Mather followed at her side, silent.

By the time they finished their second lap around the prison's lower levels, he finally spoke.

"What are you doing?"

"I've... lost Dr. Lancet," she said, eyes scanning every shadow. "I'm trying to find her."

Mather stopped walking. "Dr. Lancet?"

She turned to him, nodding. "Why... what do you know?"

He glanced both ways down the corridor, voice dropping as he leaned slightly closer.

"I've heard whispers from the other Enforcers," he said. "Rumors."

"Rumors?"

"That she's being kept prisoner," Mather said, his voice now barely more than a breath. "In a hidden bedroom. Behind The Warden's office."

Shabina stared at him. "A hidden bedroom?" Her lips curled into a shaky laugh. "You're saying The Warden is keeping her... prisoner?"

"Shh!" Mather hissed. "Someone might hear."

Her laughter died.

They walked again. Quieter now. Past the sealed med bays. Past the flickering lights. Their steps echoed down empty corridors lined with doors that hadn't opened in weeks.

"How do I get in?" she asked.

"You don't," Mather snapped.

Shabina glanced up at him. "What do you mean?"

"I mean, don't try. Don't even think about it."

She stopped. "Mather—"

"I'm serious, Shabina." He turned to face her fully, his voice shaking slightly through the filter. "That room... that man... He's not like the others. If he's hiding her in there, it's not for anything good."

"I have to know."

"No, you don't," Mather said, more forcefully now. "You want to know. But if you go in there, you won't come out. Or if you do, you won't be the same."

His fists clenched at his sides. The armor groaned with the motion.

"I've heard what happens to people who get too close to The Warden. He's dangerous, Shabina. He doesn't forget. He doesn't forgive."

She looked at him, and for a moment, something flickered behind her eyes—fear, maybe.

"I need to find her," she said quietly.

"No, you need to stay alive," Mather replied. "You don't understand what he's capable of."

Shabina stepped forward, her voice soft.

"If she really is in there. I have to find out."

Mather shook his head. "And who's going to help you if you end up locked in beside her?"

Silence stretched between them.

They walked again—laps four and five now. The corridors blurred past. Still no sign of Dr. Lancet. No answers. Just the buzz of lights and the weight of what neither of them wanted to say.

At the end of the fifth lap, Shabina slowed.

Her gaze drifted down the long, dark corridor ahead. The one that led to The Warden's office.

"Maybe the rumors are true," she murmured. "Maybe he really did lock her in there."

"Promise me you'll stay away," Mather said. "Promise me, Shabina. Please."

She looked at him, truly looked this time.

"I don't think I can."

Mather stepped forward, grabbing her arm. "Then let me go. Let me check."

She shook her head. "This is something I have to do."

She hesitated. Then reached up and pressed a gentle kiss to the edge of his faceplate.

"Keep watch. And come find me if I don't come back?"

Mather took her hand in his. "No matter what."

Shabina squeezed once.

Then turned.

And walked down the corridor toward The Warden's office—step by step, into the dark.

∞

Dr. Lancet

304

Dr. Lancet stood before the mirror, pale and trembling, her nightdress stained at the seams with deep red. Her fingers hovered over the fresh sutures carved across her torso.

"My organs," she whispered, voice shaking. "Mine."

She traced the line of her scar, fingertip trembling along the uneven ridge. The reflection rippled slightly, though the room behind her was still.

Then she saw him.

Michael.

Lurking behind her in the mirror.

He didn't blink. He didn't move. Just stood there—his smile impossibly wide, his skin ashen and waxy.

I need to get out of here. Her thoughts spiraled. *Why can't I move myself?... How is he doing this?*

Her legs refused to respond. Her arms felt numb.

Michael's grin widened. Slowly, deliberately, he lifted his hands to his chest and, with gruesome calm, pulled his ribs apart like opening a cabinet. Bone cracked. Flesh split. It was silent, but she could *feel* it.

"Mine," he growled.

Dr. Lancet's hands rose of their own accord, mimicking his motion. Her fingers trembled, resisting—barely. But the pull was too strong.

Her nails dug into the healing wound.

She screamed.

Stitches snapped one by one, blood weeping down her abdomen. She tore at herself, sobbing, powerless, as if Michael's reflection had become her puppeteer.

And then—

CLUNK.

The wall behind her groaned and hissed open.

"EVELYN!" Shabina screamed as she burst through, eyes wild, face pale.

She launched herself at Dr. Lancet, grabbing her wrists. "Stop! STOP! You're hurting yourself!"

But Dr. Lancet only laughed—a sharp, feral sound. Her hands writhed under Shabina's grip, slippery with blood. She didn't even seem to see her.

Then, she pulled a shard of glass, slick and crimson, from the gown pocket.

"No—Evelyn, no!"

Shabina stumbled back, too slow.

The mirror shard slashed across her face.

Pain bloomed white-hot as blood streaked down her cheek. She cried out, falling hard onto the cold floor.

Dr. Lancet advanced, eyes alight with manic fire. She raised the shard again.

And then—

Mather burst through the door, tackled her mid-lunge. They slammed into the floor.

Dr. Lancet shrieked beneath him, laughing, thrashing like an animal. Her limbs contorted, joints popping. She rolled, cracked her neck, and rose unnaturally fast.

Then she ran.

Straight at Shabina.

Her body twisted as she charged, mouth open in a soundless scream.

Shabina curled into herself, arms over her head, bracing for the impact.

BANG.

A deafening blast ripped through the room.

The sound echoed inside her skull, replaced by a high-pitched ringing.

Through the sliver of vision between her arms, Shabina saw Dr. Lancet falter—then collapse.

A gaping, pulpy hole marked the center of her chest, still smoking from the beanbag shot. She twitched as she fell, blood pooling beneath her.

"My organs…" Dr. Lancet choked. Her voice gurgled. "My… organs…"

She turned her head, barely, to the mirror.

Michael stood above her in the glass, his face calm, watching her suffer.

"Shush," he whispered. "You don't want your last moments to be you crying like a baby... Do you?"

Dr. Lancet howled. Her fingers clawed at the wound, digging deeper, heedless of pain. "MINE!" she wailed. "MINE!"

Mather rushed to Shabina, crouched and grabbed her arm. "We need to leave. Now."

Shabina couldn't stop staring. Blood everywhere. Lancet's broken body twisting, twitching—tearing.

"Shabina! NOW!"

She snapped to life.

Together, they stumbled back through the false wall. Mather hit the control on The Warden's desk, and the hidden passage began to seal shut.

Shabina looked back one last time—just as Dr. Lancet gave one final twitch.

Then nothing.

Only blood, and silence.

The wall hissed closed.

∞

Shabina

Shabina's legs trembled as they moved down the corridor. Her face stung, blood still warm on her cheek, but she didn't lift a hand to stop it. Her eyes were locked on the ground. Red smeared across her palms. Her breath hitched.

"What are we supposed to do, Mather?" she whispered, her voice cracking under the weight of it. "You *killed* her!"

"Shush." Mather raised a gloved finger to the mouthpiece of his helmet. "We don't say a word to anyone about this, okay?"

She looked up at him, eyes wide, lips trembling. Then she nodded.

"What if…" she started, but Mather cut her off.

"Not even to each other," he said, his voice colder now. "Not now."

He glanced up and down the corridor. Empty.

"Now go home, Shabina."

She stopped walking. "Mather… I…"

Something in his tone had shifted. It wasn't the warmth from earlier. He felt distant now—harder.

Mather paused, then exhaled through the modulator.

"I'm sorry," he said, quieter this time. "Are you okay?"

She gave the smallest nod.

"Why isn't anyone coming?" she asked, voice trembling as she looked around. The hallway was still, silent, untouched. Not even an echo.

"I heard The Warden had that room soundproofed…" He trailed off. "I guess that rumor's true too."

Shabina wrapped her arms around herself.

"Mather," she whispered, "I… I live here. Under the prison."

She stared at the floor.

"Like I said… No one can know about…" She hesitated. Her voice dropped lower. "About my father."

She looked up, eyes pleading.

"So I live in an abandoned mineshaft. There are hundreds of them. Old service tunnels no one uses anymore."

Mather didn't speak.

"Please," she said, voice fragile. "Say something."

A long silence.

Then—

"Show me."

Shabina stared at him for a moment, uncertain. Then she gave a small nod and turned.

They moved down a narrow corridor, darker than the others, the lights overhead flickering intermittently. At the end, a blank concrete wall waited—featureless, still.

She reached forward and pulled a thin, rusted piece of pipe from a crevice, then used it to press inward on a specific panel.

With a faint *click,* the section of wall shifted.

"Down here," she whispered, glancing over her shoulder.

Then she slid inside.

Mather followed Shabina down a long, narrow flight of stairs. The air grew cooler with every step, thick with earth and silence. Every so often, a flickering torch cast a dim pool of light over the path, throwing their shadows in warped, stretching shapes along the walls.

"After so many years," Shabina whispered, "most of these old tunnels have been forgotten. So it's the perfect place to stay hidden."

Mather scanned the jagged walls, listening to the gravel crunch beneath his boots. "How long have you lived here?"

They reached the end of a carved-out tunnel. A small cavity had been hollowed from the rock, just large enough to fit a narrow bed, a leaning wardrobe, and a tattered armchair that sagged beneath its own weight. The ceiling hung low. Dust floated in the air like suspended ash.

"Since I left The Farm," Shabina said softly. "It's not much… but it's home."

Mather's voice rose, sharper than she expected. "I thought Dr. Zygote would've given you better than this!"

Shabina flinched and stepped back. The heat in his tone startled her.

Mather immediately stopped and held up his hands. "I'm sorry. Hold on."

He leaned his gun against the wall and reached up to his helmet. "Are you sure it's safe?"

Shabina nodded.

Mather unclipped the locks and lifted the helmet free. The balaclava came next, revealing his fiery red hair, damp with sweat, falling slightly into his eyes.

Soft flickering light illuminated his face—his deep hazel eyes, angular cheekbones, and chiseled jawline.

Shabina froze.

He's… handsome.

Mather noticed the pause. He shifted awkwardly.

"Are you… disappointed?" he asked.

Shabina blinked, then slowly reached out and took his hand. "No. Not at all… I'm just… nervous."

He smiled faintly. "What are you nervous about?"

"I've lived here since I left The Farm," she said, voice small. "*Alone.*" She looked up at him. "I've never had a visitor. A friend. A man."

Mather exhaled, his voice quiet. "I… I understand."

He glanced away, a slight blush rising to his cheeks. "Neither have I. Had a woman, I mean."

The two stood in silence, the closeness between them delicate and new.

"How about we just sit down," Mather offered gently, "talk a while. Get to know each other."

Shabina smiled. "I think I'd like that. But… can you even sit in that?" She gestured to the bulky armor still strapped to his torso, arms, and legs.

Mather chuckled. "I suppose I'm going to need your help."

Piece by piece, she helped him unclip the remaining plates—forearms, thigh guards, chest piece. With each section gone, he seemed to shrink just slightly, human beneath all that weight.

"What about work?" she asked. "Won't someone notice you're missing?"

He shook his head as she set the last of the armor aside. "No. My shift ended when we left the roof. We have some time."

He sat on the armchair with a sigh of relief, and Shabina settled gently onto the edge of her bed.

"Uh…" she started, then paused. Her hands fidgeted in her lap. "I don't really know what to say."

Mather laughed softly. "It was easier upstairs."

Shabina dropped her head. "Sorry," she whispered—and then she cried.

"Hey, whoa," Mather stood and moved to her. "I was only joking."

"It's not that," she said, wiping at her tears with the heel of her hand. "I just… Why are you here?"

He sat beside her and placed an arm gently around her shoulders.

"You invited me, silly," he said with a crooked smile, trying to lighten the mood.

But Shabina kept crying.

"Tell me what's going on," Mather said gently. "Please."

"You killed her, Mather," Shabina said finally. "You killed Dr. Lancet. What if there are cameras in there?"

Mather let out a slow breath. "There are no cameras in Augmentation Bay, Shabina," he said. "There isn't enough power. Everyone who works here knows that."

Shabina shuddered. "I didn't think there'd be enough power for that… that sex dungeon hidden in the walls," she said. "But there it was. What do we do now, Mather?"

"We go to work like normal," he said. "Act like nothing happened. They don't know it was us."

Shabina sniffled. "Even if they find out… you were protecting me. They can't go too hard on you… can they?"

Mather pulled her into a tighter hug. "I don't know," he admitted. "But I'd do it again. No matter what."

His eyes drifted to the bandage on her cheek—half-saturated with fresh blood.

"Let me clean your wound."

He stood and walked back to his armor, pressing the Enforcer insignia at the chest. A small hatch popped open with a hiss, revealing a compact first aid kit.

"Here's a nifty little trick only us Enforcers know about," he said, returning to her side. "Comes in handy more than you'd think."

He sat beside her again and gently peeled away the bloodied bandage, revealing the gash that stretched over the three thinner scars beneath— the ones from the cat.

He frowned. "Same spot," he muttered. "It's like she aimed for it."

Shabina winced slightly as he cleaned the wound with practiced care.

The air between them went still—thick with pain, silence, and something unspoken.

∞

The Warden

"EVELYN!"

The Warden's voice echoed through the room like a war cry, full of rage, confusion, and something eerily close to panic. He dropped to his knees beside Dr. Lancet's twisted, bloodied form and grabbed her by the shoulders, shaking her violently.

"EVELYN, WAKE UP!"

Her head lolled back, mouth slightly agape, blood drying at the corners of her lips. Her chest, torn open and ragged, no longer rose or fell.

The Warden froze.

Then slowly, he let her go. Her body hit the ground with a sickening thud, limbs splaying unnaturally.

He stumbled to his feet, pacing in tight circles above her.

"Fuck… what do I do now?" he muttered, dragging his hands through his hair. "You fucking idiot," he spat, glaring down at her lifeless form. "How the fuck did you even do that to yourself?"

His eyes scanned her ruined chest, the ragged incision still leaking blood.

His lip curled.

Then something caught his eye. Embedded in the wound—partially buried beneath blood and broken flesh—was something foreign. Something man-made.

"What's this?" he muttered.

He reached into the gaping cavity with gloved fingers and pulled it free. It was misshapen, scorched, slick with blood.

A beanbag round.

He stared at it for a long time, face unreadable. Then his jaw clenched, eyes darkening.

"So one of my Enforcers did this to you," he growled. "You didn't die alone down here… someone was with you."

He looked up, eyes scanning the sealed walls around him. "Someone *was in here.*"

He rose, gripping the beanbag so tightly his knuckles turned white.

"Don't worry, Evelyn…" he said, voice low and venomous. "I'll find whomever it was… and I'll make them pay."

His gaze dropped back down to her.

She lay in a pool of blood, her nightdress hiked slightly from her final spasms. Her face, though lifeless, still wore the tension of her final moments. Her body, though damaged, was exposed enough to stir something twisted behind his eyes.

The Warden crouched beside her again, his expression shifting into something grotesquely tender.

"Even in death," he murmured, voice warped with hunger, "you're still… sexy."

He bit his lip, tilting his head.

"I know it's wrong," he whispered as he reached down, slowly unzipping his jeans. "But I won't say anything if you don't."

He slid his hand along the fabric of her nightdress, pushing it up.

And he smiled.

∞

Dr. Zygote

"Fuck," The Warden muttered, his head dropping into his hands. His voice cracked with something rare—panic.

"Fuck."

Dr. Zygote cleared his throat from the doorway.

The Warden looked up, eyes bloodshot and unfocused.

"Is everything all right?" Dr. Zygote asked carefully.

The Warden's voice was low. "Zayne… close the door."

He hesitated.

"Lock it," The Warden added.

Dr. Zygote entered and turned the bolt. The click echoed like a gunshot.

He moved toward the desk and sat down, folding his hands neatly in front of him. "Tell me what's going on, sir."

The Warden exhaled slowly, as though preparing to vomit his sins. Then he stood, walked around the desk, and pressed a button underneath it.

A soft hiss followed.

Then the wall slid open.

Zygote stood, the chair scraping behind him.

His breath caught. "No…"

The hidden chamber revealed itself—opulent, grotesque, silent. His eyes landed first on the wide bloodstain beneath the broken mirror. A deep, sprawling pool, now partially dried, glinting under the overhead light.

Shabina was right.

"I… I need your help, Zayne," The Warden said, voice unsteady. "It's Evelyn."

He gestured toward the open bathroom door. Dr. Zygote followed him in, footsteps sticking slightly against the floor.

Dr. Lancet's body lay in the bathtub, stiff, twisted, her chest a gaping ruin. The water around her was dark and thick. A few strands of blood-matted hair clung to her face.

"This needs to be kept quiet until I can find out who it was," The Warden said. "All I know is it was one of my Enforcers. If anyone finds out before they're punished... there'll be a riot. Or worse."

He looked down at her, something unreadable in his expression. "Can your friend help with... this?"

Zygote blinked. "Sorry, sir. I haven't heard from him in a while now."

"FUCK!" The Warden roared, slamming a fist into the bathroom mirror. A crack split the glass down the center—right where Michael's reflection had once stood.

Dr. Zygote stepped forward. "I can sort it out. Don't worry."

He placed a hand on The Warden's forearm, firm but reassuring.

"Go home. You haven't left this place in weeks. Take a shower. Eat something. Sleep. I'll call you when I'm done."

The Warden hesitated. Then gave a slow, reluctant nod. "Thank you, Zayne. You're a good friend."

Once the door sealed behind him, Dr. Zygote exhaled and turned back toward the tub.

He crouched, studying her slackened face.

"Well, well, well," he murmured. "I told you I'd outlive you, Evelyn. You wrinkled old prune."

He smiled, briefly.

Then his expression faltered.

"It's not fun when she's dead," he muttered.

A pause.

"But it will be fun getting rid of the body."

He stood and returned to the main room. The bloodstain on the carpet was still wet at the edges, the fibers soaked through in a deep pink ring.

Dr. Zygote knelt and ran a gloved hand along the edge of it, frowning.

"This will take some time," he mumbled. He straightened up, wiped his hand on his coat, and left the chamber briefly, returning with a container of cleaning agents and bleach.

But his mind wasn't on the stain.

"Where is she?" he muttered as he scrubbed. "Where the hell is Shabina?"

After searching the prison for nearly an hour and failing to locate her, he gave up.

"She should be doing this," he hissed.

He poured the remainder of the chemical solution across the pale pink stain. The fumes rose like steam.

"If that doesn't work… I'll just move the bed over it."

He stood, stretched his back with a groan, and walked back into the bathroom.

The air was heavier now. Claustrophobic.

Dr. Lancet hadn't moved. Her face was slack. Her limbs stiff. Rigor mortis had set in.

"Well," he muttered, donning gloves and grabbing a sheet from a nearby drawer, "my job just got a lot… harder."

He chuckled.

And set to work.

∞

Shabina

Mather and Shabina had fallen asleep curled together on the narrow bed after hours of quiet conversation. Between stolen glances and laughter, between the unraveling of guarded truths and long-held fears, their exhaustion had finally overtaken them.

When Mather woke, Shabina had nuzzled herself into his chest, one hand resting gently over his heart. His arm was still wrapped protectively around her waist.

He blinked at his watch.

"Shit," he breathed.

Shabina stirred at the sound of his voice, blinking sleepily as she pressed a hand to her cheek, wincing slightly at the tender throb of the healing wound.

"What time is it?" she mumbled, yawning.

"It's almost seven in the morning." Mather swung his legs over the edge of the bed and reached for his armor. He paused, holding his chest plate out to her. "Do you mind?"

Shabina smiled softly and nodded.

They worked in quiet rhythm. She helped him strap in the plates, smoothing her fingers along each latch and buckle with practiced care. It was more intimate than she expected—her touch lingered longer than it needed to. Mather didn't flinch. He didn't rush.

Once he was almost fully suited, Shabina stepped behind the small divider nestled beside the wardrobe. A bit of curtain, hung years ago, gave her the smallest measure of privacy. She changed quickly, tucking her shirt into her waistband, brushing out her hair with her fingers.

They emerged together into the mineshaft, the silence between them no longer awkward, but warm. Familiar. The kind that asked nothing and still said everything.

They climbed the narrow stairs slowly, each footstep echoing off the walls. The early morning chill curled through the tunnel, tugging at Shabina's clothes.

"This prison isn't very secure when you think about it," Mather murmured as they reached the top. "Anyone could wander through these mineshafts and make their way in."

"Or out," Shabina added with a sideways glance.

As they reached the door hidden in the wall, she touched the edge of it, hesitating.

"You should put your helmet on now."

She pushed the door open slightly and peeked through the crack.

When she turned back, Mather was still holding his helmet in one hand, unmoving.

"Mather?" she asked, a touch of confusion in her voice.

He looked at her—really looked—and in one step, he closed the distance between them.

He kissed her.

This time there was no hesitation. No rush. His free hand cradled the side of her face with surprising gentleness, careful not to press the wound. Shabina's breath caught as her fingers curled into his thick, fiery hair, pulling him closer.

She could feel his heart racing beneath the armor. She melted into him, every ounce of tension unraveling between their lips. It wasn't hurried or desperate—it was soft, patient, and real. The world didn't fall away, but for a moment, it didn't matter.

They parted slowly.

Shabina didn't open her eyes right away. She stayed there, forehead resting against his, her hand still tangled in his hair.

Then, silently, they slipped through the hidden door and into the waking corridors of Augmentation Bay.

∞

By the time they reached Dr. Zygote's office, their moment in the mineshaft had already begun to fade behind them.

"Shabina!" Dr. Zygote barked the moment she stepped into the room.

She flinched like a child caught sneaking in after curfew.

"Where have you been?"

"I… uh…" Her heart pounded. "My shift was over," she blurted, the words tumbling out in a breathless rush.

Dr. Zygote's eyes narrowed, flicking between her and Mather, who lingered in the doorway. His gaze sharpened.

"Leave us," he snapped at Mather.

Without a word, Mather gave a stiff nod and turned on his heel, the door hissing shut behind him.

Dr. Zygote watched him go, then slowly turned back to Shabina.

"I have good news," he said, almost sweetly. "It's Evelyn."

Shabina's stomach dropped.

Her breath caught. Her limbs turned to ice.

He knows.

He knows what Mather and I did to her.

She couldn't think. Couldn't breathe.

"What's going on with you?" Dr. Zygote asked, studying her. "You look like you've seen a ghost."

"I… I…" *Say something. Anything.* "I couldn't find her," she squeaked, her voice two octaves too high.

He tilted his head.

"Of course you didn't," he said, drawing out the words. Then his smile returned—sharp, cruel. "Because she's dead."

He leaned in, his voice dropping to a hiss.

"You were right, Shabina… There was something hidden. Not a passage—a room. Wyatt had her in there."

Shabina stared at him, wide-eyed.

This is a test. He's watching my every move. If I say the wrong thing…

Before she could decide what to say, he kept going.

"He claims one of his Enforcers did it. But I'm not so sure…" Dr. Zygote's tone shifted, darker. "I think it was him. Why else would he be so desperate to keep it quiet?"

"So… no one else knows?" Shabina asked, her voice cautious. Her shoulders loosened slightly.

Dr. Zygote smiled like a man who had just won something.

"Secrets are hard to keep here…"

He walked behind the desk, his fingers tapping thoughtfully against the glass. "I'm Wyatt's number one now. *Me.* And I can't have anything ruining that."

Then he looked at her sharply.

"Shabina," he said slowly, "what aren't you telling me?"

Her eyes darted to the surgery doors. The room felt suddenly too small. Too quiet.

"I'm worried about taking over from her," she said quickly. "I'm not ready. I still have more to learn."

Dr. Zygote raised an eyebrow, then gave a short, derisive laugh.

"What are you worried about? Killing one of your patients? They're dead already." He chuckled to himself. "This is how you learn, Shabina. Evelyn wouldn't have taught you anything. She was too paranoid. Thought you were after her job."

"Was it paranoia," Shabina said before she could stop herself, "when she was right?"

The room turned colder.

Dr. Zygote's eyes darkened. His smile vanished.

"Who changed your dressing?" he asked, voice like steel.

"I— I did. This morning." She reached up and touched her cheek, trying to make it look natural. "It was starting to bleed again."

He stared at her for another beat. Then looked away.

"Well, anyway," he muttered. "We'll know who killed her soon enough. The beanbags—each has a serial number. We match it to a gun... and we find her killer."

Shabina's blood turned to ice.

Dr. Zygote looked up just in time to see the color drain from her face.

"What's wrong with you, girl?" he snapped.

"I... I need some Vitality Serum," she said quickly. "My cheek."

Dr. Zygote scoffed, waving her off. "Your generation is so weak. I grew up without that shit. Never had it. Never will."

Shabina stared at the floor.

"Well? Go on," he snapped. "And don't come back until you can be of use."

She turned and fled the room, the door hissing shut behind her. Her breath caught in her throat as she sped down the corridor.

What do I do?

They're going to find him.
They're going to find us.

As Shabina rounded a corner, lost in her racing thoughts, she slammed hard into a Black Enforcer. The collision sent her stumbling backward, landing with a thud against the cold ground.

"Watch where you're going!" the Enforcer snapped, their voice a low, venomous rasp behind the modulator.

Shabina scrambled to her feet, heart pounding. "Sorry, I just—"

"You just weren't looking where you were going," they cut her off, stepping forward.

Shabina instinctively backed up a step.

"Watch your manner," she snapped, trying to inject steel into her voice. "I'm the new Harvest Surgeon."

But the words trembled as they left her lips. The Black Enforcer towered over her, all shadow and steel, and the air between them tightened like a snare.

"Watch yourself," they growled, their fingers tightening on the grip of their gun. "I hear someone killed the old surgeon… You don't want the same thing happening to you… Do you?"

Shabina stood her ground, chin raised. Her fists clenched as she stared into the featureless black slit where their eyes should be.

Then—

"What's going on here?" came another voice from behind.

Another Black Enforcer rounded the corner. The first one didn't turn to face them.

"Just bumped into this lovely young lady here," they said flatly.

Then they tilted their head ever so slightly toward Shabina. Even with the helmet, she could feel it—the weight of their menace. A heatless stare burning through the visor.

"My apologies, Miss."

And with that, the Enforcer walked past her, disappearing around the corner, boots clicking in perfect rhythm.

Shabina stood frozen.

"What was that about?" the second Enforcer asked.

Shabina stared at them blankly.

"It's me," they added, voice softer now. "It's Mather."

Relief flooded her face. She stepped closer to him. "We need to talk… in private."

She didn't wait for confirmation. She turned and hurried down the corridor, glancing over her shoulder as she reached the hidden door that led to her home.

"Quickly," she whispered after checking that no one had followed.

They slipped inside.

∞

Mather stood at the top of the stairs, helmet still on, silent.

In his hand was the gun—the one he had used to shoot Dr. Lancet.

Mather spoke first. "Well… it's probably best if I turn myself in."

Shabina's breath caught.

"I'll tell them I found the room alone," he said, staring at the weapon. "That she was mad. That I had no choice. Maybe The Warden will go easy on me."

He sighed deeply. Not believing his own words.

"No," Shabina said quickly. She stepped toward him and took his hand in hers.

"We're in this together. I won't let you take the fall for me. She would have killed me if it weren't for you."

She met his gaze, her voice trembling. "We'll see The Warden… together."

Mather's shoulders slumped. Slowly, he dropped his arms to his sides. The helmet slipped from his fingers and landed on the ground with a soft *thud.*

"I'm sorry," he whispered, his voice raw. "I never meant for this to happen."

Shabina stepped closer.

"If I hadn't gone in there…" Her voice cracked. "*None* of this would have happened."

She reached up and cradled his face, brushing her thumbs along the sharp line of his jaw.

"I just wish we'd had more time."

She kissed him.

It wasn't frantic. It wasn't desperate.

It was full of sorrow. Of all the things they couldn't say. Her hands tangled in his hair as she pressed into him—one last time, one last warmth.

Then she pulled back, picked up his helmet, and handed it to him.

"No matter what," she said, forcing a smile.

Mather took it from her, nodding. "No matter what."

He fastened the helmet back into place.

Together, they stepped back into the corridor, walking side by side in silence.

Their footsteps echoed against the walls, the sound rhythmic, solemn—like a funeral march.

Shabina wavered slightly, her balance off.

"I need something first," she said, turning down the Light Mile. Her voice was quiet, but resolute. "Wait here."

She paused outside Dr. Lancet's office.

Shabina drained the last bitter sip of Vitality Serum, wincing as the warmth flooded through her limbs. Her body still ached, but the fog in her head began to lift.

She turned to the locked cupboard nestled in the corner—the one she'd seen Dr. Lancet open countless times for a smoke and a drink.

"I know the key is here somewhere," she muttered, rummaging through the left-hand desk drawer.

Her fingers brushed against cool metal.

"Aha," she whispered, pulling free a small, tarnished brass key.

She unlocked the cupboard and pulled out a half-full bottle of vodka and a pack of untouched cigarettes. Pouring herself a glass, she lit a cigarette and took a drag—coughing immediately as the smoke hit the back of her throat.

That's when the door creaked open.

A Black Enforcer stepped inside.

"I thought I asked you to wait," Shabina coughed, eyes watering from the smoke.

But as she stood, she realized—this wasn't Mather.

The Enforcer towered over her.

"Did you think I was someone else?" they asked.

Shabina stayed silent.

"Have you been getting up to no good with an Enforcer?" the voice sneered. "Perhaps that clumsy fucker I saw you with earlier?"

They stepped closer, the room shrinking by the second.

"It's funny…" they continued, their tone turning taunting. "I thought you would have figured it out by now."

The Enforcer grabbed her wrist—tight, bruising.

"But that just shows how gullible you are, *Shabby*."

Her breath caught.

Shabby.

Only one person had ever called her that.

"No," she whispered. "Jaidon?"

The Enforcer nodded and let out a chuckle. "I thought you'd know it was me the moment we saw each other. You always said you'd recognize me in the armor." He tilted his head. "I guess you lied about that too."

He squeezed her wrist tighter. "What did I expect though? You sneak into Command. You weasel your way into Augmentation Bay…"

She yanked at her arm, but his grip didn't loosen. His other hand came up fast, wrapping around her throat.

"You disappeared on me once before, *Shabby*. I won't let it happen again."

Before she could gasp, there was a knock.

Jaidon froze. Then let go.

Mather stepped into the room.

"Is everything okay?" he asked.

"Sure is, mate," Jaidon said casually. "Just getting to know our new surgeon." He tipped his head mockingly. "Have a lovely day, Miss."

He turned to leave, but Mather stepped forward—too quickly. Their shoulders collided. The two men stumbled and hit the floor in a tangle of armor.

"You fucking idiot," Jaidon snapped, scrambling to his feet.

Shabina rushed over, helped Mather up, then spotted both weapons lying on the floor.

She grabbed one and pressed it into Mather's hands.

The other, she pushed toward Jaidon with the toe of her boot. "Oops," she said with a smirk, eyes locked on the back of his helmet as he scooped it up and stalked out the door.

The moment it closed, she turned and locked it.

"Are you okay?" she asked, breathless.

Mather nodded. "Just a bruised ego," he said with a weak chuckle. "What was *their* problem?"

Shabina let out a shaky sigh. "I need to tell you something," she whispered. "I know that Enforcer… His name is Jaidon."

She looked down.

"Years ago, I used to sneak into Command. I'd watch the Enforcers training… from the air ducts."

Mather arched an eyebrow. "Of course you did. But how?"

Shabina gave a small, sad smile. "I told you… there are hundreds of old mineshafts. They go everywhere. One day, one of the trainees—Jaidon—caught me."

She wrapped her arms around herself. "At first, he was kind. Said he'd keep my secret. So I kept visiting him."

Mather stepped closer, wiping a tear from her cheek.

"They're locked?" he asked, glancing toward the doors.

She nodded.

He removed his helmet and looked at her gently. "You can tell me anything, Shabina."

She took a deep breath.

"He became obsessive. Controlling. Abusive. One night, we were alone… and he told me he wanted to be with me. I told him I didn't feel the same."

She swallowed.

"He got angry. Said I'd been leading him on. He grabbed my throat… said he deserved to have me. That I *owed* him."

Mather's hands clenched. His jaw tightened.

"What did he do to you?" he asked through his teeth.

"Nothing. I was lucky. He tried to open my shirt… but another trainee heard him yelling. They came to check. I got away."

She looked up, tears welling again. "So I ran. I ran and I never looked back."

Mather pulled her into his chest, wrapping his arms around her.

"I knew it was you," he whispered.

"What?"

"I was the trainee who heard him yelling," he said softly. "I thought I saw someone—a girl—running away crying. Then I bumped into Jaidon. He said I was just seeing things."

Shabina's face crumpled.

"I thought I was going to die," she choked. "You've saved me twice, Mather. Now it's my turn to save you. I'll make sure you don't get caught."

"You can't change my gun's serial number, Shabina," Mather said. "They're going to inspect all of them until they find me."

Shabina wiped her cheeks. "I can't," she said. "But I can change your gun."

Mather stared at her.

"That's too risky," he said. "I'm not going to let you do that. You'd get caught."

Shabina smiled slyly, brushing the last tear from her cheek.

"I didn't," she said.

Mather blinked. "What?"

"I didn't get caught," she said. "When you and Jaidon fell... I swapped your guns."

$$\infty$$

Valentino

Two weeks had passed.

At least, he *thought* it had been two weeks.

There was no light. No clock. No rhythm to mark the days—only the sound of his own breathing, the drip of unseen condensation, and the creaking groan of shifting metal.

Still no sign of Connor.

Valentino sat slumped against the cold wall, knees tucked to his chest. His voice rasped from disuse.

"Where is he?" he muttered. "He should be here by now. Doesn't he want to know where his brother is?"

He ground his teeth, fingers twitching on his thighs.

Then suddenly sat upright, as if the thought had struck him for the first time.

"Where *is* his brother?" he asked the darkness. "Father never told me that part."

His eyes flicked side to side, unseeing.

"Did he... did he kidnap a child?"

Valentino's breath caught.

"No... no, he wouldn't do that," he said aloud. "Would he?"

Silence pressed in like a second skin.

He laughed—once, short and bitter. Then whispered, "*Would* he?"

No answer.

Only the low, ambient hum of the facility—its machinery groaning like distant thunder.

Valentino's hands trembled as he hugged his knees tighter to his chest. His body ached from disuse, and his thoughts frayed at the edges.

Time had melted into something meaningless. He couldn't remember how long it had been since he'd last eaten. Since he'd heard another voice.

He stared into the dark—where the wall should have been—and focused on it as though it might open if he stared hard enough.

"Rachel?" he whispered.

His voice cracked on her name.

"Rachel? Are you there?"

Nothing.

Just the drip.

Drip.

Drip.

"I'll find you," he muttered. "Sleep… that's where I'll find you. I know I can save you."

He lay down slowly, curling into himself, rocking ever so slightly on the hard floor.

"Sleep," he murmured. "That's where she is. She's waiting for me. I'll find her there. I'll tell her… I'll tell her I'm coming."

His voice faded into mumbles. Then into silence.

And eventually, sleep consumed him.

∞

Valentino was at the beach.

The sky was soft and blue, the sun warm against his skin. The waves rolled gently toward the shore, catching the light like sheets of glass.

Pandora was in the water.

She laughed as she dove beneath the surface, then broke through the waves again—her long black hair slicked back, her eyes shining. She was radiant. Alive. Free.

Valentino sat on the sand, watching her, a peaceful smile softening his features.

For a moment, everything felt right.

Then a shadow fell over him.

"What did I tell you?" The Architect's voice growled from above.

The smile vanished.

Valentino looked up—and there he was.

The Architect. Towering. Expression unreadable. Voice like iron on bone.

Valentino turned back toward the water—and his blood ran cold.

Marcus was there.

He was dragging Pandora out of the surf by her hair, water streaming from her limbs as she kicked and clawed against his grip.

"PANDORA!" Valentino screamed, scrambling to his feet, sand slipping beneath him.

"VAL!" she cried back, trying to reach for him.

Her voice was raw with fear.

Valentino turned to The Architect, panic rising in his throat. "Please, Father—I haven't told her anything!"

The Architect's face twisted into something cruel.

"You haven't told her anything… yet," he said.

"You've become too attached. You've become sloppy. It ends now."

"NO—" Valentino choked, spinning back toward the shore. "NO, MARCUS!"

He broke into a sprint, feet pounding against wet sand.

"PLEASE!"

Marcus looked up as Valentino ran.

He leaned down and whispered something into Pandora's ear.

Her head jerked up.

Her eyes locked on Valentino's.

"VAL!" she screamed again, louder this time, just as he neared.

The Architect gave a nod.

And before she could say another word, Marcus slit her throat.

"NO!" Valentino howled as he dropped to his knees beside her.

Blood poured from the wound, soaking the sand beneath her. He caught her in his arms as she fell, her eyes wide, lips trembling.

"Val…" she gurgled, trying to speak.

"Your… your br—"

But the rest of the word never came.

She went limp.

Valentino pressed her against his chest, rocking back and forth in the wet sand. "No… no… no…"

Her blood stained his hands. His arms. His soul.

Above him, The Architect loomed once more.

"THIS IS YOUR FINAL WARNING!" he thundered. "NO ATTACHMENTS!"

Valentino wailed, cradling Pandora's lifeless body. Her long black hair draped over his arm, still warm from the sun.

And then it began to fall away.

Strand by strand, it slid from her scalp.

He looked down in horror.

Her hair was coming out in clumps.

"No…"

His voice broke.

"No!"

He tried to catch it, to hold it in place—but it kept falling.

And when he looked up, Marcus stood over them again—smirking, Pandora's hair balled in his fist.

"I'll have you, Pandora," he said, voice low and sickening. "One way or another."

∞

Valentino woke with a gasp, drenched in sweat.

His body trembled. His breathing came in short, ragged bursts, and unintelligible phrases spilled from his lips like broken static.

"Rachel…" he croaked.

His eyes darted to the entrance of his makeshift shelter.

For a moment—just a moment—he saw her.

A silhouette. Slim. Familiar.

"Rachel?" he whispered, sitting up.

She slipped out through the hanging covers and into the roof space beyond. Silent. Ghostlike.

"Rachel!" Valentino cried, scrambling to his feet.

He didn't stop to grab his night vision glasses. His legs carried him forward, unsteady and desperate, straight into the blackness.

"Rachel?" he called, his voice cracking.

He stumbled through the Detachment Gibbets, bumping into hanging cages with dull, metallic thunks. One by one, voices stirred in the dark.

"Shut up…"

"Quiet…"

"Go back to sleep…"

The cageys groaned and grumbled in irritation, but Valentino didn't stop.

He pressed deeper into the maze of suspended cages and narrow walkways, blindly calling her name into the void.

"Rachel?"

A shape appeared ahead—blurry and low to the ground.

Kneeling.

It was her. Her silhouette. Still. Fragile.

Kneeling in the middle of the roof's dark expanse.

And behind her… a figure loomed.

Tall. Menacing.

Marcus.

He stood above Rachel, blade in hand.

Valentino's chest seized.

"RACHEL!" he screamed, bolting toward them.

But before he could reach her—

Marcus moved.

The blade arced clean through Rachel's throat.

Both figures vanished instantly into the darkness, as though swallowed by it.

"NO!" Valentino cried out, stumbling.

He tripped over a loose beam, fell hard, and struck his head on the steel grating beneath his feet.

The last thing he heard before everything went black was the faint groan of the cages swinging around him.

Then—

Silence.

∞

The distorted voice crashed through Valentino's haze as someone shook him hard, jolting him from unconsciousness.

"Get up—quickly. They're coming."

Valentino flinched and tried to crawl away, limbs sluggish, breath hitching in panic.

"It's me, mate—it's Fred!" the voice hissed, still filtered through a modulator. "Now get back to your shelter!"

Valentino blinked wildly, trying to focus on the armored figure crouched over him. His head throbbed. The blackness around him shifted and spun.

"I... I don't have my glasses," he stammered, voice hoarse and trembling.

"Fuck," Fred muttered under his breath.

He grabbed Valentino by the scruff of his shirt and hoisted him to his feet with a grunt. "Come on. Hurry!"

Half-dragging him, Fred pulled Valentino through the dark, weaving between swaying cages and groaning cageys. Somewhere nearby, metal creaked and echoed—voices murmured in the dark.

"Quickly—get in!" Fred snapped, hurling him through the flap of hanging covers that concealed the small shelter.

Valentino collapsed inside, gasping. He crawled to the corner, wrapped his arms around himself, and began rocking back and forth.

What just happened?

Come on, Val. You're stronger than this.

His breath was sharp and shallow.

The covers flung open after a long while, and Fred shuffled in, his boots scraping against the rusted floor grates. He switched on a flashlight, its weak beam cutting through the gloom. Then, with a heavy exhale, he removed his helmet.

"What the fuck were you doing out there, Val?" he asked, crouching beside him. "And without your glasses? If someone else had found you…" He shook his head. "You would've been stuck here. *For life.*"

Valentino didn't respond at first. He stared down at the floor, the flicker of the flashlight dancing across his shaking hands.

"I… I don't know…" he finally whispered. "This place… it makes you see things."

His voice cracked. He looked up, eyes haunted. "Things that aren't there."

Fred's expression softened. He placed a hand on Valentino's shoulder. "It'll be all right, mate. It's happening in a week. You'll be out of here soon."

Valentino nodded slowly, but his body kept rocking. Back and forth. Back and forth.

Fred swallowed. "I'll come back and check on you… as soon as I can," he added, but the reassurance fell flat, swallowed by the oppressive silence.

"Don't go anywhere… okay?"

Valentino stopped rocking for just a moment. He looked up at Fred and offered the faintest, most fragile smile.

"Where would I go?"

Then he dropped his gaze and resumed rocking.

Fred sighed. "You're going to be okay, Val. Just hold on a bit longer."

He stood, hesitated, then pulled his helmet back on.

∞

Fred

As he pushed through the covers and stepped out into the void of the Detachment Gibbets, the darkness swallowed him.

Vince stood nearby, silent and still, one hand resting on his gun.

Fred didn't look at him as he spoke. "I'm not sure how much more of this he can handle."

He flipped on his night vision glasses. "I think he's going mad."

Vince didn't blink.

"We may need to sort him out," he said coldly. "We can't have him ruining the mission."

Fred stiffened.

"He's our only connection to The Architect, Vince. If we do that… no more jobs. We have to look after him while he's up here. *You know that.*"

Vince scoffed, then chuckled darkly.

"Val isn't The Architect's son. You know that. He's just some ratty orphan the old man dragged off the street to do his dirty work."

Fred hesitated. "I don't know, Vince… I think we might be getting in too deep."

Vince turned to him, his expression unreadable beneath the helmet.

"If we let him go mad… if he dies… or better yet, if he's caught?"

He shrugged.

"Then we're out."

Fred turned, glancing back toward the curtain that marked Valentino's shelter.

"So what… we just don't come back?"

Vince nodded. "If The Architect comes asking questions, we say he lost it. There was nothing we could do."

He paused.

"Anyway, we still have The Renegades."

Fred didn't answer.

"Come on," Vince said. "Let's get back downstairs before someone notices we're missing."

The two Enforcers melted into the darkness, their footsteps swallowed by the hum of the prison's machinery.

PART TWO

CHAPTER EIGHT

The Point Of No Ret/rn

Xavier

It was two days before the next full moon, and the top-level cageys were beginning to unravel. They howled at the bars, fought over scraps, and screamed into the dark as if the moon had already taken them.

Inside Charlie's cage, the covers had just reached the floor. The stale hush that followed made the air feel heavier than usual.

"I'm worried about Lincoln," Charlie said quietly. His voice was low, almost lost in the thick dark. He flicked on his flashlight and looked toward Connor, Jaysen, and Xavier. "He's become reclusive. Withdrawn. Just… promise me you'll keep an eye on him after I'm gone. At least until you escape."

Connor sat up on his bunk and smacked his head on the cage roof. "For fuck's sake—that bloody hurt." He rubbed his scalp and grumbled. "I don't think I'll ever get used to this place."

"You will," Charlie said with a soft smile.

Connor dropped down beside him. "You're going to come back. Just like last time."

Charlie sighed. "Maybe. But just in case I don't... promise me. I know he can be a right pain, but he's not a lost cause. Not yet."

Connor's jaw tightened. "How many more chances are we supposed to give him? It's the same pattern, Charlie. He lies. He apologizes. Then he does it all again."

Xavier stood and walked to the chamber pot. "He's been through a lot. We all have." He shrugged, glancing back. "I'll look out for him. Even with the eye patch and the attitude, he's still easy on the eyes."

Jaysen said nothing.

He took a long sip from his flask, then began pacing in the dim light, steps short and sharp.

"What if we break out on the full moon?" he asked suddenly. "We could get Izzy. And you, Charlie."

The cage fell silent.

Xavier's eyes dropped. "So it's happening on the full moon?"

Connor didn't hesitate. "You knew this was the plan."

"I did," Xavier muttered. "Just didn't think it'd be so soon. I was hoping I'd be taken to The Harvest before you left."

His voice cracked.

"I'm going to miss you idiots," he said, wiping a tear from his cheek.

"You could still come with us," Charlie offered. "It's not too late."

Xavier gave a faint smile. "You know I can't. My family needs what comes from this place. And someone has to keep Lincoln from going completely feral."

The four men exchanged a look—bittersweet and weighted with unspoken things.

"So it's really happening," Charlie whispered.

"This is happening," Jaysen confirmed.

Silence swelled around them again.

Tomorrow, Charlie would walk the stage again. Jaysen and Connor would ascend into The Detachment Gibbets. And Xavier—Xavier would be here. Alone.

"What are you going to do to get sent to Detachment?" Xavier asked, trying to fill the stillness.

Connor nudged Jaysen. "We'll get into a fight. Tomorrow. In The Big Cage."

"Suppose there's no better time." Xavier reached into his pocket and pulled out a small tin. "One last hurrah?"

He opened the lid—three hand-rolled joints rested inside like treasure.

"You'd better have your own drinks. I'm not made of favors."

They drank. They smoked. They talked until the haze dulled the weight of what was coming.

"Maybe I'll join the fight," Xavier said as they settled into their beds. "Still need a life sentence, don't I?"

Jaysen laughed. "Just don't hit me too hard. I'll need my brain intact."

Charlie remained awake a little longer, scribbling symbols onto a scrap of paper—triangles, squares, circles, and lines intersecting in strange combinations.

Connor peered over. "What's that?"

"Oh, nothing," Charlie said with a chuckle. "Just some scribbles. Never been much of an artist."

He folded the paper, tucked it into his pocket, and clicked off the flashlight.

Darkness claimed the cage.

Sleep didn't come easy.

But it came.

∞

A dry stillness clung to the morning air, brittle as old parchment.

As the covers rose, the silence inside the cage felt heavier than usual—like the calm before a storm. Every breath scraped their throats, rough and dry, like sandpaper dragging through their lungs. Words tried to rise but stayed lodged somewhere deep, unspoken.

The four men hadn't said much that morning. Only glances. Determined. Apprehensive.

This is it, Xavier thought as they were marched toward The Big Cage. *Once they're gone, it'll be just me… Barry… and Lincoln.*

As they reached their usual spot and Xavier dropped down onto the bench, a voice hissed behind him.

"I need more smokes."

Xavier jolted. "Zoti's tits, Link—stop creeping up like that. It's… well, it's creepy."

Lincoln smirked. "What's got you on edge? You lot look like you've just been to a funeral."

Xavier rubbed his temples and feigned a groan. "Hungover. Big night last night."

Lincoln's gaze slid between him, Charlie, Jaysen, and Connor. He raised his good eyebrow slowly. "Sure…" he drawled, clearly unconvinced. "What's going on?"

No one spoke at first. Then Xavier turned to face him fully. "You want more smokes?"

Lincoln narrowed his eye. "Obviously."

"Then hit me."

Lincoln blinked. "You want me to hit you?"

"You'll have to take a few from us, too," Xavier added. "You know… for realism."

Now Lincoln looked outright suspicious. "Take a beating for smokes?" he scoffed. "Not exactly a fair trade."

Jaysen stepped forward, voice calm. "It clears your debt to me. And you get to give it back—properly. Just don't touch Charlie. He's off limits."

Lincoln considered that, running his tongue across his teeth. Then, to Xavier, "Not the face," he said with a wink. "And I want the smokes up front. Double."

"I have a few people to speak to," Charlie blurted suddenly, rising from the bench before anyone could respond. He walked off quickly, heading toward the Black Enforcers.

"He's acting weird," Jaysen muttered.

"You would be too, if you thought you were about to get harvested," Connor replied.

Jaysen placed a steady hand on Connor's back. "Don't worry. We'll get him out before then."

Connor nodded, watching as Charlie slipped a folded piece of paper into one of the Enforcer's gloves with practiced subtlety—the same paper he'd been scribbling on the night before.

Later, after Xavier had returned from meeting Barry, Lincoln tossed him a roasted corn cob.

"I won't fight a weak man," Lincoln growled, his tone cutting despite the gesture.

Xavier smiled at the gift. "And here I was thinking you were just being nice."

He handed over the promised goods—two small aluminum tins and a pack of smokes.

"Double," Xavier said. "Just like you asked."

∞

Lincoln

Lincoln grunted as he took the smokes, stuffing them into his pockets. "What are you guys planning?"

"We can't tell you," Connor replied through a mouthful of corn, then winked.

So it's something to do with that voice I heard in the roof. Lincoln's jaw tensed. *But why's Xavier involved? And Jaysen? He wasn't supposed to tell anyone.*

"You ready?" Xavier asked, tossing the stripped cob aside. Charlie had just returned and sat with the group again, more distant than usual.

"I've been waiting for this since I met you," Lincoln said as he stood. "Didn't expect you to ask for it, though."

He grabbed Xavier by the scruff and hauled him upright. Xavier's feet lifted from the ground. Lincoln drew back his fist.

Xavier gasped at the sudden force, eyes locking with Lincoln's.

But Lincoln hesitated.

Xavier saw it, and his shoulders slumped. "What's wrong, Ken? Can't bring yourself to hit me?" he teased—and then smacked Lincoln across the cheek with the soggy corn cob.

Lincoln barely flinched. "What the fuck, Xav?" he growled, brushing chewed kernels from his face. "I said not the face."

He grabbed the cob and returned the favor—smacking Xavier across the jaw. They both smirked.

"Punch me," Xavier whispered.

Lincoln's smirk faded. He drew back and slammed his fist into Xavier's gut, winding him. Xavier dropped to the ground.

Connor and Jaysen lunged. They tackled Lincoln and drove fists into his ribs—hard enough to sell the performance, soft enough not to damage him for real.

Xavier staggered to his feet and moved to join the brawl—only to feel a massive hand clamp down on his shoulder. The force threatened to tear it from the socket.

He was spun around—Robbie.

Lincoln's newest cagey.

A bear of a man, wild-eyed and feral.

Robbie raised his fist.

Xavier shut his eyes, bracing for the blow.

It never came.

Instead, he was thrown. Hard.

He landed with a thud, and when he opened his eyes, he saw Charlie leaping onto Robbie, trying to pin him by the neck with his cane.

Robbie roared and tossed Charlie like he was made of paper. He hit the benches and crumpled to the ground.

"CHARLIE!" Xavier screamed as Robbie charged him again.

Jaysen, Connor, and Lincoln all turned—eyes going wide as they saw Charlie sprawled and unmoving.

Connor broke toward him.

Jaysen and Lincoln sprinted after Robbie.

But they weren't fast enough.

Robbie's fist connected with Xavier's face. Hard.

The world spun. His ears rang with the high-pitched static of chaos. Distant screams. Grunts. The thud of fists. It was all a blur.

Then Robbie saw Jaysen.

He dropped Xavier like dead weight and tore toward him.

"ROBBIE, NO!" Lincoln shouted, but the brute didn't stop.

As the spinning settled, Xavier blinked and found them through the blur—Jaysen running, Robbie charging, fists clenched.

Then Lincoln tackled Robbie, driving him sideways into a row of benches.

Robbie growled, spitting blood. "What the fuck are you doing? I'm on your side."

"Stay out of it," Lincoln snapped, and punched the bench beside Robbie's head.

Robbie stood. So did Lincoln.

"Not likely," Robbie snarled. His grin was wicked—too wide. "Why can't I hurt him, huh? We all know he's a fag... Is there something you're not telling us, Link? Does he take it from you? Or do you take it from him?"

That grin stayed, disgusting and full of teeth.

Lincoln turned on him.

He grabbed Robbie by the throat, thumb digging into the hollow of his neck.

Then he punched.

Again.

And again.

Robbie's face darkened. Purple and slick with blood. His nose shattered. His brow split. Five teeth flew from his mouth with a single blow to the jaw.

His limbs flailed weakly.

Then stopped.

Lincoln let go.

Robbie dropped in a heap, blood dripping from his face and pooling beneath him.

Lincoln's fists dripped red.

He turned—and saw Jaysen and Xavier watching him.

"I'LL KILL YOU, LINCOLN!" a voice screamed from the crowd.

Lincoln spun just as Nathan—another of his new cageys—charged forward, jagged bedpost in hand.

Xavier moved first.

I have to do something.

He ran—not to meet Nathan head-on, but low, fast, and sliding at the last second.

His feet collided with Nathan's shins.

Nathan flew forward—impaling himself on the broken post.

He gasped. Twitched. Went still.

Connor

"JAYSEN! XAVIER!" Connor screamed.

He cradled Charlie's head in his lap, breath hitching, voice trembling. "It's going to be okay, Charlie," he whispered, though he could barely believe it himself. "JAYSEN!… XAVIER!" he shouted again, desperation clawing through his throat.

No, no, no… He can't die. Not now. We're just about to get out.

"Connor," Charlie rasped, his voice barely audible. Blood pooled in the corners of his mouth.

"Shush, Charlie." Tears welled in Connor's eyes. "Save your energy."

Charlie gave a soft smile before coughing again—more blood, this time darker. "It's okay, Connor," he said, voice shaking. "It's okay." His hand found Connor's forearm. "I love you, son."

Tears streamed freely as Jaysen, Xavier, and Lincoln shoved their way through the riot and reached them.

"CHARLIE!" Xavier cried, rushing forward.

But before he could reach them, Mitch appeared from nowhere— Lincoln's third cagey. He grabbed Xavier and hurled him back into Jaysen. The two collided and fell hard to the ground.

Lincoln's eye widened. "Mitch, you don't understand what's happening!" he barked. "Turn around. Stay out of it!"

Mitch's glare flicked between Lincoln, the boys, and Charlie bleeding on the ground. "You killed our cageys for these fags!" he spat. His fists clenched. "You're going to die with your little faggy friends… Who's first, then?"

He stepped toward Jaysen and Xavier.

Mitch was a slab of muscle, veins bulging like ropes under his skin. He grabbed both men by the neck and lifted them as if they weighed nothing.

"Link…" Xavier choked. "Help."

Jaysen clawed at Mitch's arms, but the grip only tightened. His face turned purple. Xavier's vision narrowed.

And then he saw Lincoln.

Charging.

The broken bedpost from earlier gripped tight in his hand.

Lincoln drove it forward—straight into the back of Mitch's skull.

The force was monstrous. The post burst through the front of Mitch's face, jutting out of his eye socket. His eye dangled by its optic nerve, swinging grotesquely.

Mitch didn't fall.

But he dropped Jaysen and Xavier, stumbled backward, and turned slowly to Lincoln.

"You… fucking… fag…" he choked, blood misting from his mouth and torn face.

Lincoln slammed a fist into his sternum—then another into his throat.

Mitch's eye rolled back. He toppled over the bench and hit the ground, dead.

"Link… You… You're—" Xavier couldn't finish. "CHARLIE!" he suddenly cried, remembering.

"I'm Charlie?" Lincoln blinked, confused. Then he saw. "Oh, shit."

He helped Jaysen to his feet, and together they moved to where Charlie lay cradled in Connor's arms.

Charlie's skin was waxy now. Pale. His eyes were half-lidded, blood trickling from his nose and lips.

"My boys…" he breathed.

Xavier and Jaysen dropped to their knees. Lincoln stood behind, watching—his hands still stained red. He kept the other rioting cageys at bay, shielding the final moments.

"I'm so sorry, Charlie," Jaysen said, his voice breaking. "This was my plan. I should have known…"

"It's okay, son." Charlie smiled faintly. "It's my time anyway."

He coughed, blood bubbling up, and wheezed as he spoke. "This… this beats that stage."

Tears streamed from all of them.

Charlie's breaths slowed.

"I… I love you, boys."

One last wheeze.

Then silence.

His body went still.

"No…" Xavier whispered, voice fragile.

Lincoln's bloodied hand settled on his shoulder.

"I'm sorry, Xav. But the Enforcers are coming. They need to see us fighting, or this'll all be for nothing."

Lincoln's lone eye softened.

Then someone tackled him from behind.

Xavier and Jaysen reacted instantly—leaping onto the attacker, fists flying. Xavier wrapped his arm around the man's neck.

A loud bang cracked the air.

Pain exploded in Xavier's back. He screamed and hit the dirt.

He turned just in time to see three more beanbags explode into Jaysen, the unknown man, and Lincoln, breaking up the fight.

Connor stood, gently laying Charlie's head on his scrunched-up jacket. Then he ran—straight for the Black Enforcer who had fired the shots.

He dodged expertly, weaving past the beanbags.

He was nearly on them—when the Enforcer stepped aside.

Revealing the hound.

It lunged for his throat.

Another bang rang out.

The Pearl Enforcer had fired from their post—missed Connor.

But the beanbag shattered the hound's jaw just inches from Connor's neck. Bone split through skin. The beast yelped and dropped, whimpering.

The Black Enforcer stepped forward and cracked Connor across the back of the skull with the butt of their weapon.

He collapsed.

∞

Jaysen

The Black Enforcer stared down at Connor for a moment.

Then they looked up at the Pearl Enforcer.

Without a word, they turned and began dragging Connor by the arm, his limp body trailing behind them toward The Aviary.

Jaysen staggered upright, blood pounding in his ears. Lincoln groaned nearby, pushing off the dirt. Xavier was on his hands and knees, spitting blood.

Then he saw it.

Charlie.

Lying still.

No… not Charlie…

The grief nearly knocked the air from his lungs. His legs wobbled beneath him. But before he could take a step, three more Black Enforcers marched toward them.

The closest one raised their weapon.

Jaysen barely had time to react.

The butt of the gun slammed into his stomach. He crumpled.

Then—another blow.

To the face.

Crack.

Blood burst from his brow, warm and blinding.

As the world began to spin and fade, he looked one last time at Charlie's body on the ground.

Still.

Silent.

Gone.

And then darkness took him.

∞

Xavier

Xavier shook as he watched the two remaining Black Enforcers close in on him and Lincoln.

The nearest one raised the butt of their gun, aiming straight for his face—

But Lincoln lunged first.

He tackled the Enforcer to the ground, and in the scuffle, their helmet rolled away. Lincoln seized their balaclava, yanked it upward—

And froze.

He stumbled back, breath catching.

"D… Dad?" His voice trembled. "No… you're… You're dead!"

The Enforcer sneered, blood on his lip. "I am now, you fucking idiot."

Lincoln's chest rose and fell, panic taking hold.

"That'll teach me for raising a fucking faggy little bitch like you. You're not my son."

The words sliced through the air.

Lincoln's fists clenched.

He grabbed the fallen helmet.

Then he snapped.

He lunged and smashed the helmet into his father's face. Again. And again.

The gas mask shattered first. Filters split open. Bone followed. Blood sprayed outward in brutal arcs, soaking the dirt.

His father laughed—choked, wet, hideous.

Lincoln roared louder.

The Pearl Enforcer left their post and charged.

But Lincoln didn't stop.

He kept smashing the helmet down. Splintering cartilage. Crushing sockets. Pulverizing whatever was left of the man who'd once been his father.

The Pearl Enforcer struck him in the back of the head.

Lincoln didn't flinch.

Another blow—harder.

Still, Lincoln screamed unintelligible rage, hammering the helmet into pulp and flesh.

The Pearl Enforcer signaled for backup.

Black and Argentine Enforcers rushed in.

Lincoln ripped a chain from his father's neck, holding it up like a trophy. "This is mine," he growled, stuffing it into his pocket.

"Mine."

Smash.

"Mine."

Smash.

The Enforcers surrounded him. Five of them. It took all of them to pull him off the corpse.

He howled like something feral—inhuman—as they dragged him away.

Xavier met his eye.

It wasn't Lincoln's anymore.

There was no blue. No white.

Only a blown-out, ink-black pupil, wide and vacant.

Something else had taken over.

Something wild.

Something hungry for blood.

Lincoln's laughter echoed, infernal and jagged.

It sent chills racing up Xavier's spine, freezing him in place.

And then—blackness.

The butt of a rifle cracked against the side of his skull.

And Xavier knew nothing more.

∞

Jaysen

When Jaysen woke, the infirmary was chaos.

Crowded. Noisy. The air thick with antiseptic and pain.

Jessica rushed between tables, tending to the wounded. Each cagey had a Black Enforcer looming beside them like shadows. Her eyes were swollen, red-rimmed.

She'd been crying.

She must know about Charlie.

A tear slipped down Jaysen's cheek.

352

This is all my fault.

He tried to wipe it away. His hand didn't move.

Heavy shackles pinned his wrists and ankles to the metal table.

The Black Enforcer beside him looked down. "Sit still."

Jaysen obeyed.

He turned his head as far as he could. Connor was on the table to his left. Xavier to his right. Both shackled, silent. Lincoln wasn't there.

The hours blurred.

Jessica eventually made her way to Jaysen, tending to his wounds with mechanical movements. She didn't speak. None of them did. The silence screamed louder than words ever could.

One by one, the other cageys were wheeled out.

Only Jaysen, Connor, and Xavier remained.

Still shackled. Still watched.

The doors opened again—this time, it was The Warden.

He walked with calculated steps, stopping in front of the three of them.

"Uncuff their wrists," he ordered the Enforcers.

Metal clinked as their shackles released. The men sat up, groaning through bruises and aching muscles.

His eyes settled on Jaysen first.

"Why are you always involved, Mr. Masters?" His voice was sharp. Controlled. Like a blade just before the strike. "Do you want a life sentence? Because the way you're going, it's looking more and more likely."

He shifted his gaze to Xavier.

"I've added twenty years to your sentence," he said.

Then, to Connor.

"And you, Mr. Matthews." He raised one finger. "Once more… If I have to see you again, it's a death sentence."

He dropped his hand. The room felt colder.

"Four days in The Detachment Gibbets. For all of you."

Then he turned. "Take them. The Pearl Enforcer is waiting."

The Enforcers unchained their ankles and hauled them to their feet.

The men expected to be dragged to the end of the corridor—turn right, up the stairs, to The Detachment Gibbets.

But halfway down, the Pearl Enforcer stopped.

They stood beside a set of steel double doors, marked by a strange brightness leaking through their edges.

A white hallway.

"The Light Mile," Connor whispered.

The doors groaned open, spilling sterile light across their faces.

The group stepped through.

But they didn't go far.

Just a few feet in, they stopped before a second set of double doors.

To the left: Dr. Z. Zygote.

To the right: Dr. S. Valentine.

Connor frowned. "S. Valentine… What happened to Dr. Lancet?" he whispered.

None of them answered.

$$\infty$$

Xavier

Moments later, the door beside Dr. Zygote's office swung open.

Dr. Zygote stepped into the corridor, clipboard in hand, followed by two Black Enforcers—each flanking a cagey.

Lincoln.

And the man who had tackled him just before the fight ended.

Both of them looked bruised, bloody, and broken in different ways.

Lincoln's eye scanned the hallway. It landed on Xavier.

For a moment, time slowed.

That single, piercing blue eye—once so full of fire, of fight, of something that felt… human—met Xavier's.

But Xavier couldn't hold the gaze.

354

He looked away.

That blue doesn't feel like Lincoln anymore. Not after what I saw. It feels like a mask. A disguise. Hiding that… thing.

The thing that laughed while ripping flesh from bone. The thing that had to be dragged off his own father.

"Xav?" Lincoln said softly as he was guided forward.

Xavier said nothing.

"Xavier?" he tried again, a little louder now. There was desperation in his voice.

Xavier kept his eyes down.

I don't know who you are anymore.

"Quiet," the Black Enforcer snapped. They slammed the butt of their gun into Lincoln's shoulder, knocking him forward.

Lincoln grunted but didn't retaliate. He simply shuffled into line beside the others.

Dr. Zygote didn't acknowledge the exchange. His pen scratched at the clipboard, as clinical and detached as ever.

The hallway was silent again—too silent.

Xavier stared at the ground, heart pounding, refusing to look up.

He wasn't ready to face whatever Lincoln had become.

Not yet.

∞

Jaysen

Jaysen's breath caught.

For the first time since Charlie's death, a flicker of hope lit inside him. His eyes locked on the door just ahead—The Cell.

Izzy… she's just behind that door.

His heart pounded.

Don't worry, Izzy. I'm coming for you.

But the moment was brief.

The Pearl Enforcer turned left at the end of the hallway, and the others were forced to follow.

The corridor beyond wasn't like The Light Mile.

Gone was the sterile white glow. Here, the walls were wet, dark, and choked with mold. The familiar rot of Augmentation Bay settled into Jaysen's lungs again like poison he'd learned to breathe.

They descended back into the depths of hell.

The other set of stairs to the Detachment Gibbets… they should be just up here, Jaysen thought, remembering the stolen blueprints burned into his mind.

And then he saw them.

The curved stone walls loomed ahead, curling around a narrow spiral staircase that wound upward into shadow.

Cold. Ancient. Cruel.

The Pearl Enforcer ascended first without a word, two Black Enforcers close behind.

Jaysen followed, flanked by more Enforcers.

Connor beside him. Xavier. Lincoln. The unknown man who'd tackled Lincoln. All of them marching silently beneath the weight of blood, bruises, and secrets.

Jaysen looked up the stairs, jaw tightening.

Just a few more steps.

Just a little longer, Izzy.

∞

Lincoln

"I'm sorry if I hit you too hard, Xav," Lincoln said quietly from the darkness.

No response.

He tried again, just a little louder. "Come on… you *did* ask me to do it."

Still nothing.

"Xavier!" Lincoln barked.

He heard the sharp jolt in the gibbet beside him. Xavier had jumped.

"Quiet back there," the Pearl Enforcer growled from somewhere beyond the metal.

What the fuck is wrong with him? Lincoln scoffed to himself. *Why do I even care, anyway?*

The thick metal door slammed shut behind them, and the Pearl Enforcer's steps faded.

Darkness.

Silence.

Lincoln exhaled, then tried again. "Xavier… what the fuck, man? You asked me to hit you, and now you won't speak to me?"

He waited, listening to the hum of the air vents and the occasional creak of the cages.

Finally, Xavier's voice came from the gibbet to his left—shaky, uneven.

"That's… that's not it."

"What is it then?" Lincoln snapped.

Was that his cage shaking again? Is he scared of me?

"I… You…"

Lincoln narrowed his eyes, trying to focus on the voice.

"Xav, you okay?" came Jaysen's voice from the right.

"I think he's broken," Lincoln muttered.

"Stop being so insensitive, Lincoln," Connor's voice cut in from across the gibbets. "You had to be dragged away when Shane died. Charlie was…" His voice cracked.

"I'm sorry," Lincoln sighed. He leaned his head back and stared into the void above him. *I need to stop being such a dick.* "Look, I know I haven't been great to any of you… but maybe we could start fresh?"

"Sure, Link," Jaysen said after a moment.

Connor followed with a tired, "Why not?... Today went horribly wrong. But we all deserve a second chance."

"I... I don't know if I can do that," Xavier whispered.

Lincoln froze.

"Lincoln... You... You killed your father," Xavier continued. "You smashed in his skull until there was nothing left but a mess of blood and bone. You looked like a monster... *You were a monster.* I don't think I can be around that side of you."

Lincoln's head jerked up—hard. He cracked it on the top of the gibbet.

"What the *actual fuck*, Xav? My dad died *years* ago."

"Lincoln, you viciously murdered him right in front of me... just earlier, in The Big Cage," Xavier said, concerned, maybe even afraid.

"So I suppose Jaysen and Connor saw this too?" Lincoln spat, growing defensive.

"I saw you kill Mitch and Robbie," Connor replied firmly.

"Same," said Jaysen.

"And I saw *you* kill Nathan," Lincoln countered, voice a little quieter. "Which I'm grateful for, by the way, Xavier. You saved me. But this father thing? I think you're imagining it."

"I saw it," said a voice from the dark.

Lincoln froze.

So did the others.

"I saw you kill your father. Your eyes were completely black, man. You smashed his head in like a fucking watermelon. Then you laughed—this *crazy*, *wicked* laugh. No wonder the kid's scared of you. You took something from his neck... If you don't believe me, check your pocket."

"That's right!" Xavier said suddenly. "You put it in your pocket. You kept saying it was yours."

Lincoln hesitated.

Then slowly reached into his coat. Fingers brushed smokes... tins... lighter—

Then something else.

Cold metal.

He pulled it out.

The lighter—and a chain.

He clicked the lighter to life, its tiny flame casting strange shadows in the gibbet. Dangling from the chain was a double moon pendant.

His jaw tightened.

"I don't know how I can be around you anymore, Lincoln," Xavier whispered. "I can't get the sound of you laughing out of my head. It was like something from hell."

Lincoln stared at the pendant.

This can't be happening.

He turned it over.

There it was.

Strength comes from within.

"Don't forget to let it out," he whispered under his breath, pressing the pendant to his lips.

Then his head snapped up.

"Who are you?" Lincoln growled into the dark. "Who the fuck are you?"

No reply.

"Jaysen, do you have the flashlight?" Connor asked.

"Yeah… give me a sec."

Lincoln heard the rustle of movement. The click. Then light.

Jaysen swung it toward the sound.

The gibbet the voice had come from… was empty.

"What the fuck?" Lincoln muttered.

Jaysen swept the light around. One empty cage. Then another. Then another.

"Where did he go?" Xavier whispered.

"And where are all the other cageys?" Connor asked, unease creeping into his voice.

An eerie silence fell.

Jaysen moved the light around—and it landed on a silhouette in the distance.

He turned it off.

"Shit," Connor hissed. "Was that a Black Enforcer?"

"No…" Xavier whispered. "It was the Pearl Enforcer."

"Shush," Jaysen warned. "I'm not sure who it was… but arguing isn't going to help."

The silence dragged.

Then came the hellish grinding.

The covers were being lowered.

All four men jumped and hit the tops of their gibbets.

∞

"I see how people could go mad in here," Connor said once the grinding stopped. "I'm glad we won't be stuck here for four days."

"What do you mean?" Lincoln asked.

Jaysen turned on the flashlight again and swept the space.

"Lincoln… we're leaving tonight," he whispered.

Lincoln laughed, leaning back. "Good one," he chuckled. "Leaving tonight. You're funny."

"They're not kidding," said Xavier. "They're leaving tonight. That's why we needed to get sent up here."

Lincoln was quiet for a moment.

"And you're not going?" he finally asked Xavier.

"No. I want to volunteer… for my family."

Lincoln's stomach twisted.

Shane had said the same thing.

"Don't be so stupid," he muttered. "You should get out while you can. I *would*."

Jaysen and Connor exchanged a look.

"You should come with us, Lincoln… if you want," Connor offered.

Lincoln stared toward Xavier's gibbet. Xavier looked away.

"There's nothing left in here for me," Lincoln muttered. "Hell yeah, I'll come."

He scoffed. "How are we gonna do this?"

A clatter echoed in the distance.

Jaysen turned off the flashlight.

Silence.

Another clatter—closer now.

Then another.

Lincoln's pulse quickened.

Something's coming.

Then—nothing.

"Who's there?" Lincoln growled into the dark.

No reply.

Jaysen clicked the light back on.

A hiss.

Then they saw her.

Prison Cat.

Curled in the center of the walkway.

One pupil round and black. The other split and strange.

She stared back at them, silent.

Lincoln blinked. She reminded him of himself.

He chuckled.

So did Jaysen and Connor.

"I thought there'd be other cageys up here," Jaysen said. "It's kinda weird that no one else is here."

"I'm here," came that voice again—closer now.

The cat bolted, claws skittering on the metal floor.

Jaysen swung the flashlight around.

There he was.

The unknown man.

Standing in the center of the walkway.

Just outside their gibbets.

"How did you…" Jaysen started.

The stranger cut him off with a smirk, pulling a glinting object from his pocket. "Keys can be tricky things."

He held it up—Jaysen's stolen key.

Jaysen gasped and immediately rifled through his pockets. Nothing. Panic overtook his expression.

"How did you get that?" he snapped.

"A lot can happen when you're fighting," the man said casually, still wearing that smug grin. He didn't look at Jaysen—he *studied* him. Like he already knew every move he was going to make.

Lincoln gripped the bars of his gibbet. "Stop playing games and tell us what you want."

The man didn't move at first.

Then he stepped into the center of the walkway, his shadow stretching with the flicker of Jaysen's flashlight.

"I'm with The Renegades," he said, voice low and unsettling. "They want to help you."

Lincoln narrowed his eye. "Help?"

"Help us how?" Jaysen asked warily.

The man tilted his head toward Jaysen. "Your sister… She can't just *leave*."

Lincoln could hear Jaysen's heartbeat in his breath.

"She's in a coma," the man finished.

Jaysen jerked forward and cracked his head on the top of his gibbet. "What?" He snarled.

"The women in here… In The Cell…" the man continued. "They're all in an induced coma. You're going to need this."

He pulled a syringe from his coat.

Lincoln leaned forward, trying to make it out. The liquid inside shimmered faintly in the flashlight's glow—like mercury laced with moonlight.

Jaysen's eyes burned holes through the man. "*Why* is my sister in a coma?" he asked through gritted teeth.

"You're going to need to see that for yourself."

The quiet that followed was loaded—weighted like a ticking clock.

Xavier finally broke it. "What do The Renegades want for that syringe?" he asked. "They aren't helping Jaysen for nothing."

The stranger turned, slowly.

Walked directly to Xavier's gibbet.

He leaned in.

Too close.

Xavier recoiled, pushing his back to the bars and turning his face.

Lincoln saw him shudder.

The man's breath fogged the air, thick and sour.

"That's right," the man whispered. "They're not doing it for nothing. Aren't you a smart boy?"

His voice dropped into a rasp.

"They want *you*."

∞

Xavier

"We won't let them hurt Xavier," Jaysen snapped.

The stranger turned to him, that sly smile never leaving his face. "Not like that," he said smoothly. "They just want to talk."

"About what?" Xavier asked, his voice barely holding together.

"That's not for me to divulge," the man said. Then he dangled the stolen key and the syringe just inches from Jaysen's reach. "But if you want to get out of here…" He nodded toward Xavier. "Then pretty boy needs to come, too."

Xavier froze.

His whole body tensed.

My… my family. His heart pounded. *I can't choose between them and my friends' freedom.*

The man's voice softened, but Xavier didn't trust it. "We will look after your family if you choose to come. We know why you're here, Xavier."

His tone was disturbingly gentle—sympathetic, yet wrong. Hollow and crawling under his skin.

"A messenger is waiting with a large bag of iron," the man continued. "Enough for them to live comfortably. You only have to say yes."

Xavier looked to Jaysen, to Connor.

But not to Lincoln.

He still couldn't look at Lincoln.

All he could see was that other thing—the thing that had laughed while crushing his father's skull. The thing that had stared through him with a bottomless, black eye.

"Don't take your friends' freedom from them," the man said.

Xavier's voice cracked. "Do you swear you'll pay my family?"

"I swear," the man said, his smile stretching, wider and worse.

A moment passed. Then Xavier gave the smallest nod. "I'll come with you."

The man lifted a small radio from his pocket. "They're ready."

The roof lights clicked on, harsh and blinding.

Xavier squinted and turned away, blinking furiously.

A Pearl Enforcer marched in, cold and precise, followed by five Black Enforcers. Boots echoed through the chamber like war drums.

"You fucking liar," Lincoln growled, rattling his gibbet so hard Xavier instinctively flinched. He pressed himself against the bars and tried to shrink.

"Settle down, big boy," the stranger said. "The Renegades are everywhere."

Then he turned to greet the Enforcers. "I didn't think Charles could pull this off before the next Harvest," he said to the Pearl Enforcer. "He proved me wrong."

"Charlie?" Connor said. "What's he got to do with this?"

The Pearl Enforcer turned to Connor, their steps deliberate as they approached.

"Charlie was the lead in this operation," they said. "I'm sorry for your loss. He was a good man."

"The note!" Jaysen gasped. "That's what it was!"

The Pearl Enforcer nodded once. Then they began unlocking the gibbets, starting with Connor's.

"You three," they instructed, gesturing to three of the Black Enforcers, "take Lincoln, Connor, and Xavier to the mountains. I will take Jaysen to Isabelle with the other two."

Connor stepped forward immediately. "I'm not leaving Jaysen."

The Pearl Enforcer didn't argue. "Fine. Take Lincoln and Xavier to the mountains. I'll take Jaysen and Connor to Isabelle. We'll regroup at the abandoned mill. If we're not there by sunup, go to the hideout."

Xavier stepped out slowly, his legs shaking beneath him. He still couldn't look at Lincoln, not yet.

You agreed to this. You chose.

He kept his head down as the Black Enforcers ushered him toward the door at the end of the room.

From the other side of the stairwell, he heard Jaysen's voice, low and steady.

"Who *are* you?"

"There's no time for that," the Pearl Enforcer replied. "We only have a three-hour window. I scheduled all Renegade Enforcers on one shift to help you escape. There are still a few who aren't with us. But after three hours… there will be more. And trust me—"

Xavier looked back, just once.

The light caught Lincoln's face for a second.

Not the face from the riot.

But not the one he remembered either.

"…We want to be gone before then."

"This is it," the Pearl Enforcer said. "The point of no return."

Xavier followed the Black Enforcer through a narrow hallway.

Then another.

Then another.

Lincoln was close behind, his presence pressing at Xavier's back like a storm about to break. The two remaining Black Enforcers brought up the rear, boots thudding against concrete.

They rounded corner after corner, walked what felt like miles through endless corridors.

Something didn't feel right.

"Are you sure this is the right way?" one of the Enforcers in the back asked.

"I'm sure," growled the one leading them—sharp, dismissive.

Then they stopped.

A dead end.

Xavier's pulse jumped.

"Where do we go from here?" Lincoln asked, mockingly, from behind.

The lead Enforcer turned slowly. His silence stretched like a noose tightening.

Then he raised his gun.

"What are you doing, Vince!" one of the other Enforcers shouted.

The gun aimed at Xavier's head.

"The Architect is paying a lot of iron for you," Vince said, voice dripping with malice.

Xavier couldn't move. Couldn't breathe.

I should have said no.

He closed his eyes.

"We were supposed to wait, Vince," one of the other Black Enforcers said, panicked. Behind them, another Enforcer lifted his weapon.

"Fred!" barked the third. "This isn't the plan!"

Fred hesitated. Turned.

That was all Lincoln needed.

In a blink, Lincoln yanked Xavier into his chest, shielding him with his body. One hand grabbed the Enforcer's weapon and spun it around. The barrel aimed directly at Vince.

CRACK.

One deafening shot echoed through the hall.

Xavier flinched, hands flying to his ears as he buried his face into Lincoln's chest. The silence after the shot was more terrifying than the sound itself.

Lincoln turned them. Fred now stood frozen, weapon still raised—but not fired.

"What the fuck, Fred!" the third Enforcer yelled, panicking. "What the fuck!"

Lincoln's eye narrowed. "There's no time for this."

He raised the gun toward Fred.

"NO!" the third Enforcer shouted. "He has to answer to The Council!"

Lincoln paused, weapon steady.

"Let me cuff him," the Enforcer said quickly.

Another moment passed—then Lincoln lowered the gun.

Xavier cleared his throat softly, still cradled in Lincoln's arms.

Lincoln looked down, surprised, and quickly let him go. "Sorry."

Xavier stood shakily, staring at him.

Why did he do that? And how did he move so fast?

He locked eyes with Lincoln—the striking blue, still human.

"Link… I… I…" he tried to speak, but nothing came.

"We need to go," the third Enforcer said, already turning. "That shot will bring attention."

Just then, an alarm began to blare.

Screaming through the walls.

They ran.

Corridors blurred past as Xavier stayed close behind the Enforcer, Lincoln trailing at his side. Now, Lincoln's presence didn't chill him.

It made him feel safe.

They rounded a final corner—and hit another dead end.

"You've got to be kidding me," Lincoln muttered.

The Enforcer ignored him, began tugging at a section of old pipes. One came loose, and a hidden door creaked open.

"This way."

Xavier hesitated, turned to Lincoln.

Lincoln gave a small nod, that familiar flicker in his eye.

They stepped through. The door shut behind them.

Darkness.

Stairs spiraled downward. The Enforcer's torch flickered on—dim, but enough to see their steps.

They descended in silence.

"How high up *were* we?" Xavier asked after a long while.

"Thirty stories," the Enforcer answered. "We're almost at ground."

Xavier's heart pounded harder.

Why does The Renegade Council want to talk to me?

The ground shifted under his feet—dirt instead of concrete.

He tripped.

Fell back.

Right into Lincoln.

Lincoln caught him under the arms.

"Trust fall?" he said.

Xavier blinked. *Trust fall. What a stupid thing to say*. But for a moment, it felt… easy.

He could've sworn Lincoln almost smiled.

Lincoln steadied him, then moved forward.

Nearly an hour later, they reached a ladder. The Enforcer climbed first, cracking the hatch open and peering out.

"Looks clear. Hurry. We need to get to the mill."

Xavier hesitated.

Lincoln stepped forward. "I'll go first," he said gently. He gave Xavier a reassuring smile, then climbed up and disappeared.

Silence.

"Link?" Xavier called softly.

Lincoln's head appeared again. He held out a hand. "It's okay. We're in the mountains… You should see it."

Xavier took his hand and was lifted into the cool night air.

He inhaled deeply. It was crisp, clean.

"Isn't it beautiful?" Lincoln said, staring at the stars, still smiling.

Xavier followed his gaze. "It *is* beautiful."

They stood there, side by side under the moonlight.

"You can have your romantic moment later!" the Enforcer barked. "We need to go now."

Startled, they looked down.

They were still holding hands.

Both pulled away at the same time and followed in silence.

He was just caught up in the moment, Xavier told himself as they weaved through the trees. *It didn't mean anything.*

"The full moon's at its peak," the Enforcer said. "It's midnight. We're late."

They picked up the pace.

Xavier struggled to keep up.

A tree root snagged his foot. He tripped.

Lincoln lunged but didn't reach him in time. Xavier hit the ground, skull smacking a rock.

The world spun.

"Get him up," the Enforcer said urgently.

Lincoln dropped to his knees, lifted Xavier gently into his arms.

"You have to carry him. We're close."

Lincoln adjusted Xavier's head, shielding it as best he could. "Hold on, Xavier. I've got you."

Xavier's eyes fluttered. He looked up at Lincoln—calm, focused.

He let his eyes close again, listening to Lincoln's steady heartbeat.

Lincoln held him tighter and ran—through the dark, toward the mill, toward whatever came next.

When Xavier woke, the air was warm and still.

He was in a small, shabby room coated in dust. Cobwebs clung to the corners. The furniture was broken—splintered chairs, a cracked mirror, an overturned desk—but someone had pushed the wreckage aside to make space.

He was lying on the floor, tucked beside a small fire that flickered low but steady. Birds chirped faintly beyond the shattered window. The moonlight leaked in through broken glass.

It must be two or three in the morning.

He tried to sit up.

But he couldn't.

There was weight pressing down on him—firm and steady. Panic crept in.

He struggled, muscles tense.

Then—Lincoln grunted and shifted beside him, arms tightening instinctively.

Xavier froze.

No way... Lincoln's hugging me.

The weight wasn't threatening. It was warm. Secure. Protective.

This is so weird...

I feel... safe.

Carefully, Xavier rolled over in the circle of Lincoln's arms. He moved slowly, not wanting to wake him.

He looked up at Lincoln's face.

His breathing was even, his chest rising and falling with the rhythm of deep sleep. The firelight cast soft gold over his jawline, over the scar at the edge of his brow. His lips were curved—just faintly—into the smallest smile.

Xavier's gaze lingered longer than it should have.

Every few seconds, Lincoln's jaw twitched slightly in sleep, and the scruff of his beard brushed against Xavier's nose, tickling.

Xavier didn't move.

He didn't want to.

His eyelids grew heavier, and the fire's warmth, combined with Lincoln's steady heartbeat, made him want to drift back into sleep. He nuzzled gently into Lincoln's chest and slipped a hand over his heart.

The beat was strong beneath his palm.

Rhythmic. Steady.

Alive.

For the first time since the riot, Xavier didn't feel haunted.

He felt grounded.

Safe.

The door burst open.

Xavier jolted.

The Black Enforcer rushed in, armor clanking as they scanned the room. Lincoln stirred instantly, his gaze locking with Xavier's.

Xavier froze.

His hand was still on Lincoln's chest.

Lincoln's body tensed—and he sat up quickly, breaking their connection.

"What were you doing?" he asked, voice strained, eyes wide with something like panic.

"Sorry... I... I was—" Xavier started, but the Enforcer cut him off.

"They're not back yet," they said quickly. "We have to leave in two hours."

Then the Enforcer paused, gaze drifting between them. "I'll patrol again... give you two some... privacy."

"It's not like that," Lincoln snapped. He rubbed the back of his neck, then looked down at the floor. "I just... just... I was asleep."

His voice sounded uncertain.

Like he didn't even believe himself.

"Yeah... we were asleep," Xavier echoed, turning his gaze away.

But his heart was racing.

Not with fear.

Not with guilt.

Something else entirely.

He didn't know what to say next. Didn't know what Lincoln was thinking.

But for the first time… he kind of wanted to.

∞

Jaysen

The Pearl Enforcer switched off the lights as Jaysen and Connor stepped through the door. The Black Enforcers followed, their boots heavy on the stone like war drums echoing down the corridor.

They began their descent down the winding staircase.

I can't believe Charlie was working with the Renegades.

Every step felt heavier than the last. The deeper they went, the more the cold sank into Jaysen's bones. The stone walls pressed in around them, too close. His thoughts spun—fractured memories of Charlie's voice, the note, the look in his eyes before The Harvest.

Near the bottom, the Pearl Enforcer raised a hand. "Wait here."

Then they disappeared around the bend.

Jaysen's chest tightened. *What if this is a trap? What if we're too late?*

Moments later, the Pearl Enforcer returned, sharp-eyed and breathless. "This way," they said, already vanishing again.

Jaysen and Connor followed—then froze.

Jessica stood in The Light Mile, her auburn hair tangled, eyes red-rimmed.

"Jessica?" Jaysen whispered.

"She's one of them," Connor muttered. "A Renegade."

Jessica didn't stop to explain. She turned and moved quickly.

"We have about an hour until Dr. Zygote wakes," she said as they followed. "Another hour before he makes his rounds of The Cell."

They reached a door marked in stark, utilitarian lettering: THE CELL.

Jessica paused, glancing over her shoulder. "I'm sorry, sweetie... We didn't know. No one did. Not until we were inside."

Her voice wavered.

She pushed the door open.

Jaysen stepped through and was hit with a wall of names—boards upon boards lining the room, each neatly labeled: T-1, T-2, T-3, P.S.

"Isabelle is in T-1," Jessica said quietly, leading them through to a second door.

It opened into a cavernous room—twice the length of The Aviary, though half its width—and filled with endless rows of hospital beds.

Each one occupied.

Each woman comatose.

Jaysen stopped cold.

His stomach turned to lead.

"Connor..." he breathed. "They're all pregnant."

Connor turned, mouth falling open. "Fuck..."

Jessica nodded, swallowing hard. "The sectors mark trimesters. T-1 is the beginning." She led them deeper. "They're put into comas... Their bodies used. To create children. For The Nation."

She stopped at a bed.

Jaysen's heart shattered.

It was Izzy.

Her skin looked too pale, her lips too still. A small I.V. fed into her wrist.

He reached for the file clipped at the base of her bed: Isabelle Masters – First Pregnancy.

He flipped through the notes, eyes catching one name.

Kaylus.

I'll kill him...

He crumpled the file in his fist.

"Kaylus," he growled, rage rippling through him.

Jessica gently placed a hand on his arm. "I'm so sorry."

"Jessica," the Pearl Enforcer said, urgent now. "Wake her."

Jessica stepped forward and took the syringe. With practiced hands, she injected it into Izzy's I.V. line.

Then they waited.

Thirty minutes passed.

Izzy didn't stir.

"What's wrong with her?" Jaysen asked, voice tight with panic.

Jessica shook her head. "It's different for everyone."

She looked at the Black Enforcers. "Can one of you carry her?"

One stepped forward.

Jaysen blocked them with his arm. "No."

He turned and lifted Izzy himself, cradling her against his chest.

"I will carry my sister."

He bent his head close. "I'm sorry, Izzy. I'll never let anyone hurt you again."

They began walking back through the endless rows of women.

But Jaysen noticed something else—something even more horrifying.

Across the chamber, a section labeled P.S.

He stopped.

Tubes ran from the women's chests into a complex series of machines. Milk was collected in sealed bags, then funneled into a refrigerator unit through tubing that snaked along the wall.

Harvested. Bottled.

Like livestock.

"This is disgusting," he spat. "We have to stop this."

Connor stopped beside him, eyes wide.

Then his face drained of color.

"Genevieve…" he whispered.

He took off running.

Jaysen followed, heart racing.

Connor dropped to his knees beside a bed in the P.S. section. A woman lay there—long red hair, skin like porcelain, pumps attached to her chest, tubes feeding away from her.

"No…" Connor choked. "It can't be."

He looked to Jessica. "Do you have another needle?"

Jessica hesitated. "Connor… I don't…"

A voice spoke from behind the refrigerator.

"I do."

The unknown man stepped out of the shadows, holding a second syringe.

"We figured you'd need this."

Connor stepped forward.

The man pulled back the syringe. "You owe us a favor."

Connor didn't blink. "Done."

He snatched the syringe and gently injected it into Genevieve's I.V., removed the pumps, then laid his jacket over her trembling form.

"We have to go," said the Pearl Enforcer, more urgent now.

Connor lifted Genevieve into his arms just as a loud bang echoed through the building.

The group turned and ran.

They entered the front room. Rushing for the hallway.

"Not that way," said the Pearl Enforcer.

They pulled a pipe.

A hidden door creaked open.

They disappeared inside the walls.

Darkness wrapped around them.

Then—the alarm.

It howled through the prison like a dying animal. Augmentation Bay was awake.

"Connor…" Jaysen whispered. "Who is she?"

Connor opened his mouth to speak, but the Pearl Enforcer turned on a flashlight.

"This way."

They climbed a narrow stairwell in single file.

"Genevieve…" Connor whispered to her, voice shaking. "I'm so sorry they did this to you. I should've protected you."

Who is she? Jaysen thought. *He's never spoken of her before… but she must mean everything to him.*

They reached another hatch.

"One more flight," the Pearl Enforcer whispered. "Then we reach the tunnel. But we need to cross the wall."

The Enforcer peeked out, then raised a finger.

Three Argentine Enforcers patrolled outside.

"What now?" Connor whispered.

"We wait."

Time slowed.

Then The Warden emerged.

"Patrol the outskirts!" he barked into his radio. "Find the source of the shot!"

He paced the top of the wall, speaking with the guards.

"You two—stay here. You, come with me."

The Warden disappeared with one guard. The other two resumed patrol.

"We need to go," the Pearl Enforcer said quietly. "Wait."

They timed it perfectly.

When the guards turned their backs, the Pearl Enforcer slipped outside.

"You two!" they barked. "Go patrol The Aviary."

"But The Warden said—"

"The Warden said to patrol The Aviary," they snapped.

The guards hesitated.

Then obeyed.

The Pearl Enforcer returned to the door. "Quickly. Stay low."

Jaysen and Connor ducked, holding Izzy and Genevieve tight.

They crossed the top of the wall—and Jaysen glanced down.

A playground.

Slides. Swings. Climbing ropes.

"What… is that?"

"That's The Farm," Jessica said. "Where children go if they aren't adopted. The Cell produced more babies than The Nation needed. So instead of stopping... they built that."

Connor gritted his teeth.

"Genevieve never wanted kids. Not after what happened to her mother... or her baby sister. They both died during the birth. Then her dad killed himself."

He looked down at her sleeping face.

"They never gave her a choice."

"I'm sorry," the Pearl Enforcer said. "But we have to move. The sun's coming."

They ducked into the inner corridors.

Down narrow stairs.

Through dirt and stone.

Into a tunnel that cut beneath the earth.

At the far end—cracks of morning light.

"Quickly!" the Pearl Enforcer shouted. "The mill is just over that crest!"

Jaysen ran, heart pounding, Izzy in his arms, as the light broke over the mountains ahead.

∞

Xavier

Xavier and Lincoln sat in silence, staring at the small fire crackling between them. The room was quiet except for the occasional pop of wood and the distant chirp of early morning birds.

Every so often, Xavier glanced at Lincoln—and caught Lincoln looking back. But each time, Lincoln turned away quickly, like he'd been caught doing something he wasn't ready to explain.

Once, Lincoln opened his mouth, like he might say something.

But he didn't.

The silence stretched until Xavier couldn't take it anymore.

"Link," he whispered, voice soft. "Do you think Jaysen, Izzy, and Connor made it out?"

Lincoln kept his gaze on the fire. "It'll take more than Augmentation Bay to hold those boys," he said. "And Jaysen... he'd do anything to protect his sister. I think they'll be just fine."

Another silence.

The fire burned lower.

Xavier pulled his knees closer to his chest and shivered.

Lincoln reached for a small pole and prodded the embers, trying to coax out more heat.

"We can't let it get too big," he muttered. "Someone might see... Sorry."

Xavier curled in tighter, teeth chattering. "That's okay," he said. "It may be cold... but it beats that cage."

Lincoln moved closer.

Their shoulders nearly touched.

Xavier could feel the warmth radiating from him. He closed his eyes, remembering how it felt—being held in Lincoln's arms when the Enforcer burst in. How safe he'd felt in that brief, stolen moment.

What am I thinking? he asked himself, shaking his head.

But still, the thought lingered—how he wanted to nuzzle into Lincoln's chest again. Just to feel that warmth. That quiet strength.

The fire was almost out when Lincoln moved.

Without a word, he slipped his arm around Xavier.

"It'll be okay," he said gently, squeezing him closer.

Xavier leaned into him without thinking.

Lincoln inhaled sharply, stiffened—then let out the breath slowly. He didn't let go.

Instead, he held Xavier tighter.

"Get some rest," Lincoln mumbled. "I'm sure they won't be much longer."

He reached out and brushed a loose white strand from Xavier's face.

Xavier's eyes fluttered closed.

The fire faded to embers.

Birds chirped louder outside. The room grew lighter.

And Lincoln didn't move.

He just held Xavier as he slept.

∞

Xavier stirred at dawn.

He was curled in Lincoln's lap, a blanket draped around them both.

When he lifted his head, Lincoln was already watching him.

"I never noticed how stunning your eyes are," Lincoln said.

Xavier blinked, frozen.

I'm dreaming, he thought. *I have to be.*

Lincoln didn't pull away. He kept one arm wrapped around Xavier, the other hand gently touching his cheek.

His fingers traced the cut along Xavier's temple—the one from the fight. Then they moved lower, to the back of his head, where he'd hit it in the fall.

"Are you okay?" Lincoln asked, voice quiet, vulnerable. "You had me worried."

Xavier nodded slowly. "I… I'm okay."

His head relaxed into Lincoln's touch.

This is my favorite side of him. He thought. *The most surprising… but definitely the best.*

Lincoln's fingers trailed down his face, slow and reverent.

Xavier started to lay his head back down—but Lincoln stopped him. He lifted Xavier's chin gently, so their eyes met again.

"I'm sorry," Lincoln said. "For how I treated you."

His voice broke.

"I couldn't accept who I am. Not in there. Not even before that place. My father… he—"

Tears welled in his eye, and Xavier reached up, cupping Lincoln's cheek.

"Link," he whispered. "I understand… and I forgive you."

Lincoln closed his eye, placing his hand over Xavier's. His cheek pressed into the warmth of it, like he didn't want to let go.

Xavier leaned in slightly, then paused.

Don't rush him. I've met people with parents who never accepted them. I don't need to pry.

Lincoln opened his eye.

And then he moved.

Just a few inches—closing the space between them.

A loud clatter echoed from outside.

They jumped apart, breath caught in their throats.

The fire hissed as a breeze crept through the cracks in the boarded-up window.

Their gaze met one more time.

But the moment was gone.

"Marcus," a voice whispered loudly from outside. "Fred… Vince, are you in there?"

Xavier jolted upright, heart racing.

Connor's voice came next. "Lincoln, Xavier—it's us."

Relief surged through him.

"We're in here!" he called out, his voice shaky with a mix of exhaustion and relief.

The door creaked open, and the Pearl Enforcer entered first, scanning the room like they expected trouble. Behind them, Jaysen stepped inside, carrying a pale, semi-conscious Izzy in his arms. Connor followed, clutching a sleeping red-haired woman.

The warmth from seeing their faces made Xavier want to collapse in gratitude.

But the Pearl Enforcer glanced around. "Where are my men?" they asked sharply.

Lincoln and Xavier exchanged a look.

"Two of *your men* tried to kill us," Lincoln growled.

Xavier turned toward him in surprise just in time to catch it—Lincoln's pupil dilating.

Dark. Wide.

The same way it had during the riot.

The memory of it chilled Xavier, but he didn't move away.

He stayed beside him.

Two Black Enforcers entered the room behind the others.

Lincoln's grip tightened. In one smooth motion, he drew Vince's gun and shoved Xavier behind him, his stance wide and protective.

"If The Architect wants Xavier," Lincoln snarled, "he can come get him himself."

The Black Enforcers raised their weapons—but before anything could escalate further, the Pearl Enforcer stepped between them, calm and controlled.

"Everyone, lower your weapons," they said. "We aren't here to take you to The Architect. We're taking you to The Renegades."

A beat of silence.

Then the Black Enforcer who had stayed with Lincoln and Xavier reappeared—Jessica close behind.

Xavier peeked around Lincoln's back, heart skipping. "Jessica?"

She gave him a soft smile—but before she could speak, the Pearl Enforcer cut in.

"Marcus," they said, turning to the loyal Enforcer. "Care to explain what's going on?"

Marcus stepped forward and explained what had happened—how Vince and Fred had planned to kill Xavier and bring his body to The Architect for a reward.

"That explains the shot we heard," the Pearl Enforcer muttered.

"I have Fred tied up in the back room," Marcus added. "The Council can deal with him."

The Pearl Enforcer turned to the two Black Enforcers who had entered behind Jaysen and Connor.

"On your knees," they ordered. "Remove your helmets."

The Enforcers obeyed without hesitation.

As the helmets came off, Xavier blinked in surprise.

They're twins.

He couldn't stop himself from wondering.

Was the one Lincoln killed that young, too?

A cold shiver ran through him.

Lincoln must have felt it.

He stepped backward slightly until his back brushed against Xavier's chest—subtle, grounding.

Xavier rested his cheek gently against Lincoln's back.

His warmth calmed the storm brewing in Xavier's mind. He stayed like that, quietly taking comfort in the closeness.

"Did you have any part of this, Nick, DJ?" the Pearl Enforcer asked.

The twins shook their heads immediately.

"We'd never work with The Architect," DJ said firmly.

"Our parents are dead because of him," Nick spat, venom thick in his voice.

"If you're lying," the Pearl Enforcer said, "The Council will know."

Then they turned toward Lincoln. "Lower your weapon. Nothing is going to happen to Xavier."

Lincoln hesitated.

His hand drifted behind him, resting softly against Xavier's back— just a touch, but it made Xavier's heart stutter.

Jaysen and Connor shared a glance. Jaysen raised an eyebrow.

"Link, it's okay," Jaysen said gently. "Please. We need to go."

Lincoln looked over his shoulder at Xavier one last time—then finally lowered the gun and stepped back.

"I'll kill you all if you touch him," he growled.

Xavier stepped forward, his hands still trembling from the adrenaline, and joined Jaysen, Connor, and Jessica.

"Jessica, you're a Renegade?" he asked, his tone lit with a sudden spark of excitement.

Jessica nodded, but before she could say anything, Xavier spun toward Connor, eyes narrowing with curiosity.

"And who is this?" he asked, nodding toward the unconscious woman in Connor's arms. His tone was light, teasing, but his interest was real.

Connor looked like he was about to speak—but the Pearl Enforcer cut him off with a sharp tone.

"There will be time for this later!" they barked. "We *need* to go!"

The moment snapped. The urgency returned.

But something had changed.

Xavier glanced back at Lincoln.

And Lincoln was already looking at him.

∞

Jaysen

The group followed the Pearl Enforcer through the forest, ducking beneath low-hanging branches and weaving between gnarled trees. Their breath misted in the cold morning air. The world was hushed, as though it, too, was waiting.

In a small clearing, the Pearl Enforcer paused. They scanned the area, then crouched and brushed away a layer of leaves to reveal a wooden hatch in the ground.

They lifted it open with a creak.

Just like in my dream, Jaysen thought as a chill ran down his spine.

One by one, the group disappeared into the darkness below. Jaysen stood at the edge, holding Izzy tightly.

He looked back at Lincoln. "Do you mind?"

Izzy stirred slightly. "Jayse?" Her voice was faint. Fragile.

"Don't worry, Izzy. You're safe," he said, gently brushing a strand of hair from her face. "They can't hurt you anymore. I'll see you in just a second, okay?"

He kissed her forehead and handed her off to Lincoln, then slipped into the hatch. Lincoln crouched and carefully lowered Izzy into Jaysen's waiting arms.

Connor stepped up next, his expression guarded. "Be gentle," he whispered as Lincoln took Genevieve from his arms. "She still hasn't woken up."

Lincoln nodded and lowered her down as well.

Then, turning to Xavier, he reached out a hand.

Xavier hesitated.

Just for a moment.

Then he took it.

Lincoln helped him down, then climbed in after him. Marcus, the twins and a bound Fred, followed last, sealing the hatch above them.

The Pearl Enforcer flicked on a flashlight, the beam slicing through the underground dark. They crossed to an old wooden chest in the corner and knelt to open it.

"We have a fair walk ahead of us," they said. "Rest here for a minute."

Jaysen and Connor sank down against the dirt wall. Jaysen laid Izzy beside him, gently resting her head in his lap.

"What's happening?" she murmured, her eyelids fluttering.

Jaysen looked down, brushing her hair back as a tear slipped from the corner of his eye.

"Rest up, Izzy. I'll explain everything when we get to The Renegades."

She nodded faintly, then closed her eyes again.

Jaysen wiped his face quickly.

Xavier sat beside him.

Lincoln followed, close behind.

"So…" Xavier glanced at the sleeping woman in Connor's arms. "Who is she?"

Connor looked down at Genevieve, his fingers trailing gently through her hair.

"Her name is Genevieve," he said softly, the faintest smile tugging at his lips. "She's my wife."

Jaysen's eyes widened. "Your *wife?*"

"Shush," the Pearl Enforcer said from across the room.

Connor let out a shaky breath. "We married young. Seventeen. I thought she died... in the same accident that killed my parents."

His voice cracked.

"I should've looked for her," he said, his throat tightening. "I should never have believed she was gone." He leaned down, resting his forehead gently against hers. "All this time... and she's been just in the next room."

He clutched her tightly. "Please, baby... Please wake up. I'm so sorry."

Xavier choked up. "I'm sorry, Connor. I had no idea."

Lincoln slid his arm around Xavier's shoulders.

Xavier let himself lean into him, burying his face in Lincoln's chest. The tears came quickly—silent, hot.

Jessica sat down next to them, placing a hand on Genevieve's arm.

"It may take a while," she said gently. "She's been under for a long time."

Connor put his hand over hers. "Thank you. For everything."

He looked up at her, and they exchanged a tired, grateful smile.

The Pearl Enforcer opened a chest, then pulled out a crate of dusty water bottles.

They handed them around.

"It's not fresh," they said, "but it's better than nothing."

Everyone took one.

Jaysen drank, eyes still on his sister. Still on Genevieve. Still processing.

"We need to keep going now," the Pearl Enforcer said.

Jaysen nodded and tightened his grip around Izzy.

He was ready.

Lincoln

As the group moved deeper into the underground tunnel, Lincoln stayed close.

Close to his friends.

But mostly—close to Xavier.

The packed dirt walls curved around them, the air thick with dampness and old stone. The only sounds were footfalls and breath, the occasional scrape of a boot on the uneven floor.

Lincoln walked in silence, his shoulder brushing Xavier's every so often. Each time it happened, he stiffened.

Don't creep him out, you idiot, he scolded himself. *Back off. Give him space.*

But even when he slowed, even when he pulled away, he found himself drifting back toward Xavier—like gravity, like instinct.

What are you even doing? he thought, frustrated. *You've got no clue how to do this. No idea what he wants… or what you want, really. Just don't fuck it up.*

Xavier must've noticed the distance widening between them and the rest of the group. He slowed his pace until it was just the two of them at the back of the line.

The flashlight ahead barely reached them. They were wrapped in shadows.

Xavier glanced over, offering a small smile. "Are you okay, Link?" he asked softly.

Lincoln's throat tightened.

The question was gentle. Innocent. But it stuck in his chest.

He meant to say, *I'm fine.*

Then thought *Good* would be safer.

But what came out was: "I'm food."

The moment the words left his mouth, he felt his face erupt with heat.

I'm food.

Smooth, Lincoln. Real smooth.

He turned bright red, eyes dropping to the ground. His boots scuffed awkwardly against the packed dirt.

Xavier giggled.

Not the cruel kind. Not mocking.

It was soft. Warm.

Like the sound Lincoln imagined a sunrise might make.

Lincoln didn't say another word. Couldn't. He just kept walking, face still burning, heart pounding way too loud for comfort.

Beside him, Xavier didn't move away.

He didn't laugh again.

He just stayed there, close enough to brush hands now and then in the dark.

And Lincoln couldn't help but hope—

Maybe that wasn't so bad after all.

∞

Xavier

Xavier smiled, the corners of his lips tugging up as he glanced sideways at Lincoln.

"You're cute when you're embarrassed," he said, voice low enough for only Lincoln to hear. "You turn so red."

Lincoln's face darkened instantly, blooming into an even deeper shade of crimson. He looked at Xavier with a wide, startled eye.

That piercing blue… it was almost electric in the dim light of the tunnel. Unfiltered. Raw.

Xavier's heart hammered so loudly in his chest, he barely heard his own thoughts. The tunnel seemed to close in, blurring everything except Lincoln—his awkward posture, his twitching fingers, his heated cheeks.

Hold his hand. This shouldn't be so hard, he told himself, gaze dropping to where Lincoln's hand swung loosely at his side.

It's right there... just take it.

But Xavier hesitated.

What if he pulls away?

What if this ruins everything?

Lincoln shifted beside him, eyes still locked on Xavier's flushed face.

"Now who's turning red," he said with a teasing smirk.

Then he followed Xavier's gaze.

Down to his own hand.

His expression softened in that moment—not teasing, but something else. Something more careful. More open.

Slowly, Lincoln stepped closer, close enough that their hands brushed.

Xavier didn't overthink it this time.

He reached out.

His fingers slid between Lincoln's.

And Lincoln let them.

Xavier looked up, nerves tugging at every edge of his smile.

But Lincoln was already looking back—smiling softly, shyly.

And then he gave Xavier's hand a gentle squeeze.

Not just permission.

Reassurance.

And Xavier's heart, still racing, finally slowed just enough to let him breathe.

∞

Jaysen

"Look at this," Jaysen whispered, his voice full of disbelief as he peered over his shoulder.

Back at Xavier.

And Lincoln.

Walking hand in hand.

"What the fuck did we miss?"

Connor followed his gaze, eyes widening slightly before glancing back at Jaysen. He shrugged.

"I have no fucking clue," he muttered. "That is the last thing I was expecting to happen tonight."

DJ, walking a little ahead, turned slightly. "So… they're *not* together?"

"They were always fighting. Like, constantly—like cats and dogs," Jaysen said, shaking his head. "At least that's how it was when we left them in the roofs."

He paused.

"And well, we knew about Xav…" His voice dropped slightly. "But not Lincoln."

From beside him, a soft voice cut in.

"Xav?"

Jaysen looked down.

Izzy.

Her eyes were fluttering open again, her voice faint and drowsy.

"Xav's here?" she asked.

"He's here," Jaysen said gently, holding her a little closer. "He'll come see you soon… Once we're there."

Izzy nodded slightly and tucked her head back into his chest. Jaysen tightened his hold around her, resting his chin on her hair.

DJ slowed his pace, pointing up ahead.

"It's not much farther," he said. "The entry's just around this bend."

CHAPTER NINE

No Ma∨er What

Jaidon

Jaidon screamed, voice fraying into something wild and animalistic, as the Argentine Enforcers tore the armor from his body.

Each strap unbuckled, each piece stripped away, felt like a layer of his sanity going with it.

"The Harvest is in two days," The Warden sneered, his boots echoing as he stepped into view.

"You know my organs are worthless," Jaidon spat, desperation cutting through his words like broken glass.

"They are," The Warden agreed, too calmly. He took a slow step closer, something wicked glinting in his eye. "That's why you're going to be… the entertainment."

There was a sick pleasure in his voice. A perverse satisfaction.

Is he getting off on this? Jaidon thought, horror flooding him. *Zoti help me…*

The Warden's lip curled.

"Traitors don't get a quick death."

He turned his back without another word. "Take him to The Pitts."

"No—NO!" Jaidon thrashed, his feet skidding against the floor as two Argentine Enforcers seized him by the arms. "I'M NOT A TRAITOR!"

His voice cracked.

"I WAS SET UP!"

"I SHOULD BE HAVING A TRIAL!"

"WHAT HAVE I DONE TO DESERVE THIS!?"

"I HAVE MY RIGHTS!"

His words echoed through the corridor.

No one responded.

No one cared.

Only the cold, merciless drag of boots on stone as they hauled him toward the darkness below.

∞

Shabina

Shabina and Mather sat together in the locked surgery, the flickering light above them humming softly as silence settled over the room.

From beyond the thick walls, Jaidon's screams had finally faded— swallowed by the darkness of The Pitts.

She closed her eyes and whispered, "We did it, Mather."

Her voice trembled with exhaustion, with disbelief.

"We're going to be okay."

She reached for his hand and took it gently.

"It's okay… you can relax now."

Mather's fingers tightened around hers.

"*You* did it," he said, voice low with wonder and guilt. "*I* was ready to hand ourselves in… That could've been us. It *would* have been us— if it wasn't for you."

She looked up at him, eyes shining with fierce devotion.

"I'll keep you safe… just like you've kept *me* safe," she said. "No matter what."

"No matter what," he echoed, pulling her into his chest and wrapping his arms around her.

They stayed like that, breathing together.

"We never speak of that room… of Jaidon, again… okay?" Shabina whispered, her voice barely more than a breath against his collarbone.

"Never again," Mather said, firm and certain.

He kissed her forehead.

And held her tighter.

∞

Jaidon

They threw Jaidon into a cage better suited to a Rottweiler than a man.

"THIS ISN'T RIGHT!" he screamed at the Argentine Enforcers as they walked away.

"What you did wasn't right. Killing Dr. Lancet—the Harvest Surgeon? You're scum. You're no Enforcer," one of them called over their shoulder.

"You're getting exactly what you deserve," said the other. "These rats are going to rip you limb from limb… Traitor! HEAR THAT, RATS? THAT ONE THERE—HE WAS AN *ENFORCER*!"

The cageys locked away with Jaidon erupted, yelling and rattling the bars of their cages.

"I'M BEING SET UP!" Jaidon bellowed as the door slammed shut behind the Enforcers. "I DON'T DESERVE THIS!"

"None of us deserve this," a voice hissed from the cage beside him. "And it's because of people like you that we're here. I hope I'm the one who gets to kill you. I'll make sure you suffer."

"Fuck you, rat," Jaidon spat. "You—and every other rat in here—you deserve this. I don't. They sent you here for a reason. *I* WAS SET UP!"

Again, the cageys roared and shook their cages, their rage echoing off the walls.

After hours of screaming, Jaidon's voice had turned to gravel. The stench of the cramped, filth-slick cage was overpowering, making him gag. He slid down the bars, curling into himself.

"I don't deserve this," he sobbed, rocking back and forth. "I'm not a traitor."

Eventually, the stench overcame him. He lost consciousness, slumped in the corner. The cageys around him whispered and laughed in the dark—scheming.

∞

When Jaidon awoke, the world was still black.

"Is there no light in here?" he rasped, eyes straining.

The cageys laughed.

"You want light?" one of them asked.

"Yes. I do," Jaidon snapped. "It's basic human rights."

"Human rights?" another scoffed. "We don't have rights. And now, you're one of us."

Jaidon spat. "I'll *never* be one of you."

The laughter came again.

"That's too bad," said the man in the cage beside him, his voice oily. A flashlight clicked on briefly—just enough to sear a white blotch into Jaidon's vision—then vanished.

"Show me that again," Jaidon demanded.

Laughter again.

"But you're not one of us," the man drawled. "Why would I show you the light?"

Jaidon stared at the blotch left behind in the dark, trying to form a plan.

"Because… because…" he faltered.

"How you ever became an Enforcer, I'll never know," the man chuckled.

"You're right," Jaidon muttered. "I was never a good Enforcer. Maybe… maybe I am one of you."

The cageys howled.

"So, will you show me the light?" he asked, heart racing. *Snatch it from him. As soon as he shows you, take it.*

"Sure," said the man. "Come closer."

Jaidon crawled toward the side of his cage.

"Closer."

He pressed his face to the bars. *Perfect. Now I can—*

The flashlight flicked on. Jaidon lunged for it.

But the man caught his wrist.

"You'll never be one of us," he sneered.

The cageys erupted with cheers as Jaidon struggled.

"You want to see the light?" the man said, yanking the flashlight back. "I'll show you the light."

"HELP!" Jaidon screamed.

"No one's coming. You're not one of them anymore *either*."

Jaidon tried to wrench away, but the man's grip was iron.

"Not so strong without your armor and gun, are you?" the man laughed, pressing Jaidon's face to the bars. "You're not taking our last chance for glory. *Traitor*."

"I'M NOT A TRAITOR!" Jaidon howled. "I WAS SET UP! THEY'LL MAKE YOU PAY FOR THIS!"

The cageys cackled, banging the bars.

"They can't give us anything worse than The Pits," the man growled. "Maybe I should keep you alive… So you can *see*."

Jaidon's heart pounded. *Keep me alive?*

"But then again," the man said, voice dropping, "you're not stealing our glory."

He yanked Jaidon closer, body jammed against the cage wall.

"THIS IS WHO THEY HAVE GUARDING US!" he roared, shining the flashlight straight into Jaidon's face. "THIS… RUNT!"

Cheers erupted.

"PUT IT DOWN! KILL IT!" the cageys howled.

Jaidon thrashed—then screamed as something sharp slid down his arm, splitting it open.

Blood poured freely.

The light flashed upward.

Then—pain. Deep and blinding. A sharp stab in his chest.

The last thing Jaidon saw was the scarred, tattooed face of the man leering at him. Yellow teeth twisted into a smirk.

Then—

A bang. Echoing in the walls.

And darkness.

$$\infty$$

Valentino

Valentino's lamp had long since dried out. The battery on his glasses blinked red, warning him they were nearly dead. His water bottle was empty, the plastic walls caved in from his desperate attempts to drain the last drops.

Fred and Vince hadn't come back.

Hadn't come back in… he'd forgotten how long.

"But I still have six giant bags of jerky," he cackled to himself. The sound bounced off the walls like a threat.

With a wild grin, he hurled his lamp out of the shelter. It shattered against the ground, shards spinning into the dark.

Once, it had been sweat that glued his clothes to his skin.

Now, it was filth. Weeks of it.

Urine. Feces.

He'd stopped caring. Somewhere between hunger and madness, dignity had become a distant memory.

Valentino stuffed the bags of jerky into his backpack, slung it over his shoulder, and pushed his glasses up onto his nose. The flickering overlay of their failing interface glitched at the corners of his vision.

"I'm getting out of here…" he mumbled. "If it's the last thing I do."

He stepped out of his shelter into the stale air of the roof.

He had no idea how long he'd been up here.

The days had bled into each other.

The grinding overhead seemed louder now. Closer. The darkness more alive.

Shadows formed shapes in the corners of his vision—some familiar.

Some not.

"Where is it?" he muttered, fingers trailing along the cold piping, searching. "The door… the door…"

His glasses beeped again, louder this time.

Low battery.

Just as he found a panel in the wall.

"Wasn't it on the other side?" he whispered.

He pushed it open and slipped through.

"No… no… I just got turned around… that's it… Turned around…"

He wandered deeper into the walls, retracing steps he wasn't sure he'd ever taken. His fingers skimmed rough metal, peeled paint, half-forgotten paths.

"Wasn't there a stairwell here?" he mumbled.

He turned back.

Tried another way.

The interface of his glasses flickered—once, twice—then died. The dull image vanished into suffocating black.

"No, no, no—" Valentino gasped, heart pounding.

He sucked in the air too fast. It felt thin. Wrong.

Then—voices.

Faint. Muffled. Somewhere ahead.

He stumbled toward them.

And then—

BANG.

A sharp crack like a gunshot.

Valentino dropped to the floor, disoriented, the sound ringing in his ears.

Then the siren.

It wailed through the metal corridors, bouncing from pipe to pipe, vibrating through his skull.

He cried out, hands flying to his ears as he crumpled into the fetal position.

Everything was spinning.

He couldn't see. Couldn't think. Could barely breathe.

The siren grew louder.

The dark grew thicker.

And Valentino rocked against the cold metal wall—lost in the sound, in the dark, in his own unraveling mind.

∞

Dr. Zygote

Dr. Zygote was curled in the narrow bunk tucked behind his surgery, snoring softly, when the loud bang jolted him awake.

His eyes flew open.

"What now?" he grumbled, tossing the thin blanket aside and hopping down onto the cold floor. He yanked his lab coat from a hook and shrugged it on, fumbling for his glasses on the side table.

An alarm began to blare—sharp, piercing. It echoed through the walls of the facility.

Zygote paused, smoothing his hair with one hand while staring into the old, smudged mirror nailed above the sink.

His reflection looked wild—hair sticking out at the sides, one button misaligned, the red-rimmed eyes of someone who hadn't truly slept in weeks.

"Perfect," he muttered sarcastically, and stormed out of the room.

∞

The hallway pulsed red with the alarm lights.

He ran full tilt toward The Cell, shoes slipping slightly on the polished floors.

"WHERE IS SHE?!" he bellowed as he stormed through the rows of hospital beds.

Two beds were still warm.

But they were empty.

"JESSICA!" he screamed, spinning in a frantic circle. "JESSICA, GET HERE NOW!"

No response.

Only the alarm. Only the hollow stillness of the room.

Dr. Zygote spun again, eyes darting to every corner. With each lap around the chamber, he looked—hoped—that maybe they would just… reappear.

But the beds where Isabelle and Genevieve had been were still vacant.

Empty restraints.

Monitors offline.

Gone.

"WHERE ARE THEY?!" he roared, spit flying from his mouth as he pounded a fist on the nearest wall.

He stopped moving.

Stood trembling in the center of the room.

His shoulders slumped.

"I know," he whispered to himself. "I know, my love…"

His eyes turned distant, then dark.

"She's a traitor," he said coldly. "She took you."

His voice cracked. "She took you both."

His rage reignited, and he spun on his heel, coat billowing.

Dr. Zygote stormed from The Cell, alarm still screaming around him, and charged toward The Warden's office—with fury in his chest and betrayal twisting behind his eyes.

∞

The Warden

The Warden stood silently in his office.

There was no trace of her now. Dr. Lancet.

No blood.

No body.

No mess.

Not even the scent of her perfume lingered.

Just the memory of what he'd done—and what had been done to her.

He smirked.

"I wish you had lasted a bit longer," he murmured, voice smooth and low as he stared at the bed. "But it was fun while it lasted."

His eyes darkened.

"And don't worry… we got the fucker who took you from me."

The silence of the office wrapped around him, thick and reverent.

He remembered her mouth.

Her eyes.

Her scream.

"I know… I know," he whispered, his voice shifting into something twisted and amused. "It was wrong…"

His fingers moved to his belt buckle.

"But it felt so good."

He bit his lip, smirk widening, the tension in the room turning rotten.

Then—

BANG.

The sound crashed through the ceiling vent above him—sharp, metallic.

The Warden froze.

The smirk vanished.

He slowly raised his head, eyes narrowing toward the grating above.

The Warden's hands moved away from his belt.

His posture shifted.

His smile faded into something colder.

Alert.

Calculating.

He looked toward the door, the tension broken—but something else rising in its place.

Something worse.

∞

The Enforcers

"It came from up here," an Argentine Enforcer called out as they flipped on the overhead lights, flooding The Detachment Gibbets with harsh illumination.

The roof groaned underfoot.

"Where are all the rats?" asked the Black Enforcer, their voice low and wary as they scanned the rows of now-empty gibbets.

They exchanged a look.

Something was wrong.

They moved cautiously, boots echoing on the steel floor, rifles tight in their grips as they swept through the roof. The silence didn't feel like quiet—it felt like something holding its breath.

As they neared the gibbets where the prisoners had been locked up just the night before, the Black Enforcer spotted something on the ground.

A small piece of paper.

"And don't forget, trainee… you do what *I* say. And I say until he sees this—and figures out what it is—the fewer people who know about it, the better."

The Black Enforcer nodded silently.

They turned to leave, boots crunching faint debris with each step.

Just before turning off the lights, the Argentine Enforcer paused.

A glint caught their eye.

Near the edge of the walkway.

"Hold on," they said, raising a hand. Their voice dropped into something cautious. Controlled.

They gestured for the Black Enforcer to follow and crept toward the object.

The light flickered slightly above them.

They found the lamp.

Then the shelter.

"No one's here," the Black Enforcer said after inspecting it, sweeping the area.

"But someone *was…*" They looked at the scattered wrappers, the bedding, the makeshift walls of hoarded supplies.

"For a long time."

They stood in silence.

Then without another word, the Argentine Enforcer shut off the light—and the roof returned to shadow

∞

Shabina

"What was that?" Shabina asked, heart lurching in her chest as the muffled sound echoed through the walls above them.

She and Mather were already halfway up the narrow stairs that led from the hidden passage.

"It sounded like a gunshot," he said, slipping his helmet over his head. "But not one of ours."

The two exchanged a glance—sharp, knowing.

Shabina reached the top first, her palms damp against the concealed door. She pressed her ear to the cold metal.

Silence for a beat.

Then distant shouting.

The shriek of boots on stone.

Her fingers worked quickly to undo the latch, and she cracked the door just enough to peer through.

The corridor beyond pulsed red with alarm lights, casting sharp shadows that danced across the floor.

She took a breath.

You've done this before. Keep calm. Keep moving.

She nodded to Mather.

He nodded back.

Together, they pushed through the door and slipped into the corridor—just as the alarms began to wail.

The sound slammed into them like a wave—piercing, disorienting. It made the walls feel too close. The world too loud.

"This isn't good," Mather muttered, scanning the hallway. "I was supposed to be on patrol…"

His voice trailed off, guilt creeping into the edges of his tone.

Shabina grabbed his arm and tugged him toward her.

"You were on patrol," she said firmly, eyes meeting his behind the visor. "You were helping me… preparing for surgery."

He hesitated.

Then gave a tight nod.

But she saw the conflict still churning behind his mask.

The weight of the lie. The danger of their choice.

Neither said it aloud—but they knew: if anyone traced anything back to that hidden room…

They were both done for.

"Let's go," she said.

They broke into a run, boots pounding down the corridor in perfect rhythm.

Each corner they rounded, each hallway they passed, was bathed in flickering red light. The sirens screamed louder with every step, pulsing through the walls like a heartbeat gone mad.

As they neared the turn that would take them toward The Warden's office, Shabina glanced sideways at Mather.

Hand near his weapon.

Always ready.

She was grateful he was there.

Grateful she wasn't facing this alone.

Not anymore.

They rounded the final corner—breath sharp, hearts pounding, eyes fixed forward.

Whatever had just happened... we're about to find out.

∞

The Warden

"Has anyone else seen this?" The Warden asked coldly as he paced the floor of his office, boots thudding softly on the stone.

The coded note trembled slightly in his hand, though not from the paper.

"No, sir," the Argentine Enforcer replied. "Just us."

The Warden nodded slowly. "Good... tell no one."

His eyes never left the symbols on the page.

"Expect a bonus this week. Both of you. Leave your ID numbers there." He gestured vaguely toward a small silver tray on the edge of his desk, eyes still fixed on the message.

"That will be all."

The Enforcers didn't move.

"Sorry, sir," the Argentine Enforcer added nervously. "There's… more."

The Warden's jaw twitched.

"Well, go on then," he growled. "Spit it out."

"There's no one in Detachment," the Enforcer said quickly. "And… we found a shelter."

The words hung in the air.

The Warden's gaze snapped toward the Enforcer like a knife unsheathed.

"WHAT?" he roared. The walls seemed to tremble with the force of it. "WHERE ARE THEY? WHO WAS THERE?!"

The Enforcers stiffened, trying not to let the rattle in their armor show.

"We… We don't know, sir."

The Warden's voice turned venomous. "WELL, WHAT THE FUCK ARE YOU WAITING FOR?! GO AND FIND OUT! GET EVERYONE SEARCHING—*NOW!*"

The Enforcers bolted.

The room fell into a tense, echoing silence.

Dr. Zygote stepped forward from the shadows, his expression pale.

"This isn't good," he muttered. "Donovan is going to kill us… We lost them."

The Warden didn't respond.

He sat at his desk, tapping a pen slowly—methodically—against the wood.

Tap. Tap. Tap.

"Evelyn," he blurted suddenly.

Dr. Zygote's brow furrowed. "She's *dead*, sir."

"Yes," The Warden snapped. "I *know* she's dead."

His eyes flicked up, sharp and gleaming.

"But before that—she implanted a tracker into the incubator."

Dr. Zygote's face turned red.

He froze.

Then exploded.

"She did *what?!*" he seethed. "SHE DID *WHAT?!* HOW DARE SHE! IF SHE WASN'T DEAD ALREADY—*I'D KILL HER MYSELF!*"

He slammed a hand on the table, eyes blazing.

But The Warden simply smirked, the cold gears already turning behind his eyes.

∞

Mather

"Who are you killing?" Shabina asked as she and Mather entered The Warden's office.

Mather's boots clicked softly on the stone behind hers, his steps slower, more controlled. He was watching everything.

"What's this Enforcer doing here?" The Warden snapped. "They should be patrolling with the others."

"This Enforcer is training to be my guard," Shabina answered, not missing a beat. Her voice was calm, composed—just sharp enough to keep control. "Given the circumstances of Dr. Lancet's death, I deemed it necessary to have protection at all times... After all... I am the only Harvest Surgeon now."

"How do you know we can trust him to look after you?" Dr. Zygote asked.

"I don't," Shabina said, eyes steady. "But if something does happen to me... you know whom to look for."

Mather stepped forward. "I will protect Dr. Valentine with my life," he said. "Her safety is my priority. You have my word."

The Warden and Dr. Zygote exchanged a look—cold, assessing.

"We're going to need more than your word," The Warden said. "It's your time, too... Shabina."

"My time?" she echoed.

"Are you sure they're ready?" Dr. Zygote asked.

"We're going to find out," The Warden replied. He stepped toward the fire, removing a long iron rod glowing red in the coals.

"Remove your helmet."

Mather hesitated. "Sir… Mr. Blakewell said—"

"You do what I say now," The Warden barked. "Remove your helmet. I won't ask again."

Mather unfastened it, one slow clip at a time, then pulled off the black balaclava beneath.

"What's your name?" The Warden demanded.

"Mather, sir."

"Well, Mather… Shabina… It's time for you two to make your loyalty known to me."

He lifted the branding iron from the fire.

"Zayne. Show them."

Dr. Zygote turned around, pulling back his thinning hair to reveal the old burn seared into the back of his neck—the shape of cagey shackles, unmistakable.

"It will only hurt for a moment," he said as Shabina gasped. "This gel will help."

Mather's chest tightened.

Shabina looked at him. Her eyes said it all.

After a pause, she nodded. "Okay," she said, quieter now. Then she looked at her father.

Dr. Zygote and The Warden turned to Mather.

"Say no now," The Warden said, "and you can leave. Say yes… and you never leave."

Mather didn't flinch. "I'm not leaving her."

"Right then," The Warden said. "On your knees. Show me the back of your necks."

Mather lowered himself beside Shabina, staring down at the floor as she brushed her hair aside and closed her eyes.

When the iron struck her flesh, her scream cut through the chamber.

Mather reached for her hand and gripped it tightly, holding her steady as she trembled.

When The Warden lifted the iron, pieces of her skin clung to it, sizzling.

Dr. Zygote quickly applied the gel. Shabina's whimpers softened.

The Warden returned the iron to the fire. "Don't go anywhere," he told Mather with a smirk. "You're next."

This sick bastard is enjoying this, Mather thought, gritting his teeth. *One day… I'm going to make him pay for this.*

Then the iron came.

The searing heat lanced into his skin, and Mather bit down on the inside of his cheek so hard he tasted blood. He didn't cry out.

But the pain didn't fade.

No one moved.

No one helped.

He waited for the cool relief of the gel.

It never came.

Shabina stirred beside him. "Why aren't you putting the gel on his neck?" she asked.

"We have a limited supply," The Warden said coolly. "This one is for you only. He needs to prove his strength."

"That's fucking ridiculous!" she snapped.

"It's okay, Dr. Valentine," Mather said as he rose to his feet. His body trembled with the effort. "They're right. You need it more than I do."

The Warden smiled again. "Now put your helmet back on and get out there."

Shabina moved as if to protest, but Dr. Zygote silenced her with a glare.

"Yes, sir," Mather said before she could speak.

He pulled the balaclava over his head with trembling fingers, then eased the helmet into place, wincing as the pressure pressed against the raw burn.

Once he was fully suited, Dr. Zygote handed the gel to Shabina.

"Use it sparingly," he said. "Now go on. Back to your surgery. Lock the doors."

His voice grew darker.

"Prisoners have escaped. They're dangerous men. And they've stolen two incubators."

∞

"Please," Shabina begged, stepping in close. "I locked the doors... Let me put some of this on it. Please, Mather."

She held the gel in her hand, hope flickering in her eyes.

"Not now," he said, voice low. "They may check... We can't risk it. I'm okay."

He tried to reassure her, but inside he was crumbling. *I've never been more grateful for this helmet,* he thought as hot tears streamed down his face, soaking into the thick balaclava. The fabric clung to the fresh burn, magnifying the pain like a brand inside his skull.

"At least take your helmet off," she pleaded. "Let it breathe. It's been hours... It needs air."

Mather shook his head. Pain radiated from the branding, sharp and constant. Still, he gritted his teeth, swallowing the grunt that clawed at his throat.

"I'm fine, Shabina," he said firmly. "Please... that's enough."

She dropped her head.

The movement tugged at her own wound. She winced, letting out a small yelp as her hand instinctively went to the back of her neck.

Mather was beside her instantly. "Sorry," he murmured, softer now. "Here... let me."

He slipped off his gloves and held out his hand. Shabina hesitated, then handed him the gel. Gently, he brushed her hair aside, fingers lingering just a moment longer than necessary, and applied a small amount of the gel to the red, angry brand.

The cooling touch beneath his fingertips was soothing—even if only for her.

I wish I could feel it, he thought as she exhaled, her body relaxing under his hands.

"Will you at least let me kiss you?" she asked softly.

Mather removed the mouthpiece of his helmet. Shabina set the gel on the table behind her, then turned and wrapped her arms around his shoulders.

She kissed him gently.

Mather pulled her closer by the waist. Her hands traveled to the side of his neck, fingers slipping under the edge of his balaclava, tugging it up just enough.

"Let it get some air," she whispered.

The fresh air hit his burn and stung at first—but it was better than the suffocating heat beneath the fabric. Her kisses eased the pain, the soft press of her fingertips soothing even as they neared the raw skin.

Then—

Her fingers touched the wound.

A cool numbness followed in their wake.

Mather froze.

He stepped back sharply, instinctively grabbing the back of his neck.

"What did you do?" he asked, eyes darting to the gel remnants still slick on her hand. The sudden relief had given him away. It was there—soothing, welcome.

But fear clawed in his chest.

Fear of The Warden.

Of Dr. Zygote.

Of what they'd do if they found out.

"Shabina…"

He didn't know what to say.

"I'm sorry, Mather," she said, breath catching. "But I'm a surgeon. I *know* what will happen to you if it's not treated."

"AND WHAT ABOUT WHEN THE WARDEN FINDS OUT?" he snapped, louder than he intended.

Shabina jumped.

"I'm sorry," she whispered, retreating a step. "It was only a little bit."

Mather sighed and dropped his voice. "Please… just… don't do that again," he said, guilt softening his tone. "I'm sorry too. I shouldn't have yelled."

She nodded slowly. "I'll be talking to my father as soon as I can," she said with quiet resolve. "He's a doctor. He *has* to understand."

"I'll be all right," Mather said, stepping closer again. "You have to trust me."

He took her hand gently, wiping away the remaining gel.

"Now turn around."

She did.

He applied the rest of the gel to her neck, fingers moving with care. When he finished, he turned her gently by the shoulders.

"It's going to take a lot more than The Warden branding me to take me down," he said with a half-smile. "Especially now that I'm your guard. Nice thinking, by the way… Now we've got the perfect excuse to spend all our time together."

"This place…" she whispered. "There's something wrong with it. Something terribly wrong. I don't know what it is, but I'm sure it starts with The Warden… and I *will* find out."

Mather removed the rest of his helmet and balaclava, laying them beside the table.

"Shabina…" he said, tone worried. "You shouldn't mess with him. He's—"

"Dangerous," she finished. "I know. But I'm smart."

He looked at her, concern etched into every line of his face.

"I'm not saying you aren't," he said. "I just… I don't want you getting hurt. The Warden—he's not just dangerous. He's *insane*."

Shabina cupped his face in her hands.

"I've known insane my whole life, Mather," she said gently. "I mean, I grew up here. And look at my father. Did you know he talks to my mother? She's an incubator in The Cell. She's in a coma, and he talks to her. He thinks… she talks back."

Mather stared at her, stunned.

"The best thing about insane?" she added. "It's easy to outwit."

"He talks to your mother?" he asked quietly.

She nodded. "It sounds like mumbling, but he isn't talking to himself. He's talking to *her*."

"Who is she?"

"I don't know," Shabina said, her voice low. "All I know is her name is Maya… At least, I think it is. He mutters a lot about how she and my sister were given the wrong name. He calls them *both* Maya."

"How do you know all this?"

"I've lived under this prison for so long," she explained. "I know how to get around without being seen. I heard him talking when he thought he was alone. He said he wants to wake her up soon. He says a lot when he thinks no one's listening."

"So… does he actually *know* your mother?" Mather asked.

She shook her head, a flicker of sadness crossing her face. "No. She was already asleep when he first saw her, years ago. He made it all up in his head."

She paused.

"I know my father's insane. I know I could never trust him. But… this is the only way to discover who I am."

Mather clenched his fists. "This place," he growled.

"There's something wrong with it," she echoed.

"And we're going to find out what it is," Mather said. "Together."

"No matter what," she whispered as she melted into his arms.

"No matter what," he echoed, holding her close.

I need to keep her safe, he thought. *She's all that matters… The only good thing about this place is her.*

∞

Dr. Zygote

"What do you mean you can't get into it?" Dr. Zygote snapped, pacing like a caged animal inside The Warden's office. "You let that *troll* into my Cell... You let her put a tracker into my incubator... and now you can't even access it?"

The Warden didn't look up. He was hunched over Dr. Lancet's laptop, punching in another password.

Incorrect.

Again.

"You forget your place, Zayne," The Warden said, voice cold and flat. "Do you need help remembering it?"

Dr. Zygote stiffened but forced a controlled breath through his nose.

"Was I wrong to assume," he said slowly, "that you would be capable of accessing a tracker you approved?"

The Warden's jaw twitched. He typed again—failed again—and slammed his fist onto the table.

"Yeah, well, I didn't plan on her dying, Zayne!"

Dr. Zygote didn't flinch.

"Maybe the new surgeon can figure it out," he said coolly.

"Maybe," The Warden echoed, glancing sideways. "Take it to her. See if she can help. What's the worst that could happen? If she betrays me... she can join Evelyn."

Dr. Zygote's expression remained carefully neutral as he collected the laptop.

Shabina had better not fuck this up, he thought bitterly, marching into the corridor. *If she can do this... we go straight to Cypher. Or better yet... The Architect.*

His thoughts twisted, moving faster than his feet. *But I still need Valentino... Where is he?*

He reached Shabina's surgery and rapped on the door. "Shabina. I need to speak with you."

The lock clicked.

The door cracked an inch.

"Is it safe?" she asked, voice low. "Have they found the men?"

Dr. Zygote shook his head. "No. But if you can help… we might."

He watched her glance over her shoulder.

Mather stood near the wall, helmet clipped in place. He gave a small, wordless nod.

Shabina opened the door.

"Come in," she whispered, locking it again once he stepped through.

Dr. Zygote didn't wait. He crossed the room and placed the laptop on the workbench with more force than necessary.

"Can you get into it?" he asked.

"I don't know," Shabina admitted, studying the device. "I've only ever worked with pagers and radios… you know, older tech. This might be beyond my skills."

Dr. Zygote looked like he might combust.

"Figure it out," he hissed through clenched teeth. "The Warden is expecting it."

"What's on it?" she asked.

"Information," he said flatly.

"Okay, Dr. Zygote," she said, polite and cool. "I'll notify you when I'm finished."

He gave her a sharp nod, then turned toward Mather.

"How's your neck?" he asked wryly, his tone edged with mockery.

"Fine, sir," Mather said bluntly.

Zygote scowled, then stormed out of the surgery—muttering curses as he fumbled with the locking mechanism on the door.

∞

Shabina

415

Shabina stared down at the laptop on the workbench like it might detonate.

Dr. Lancet's laptop.

Heavy. Locked. Full of secrets she wasn't meant to uncover.

"I've never hacked anything, Mather," she said quietly, not taking her eyes off it. "I fixed a couple of pagers and broken radios I found down in the tunnels. That's it. How am I supposed to get into the laptop of a woman I hardly know?"

Her voice cracked on the last word.

Mather stepped beside her and placed a reassuring hand on her shoulder.

"If he comes asking questions," he said gently, "just tell him it'll take time. Make it sound complicated. Keep him distracted."

Shabina nodded slowly, fingers twitching with the need to *do* something—but afraid to even touch the laptop again.

"I have a friend," Mather continued, "at Command. Her name's Locklan. She's always tinkering with tech—radios, computers, circuit boards. If anyone can crack this, it's her."

Shabina looked up at him. Her voice was barely a whisper. "We can trust her… right?"

A tear slipped down her cheek before she could stop it.

Mather wiped it away gently with his thumb. "Locklan is one of the most trustworthy people I know," he said. "I'd trust her with my life."

His words held steady, solid like stone beneath her feet.

"We'll visit her in a few days," he added. "Can you show me where you used to sneak in?"

Shabina nodded.

Maybe she couldn't break into the laptop herself.

But with Mather, and Locklan…

She just might have a chance.

∞

Fred

"What happened, Fred?" a calm voice echoed from the mouth of the small cave.

Fred looked up slowly from where he sat on the cold stone floor, his wrists shackled, his back against the rough wall. The cell was little more than a carved-out pocket of rock, converted into a holding room for traitors.

Lance stepped closer, his silhouette backlit by the faint light from outside. "If you don't talk… you know what happens."

Fred scoffed weakly. "Lance," he muttered, shaking his head. "You wouldn't understand."

Lance sat down beside the bars, his voice softer now. "Try me."

Fred didn't answer at first. He looked back down at the ground, fingers nervously tracing the edge of a scab on his knuckle.

"We're friends, Fred. Please…" Lance urged. "Just tell me what happened. What exactly does The Architect know?"

Fred hesitated.

Then, quietly, "Vince… He said it would be okay." His voice trembled as he dropped his head into his hands. "He said if we did it… we would be free."

Lance tilted his head. "Free?"

"Free to leave. To finally be together."

A pause stretched between them.

"The Architect was paying you to bring him Xavier?"

Fred nodded slowly.

Lance's voice darkened. "Do you even know who The Architect is?"

Fred shook his head. "There was a middleman. Val. He gave us the job. When The Architect got word the job was done, we were supposed to meet Val again… and get paid."

His eyes welled. "We were so close to escaping The Nation… So close."

"Where's Val now?" Lance asked.

Fred let out a hollow, bitter laugh. "He's probably rotting in the roof of Augmentation Bay by now. He started losing it. Vince convinced me to leave him there. Said he was a liability."

He leaned his head back against the wall.

"The last time I saw him... he was covered in shit and piss, running around the roof chasing ghosts."

Lance exhaled heavily. "I told you to stay away from Vince. He wasn't a good person, Fred. You see that now... don't you?"

Fred didn't answer.

Lance pressed on. "If you tell me everything—*everything*—maybe I can help you."

Fred let out a laugh that bordered on a sob. "You can't help me now. You were right. And now it's too late."

"Well..." Lance's voice softened. "Maybe *you* can help *me*, Fred."

Fred looked up.

"How long have you been doing jobs for The Architect?"

A long pause.

"A year now," Fred admitted.

"Where do you meet Val?"

"The lookout. After dark."

"And how does he contact you?"

"Smoke signal," Fred replied. "Northeast mountain side. Ten miles out. The day before the meet."

Lance stood, brushing the dust from his knees. "Thank you, Fred," he said. "I'll have some food and water brought down."

Fred looked up, a sliver of hope in his eyes. "You could unlock the gate." He forced a weak smile. "I mean... aren't we friends?"

Lance's expression flickered. Regret. Sadness. Duty.

"You know I can't do that, Fred. I'd be kicked off The Council. Then you'd have no one left to fight for you."

He turned and walked away.

Fred stared at the door as it closed behind him.

"Why did I follow Vince?" he whispered, voice brittle. "I should've listened to Lance… I should've never started working for The Architect."

He leaned forward, burying his face in his hands.

"If The Council doesn't kill me… *he* will."

∞

Shabina

"Mather, you need to let me treat your neck," Shabina demanded as they made their way through the narrow tunnels of the mineshaft. Her voice echoed off the stone, urgent and strained.

"I'm fine, Shabina…" Mather muttered, his words staggered and unconvincing.

She could hear the pain in every breath he took.

He pulled off his helmet and then his balaclava, and a groan tore from his throat as the fabric peeled away from the raw, festering brand.

Pus and blood clung to the edges. Dead skin came with it.

The smell hit her.

"NOW JUST STOP IT!" she yelled, stomping her foot. Her eyes welled with frustration. "YOU NEED TO LET ME TREAT YOU… OR… OR YOU'RE GOING TO DIE, MATHER! IT'S GOING TO GET WORSE!"

Mather dropped his head, shame coloring the edge of his voice. "I… I just can't. The Warden…"

Fear.

It still had its claws in him.

He wanted to say yes. She could see it in the way he avoided her eyes. In the way his hands trembled at his sides.

"Fine," Shabina snapped, folding her arms. "If you won't let me treat you, then I won't treat myself either."

His head jerked up. "You can't do that to me, Shabina."

"Well, *you* can't do *this* to me!" she shouted. "If you won't treat your neck... I'm not treating mine. It's that simple."

He sighed—deep and broken.

"Please, Mather," she whispered, her tone cracking. "You're so pale."

Mather stepped toward her, unsteady.

He opened his mouth to speak, but his knees buckled before any words left.

"MATHER!" she screamed, rushing forward as he collapsed to the stone floor.

She dropped to her knees beside him, cradling his head. "Please be okay," she begged, her hands trembling as she turned his face toward her.

The back of his neck was a disaster.

The skin was red, cracked, and slick with yellow pus. Strands of black cotton were fused to the wound, baked into the flesh. The heat coming off it was searing.

He had been burning under that helmet for hours.

Shabina sobbed as she applied the gel, her fingers moving carefully despite her panic. "I'm sorry," she cried. "I'm so sorry. Please... Please wake up."

She stayed on the cold floor, his head in her lap, tears streaming down her cheeks.

"Please," she whispered again and again, rocking slightly. "Please, Mather... Please wake up... I love you."

It was the first time she'd said it aloud.

She didn't take it back.

Later, after her tears had dried, she managed to drag his unconscious form to the bed nestled into the wall of her secret cavity. She laid him down gently, brushing hair from his forehead.

"You're going to be okay," she whispered, unclipping his armor piece by piece, setting it aside in a neat pile. "You're the strongest man I know."

She curled into the armchair nearby, eyes locked on the slow rise and fall of his chest.

She didn't sleep.

She couldn't.

Hours passed. The temperature dropped.

"I need to get some more of that gel," she murmured to him. "And a few things from the surgery."

Mather didn't stir.

Shabina leaned down and kissed his forehead. Then, she crouched beside him and inspected his neck again. The redness was still strong, the wound still hot. Her fingers hovered a moment before pressing the gel to the burn.

"You've got this," she said quietly. "You can't leave me. I still need you."

CHAPTER

TEN

The Renegade◇

∞

Isabelle

When Izzy woke, the first thing she noticed was the heaviness in her limbs.

The second was the stillness.

The room was large but stuffy. The air smelled faintly of antiseptic and damp stone. A slow drip of fluid slid through a line into her arm, and when she looked to her side, she saw another bed—occupied.

A woman with fiery red hair lay unconscious beside her, unmoving.

Izzy's eyes wandered across the room. Jaysen sat slumped in a fraying armchair in the corner, his head tilted back, mouth slightly open in sleep. A man paced at the end of the red-haired woman's bed, brow furrowed in thought.

Everything felt… wrong.

Her mouth was dry. Her body ached. And her mind—fogged.

She tried to speak but could only manage a raspy breath.

The man turned sharply, his eyes widening. "Jaysen," he said quickly. "Izzy's awake!"

Jaysen startled upright and blinked away the remnants of sleep. He was across the room in seconds, falling to his knees at her bedside.

"Izzy," he breathed, grabbing her hand tightly. "Izzy, I'm so sorry this happened to you."

His voice cracked. His whole body shook as sobs overtook him. "I'm so sorry," he repeated, head bowed, tears dropping onto the blanket.

Izzy blinked, still trying to piece things together.

"What… What happened?" she croaked, rubbing at her eyes. "I was with Mother and Father, and… and…"

She trailed off, her voice trembling. "Mother was crying," she whispered. "And I… I can't remember anything else."

Her gaze snapped to Jaysen. Panic flared behind her eyes.

"Jayse… what happened?" she asked, voice cracking. "Where's Mother and Father?"

Jaysen's head dropped.

He hadn't even thought about their parents—not since the day it all fell apart.

"I don't know," he said softly. "I don't know what happened to them."

He opened his mouth to say more, but nothing came out. He shook his head, helpless.

"I don't even know where to begin."

The man stepped forward, resting a hand on Jaysen's shoulder.

"It's okay, mate," he said quietly.

Izzy looked up at him. "Who are you?"

He offered a small smile and extended his hand. "I'm Connor," he said. "Jaysen's cagey. But we're more like brothers now."

She shook his hand, though confusion still clouded her expression.

"What's happening?" she asked, voice barely more than a whisper.

Connor looked at Jaysen, who gave a nod.

So Connor sat gently on the edge of her bed.

"Izzy… we broke out of Augmentation Bay," he said. "We had to get you out."

"Me?" she repeated, frowning. "But… that's the *men's* prison."

Jaysen squeezed her hand. "Turns out," he said, his voice shaking, "it's not just a men's prison."

He couldn't go on. His throat closed around the rest.

Izzy turned to Connor again, eyes pleading. "What do you mean?"

"There's more to Augmentation Bay than anyone knows," Connor said, pulling out the old, creased blueprints Charlie had given him.

He unfolded the page, pointing to a segment labeled in small, scribbled text: The Cell.

"This is where you were. Where Genevieve was."

Izzy's eyes moved to the unconscious woman next to her.

"That's Genevieve?" she asked quietly.

Connor nodded.

"There were other women too," he said. "A lot of them."

"Tell me what's going on," Izzy said, her tone shifting. It was stronger now—sharper.

Connor hesitated for only a moment, then answered.

"All the women in there… they were in induced comas. And they were all…"

He looked at her stomach.

Izzy followed his gaze.

She pulled her hand away from Jaysen's and pressed it slowly to her abdomen.

Her fingers trembled.

"I'm…" her voice caught. "I'm pregnant?"

Jaysen reached for her hand again. "I'm so sorry, Izzy."

She pulled away.

"I… I need to be alone," she said, her voice distant, hollow.

"Isabelle—" Jaysen tried again, his heart cracking in his chest.

But she didn't look at him.

Connor glanced over at Genevieve.

"I'll call out if she wakes up," Isabelle said softly. "I need to be alone," she said again, more firmly this time.

She turned her face toward the wall and didn't say another word.

The silence in the room was heavy, but her message was clear.

Izzy lay there, hand still on her stomach, eyes burning as she tried to process the unthinkable.

Jaysen stood, desperation in his voice. "Izzy, please, don't shut me out."

Izzy kept her gaze down, staring at the edge of the blanket twisted between her fingers. "I need to be alone, Jayse," she whispered. Then she looked up and managed a soft, bittersweet smile. "It's okay. I'm not going anywhere… I promise."

When the room finally fell silent, and the door clicked shut behind them, she let out a sharp breath.

She looked down at her stomach.

This seems so surreal, she thought. Her fingers hovered above her belly. "Are you really in there?" she whispered. "A baby… growing inside me?"

She rubbed small circles over the soft fabric of her shirt. A motion meant to soothe—but the longer she sat with it, the more the panic built.

Her hand froze.

Then her head snapped up.

"Who's your father?" she snarled, voice trembling. "Who did this to me?"

The tears came fast and unbidden.

She'd always dreamed of being a mother. But not like this.

Not like this.

"How could someone do this?" she cried, her voice cracking as it echoed in the quiet. She turned to look at the woman still unconscious in the bed beside hers.

Genevieve.

Izzy stood slowly, tugging the I.V. pole with her. Her legs felt stiff, heavy. She moved to Genevieve's side and took her hand, studying the sharpness in her cheekbones, the gentle flutter of her lashes.

"I'm sorry this happened to you," she whispered. "We didn't deserve this."

Genevieve's hand twitched.

Then it squeezed.

Izzy's breath hitched. "Connor!" she gasped. "Connor, she's waking up!"

The door burst open. Connor was the first through it, eyes wide with hope. Jaysen followed. Then Xavier. Lincoln. Jessica. The twins.

The room was suddenly flooded with movement and voices.

Izzy's knees gave out beneath her.

Xavier caught her before she hit the ground. "It's been a minute," he said with a small smile, guiding her gently back to the bed.

She looked at him—and broke into tears.

"Xav," she sobbed, throwing her arms around his neck. "What are you doing here with my brother?"

Xavier hugged her tightly. "It's a long story. For another time."

She leaned back and caught sight of Lincoln, standing protectively near Xavier's side.

"Who's your friend?" she asked, eyeing their closeness.

"This is Link," Xavier said, cheeks flushing. "He's... well, he's my..."

He couldn't finish.

Izzy smiled. "It's okay," she said gently. "Who needs labels?"

The tension broke slightly. Xavier laughed, and Lincoln turned equally red.

"Give her some space," Jessica said firmly, directing the crowd away from Genevieve's bed.

Everyone turned as a weak voice croaked from behind them.

"What's... what's happening?"

Genevieve's eyes fluttered open. Connor dropped to his knees at her side.

"Genevieve," he said, voice barely holding steady. "My love... I'm so sorry."

She blinked at him, studying his face.

"Connor?" she whispered.

"Yes, darling. It's me."

He took her hand, pressing it against his chest.

She stared at him, confused. "But you're... older."

Connor looked up at Jessica, his voice suddenly sharp. "How long was she in there?"

Jessica flinched. "I... I don't know. She was already there when I started."

"When was that?" Connor barked, his voice rough and rising.

"Seven years ago," Jessica said softly. "I'm so sorry."

Her eyes dropped, and Connor turned back to Genevieve, haunted.

"What are you talking about?" Genevieve asked, voice cracking. "Where was I?"

"Darling, get some rest," Connor whispered, brushing her hair back. "I'll explain everything later."

"No." Her voice broke. "Please... please tell me what's going on."

Connor froze.

"Oh, for fuck's sake," Izzy snapped. "She needs to know. She *deserves* to know."

She returned to Genevieve's bedside and sat beside her, placing a hand over hers.

"It's my turn to help you now," she said softly, glancing at Connor with warmth and strength.

"Genevieve, we've both been in Augmentation Bay. We were put into comas. Used to... to have babies."

She placed her other hand protectively over her own stomach.

"They stole our bodies. Took everything. And we need to make them *pay*."

Genevieve's breath caught in her throat. Her eyes went wide as she looked down.

"I'm pregnant?" she choked out.

"No, sweetie," Jessica stepped forward quickly. "You're not."

Izzy's head snapped toward her.

"You've been in the Pumping Station," Jessica said gently. "After the birth—or when they can no longer have children—they send the women there. To produce milk. For the rest of their sentence."

Jessica's voice cracked. She dropped her head. Tears fell freely.

Genevieve turned to Connor, her face crumpling. "Connor…" she whispered. "Tell me this isn't happening. Please…"

He said nothing.

He couldn't.

She tried to sit up, but her body wouldn't move.

Jessica was at her side in a flash. "This is going to take time," she said. "There's a physio program in The Cell, but… it's minimal. Izzy was only there for a short time. I'm not sure how long you were there. You'll need to retrain your legs."

Genevieve sobbed harder.

Connor hugged her tightly.

"She needs space," Izzy said suddenly. "All of you. Out. I'll look after her."

She placed her hand on Connor's shoulder.

Connor looked at Genevieve.

"She's right," Genevieve said, voice trembling. "I need some time."

Connor nodded, brushed a kiss against her brow, and held her hand to his chest a moment longer.

"You've aged well," she whispered when he pulled away. "You look just like your father."

Connor's breath caught, and he turned quickly before she could see him cry.

Then the group filed out.

And the door clicked shut behind them, leaving only the two women behind—haunted, wounded, and finally alone to grieve what had been done to them.

∞

Lincoln

When Connor walked into the hallway, Jaysen, Xavier, and Lincoln were waiting. His face crumpled the moment he saw them. He dropped to his knees, sobbing.

"It's her… it's really her," he said. "I never thought I'd see her again."

Jaysen knelt and wrapped his arms around him. "I can't imagine what you must be feeling," he said gently. "I just wish I knew what I could do to help."

"I think I can help," Lincoln muttered from above them, pulling the smokes and aluminum tins from his pocket.

But before he could say more, two voices echoed in eerie unison from around the corner.

"What do we have here, then?"

The twins emerged—Nick and DJ—smiling like they'd caught them red-handed. Lincoln instinctively lowered the tins, half tucking them back into his coat.

"Don't worry," said Nick, offering a hand. "We know everything you got up to inside."

"I'm Nick," he said, as Lincoln shook it warily.

"This is DJ," Nick added, nodding to his mirror image. DJ extended his hand, and Lincoln hesitated a moment before shaking it.

They weren't much taller than Xavier, but there was a confidence about them—twinned in expression and stride. Nick wore his black hair braided back, DJ's hung loose. Both had tanned skin and dark, expressive eyes. And despite their mirrored appearance, their presence felt grounded. Like they belonged here.

DJ glanced at the tins. "Mind if we share?"

"You're too young," Lincoln grunted.

They laughed.

"You flatter us," said DJ.

"We're twenty," said Nick.

Lincoln furrowed his brow. "This is creepy."

Xavier elbowed him in the ribs. "What?" Lincoln protested. "I've never seen twins before."

"Not many people have," said Nick. "That's why they wanted us."

"The Shepherd. The Architect," DJ continued, his tone hardening. "They went after our parents."

Nick's eyes darkened. "We went into hiding… but our uncle betrayed us. Killed our brother. Then himself."

"The Renegades found us a few days later," said DJ.

Lincoln's head dipped. "I'm sorry," he murmured. "I didn't…"

"Don't sweat it," they said in unison, brushing it off.

Nick held up a bottle of vodka. "You scratch our back…"

"…we'll scratch yours," finished DJ.

They led the group to a cavern with a stream running through it—crystal clear and cold. A rare luxury.

Armor was peeled off with collective sighs of relief.

"You're all gonna enjoy this," DJ called as he and Nick stripped down to boxers, wading into the water.

"Don't be shy," Nick added with a grin. "When's the last time any of you had a bath?"

Connor was the first to dive in. Jaysen wasn't far behind. Even Xavier was laughing, splashing as he pulled off his shirt and jumped into the bay.

Lincoln stayed back.

He stood at the edge of the water, watching. Thinking. His body locked.

They're going to see. He's going to see.

He couldn't do it.

Xavier surfaced, water rolling down his face, eyes already scanning the shore.

When he spotted Lincoln still standing, he swam to the edge.

"The water's perfect. You should join us."

"I think I'll stay here," Lincoln said, sitting at the edge and rolling up his trousers. He dangled his feet in the icy water, trying to look casual.

Xavier studied him, but said nothing. He reached out and gently rested his hand on Lincoln's knee.

"I'm here if you change your mind," he said softly.

Then he leaned forward and pressed a brief kiss to Lincoln's knee before diving back beneath the surface.

Lincoln blinked.

His heart thundered against his ribs.

He pulled out the tins and handed one to the twins without looking up.

"Thanks, big boy," Nick said with a wink.

"I think you need the first drink," said DJ, passing him the vodka.

Lincoln opened it with a grunt and took a long swig. The burn steadied him.

"Not very chatty, are you?" Nick asked.

DJ smirked, nodding to Xavier. "I can see how that gorgeous specimen broke you, though."

"Keep it in your pants," Nick laughed. "You don't wanna make the big guy angry."

Lincoln passed the vodka to Jaysen, who had joined them at the edge.

Connor smiled faintly. "Genevieve and I used to swim all the time. I'll bring her here one day... Maybe it'll help."

"I'm glad you're feeling better," Jaysen said, chuckling. "You smell better too."

The group laughed as Nick sparked a joint, passing it around.

Lincoln stood and stepped away, moving toward a darker edge of the cavern where the stream curved behind a cluster of rocks.

He sat alone, watching the water ripple.

Xavier noticed instantly.

"What happened between you two?" Jaysen asked quietly.

Xavier sighed. "It's… complicated."

Then he swam around and pulled himself up beside Lincoln.

"For someone who just escaped a living nightmare, you don't seem thrilled," he said gently. "What's up?"

Lincoln looked at him. Tried to smile. Failed.

"Please," Xavier said, resting his chin on his hands. "Talk to me. You can trust me."

Lincoln's pulse raced.

How does he do this to me?

"I… I just…" Lincoln's breath hitched. His vision blurred. "I can't do this."

And before Xavier could stop him, Lincoln stood and left—rushing out of the cavern, joints forgotten behind him.

∞

Xavier

Xavier watched Lincoln disappear into the tunnel they'd come through, his tall frame swallowed by shadow.

Then he dropped his head.

What just happened?

Before he could make sense of the ache forming in his chest, DJ swam up and handed him the bottle of vodka. "Are you okay, gorgeous?"

Xavier blinked.

Did he just call me gorgeous?

He nodded faintly, taking the bottle.

DJ offered a warm smile. "Come back and join us," he said, voice low, a gentle invitation. "Your friends… uh, they're missing you."

He reached out and gave Xavier's waist a soft, reassuring squeeze before pushing back through the water to rejoin Nick, Connor, and Jaysen.

After a moment, Xavier followed, taking a place across from DJ. When their eyes met, DJ winked.

Xavier looked down quickly, cheeks flooding with heat.

He passed the vodka to Jaysen without a word.

They were laughing again soon—talking in low voices, drifting toward comfort. The water helped. But something still sat heavy in Xavier's chest.

Then, a tall woman entered the room.

She had striking auburn hair and eyes to match. Her presence alone quieted the bay.

"Genevieve and Isabelle are ready to see you two," she said calmly.

Connor and Jaysen exchanged a look and rose quickly from the water.

"Sorry, boys," said Connor, with a hint of pride. "Let us pick this up later. *My wife* needs me."

He didn't miss the chance to say it—*my wife*—and the way his voice caught slightly made Xavier smile despite himself.

Then it was quiet again.

Just Xavier, DJ, and Nick.

Xavier shifted awkwardly, unsure what to say.

"We know why you went to Augmentation Bay," Nick said suddenly, breaking the silence.

"You're a good man," DJ finished.

Xavier looked up, surprised.

He thought of the deal—the one that promised to protect his family if he went with them.

"My family…" he murmured. "They're going to get paid, right?"

Nick and DJ slid closer—one on either side of him.

"Of course," said Nick.

"The Council looks after us," DJ added, placing his hand gently on Xavier's thigh. "We look after our own."

Xavier glanced at him, wide-eyed.

"I have something I need to do," Nick said, standing. "I'll leave you two to it."

He gave DJ a knowing smirk before disappearing from the room.

Xavier sat still.

He could feel DJ watching him. He tried to focus on the patterns in the water, but the warmth of DJ's hand was distracting.

When he looked up, their eyes locked again.

DJ moved his hand slightly higher.

"Lincoln doesn't deserve you," he whispered.

Xavier swallowed hard. "DJ... I... I can't—" he trailed off, staring down at the water between them.

DJ lifted his other hand and cupped Xavier's cheek. "You deserve the world," he said, voice full of longing. "And I want to give it to you."

Xavier opened his mouth, but no words came.

DJ leaned in, his eyes searching Xavier's.

"I know we just met... but I feel like I've known you forever," he said, his fingers brushing the back of Xavier's neck. "I knew about you the moment you were charged. I heard about your plan. Studied you. How to get you out. And the more I did..."

He drew in a shaky breath.

"The more I fell in love with you."

Xavier froze.

Then DJ closed the gap between them and kissed him.

Xavier melted into it.

His arms wrapped instinctively around DJ. The ache Lincoln had left behind—the confusion, the rejection—it all gave way to warmth, to touch, to distraction.

DJ pulled him closer, sliding his arms around Xavier's waist, guiding him gently onto his lap.

Xavier's hands tangled in DJ's hair. He kissed him back—neck, jaw, lips—his breath catching as DJ's lips found the hollow of his throat.

I don't know what's going on... Xavier thought. *But I don't care.*

His fingers moved softly down DJ's chest.

Then—

"Lincoln!"

Xavier gasped, jerking backward as he caught sight of the figure standing in the archway.

Lincoln's expression was unreadable. Frozen. His eye locked on them—on Xavier straddling DJ's lap.

After a long pause, his head dropped.

And he turned.

And left.

Xavier scrambled out of the water. "Lincoln, wait!"

But he was already gone.

Xavier moved to grab his clothes.

"Wait!" DJ caught his wrist.

Xavier looked down at DJ, then back at the dark hallway where Lincoln had vanished. His breath trembled. So did his hands.

"I… I don't know what to do," he said, tears spilling from his eyes.

He sat down hard on the ledge, burying his face in his hands.

DJ slid closer, but didn't speak.

After a long silence, Xavier looked up—his face blotchy, his eyes bloodshot.

DJ exhaled quietly. "Actually. I should go."

Then he stood, stepped out of the bay, and left—leaving Xavier alone in the water.

The quiet returned.

But this time, it hurt.

∞

Genevieve

When the others had gone, Genevieve turned to Izzy.

"How can you be so calm?"

Izzy shrugged, her voice soft but resolute. "I have no choice."

Genevieve let out a shaky breath. "I'm just so angry. Connor was twenty the last time I saw him… but it only feels like yesterday."

Izzy's eyes widened. "How long were you in there?"

Genevieve shook her head. "I was taken… the day Connor's parents died. Locked in a small cell for—I don't know how long. Years, maybe. Then I woke up here. I don't know what happened or who took me, but I think… I think they caused the accident that killed his parents. They kept talking about Sammy."

Suddenly, she sat up. "Sammy!"

Izzy leaned in. "Who's Sammy?"

"Connor's little brother. He was sick… so cheeky, but very sick. Connor loved him so much. Sammy adored Connor. He used to follow him around like a lost puppy, dressing up just like him whenever he could. It was adorable."

A faint smile tugged at Genevieve's lips, warm and aching with memory.

"We have to make them pay for what they did to us," Izzy said, her voice rising. "For what they took from you. You missed your life. Your marriage. You missed Sammy growing up!"

Genevieve nodded slowly, her voice barely above a whisper. "Sammy will be all grown up now. I guess… he's a man. Not a little boy."

A gentle knock at the door interrupted them. Jessica popped her head in, smiling kindly. "I'm sorry, ladies. I need to give you both a checkup."

She entered, pushing a small medical table. "Are you hungry?"

"Starving," Genevieve admitted. She realized she couldn't remember the last time she'd eaten.

"I could eat," Izzy added, her stomach rumbling on cue.

Jessica chuckled. "I'll see what I can find." She checked them over quickly, then headed for the door. "I'll be back with some breakfast."

As the door clicked shut, Genevieve turned to Izzy again.

"So… if I was at the Pumping Station… that means I had a baby, right?"

Izzy's expression tightened. "I think so. Probably more than one, in all the time you were there."

Genevieve's face fell. "How long were you in there?"

"Two months… I think," Izzy murmured, placing a protective hand over her stomach.

"So you're not very far along then," Genevieve said flatly.

"I guess not."

Genevieve hesitated. "Then maybe… maybe you don't have to go through with this."

Izzy blinked, looking down. "It never crossed my mind," she whispered. "I never thought I'd be in this situation. I always wanted to fall in love, get married, and then have kids… but I've always wanted kids."

Genevieve's voice softened. "I know. But wouldn't you want your husband's kids?"

Izzy didn't answer.

"I'm sorry," Genevieve said gently. "I hate that I'm the one saying this. But if you decide you don't want a stranger's baby—one that was put there without your consent… I can help you."

She glanced toward the door, then back.

"Before they took me. I helped other women. Women who were raped. Sometimes… young girls."

Her voice broke. "Your situation isn't any different."

Izzy stared down, silent for a long time. "I… I don't know. I need time to think."

Genevieve nodded. "Of course. Take all the time you need… well, not all the time," she added with a sad smile. "You probably have about eight more weeks. But the longer you wait… the harder it gets."

Just then, Jessica returned with a tray of food.

"It's not much," she said, "but it'll help."

She placed plates of boiled eggs and toast into their laps. The women ate quickly, devouring the meal in minutes.

"Thank you," Izzy said through a mouthful of toast.

Genevieve nodded gratefully, finishing the last bite.

Jessica laughed. "Still prettier than the men eating," she teased, handing out napkins and water.

Before she could leave, Izzy stopped her. "Would you mind sending Jaysen back in?"

"Connor, too?" Genevieve added.

"Of course," Jessica said warmly. "I'll see if Aubrey can find them."

A short while later, the Pearl Enforcer stepped into the room.

"You paged?" they asked.

Izzy froze. Genevieve screamed.

"Shh, sweetie, it's okay," Jessica said quickly, rushing to her side. "That's just Aubrey."

She turned toward the Enforcer. "Don't you think you should get changed, Aubrey? You're going to give these poor women a heart attack."

The Enforcer pulled off their helmet. A woman with long auburn hair emerged, smiling apologetically. "Sorry. After so long in there, I'm kinda used to it."

She turned to go.

"Will you find Jaysen and Connor after you change?" Jessica called.

"No worries," Aubrey said over her shoulder. "They're out with the twins—probably getting up to no good."

Genevieve looked at Jessica. "The Enforcers are Renegades?"

"Not all of them," Jessica replied. "But a few. Aubrey's been undercover for four years now. The best way to know your enemy is to become them."

Jessica sat on the edge of Genevieve's bed and dropped her hands into her lap.

"I saw so many horrible things in that place. And I couldn't do anything about it... until now."

She reached for Genevieve's hand. "I'm so sorry. To both of you. I wish I could've done more."

Genevieve gave her hand a reassuring squeeze. "It's okay. You did everything you could."

∞

Connor

The doors to the infirmary burst open, and Connor and Jaysen rushed in, dripping wet from head to toe.

"Baby, how are you feeling?" Connor asked, hurrying to Genevieve's side.

She blinked up at him, confused. "Why are you all wet?"

Connor grinned. "Remember when we used to swim at the beach?" he asked softly.

"Yes," she said, her voice distant. "It seems so long ago."

Connor reached for her hand, wrapping his fingers around hers. "We can go again if you want."

Genevieve tilted her head slightly. "To the beach?"

"Well, not the beach," he said. "But we can go swimming. There's a river that runs through the caves… it's beautiful."

Genevieve glanced down at her legs. They looked so foreign. Useless. "I'm not sure I'll be able to go swimming anytime soon," she said, her voice laced with defeat, her hands twitching as she tried—and failed—to move her legs.

Connor looked over at Jessica. "How long until she's off the drip?"

"She's eating and drinking," Jessica said, nodding gently. "So as long as she can keep it down, we can take it out soon."

"Connor…" Genevieve whispered. "Where is Sammy?"

His throat tightened. He looked at her, and pain sliced across his face like a fresh wound. "I've been in Augmentation Bay for twenty years, baby… I… I don't know what happened to him." His voice cracked.

Genevieve sniffled. "But his medication. Without it, he would've died."

Connor leaned in, pulling her gently into his arms. He held her close, wanting to protect her from the ache in her chest—but not knowing how anymore. Too much time had passed. Too much had changed.

What if we can't get through this?

"I love you," he whispered against her forehead.

She placed her hand on his chest and rested her head on his shoulder. "I love you too," she breathed.

Connor pulled the curtain around the bed. "Sorry, guys. We'd like some privacy."

∞

Jaysen

"I don't feel well," Izzy suddenly mumbled. "I think I'm going to be sick."

Nick entered just in time to see her vomit on the floor beside her bed. "Shit!" he exclaimed, then darted toward the cupboard. He yanked out a metal bucket and rushed it back to her. "Here, use this."

He spun toward the sink, ran the tap, and soaked a washcloth before wringing it out. In moments, he was back by Izzy's side, placing the cool cloth gently on the back of her neck.

Jaysen was already there, sitting protectively at her side, holding her hair back. "Thanks, Nick, but I've got it from here," he said, his tone a little too sharp as he took the cloth and started dabbing her neck himself.

"Oh, yeah—sorry," Nick muttered, stepping back awkwardly. "Hope you feel better soon," he offered to Izzy.

She gave him a small smile, one of apology—right before vomiting again.

"Just like when you got that stomach bug," Jaysen said, brushing her hair from her face. "Don't worry. I'll look after you this time."

Izzy gave a weak chuckle. "You were horrible. You called me *Chunderella* the whole time!"

Once she'd set the bucket aside, Nick handed her a clean washcloth to wipe her face. "Thanks," she said.

"I said I've got it," Jaysen snapped, snatching the cloth from Nick.

"Sorry," Nick said quickly, retreating toward the door. He disappeared without another word.

"Jayse!" Izzy hissed, smacking his arm. "He was only trying to help. Don't be so pigheaded."

Jaysen frowned, his expression darkening. "I'm the one who should help you," he muttered. "Not him. He's not your family. I am."

Izzy glared at him. "Well, *Xavier* is like family to me," she said coldly. "And right now, I think I'd rather have *his* help."

"Why do you have to be so stubborn?" Jaysen growled—and without waiting for an answer, he stood and stormed out of the room.

∞

Xavier

Xavier didn't know how long he'd been alone, but he cried the entire time.

What's wrong with me? he thought as he finally stood and climbed out of the water.

"You're still here," came a soft voice from the hallway.

Xavier jumped and dropped back into the water with a splash. "Who's there?"

"It's only me," said Lincoln as he stepped into view.

"I'm sorry," Xavier said, his voice cracking. "I don't know what came over me."

Lincoln walked to the edge of the pool and sat down, letting his feet dangle into the water.

Xavier swam toward him, stopping just in front. "Will you swim with me?" he asked, placing his hands gently on Lincoln's knees.

Lincoln hesitated.

Xavier reached up and took his hands. "Come swim with me," he breathed, guiding Lincoln slowly down into the water.

Lincoln lowered himself in. His head never went under, but still he held his breath.

"Xav…" he said, voice shaking. "I… I'm sorry. I know I haven't treated you well. I will now. I promise. Please… forgive me."

Xavier's heart cracked open at the rawness in Lincoln's voice. He moved instinctively, reaching for him. The kiss he gave was soft—cautious—but full of trembling need. A plea for closeness. For trust. For something real.

Lincoln froze—but only for a moment. Then he melted into the kiss, arms slipping around Xavier as if he didn't want to let go. His fingers tangled in Xavier's wet hair, pulling him closer, deepening the kiss until neither of them could tell who had started it.

When Xavier's hands drifted down to the edge of Lincoln's shirt, Lincoln caught them. His eyes locked with Xavier's, wide and vulnerable. He shook his head, breath catching in his throat.

"What's wrong?" Xavier asked gently, letting go.

Lincoln's body stilled. "You don't know me."

"No… I don't," Xavier admitted. "But I want to. I want to know the Lincoln I see when we're alone. The gentle, kindhearted Lincoln who protects me… even when I don't need it."

Lincoln moved closer. "My father… he wasn't a good man."

He looked down at the surface of the water, his voice splintering.

"He hurt us. In so many ways."

Xavier raised his hands to Lincoln's face and cupped it with aching tenderness. "Why would I ever think less of you for that?"

Lincoln didn't look away. "Because of this," he whispered, turning around.

He lifted his shirt.

Xavier's breath caught in his chest. Lincoln's back was laced with scars—each one a silent story of pain.

"I'm so sorry," Xavier whispered. He raised a trembling hand and touched them—just barely. Lincoln tensed beneath his fingertips.

Xavier stepped forward and wrapped his arms around him from behind, holding him as if to shield him from everything the past had done. Then he gently turned Lincoln to face him again.

Their eyes met.

And then Xavier kissed him a second time.

This kiss was deeper—slower. There was no hesitation. Just heat, sadness, and something electric blooming between them. Xavier poured every ounce of compassion he had into it. It wasn't just a kiss. It was a promise: *I see you.*

When Lincoln stepped back, Xavier saw the scars that curved across his torso, some crossing over his heart.

"What did he do to you?" Xavier asked, voice catching as a tear slipped free.

Lincoln sank lower into the water.

"Let's not talk about that," he murmured.

Then he vanished beneath the surface.

Xavier waited, scanning the ripples—until hands suddenly clamped around his ankles and dragged him under. He surfaced with a startled gasp to find Lincoln in front of him, grinning.

Xavier coughed, then splashed him.

"I've missed the water," Lincoln said, laughing freely for the first time.

"Link…" Xavier hesitated. "How long were you in Augmentation Bay?"

Lincoln's smile faded.

"Six years," he whispered. "I thought I was going to die there."

"I'm not surprised," came Jaysen's voice from behind them. "Considering how you were carrying on in there. Try not to be such a dickhead here."

He was smiling when he said it, but Lincoln tensed immediately.

He pulled his shirt on quickly before Jaysen could get close enough to see.

"I should go," Lincoln muttered—and without another word, he climbed out of the water and hurried from the room.

Jaysen looked at Xavier. "What's going on with you two?"

Xavier dropped his head into his hands. "I have no fucking clue. And it just got even more complicated… DJ kissed me earlier."

Jaysen blinked. Then he placed a hand on Xavier's shoulder.

"Who'd have thought—the day we escape, and you've already got two men after you." He let out a small laugh. "Izzy's asking for you."

When Xavier didn't respond, Jaysen gave him a gentle nudge. "Maybe she's got some advice."

Xavier nodded weakly, and the two of them walked toward the infirmary—toward Izzy and Genevieve.

∞

When Xavier stepped into the infirmary, he was alone.

"Jaysen had something he needed to do," he mumbled, offering a half-hearted shrug.

Izzy stretched out her arms. Without hesitation, Xavier rushed to her, burying himself in the comfort of her embrace.

"I'm so glad you're here with me," he whispered.

Izzy pulled back just enough to look at him. "What's wrong?"

"I… I've finally met someone," Xavier said.

Izzy tilted her head. "Why are you upset about that?" she asked gently, brushing her fingers through the white streak in Xavier's hair.

Xavier let out a shaky breath. "Because… then I met someone else. I think."

His voice cracked, and Izzy sat up straighter, taking both his hands in hers.

"Well," she said with quiet resolve, "I'm going to need to know everything about both of them. Sit down." She tugged him gently beside her. "Let's figure this out together."

Before Xavier could say anything more, the privacy curtain was drawn back.

"Uh, sorry, Xav," said Connor, wincing slightly. "It's hard not to overhear."

He smirked. "When the fuck did you meet someone else?"

Xavier's face flushed deep red. He hadn't realized Connor and Genevieve could hear everything.

"Um… DJ kissed me," he admitted. "He said he's in love with me."

Connor blinked—and then barely held back a laugh.

"He doesn't even know you," he said. "We met, what, twelve hours ago? And most of that time we were running for our lives."

Xavier shifted uncomfortably. "They've been planning this for a while," he said. "Studying the plan… and us."

Connor's expression darkened.

"We need to find out what's going on here," he said, rising to his feet. He turned to Genevieve and kissed her forehead.

"I need to go, darling. I'll be back soon, I promise."

∞

Connor

Connor stepped out of the infirmary and into the main hall.

The space was vast—a dome-shaped chamber carved into the mountain itself. Flame torches flickered weakly along the uneven stone walls, casting long shadows that danced across the room. Around the edges, narrow tunnels branched off in different directions, like the arms of some sleeping beast.

Connor made his way toward the center, where Jaysen sat at a table with Lincoln and Jessica. About thirty others were scattered across the nearby tables, hunched over mismatched plates of breakfast. Some looked up as he passed. A few whispered to each other.

He didn't care.

Connor dropped into the seat beside them. "What's going on, Jessica?" he asked, his voice low but firm. "Xavier said The Renegades have been planning this for a while. That they've been studying us."

Jaysen and Lincoln both choked on their eggs.

"What?" they said in unison, coughing.

Jessica didn't meet his eyes. She looked down at her plate instead. "Sorry," she said quietly. "I don't know. They just told me to help with the escape. I was already deep cover, so I guess I was convenient for The Council. I'm in the dark, same as you."

Connor and Jaysen exchanged a look—wary, unspoken tension passing between them.

"We need answers," Jaysen said, rising to his feet.

"We'll talk to DJ," Connor agreed. "He's the one who told Xavier."

Jaysen turned to Lincoln. "You coming with us, Link?"

Lincoln's fists clenched at the mention of DJ's name.

He could still see Xavier—his hands tangled in DJ's hair, the way his eyes had lit up with something Lincoln hadn't been able to give him. That look haunted him. Burned behind his eyelid like a scar.

"No," he growled, his voice low and tight. "I'll stay with Jessica."

Connor gave him a quiet nod, one filled with unspoken understanding, then followed Jaysen toward one of the tunnels.

Behind them, Lincoln exhaled slowly.

"You don't have any painkillers, do you?" he asked Jessica without looking at her.

She glanced over at him as the others disappeared into the dark.

∞

"Where are we going?" Connor asked, his voice echoing slightly as he followed Jaysen through the twisting darkness of the cave.

"I saw Aubrey head this way," Jaysen replied, keeping his voice low. "She'll know where DJ is. And she used to be the Pearl Enforcer, so I'm guessing she has some idea what The Renegade Council really wants with us."

Connor frowned, squinting in the low light. "The woman with the auburn hair? That was her?"

"Yeah," Jaysen confirmed without looking back.

Connor let out a slow breath. "She's kinda scary now that I know that was her."

"If you say so," Jaysen muttered, glancing over his shoulder with a smug grin.

Connor narrowed his eyes at him. "You're a real smartass, you know that?"

"I've been told," Jaysen replied, clearly enjoying himself.

They walked in silence for a while, the only sound the crunch of loose gravel under their boots and the occasional drip of water echoing from deeper within the tunnels. The passages felt ancient—raw and untouched, as if the mountain had been carved by nature and claimed by ghosts long before The Renegades arrived.

The flickering light from their stolen torch cast distorted shadows along the walls, making each narrow turn feel like it might be hiding something.

Eventually, they reached a fork. Then another. Then another.

"I think we're lost," Connor muttered.

"We're not lost," Jaysen said quickly. "We just… don't know exactly where we are."

Connor groaned. "That's literally the definition of lost."

"She has to be down here somewhere," Jaysen insisted.

Just then, a faint glow illuminated the end of a corridor to their right. Voices followed, muffled but growing louder.

Jaysen raised a hand and signaled Connor to stay quiet. They edged closer to the bend in the tunnel, stepping lightly until they reached the stone wall just before the opening.

From there, they could see a larger cavern lit by lanterns strung haphazardly across the ceiling. Shadows danced on the jagged stone, but they could make out the outlines of people surrounding a long table covered in maps and scattered papers.

"What does The Architect want with them?" a man growled—his voice deep, angry.

"I don't know, Ethan," a woman replied coolly. "But if he wants them, then we need them."

"We were only supposed to get the heir," Ethan said through clenched teeth.

"We had to act," she snapped back. "When word came that The Architect was after the others, we didn't have a choice. We couldn't risk leaving them behind."

"What about Lincoln and the women?"

"They weren't going to leave without them," the woman said. "You were away, Ethan. We couldn't wait for you to get back. It would've been too late."

Connor's brow furrowed. *The heir? The Architect?* What the hell is going on?

He glanced at Jaysen, who looked equally rattled.

Connor barged past Jaysen, fury burning behind his eyes.

"What's going on?" he demanded, storming into the room. Jaysen scrambled after him.

"What do you want with us?"

"Sorry," Jaysen said quickly, trying to smooth things over. "We got lost looking for Aubrey and DJ. Connor's just worried."

"I'm not just *worried*," Connor snapped, turning on him. "I'm pissed off. First, we find out they've been studying us… and now we find out some of us weren't even supposed to make it out?"

His voice rose, echoing through the cavern. "WHAT DO YOU WANT WITH US?!"

"Calm down, Connor," Ethan growled from across the room. "Yelling won't change anything. And I'm not hiding that I didn't want you here in the first place."

A middle-aged woman with a gentle smile approached. She placed a calming hand on Connor's shoulder.

"We're not hiding anything from you," she said warmly. "Ignore Ethan. He's just a grump. I'm Nora, and this is Zara, Lance, Ethan, Evie, and Thomas." She gestured to the others gathered around a long table littered with maps and documents. "We're The Renegade Council. If you'd like to sit, we'll tell you everything we know."

"You're too trusting, Nora," piped up Evie from the back. "We don't know them well enough."

"You don't trust *anyone*, Evie. Shut up," Ethan snapped.

"Make me," Evie seethed, standing halfway from her seat.

"You two seriously need to stop bickering," muttered Zara as she lowered herself into a chair. "It messes with our vibe."

"Everyone *sit down* and *calm down*," Thomas said sternly. "We are on the brink of war, and you're all acting like children. The only people here who seem to have a head on their shoulders are me and Lance."

Connor stared at the group, stunned. *This is the Renegade Council?* he thought. *We're doomed.*

"My father trusted them," Nora said calmly. "So I trust them."

Her father? Connor turned and met Jaysen's eyes.

"Let's hear them out," Jaysen said gently.

They sat.

The Council followed suit—except Nora, who remained standing a moment longer, her gaze fixed on Connor with something like reverence.

"My father used to be on this Council," she said. "He was caught during a scouting mission and sent to Augmentation Bay when I was fifteen. After that, the Renegades began planning deep cover operations. We needed eyes on the inside… on him."

She stepped closer.

"Thank you," she said, her voice breaking. "Thank you so much, Connor. You gave my father hope. A reason to keep going."

Connor blinked rapidly. His throat tightened.

"Your father was Charlie," Jaysen whispered.

Connor turned away. "Why didn't he tell me?" he asked, voice low.

Nora sat beside him and took his hand. "That's my fault," she said gently. "I'm a Renegade. He was protecting me."

She paused, gathering herself.

"Thirty years ago, The Shepherd came after me. But now… he's dead. No one could know about me—and they still can't. He had spies everywhere."

Jaysen leaned forward. "Why was The Shepherd after you?"

Nora's expression darkened. "Because I know something that could destroy him."

"This is a bad idea," Evie muttered, shifting in her seat.

"They need to know," Lance said, speaking for the first time. "Let Nora speak."

Evie huffed, but went quiet.

Nora looked around the room. "The Shepherd died. His son took his place. He's seventeen."

"We already know that," Connor said impatiently. "He toured the prison."

Nora gave a knowing smile. "Yes. But he's *not* the true Shepherd."

Jaysen's brow furrowed. "Then who is?"

Ethan scoffed. "Already forgotten your own jokes after the tour?"

Connor and Jaysen sat up straight, glancing at each other.

They gasped in unison.

Their eyes flicked to the Council.

Nora nodded. So did the others.

"Xavier," she said, "is the eldest son of the late Shepherd. The Nation's rightful leader. And the key to winning this war."

Her words hung in the air like a storm cloud.

"Xavier is The Hidden Heir."

Jaysen stared, stunned. "How?"

"The couple who raised him—Ruben and Amara—they're not his biological parents," Nora said. "His mother was the Shepherd's chambermaid. He took a liking to her."

Connor's fists clenched under the table.

"She died giving birth to Xavier. Some of our people took him in and raised him as their own."

She lowered her gaze. "I know how much he loves his family. This is going to break his heart."

"We'll tell him," Jaysen said firmly. "It'll be better if it comes from us."

Ethan stood. "He needs to take it *well*. There's too much at stake."

Connor snapped. "How well can you expect him to take it? His parents aren't his parents, his real ones are dead, and now he's royalty—with a fucking *war* on his shoulders."

Jaysen reached across the table and placed a hand on Connor's arm. "You're right. It'll be hard."

He looked toward the tunnel they'd come from.

"Lucky he has *us*."

CHAPTER ELE+EN

The Hidden Heir

∞

Xavier

Xavier stared at Jaysen and Connor, eyes wide, lips parted slightly—silent.

Then he laughed.

It started as a short chuckle, but quickly grew louder. Sharper.

"Really?" he said, voice tinged with disbelief. "You've got an *entire* story now?"

He took a step back and shook his head, still smiling—but it wasn't joy. It was panic dressed as sarcasm.

"Xavier," Jaysen said gently, "I'm sorry… That joke we played—about the tour—it makes this sound insane. I get it. But we're not fucking with you this time. This is why The Renegade Council wanted you."

Connor stepped forward, placing a hand on his shoulder. "It's the truth, Xav."

Xavier shrugged him off.

He stood there for a moment, frozen, then started pacing—slowly at first, then faster, as if the motion might help him outrun what he'd just heard.

"So let me get this straight," he said, voice rising. "I'm supposed to be The Shepherd? *Me?*"

He turned on them, face flushed. "A *gay man* raised by a mechanic and a baker in a backwater mining settlement is supposed to *lead a revolution?*"

He threw his hands in the air. "And my mother and father—Ruben and Amara—they're not even my parents?! They were assigned to me? Like a project?"

Tears sprang to his eyes, and this time, he didn't try to stop them.

"And my real father?" he spat. "Some monster who *raped* a chambermaid? And she *died* giving birth to me? And now—on top of *all that*—I'm supposed to end a fucking war?"

His voice broke completely on that last word. His knees wobbled, and he clutched the back of a nearby chair, trying to steady himself.

Connor stepped toward him again. "We're going to be here with you," he said, soft and steady. "Every step of the way."

Jaysen nodded, eyes shining with emotion. "You're not alone in this, Xav. We're with you."

Xavier's expression hardened.

"Why didn't DJ tell me?" he hissed. "He said he *loved* me. He kissed me. And he *lied* to me."

He wiped his face roughly with the sleeve of his shirt, trying to hide the tears.

"He should have told me."

He stood up straight, jaw clenched, heart pounding. "I need to go."

"Xavier, wait!" Jaysen called after him as he turned and stormed off across the main hall.

But Xavier didn't stop.

He didn't look back.

He just walked—past the flickering torches, past the gawking Renegades—until their voices and the weight of the truth were behind him.

As Xavier walked through the tunnels, he didn't bother wiping away the tears. He let them fall. Let the whole mountain know he was breaking.

I'm the bastard son of a tyrant.

His boots scraped against the stone, dragging more than stepping. His body felt heavy, leaded with grief and betrayal.

I should've died with my mother.

He stumbled forward, aimless now, searching for DJ but unsure what he wanted to say. A confrontation? An answer? A place to collapse?

His pace slowed. His fingers twitched as strands of white hair slipped into his eyes.

So much for poliosis, he thought bitterly. The streak that had made him feel unique now felt like a brand. A mark of something dark inside him.

He brushed it away roughly. "I'll have to do something about that."

"Do something about what?"

Xavier froze.

DJ stood in the glow of a lantern, leaning in a doorway just behind him. His smile was soft. Casual. "Hi, you. What brings you to my neck of the woods?"

Xavier turned. His hands curled into fists.

"Why didn't you tell me?" he snapped.

DJ's smile faltered. "Tell you what?"

"ABOUT MY PARENTS!" Xavier shouted, the words cracking down the corridor like a whip.

DJ took a step forward, confused. "I'm sure they're going to get paid, Xav. It just might take some time—"

"That's not the parents I'm talking about," Xavier cut in, seething. "I'm talking about my *real* parents."

DJ's expression shifted—slow realization creeping into his features. His shoulders dropped. "Your real parents?"

"Don't pretend you don't know," Xavier growled. "You said you studied me. Every move. Every detail."

"Please… come sit down. We can talk about this."

DJ stepped aside and motioned toward the room behind him. His tone was soft—maybe even pleading. "Please."

Xavier hesitated.

Then he walked past him.

DJ's room was dimly lit by candlelight, flickering shadows playing across the stone walls. There was a small table in the corner, buried under scattered papers and maps. A narrow bed sat neatly made, a shelf of books and small crystals above it. A worn wooden wardrobe loomed beside the door, its handle hanging slightly loose.

"Now," DJ said gently, sitting on the edge of the bed, "what's going on?"

He patted the space beside him.

Xavier stayed standing. "You can't tell me you studied me and didn't know who my father was," he said tightly, jaw clenched.

DJ met his gaze with quiet sincerity. "Everything I know about you is on that desk—over there." He nodded toward the mess of papers. "I swear, Xavier… I don't know what you're talking about. The Council never told me anything about your family—only that they were struggling. That you had yourself sent to Augmentation Bay to support them."

He gestured helplessly. "I studied you. Your friends. How to get you out. That was all."

Xavier crossed the room and hovered over the desk. There were photos—grainy, low-resolution—of him. Of Jaysen. Connor. Lincoln. Charlie.

"Charlie…" he breathed.

His hand hovered over the image of the older man, fingers trembling. *I wish you were here.*

He rifled through the files—notes, timelines, patterns of behavior. Everything felt clinical. Mechanical. Nothing personal. Nothing about the truth.

He turned slowly to DJ.

"You really didn't know?" he asked.

DJ looked up at him, eyes searching, almost desperate.

"I really didn't know."

Xavier's body gave out. He sat heavily on the edge of the bed and dropped his head into his hands. The tears came fast now, slipping through his fingers like something he couldn't stop even if he tried.

"My parents..." he choked. "They're not really my parents."

His shoulders shook.

DJ hesitated, then placed an arm around him.

"I'm so sorry, Xavier," he whispered. "If I'd known, I would've told you straight away."

Xavier sobbed harder. "That's not the *worst* part."

He could barely force the words out.

"My mother died giving birth to me. And my father..."

He sucked in a breath, trembling.

"My father is The... The Shepherd."

DJ didn't speak.

He just wrapped both arms around Xavier and held him tight. Xavier collapsed into his chest, pressing his cheek against the warm fabric of DJ's shirt. DJ's heartbeat thudded beneath his ear.

Neither of them spoke for a long time.

The mountain was silent. The war outside forgotten. There was only this room, these tears, and the truth that would never go away.

∞

DJ

"I'm sorry," Xavier sniffled. "I thought you knew."

DJ gave him a small, reassuring smile. "It's okay. I understand why you thought I did," he said gently. "I suppose The Council didn't tell me because of *my* parents."

He didn't add the rest—how The Council always walked on eggshells around the subject. How his parents' deaths were treated like a footnote in a much bigger plan.

"My father was a monster," Xavier murmured. "What if I am too?"

DJ immediately moved closer, his hands gripping Xavier's shoulders.

"You're *not* a monster," he said firmly. "You're kind. You care about people. You risked your life for your friends. You chose to go to Augmentation Bay to help your family. That's *not* what monsters do."

Xavier looked away, lost in the whirlwind that had become his life.

"The Council wants me to overthrow… I guess he's my *brother*," he said bitterly. "They want me to be *The Shepherd*."

DJ didn't hesitate. "We'd be lucky to have you as our Shepherd," he said, voice calm but full of conviction. "You'd be able to do so much good."

Xavier was silent for a long moment.

"What if I don't want to be The Shepherd?"

"Then you don't have to be," DJ said. "It's your choice—no one else's. Just know that I'll support you no matter what you decide."

A faint smile touched Xavier's lips, but it was brief—worn down by exhaustion and pain.

"It feels like my world has fallen apart."

"I don't doubt it," DJ whispered. He reached for him again, wrapping him in another hug. "Look what I still have," he added with a small smile, pulling out a half-full bottle of vodka and a neatly rolled joint. "I think a distraction is in order."

He crossed to the wardrobe and grabbed two mismatched metal cups. He filled them, turned, and handed one to Xavier.

"Here. Let's just try to relax."

He sank onto the bed and leaned back against the wall, watching as Xavier took a sip and sat beside him.

"It's going to be okay."

"You can't know that," Xavier said, voice barely audible.

"You're right," DJ said. "I can't. But I can do my best to make it okay. I'd do anything to see you happy, Xavier."

A single tear trailed down Xavier's cheek.

Back off, idiot, DJ thought, panic rising. *Can't you see you're hurting him? He wants Lincoln, not you.*

"Sorry," he blurted. "I know you want Lincoln. I'll back off."

"That's not it," Xavier said quickly. "I don't know what I want. Until the escape, Lincoln and I weren't even friends. Actually, he was kind of a jerk."

"He still is a jerk," DJ mumbled under his breath.

Xavier gave a weak chuckle. "Maybe. But… sometimes he's different. Kind. Gentle."

DJ bit his tongue. He wanted to say: *If he only shows you that side when no one's watching, it's not love—it's shame.* But he held it back. *You'll only push him away.*

Instead, he said carefully, "I'd never treat you like that. I'd proudly have you by my side—always. And I'd always be kind… gentle."

He slid his arm around Xavier's shoulders.

"I'll spend as long as it takes proving that to you."

Xavier exhaled and leaned into him, settling in the crook of DJ's arm and chest. His presence felt warm and heavy, like he was finally allowing himself to let go.

"You'd always be by my side… even though I'm the bastard son of the man who killed your parents?"

DJ's throat tightened.

"What *he* did to my parents has nothing to do with *you*," he said, his voice soft and sure. "You're not your father's mistakes."

He pressed a kiss to the white streak in Xavier's hair. "You're better than him in so many ways."

They drank slowly, quietly. When the vodka was nearly gone, DJ lit the joint with awkward precision, careful not to disturb Xavier.

"Do you think your brother knows about you?" he asked, exhaling gently.

"Probably not," Xavier murmured. "He didn't seem to recognize me when he toured Augmentation Bay."

DJ shook his head. "I can't imagine what it must've been like for you in there. I was only there a few days. That was horrible enough… and I wasn't even a prisoner."

"It was easier with my friends," Xavier said. "They made it bearable. I don't know what I would've done without them."

DJ tightened his arm around him. "Yet you were still going to stay behind to help your family," he said. "That's how I know you're a good person."

Xavier sighed. His body softened, his breath evened. He sank deeper into DJ's side.

A minute later, he was asleep.

DJ stayed where he was, barely daring to move, staring into the low flicker of the candlelight as Xavier slept against him.

And for the first time since this all began, DJ let himself hope.

∞

Xavier

When Xavier woke, he was still in DJ's bed. DJ's arms were wrapped around him, their bodies curled together in the dim candlelight. DJ was smiling in his sleep, soft little snores fluttering against Xavier's cheek.

Xavier didn't move—just watched him.

He's so handsome. So kind. DJ felt safe, grounding. He'd held Xavier through the storm, and hadn't let go once.

I know it should be clear. I should be with him…

But then Lincoln's face slipped into his mind. The way he had carried him through the mountains. The way he had flinched at the idea of being seen—but had still held him like he mattered.

Lincoln saved me. More than once. There's good in him. I know there is.

Xavier rested his head back on DJ's chest, listening to the steady rhythm of his heart.

"You're awake," DJ murmured.

Xavier sat up abruptly—head colliding with DJ's nose.

"Fuck!" Xavier winced, clutching his head. "Sorry!"

"Shit," DJ gasped, blinking fast. He looked at Xavier—and his eyes widened. Blood was dripping down from Xavier's hairline.

Without a word, DJ yanked off his shirt, balled it up, and pressed it gently against Xavier's head. "We need to get you to Jessica."

He looped an arm around Xavier's waist and helped him through the tunnels, guiding him with surprising ease.

"How do you even know where you're going?" Xavier asked, wincing as DJ applied light pressure to the cut.

DJ chuckled. "It gets easier with time. Nick and I have been here twelve years. We know this place like the back of our hands."

They stopped in front of a small wooden door. DJ knocked softly.

"This isn't the infirmary."

"Nope. It's two in the morning. Everyone's asleep. Jess stays in here."

Moments later, the door creaked open, revealing Jessica in a rumpled robe, her hair a sleepy mess.

"Sorry, Jess," DJ said. "We need your help."

Jessica's eyes widened the moment she saw Xavier. "Oh, sweetie," she gasped, reaching for his hand. "Come in, come in."

She led them inside and quickly pulled a small first aid kit from her bedside drawer. "Sit," she ordered gently.

Xavier obeyed, and Jessica knelt in front of him, inspecting the wound.

"You're going to need stitches," she said with a frown. "Unfortunately, we don't have anything to numb the area."

"We only bumped heads!" DJ said, incredulous. "How can he need stitches from that?"

"I fell," Xavier said quickly, remembering flashes of tree branches and rocks… and Lincoln's arms around him. "In the forest. It must've happened then."

I deserve to feel the stitches, he thought. *Let the pain match the chaos in my head.*

"That's okay," he said to Jessica. "I'll be fine."

DJ sat beside him and took his hand. "Squeeze as tight as you need to. I can take it."

Xavier managed a small smile.

"You ready?" Jessica asked.

"As ready as I'll ever be," he whispered.

The needle pierced his skin.

Xavier closed his eyes tight, clenching DJ's hand hard. The pain was sharper than he'd expected. His jaw locked. His breath hitched.

"You're doing great," DJ said, trying to sound calm—though his voice had a nervous tremor.

Jessica worked fast, but every tug of the thread made Xavier want to scream.

"How many more, Jessica?" DJ asked, concerned.

"Three," she answered.

"Hear that? Just three," DJ whispered. He placed his free hand gently over Xavier's knuckles.

A tear escaped Xavier's closed eye.

DJ wiped it away with a soft touch. "We'll get you cleaned up after this. You can borrow some of my clothes. I'll take you to the bathhouse."

"There's a *bathhouse*?" Xavier gasped as Jessica clipped the final stitch.

"And I'm only just hearing about it now?"

DJ laughed. "If you give me back my hand, I can take you."

Xavier looked down and realized he was still crushing DJ's fingers. "Sorry," he mumbled, face flushing as he let go.

They stared at each other for a long beat—until Jessica handed Xavier a glass of water and a couple of pills.

"I managed to swipe these during the escape," she said with a mischievous little grin. "It was all quite exhilarating, wasn't it?"

She looked like a schoolgirl who'd gotten away with skipping class.

Xavier chuckled. "Thank you, Jessica."

"We'll let you get back to sleep now," he added, standing slowly. "Sorry for waking you."

Jessica waved him off with a smile. "You're worth it."

Xavier and DJ left Jessica's room quietly, letting her return to sleep. The tunnels were hushed and still, the mountain breathing around them in soft drips and echoes.

"I thought we were in the bathhouse earlier?" Xavier asked as they walked.

"Nah," DJ replied with a grin. "That was the pool house."

Xavier laughed. "Wow. For a secret hideout, this place sure is fancy."

DJ smirked. "We do like to have some luxuries down here."

They turned down a tunnel that dipped sharply downward, descending deeper than any of the others. The air thickened as they moved—warmer, heavier with steam. Xavier's skin prickled. By the time they reached the end, he felt flushed, as if the mountain itself were exhaling heat.

The chamber before them opened wide, carved by nature and steam. Several small rock pools shimmered under soft torchlight, water bubbling gently from fissures in the stone. Mist clung to the air like a veil.

"The water's much warmer down here," DJ said. "You'll love it."

He plucked a torch from the wall and led Xavier to one of the pools tucked beneath a rocky alcove.

"This one's my favorite," he said. "The seats are better than the others."

He mounted the torch beside the pool, its flame dancing across the water. Then, without hesitation, DJ undressed and stepped in, hissing softly as the warmth enveloped him.

He turned, hand outstretched. "The water's beautiful."

Xavier hesitated for only a moment, then undressed and took DJ's hand. The heat wrapped around him like a blanket as he stepped in, muscles loosening instantly.

"This is beautiful," he said, voice hushed by the atmosphere.

"It is," DJ replied, his gaze steady and unwavering. "Here. Sit down."

DJ guided him to a submerged ledge and sat behind him, gently pulling Xavier back to lean against his chest. Then, with careful fingers, DJ scooped warm water and poured it over Xavier's hair.

"Let's get that blood out of your hair," he said softly. "It's gotten all through that gorgeous white streak of yours."

"It's not gorgeous," Xavier muttered. "I got it from my father."

DJ stilled.

Then he turned Xavier gently to face him.

"Hey. Now you listen to me," he said, voice low but firm. "Everything about you is gorgeous. Everything."

Xavier dropped his gaze.

"It doesn't feel like that anymore," he whispered. "Everything I thought I knew about myself was a lie. I killed my mother…"

DJ's expression softened. He reached for more water and let it flow gently over Xavier's head, soothing.

"Please don't talk like that," he said. "You didn't kill anyone. You were just an innocent baby, born in a terrible, violent world."

Xavier closed his eyes as DJ's fingers combed softly through his damp hair.

"What if I overthrow my brother?" he asked. "Will I have to kill him?"

DJ hesitated. "I don't know. Maybe."

Xavier let out a long sigh, ripples spreading across the water.

"What if I screw it up? What if I take power, and The Nation becomes worse than it already is?"

DJ combed his fingers through another tangle. "I don't see how things could be worse with you in charge. People like us… we wouldn't have to hide anymore."

464

"Or it sparks another war," Xavier said bitterly. "An uprising because there's a gay Shepherd. Thousands could die because of me."

"Thousands are already dying," DJ replied. "But you? You could stop it. I believe you will stop it. That's what you were born to do."

Xavier looked down at the water, chest tight with fear and doubt.

"Hey," DJ said gently.

Xavier looked up.

"You have the most beautiful eyes I've ever seen."

DJ reached up and cupped Xavier's cheek. His touch was light, reverent, like Xavier might break if handled too roughly.

"DJ, I…" Xavier began—but the words faltered. His heart thudded against his ribs. *Why am I hesitating?* he thought. *This kindhearted, beautiful man wants me. This shouldn't be so hard.*

DJ lowered his hand slowly. "It's okay," he said. "I can wait."

When Xavier and DJ made their way back through the tunnels, it was nearing five o'clock. The air had shifted—cooler, lighter. A few people were already drifting from their rooms toward the main hall, rubbing sleep from their eyes, stretching limbs that had grown used to confinement.

Xavier's stomach grumbled. "Are we going to breakfast?" he asked hopefully.

"We are," DJ said, his tone playful. "Just not in the main hall. I've got something to show you."

They took a turn away from the waking bustle and followed a narrow offshoot tunnel Xavier hadn't noticed before. The further they walked, the more the rock around them thinned—until, with no warning, they stepped out onto a small, rocky cliff.

Xavier stopped.

The sky stretched out in front of them—vast, golden, and pulsing with the color of sunrise. Splashes of red and orange bled across the horizon, turning the clouds into smoldering embers. Below them, the forest canyon slept in a gentle mist.

DJ led him a little farther, toward a small clearing at the cliff's edge. A blanket had been spread across the ground. On it were two large plates piled with eggs and bacon, still steaming.

"I thought you might like to have breakfast outside," DJ said as he sat down, gesturing to the space beside him.

Xavier stood silently, letting the view sink in.

"It's beautiful," he whispered.

"It is," DJ agreed—though his eyes were fixed only on Xavier.

A voice behind them broke the moment.

"You have *no* idea what I went through to set this up," Nick grumbled as he emerged from the tunnel, holding a jug of fresh orange juice. He raised an eyebrow at DJ. "You owe me."

He handed DJ the jug with a smirk and turned right around, disappearing back into the tunnel.

Xavier chuckled and sat beside DJ on the blanket. "I hope you know I'm going to devour all of this."

"I'm counting on it," DJ grinned. "I hope you like bacon and eggs."

"I *love* bacon and eggs," Xavier said. "I'm so sick of eating oats and corn."

He picked up a piece of bacon and stuffed it into his mouth with a satisfied hum. "I know I wasn't in Augmentation Bay for long, but man, I missed good food."

DJ laughed and poured him a glass of juice. "Here," he said, handing it over. "Don't choke. I'd hate to have to give you CPR."

He winked.

Xavier nearly choked anyway.

He swallowed quickly and took a long sip of juice, eyes wide with embarrassment. *Don't act like such a pig,* he told himself, cheeks flushing.

"Thank you," he said after catching his breath. "I never thought I'd see anything so amazing again."

DJ reached over and took his hand.

"And it's all yours."

Xavier's heart skipped. He looked out at the sunrise, then back at DJ.

"It's all mine," he echoed, voice quiet. Nervous.

But not afraid.

They sat together on the blanket as the sun climbed higher, warmth spreading across the cliffs and into their bones. They ate slowly, talked softly—about their lives, their memories, their fears. And for a little while, Xavier let himself believe this could be real. That a morning like this could exist after everything he'd endured.

That maybe he could still have a future worth holding onto.

"There you are!"

Xavier looked up at the sound of Jaysen's voice echoing through the tunnel.

"We were starting to worry," said Connor, stepping out beside him. "We haven't seen you since you stormed off yesterday, and here you are on a romantic date!" His tone was teasing, but the smirk said he meant every word.

Xavier turned bright red.

I never thought of this as a date... but now I do.

Connor didn't wait for a reply—he flopped onto the blanket beside them and immediately sniffed the air.

"I *smell bacon*!" he shouted with the excitement of a child.

DJ laughed and handed him the nearly empty plate. "There's not much left, but you can have it."

Connor's eyes lit up as if DJ had just handed him gold. "Twenty years I've been in Augmentation Bay, eating that godawful trail mix," he said, holding the plate like it was sacred. He brought the bacon closer to his nose and inhaled deeply. "Do you have any idea how much I missed you?"

Jaysen, Xavier, and DJ looked at each other.

"He's talking to the bacon," Xavier whispered, giggling.

"I think you just made him the happiest man on earth," he added, nudging DJ with a smile. "I hope I don't have some competition now."

DJ froze for a second, then smiled—wider, warmer.

"So I have a chance?" he whispered back.

Xavier met his gaze, heart fluttering. He smiled.

But before he could say anything, Jaysen interrupted, flopping down onto the grass beside Connor.

"How are you feeling today, Xavier?"

Xavier paused for a moment, watching the golden sun creep higher over the forest edge.

"I'm okay," he said finally. "I still have a lot to process... but I'm better than yesterday."

"Good," said Connor through a mouthful of bacon, licking the grease from his fingers. "Because The Council wants to see you."

Xavier's smile faltered.

Just like that, the weight returned.

DJ slid a hand onto his shoulder, grounding him. "I'm sure they just want to meet you," he said, trying to soothe the tension.

"Or they want to know if I'll overthrow my brother and take his place," Xavier said quietly.

DJ met his gaze. "Your rightful place."

Xavier's stomach tightened. The view, the sunrise, the laughter—it all suddenly felt like something he wasn't sure he was allowed to have.

DJ gave his shoulder a light squeeze. "Go on. I'll clean up here. Can you find your way back?"

Jaysen pulled a folded paper from his pocket and waved it like a flag. "Yeah, your brother gave us this."

Xavier blinked. "My brother?"

Jaysen nodded. "DJ's brother. Nick. He's got everything down to a science."

DJ grinned. "If you see him, tell him I need to speak to him, will you?"

Xavier gave him a small nod and looked back toward the rising sun. A few more seconds of stillness. Then he stood and followed his friends into the tunnels, the warmth of DJ's touch still lingering on his skin.

Jaysen led Xavier and Connor through the tunnels, their footsteps echoing in the silence.

"So, you're not mad at DJ anymore, I see," Jaysen said with a sly grin.

"He didn't know," Xavier replied, his voice soft. "He was… helpful."

Connor nudged him. "I bet he was."

Xavier blushed. "It wasn't like that. He just… comforted me. And took me to Jessica to get stitches."

"Stitches?" Jaysen and Connor said in unison, stopping in their tracks.

"I split my head open during the escape," Xavier explained. "And when I head-butted DJ's chin this morning… it made it worse."

Jaysen turned around fully, raising a brow. "So you spent the night with DJ… and *nothing* happened?"

"Well…" Xavier hesitated. "We had a bath together. And… he washed my hair."

"He *washed your hair?*" Connor burst into a chuckle.

Xavier turned bright red. "It was romantic, okay? Let's just go see the Council already."

Connor smirked. "Okay, then. After we see them, you should go have another bath. I can check if DJ's free… or maybe you'd prefer Lincoln?"

Xavier rolled his eyes and punched Connor's shoulder playfully. "I knew you weren't going to go easy on me for this. What am I going to do?"

Connor threw an arm around him. "Maybe they'd be into being a thruple."

"Thruple?" Xavier blinked.

Connor laughed. "So young… so innocent. A three-way relationship."

"That's enough, Connor," Jaysen said with mock sternness. "We're almost there."

Xavier and Connor exchanged a smirk as they arrived at the entrance to the Council Chambers.

"Xavier!" a warm, excited voice called out.

A woman with curly brown hair rushed toward him, her eyes bright. She threw her arms around him.

"It's so lovely to finally meet you."

"Uh… hi," Xavier said, awkwardly returning the hug.

"Please, come in," she said, already turning and sweeping back into the chamber.

"Well, she's friendly," Xavier said under his breath.

"She's Charlie's daughter," Jaysen explained.

Xavier's jaw dropped. "Charlie had a *daughter*?"

"None of us knew," Connor added, a faint shadow in his tone.

Xavier's stomach twisted as they entered the chamber. Everyone was already seated, their eyes on him. He sat slowly, unease creeping in with every stare.

"Who died and made me Shepherd?" he asked shakily, trying to break the tension with a joke. "Oh, wait… my father."

The silence that followed was immediate and sharp.

"This isn't a time for jokes," Thomas said flatly. "We need to know if you're going to take your rightful place. If you're going to fight with us."

Xavier opened his mouth, but no words came out. His throat tightened. His fingers fidgeted in his lap.

"Cut it out, Thomas," Nora said, sliding into the seat beside him. Her voice was kind, steady. "Take your time, Xavier. I know this is a lot. Do you have any questions?"

Xavier exhaled shakily. "Questions are all I have. Like… you know I'm gay, right?"

Nora smiled gently. "We know," she said. "DJ seems to have taken quite a liking to you."

"Why didn't you tell him?" Xavier asked.

"We weren't sure how he or Nick would react," she admitted. "They were risking their lives to rescue the son of the man who murdered their parents. I'm guessing they took it well, considering DJ's request for bacon this morning."

"I'm not sure if Nick knows… but DJ's been… amazing," Xavier admitted, blushing.

"How are you feeling about all this?" Nora asked softly.

"I don't know. I'm so confused." Xavier dropped his head into his hands. "I was going to *die* for people who were assigned to me."

Nora rubbed his back gently. "I can't imagine how much you must be hurting. But I know the Renegades who raised you love you very much. They see you as their son, Xavier. That's why they never told you. If The Shepherd had found out… he would've had you killed. When we discovered your plan to volunteer, we knew we had to get you out before it was too late."

"Well… that answers one of my next questions," Xavier said. "I was wondering if my father knew about me. Or my brother."

"There have always been whispers," Nora said. "Legends of a hidden heir. The Shepherd denied them, over and over. Eventually, people stopped believing."

Xavier stared down at his hands. "If the people who raised me love me so much… why haven't they come to see me?"

"They're being watched," Nora said. "If they came here now, it would put everyone in danger."

Xavier went quiet for a long moment. Then:

"Will I have to kill my brother?"

Nora's eyes softened. "I'm sorry. But I don't think he'll give up the cloak easily. I believe that's what it's going to take."

"I might be able to change his mind," Xavier said. "Convince him to step down."

Nora gently took his hands. "Xavier, he—"

"He's a spoiled brat," Ethan interrupted harshly. "Mad with power. He's a murderer and a rapist, just like your father. He's *never* going to step down."

Just like my father, Xavier thought, and he shuddered.

"I… I need more time to think about this."

"Of course," Nora said, squeezing his hands. "Take all the time you need."

"We don't *have* all the time in the world, Nora," Evie interjected. "We need an answer—sooner rather than later."

"Evie, mind your tone," Nora snapped. "Xavier is understandably confused. He needs time."

She turned back to him, her voice soft again. "Go on, Xavier. Go find your friends."

∞

Mather

"Shabina?" Mather croaked as his vision came into focus, the room slowly sharpening around her face.

"Mather!" Shabina cried, rushing from her chair and falling to her knees beside him. "You're okay!"

His throat was dry, his voice thin. "Wh… what happened?"

"Your neck," she said through tears. "It was infected. Badly. I… I'm so sorry, Mather. I had no choice. I had to treat it."

He reached up and wiped her tears away with the back of his hand. "Hey… it's okay," he whispered with a soft smile. "I should've listened to you from the start."

With her help, he sat up slowly, groaning softly from the strain. She supported him with gentle hands, careful not to jostle his wound.

"You really are amazing."

"I thought I was going to lose you," she said, her voice cracking as more tears slipped down her cheeks.

He took her hand and held it tightly. "It's going to take more than that to take me from you," he breathed.

Then, with quiet reverence, he leaned in and let his lips graze her ear.

"I love you."

Shabina closed the space between them in a heartbeat, her mouth on his—urgent and warm. "I love you too," she said between kisses. "So much."

He pulled her gently into his lap, cradling her close as he kissed the side of her neck, slow and lingering. His hands moved along her waist, her back, her hips—memorizing every inch. Shabina's hands slid beneath his shirt, tracing the hard lines of his chest and stomach, pausing at the waistband of his jeans.

She looked up into his eyes, breath shallow. "Can I?"

He nodded without hesitation, heart pounding.

There was no need to speak. They both knew this was their first time. But there was no fear. No awkwardness. Just trust.

They undressed each other slowly, carefully. Every movement was deliberate, intimate. Shabina kissed the fresh scar on his neck again as she slid his shirt off. Mather brushed her hair behind her ear before tugging her top over her head. His breath caught at the sight of her—raw and beautiful in the flickering candlelight.

Their hands explored with a quiet mix of wonder and urgency. The air around them grew warm, hazy with the soft sound of skin on skin and the hum of breathless anticipation.

When their bodies finally came together, it was slow. Gentle.

Mather held her like she might disappear. Shabina cupped his face like he was something sacred. They kissed through every shift, every stumble, every moment of hesitation—guided not by experience but by instinct, by love.

Their breathing synced. Their bodies moved together with careful rhythm. And when they reached the edge, it wasn't loud or dramatic.

It was quiet. Full of feeling. Full of trembling gasps and unspoken promises.

It wasn't perfect.

It wasn't practiced.

But it was *theirs*.

And it was everything.

Afterward, they lay tangled in the warmth of the sheets, their skin still flushed, hearts still racing.

Mather held Shabina against his chest, his fingers tracing the shape of her spine, slow and steady. Her head rested just beneath his chin, and her fingers curled over his ribs.

He kissed her forehead. "You're everything to me."

Shabina smiled against his chest, her voice barely above a whisper. "I never dreamed I'd find someone like you in a place as cruel as this."

Mather brushed his knuckles against her jaw, his voice hushed and full of awe. "We made something good in the middle of all this. Something real."

And for the first time since either of them arrived at Augmentation Bay, they didn't feel broken.

They just felt loved.

∞

Xavier

When Xavier, Connor, and Jaysen entered the main hall, it was already buzzing with the chatter of nearly two hundred people. The hum of conversation echoed off the stone walls, but Xavier barely heard it.

He could feel it.

Eyes.

All on him.

He lowered his head quickly, letting his hair fall forward to hide his face.

There's that white streak again…

His breath caught.

Who I am has been right in front of me this whole time… I'm so stupid.

His mind spiraled, gaze locked on that glaring white slash of hair— and he didn't even see Lincoln until he walked straight into him.

He stumbled back, startled, but Lincoln reached out, steadying him with a firm hand on his arm.

"Be careful," Lincoln said gently. "I wouldn't want you to fall again."

His voice was soft. Almost affectionate.

Then he turned, gesturing toward a small table in the corner. "I didn't see you at breakfast, Xav," he said, leading them toward it. "So I saved you some eggs and toast."

Xavier's heart dropped.

All this time… I've been with DJ. And Lincoln's been here. Waiting for me. I'm such a horrible person.

"What's wrong?" Lincoln asked, his eyes narrowing with concern.

"I… I…" Xavier couldn't get the words out. His throat was too tight.

"Here, Xav," said Jaysen, taking his arm and guiding him down to a chair. "Xavier's gotten some news that was hard to hear."

Lincoln sat beside him, the worry etched deeper now. "You can tell me."

Xavier took a shaky breath.

"My father," he said, voice low, "was The Shepherd."

Lincoln blinked. "Isn't he like… sixteen?"

"Seventeen," Xavier muttered. "And no. Not him. He's my *brother*. We have the same father. The Renegade Council… They want me to take his place. They say I'm The Hidden Heir."

Lincoln went still. He stared at Xavier for a long moment.

"You're… The Hidden Heir?" he said, disbelief thick in his voice. "*You*?"

The noise in the hall quieted around them. A few heads turned. Then more. Whispers began weaving through the tables.

"My mother used to tell me bedtime stories about the Hidden Heir," Lincoln said, voice distant but speeding up with excitement. "She said you were taken when you were born. That The Shepherd had your mother killed, but someone stole you before he could kill you too. That they locked you away in Cypher Industries to experiment on you, but you escaped. She said you'd bring peace to The Nation."

He laughed quietly, in awe. "She also said you were a woman, though. I never believed it, but it made her happy to tell the stories."

Xavier stared at the table, pulse pounding.

"No one locked me away in Cypher Industries," he said. "I lived with some random Renegades. I thought they were my parents."

Lincoln's face fell. "I'm sorry," he said quickly. "I wasn't thinking. I just... I've heard the story so many times. I can't believe it's real. My mother always said you had white hair with black streaks that looked almost blue. I guess I didn't make the connection."

Xavier looked up sharply, his voice suddenly sharp and brittle. "Yeah? And your mother also said someone locked me away in Cypher Industries. I guess she was wrong about a lot of things!"

He stood, the scrape of his chair loud against the floor, and stormed from the hall without looking back.

∞

Xavier wandered the tunnels aimlessly, lost in the noise of his own thoughts.

You shouldn't have stormed out, he scolded himself. *Lincoln didn't deserve that... But he was so insensitive about it!*

He turned a corner sharply—and collided with someone.

A young woman stumbled backward, a bowl slipping from her hands. Crystals scattered across the floor like marbles, clinking softly as they rolled.

"Oh no!" she gasped, dropping to her knees. "I'm so sorry—I didn't mean to drop you!"

Is she... talking to the crystals? Xavier wondered as he knelt to help.

She had long, curly black hair that cascaded down her back, one side shaved and now beginning to grow back. Her eyes were bright blue, startling and vivid against her warm skin. She was short, smaller than Xavier had expected for someone who carried such calm.

"Sorry," Xavier said, handing her a crystal. "I wasn't watching where I was going."

She smiled up at him, sweet and unbothered. "That's okay. Everything happens for a reason."

She looked down at the crystal he still held, then back up at him.

"Keep him," she said, her voice soft with certainty. "He must have been calling to you."

Xavier looked at the stone in his hand—a rough stone with dark green hues, streaked with scarlet and warm amber. Near its center was a striking vein of pure white.

"They do that, you know," she added. "Crystals. They call out to people who need them. It's nice to meet you. I'm Pandora. And that little guy is a bloodstone. He must think you need him."

She held her arms out.

"Thanks, Panda," Xavier said, chuckling as he hugged her. "I'm Xavier."

Pandora giggled. "My name is Pandora, silly. But I don't mind Panda—so either is fine for you."

There was a warmth to her. A joy that radiated without effort. Xavier couldn't help but feel lighter around her.

"I have to go, though," she said suddenly, already hopping to her feet. "Sorry! I'll see you again soon, Xavier."

And just like that, she was off—skipping cheerfully down the tunnel, disappearing into the misty quiet.

Xavier blinked after her.

She skips, he thought, smiling. *Who skips these days?*

Still smiling, he looked down at the crystal in his palm. *It's beautiful.*

He kept walking, fingers curled around the bloodstone, until he found himself back at the cliff where DJ had taken him for breakfast. The blanket was gone, but the view remained.

The sun was high now, casting a golden sheen across the canyon. The morning dew was gone, but the grass still shimmered faintly with residual dampness.

I've never seen so much green in my life.

Xavier sat down where the blanket had been and pulled the bloodstone from his pocket. He studied the white streak running through it.

Did you really call out to me?

"I see you've met Pandora," a voice said from behind.

Xavier jumped.

Nick stepped into view and sat beside him.

"Sorry," Nick added casually. "That girl… she's always running around talking to her stones. Giving them out to people."

He gave a small smile. "But don't worry, she's harmless. She's one of the kindest people you'll ever meet. Some folks say she's strange… I say she's just quirky."

"I'm not worried," Xavier said, still holding the crystal. "Everyone here has been kind. Well… maybe not Ethan and Evie. Those two are… intense."

Nick laughed. "Yeah. Those two have been intense since before I had facial hair. Don't take it personally."

They sat quietly for a moment, both staring out at the view.

Then Nick shifted. The air changed.

"I need to talk to you," he said, his voice dipping into something more serious.

Xavier tensed. "Okay…"

"My brother cares about you," Nick continued, tone guarded. "I can see you're confused—and that's fair. But…"

He turned to face Xavier fully, his expression sharpening into a glare.

"Don't hurt him. If you're just going to string him along, end it now."

Xavier opened his mouth, but Nick wasn't finished.

"I was born first. It's my job to protect him. And if you hurt him, I will protect him—from you."

He held Xavier's gaze firmly, without hostility, but with a heavy kind of promise. "Don't get me wrong. I like you. But I love my brother."

The silence hung heavy.

Xavier looked down at his hands. "I don't want to hurt DJ. And I don't want to hurt Lincoln either…"

His voice broke slightly. "But someone is going to get hurt eventually. I just… I need time. I'm still trying to process that I'm The Hidden Heir."

Nick went completely still.

"You're… The Hidden Heir?"

"Yeah," Xavier said quietly. "I thought DJ would have told you."

Nick's face hardened. His voice dropped, cold. "No. He *didn't* tell me that the man who killed our parents is your father."

Xavier's head shot up. "I—"

But Nick was already standing.

He turned and stormed back into the tunnel, footsteps echoing behind him.

Xavier sat frozen.

His stomach churned. His chest ached.

I knew there would be bad reactions to who I am…

He looked back out at the trees.

I just didn't know it would hurt so much.

The sound of someone clearing their throat snapped Xavier out of his thoughts, making him jump.

How long has it been? he wondered. *The sun has moved so much.*

He stood and turned—only to see Aubrey standing behind him, cheeks flushed red.

"Sorry, m… my Lord," she stuttered, then dropped to one knee in a deep, formal bow—the same kind of bow the Enforcers used when The Shepherd had visited Augmentation Bay.

Xavier stood frozen, mouth slightly agape.

"If I'd known who you were sooner," Aubrey said, "I never… never would have left your side."

Her voice was steady now. Loyal.

"I swear to you—I will fight by your side with everything I am and everything I have. I will give my life for yours and protect you from all who intend to harm you. I will guard you by day and night… This is my vow to you."

She remained bowed.

Xavier blinked, still in stunned silence. After a long pause, Aubrey raised her head to look up at him.

"Well?" she asked. "Are you going to say something?"

"Say what?" Xavier asked, clearly still trying to catch up.

"I don't know," Aubrey said, flustered. "I've never actually done this." She giggled nervously.

Seeing her awkwardness, Xavier straightened his back, dusted off his clothes dramatically, and cleared his throat.

With mock authority, he lifted a stick from the ground and declared, "Lady Aubrey of The Renegades, I accept your most noble of offers."

He tapped her shoulders with the stick. "Arise now as *Sir Aubrey, Protector of The Hidden Heir.*"

There was a beat of silence.

Then both of them burst out laughing.

"Did you just knight me with a *stick*?" Aubrey asked, wiping tears of laughter from her eyes. "Like, you're royalty. Am I *actually* a knight now?"

"I didn't even think about that!" Xavier laughed again. "And besides… this is *not* a stick. This is my *royal staff.*"

"It's an honor to meet you… and to serve you," Aubrey said, her tone softening. "I only hope I can serve you well."

Xavier's laughter faded. He looked down, his cheeks coloring.

"Sorry, Aubrey," he said quietly. "This is all… a little weird for me. I mean, just a few days ago, I was in Augmentation Bay—a normal guy from a poor mining town. Now I'm royalty… and the fate of an entire Nation rests on a decision I have to make. People are swearing vows to me now. It all seems… surreal."

His voice cracked. A tear slipped down his cheek.

Aubrey's smile faded. "No, I'm sorry," she said. "I should have waited longer. I just… when I found out who you were, I felt awful for leaving your side during the escape. And before I knew it, I was bowing. I couldn't stop myself."

"Yeah, about that bow…" Xavier said, managing a small grin. "Please don't do that again. No one should bow to me. And anyway, I had to stay in that position for *so* long when my brother visited the prison. I *hated* it. I think I'll eliminate it when I take my place."

"So, you're saying yes?" came DJ's voice, bright and hopeful, from the tunnel.

He jogged out toward them. "You're going to say yes?"

Xavier stood frozen. "I… uh… I don't know," he stammered.

"Sorry," DJ said, slowing his approach. "When you said *when I take my place,* I thought that meant you'd decided."

"I didn't even realize what I said," Xavier admitted, shrugging.

DJ turned to Aubrey. "Mind giving us some time alone?"

Aubrey glanced at Xavier, waiting for his cue.

"It's okay, Aubrey," he said softly.

She nodded. "I'll be within shouting distance. Call out if you need me."

She disappeared into the forest, and DJ turned back to Xavier.

Xavier lifted his palms, half-smiling. "She swore a vow."

"A vow? Typical Aubrey. She's sooo honorable," DJ said with a laugh.

Xavier smirked.

"I just saw my brother," DJ continued, his tone dimming. "I'm so sorry about him."

He stepped closer, placing his hands gently on Xavier's shoulders.

"Please… give him time. He'll come around."

"It's fine," Xavier said quietly. "I was expecting some bad reactions to who I am. At least he didn't treat me like some celebrity like Lincoln did."

He stepped forward, wrapping his arms around DJ's waist and resting his forehead gently against DJ's shoulder.

"Thank you," he whispered. "For being so good to me... and so helpful."

DJ raised his hands and cupped Xavier's face. His thumbs stroked softly over Xavier's cheeks as he leaned in.

"SERIOUSLY!" Lincoln's voice echoed from the mouth of the tunnel. "I'M FUCKING DONE WITH THIS!"

Xavier turned toward the sound just in time to see Lincoln storm back into the darkness.

He froze, heart pounding.

Then DJ touched his arm gently. "It's okay," he said quietly. "Go after him."

As Xavier disappeared into the tunnel, Aubrey burst through the tree line.

"He'll be with Lincoln," DJ called after her as she ran.

∞

"LINK, PLEASE!" Xavier shouted, sprinting into the dark. "LET'S TALK!"

When he finally caught up, Lincoln was slamming his fists into the stone wall. Again and again. Blood smeared across his knuckles, his breath ragged. A tear slipped down his cheek.

"Lincoln..." Xavier's voice was soft. "I'm sorry."

Lincoln didn't turn. "Let me guess," he growled, fists still flying. "You don't know what came over you?"

Xavier reached out, trying to grab his hand—to stop him.

Lincoln shoved him back.

Xavier stumbled, hitting the stone wall hard. His head smacked the rock with a sickening thud.

Lincoln froze.

"Shit—Xavier!"

He rushed forward. "I'm sorry, are you hurt?"

Xavier pressed his palm to the side of his head. He felt blood—warm and wet—seeping from the stitches Jessica had placed just last night.

"I'm okay," he said, though his voice trembled.

Lincoln helped him to his feet, his touch gentler now.

"Are you okay?" Xavier asked, holding Lincoln's hands and inspecting the torn, bloody knuckles. "You're torn up."

"We should go to Jessica—"

"No," Lincoln cut in. "I know a place."

Without another word, he led Xavier through a twisting path of tunnels. The air turned cool, damp. Then they emerged into a forested canyon, filtered light dancing down through the leaves.

Lincoln didn't let go of Xavier's hand.

He guided him through an overgrown mossy path, barely a trail at all. After several winding turns, they stepped into a secluded clearing.

"We can both get cleaned up here. No one will walk in on us. Not many know it exists… Aubrey showed me."

He peeled off his shirt, then his pants, and stepped into the spring.

"Don't worry," he added, glancing back. "The water's warm."

Xavier stripped off his clothes and followed. The water was surprisingly soothing—soft against his skin, heating him from the outside in.

"Now show me your hands," Xavier said, stepping close.

He gently took Lincoln's hands in his own and began washing the blood from his knuckles. Lincoln winced.

"I've never seen you wince before," Xavier teased softly. "I'll try to be gentle."

Lincoln exhaled. "I'm sorry I've been acting so… erratic. It's just… seeing you like that with DJ—it hurt. A lot."

He held Xavier's hands tighter.

"I want to be the one who makes you feel that way."

Then, quieter: "I want to give you that same feeling of passion I saw on your face when you were with him."

Xavier's breath caught.

He raised one hand and traced Lincoln's jaw with soft, trembling fingers.

"I'm sorry," Xavier whispered. "I never meant to hurt you."

Lincoln closed his eyes. "The way I've treated you… I deserve it."

The words cut deep. Xavier's chest ached.

How could I do this to him?

This man who had protected me. Cared for me. Wanted me.

Xavier didn't think—he moved.

He kissed Lincoln.

Lincoln stiffened for a moment.

Then melted.

He wrapped his arms around Xavier, kissing him back like he meant it—like he *needed* it. Xavier's hands tangled in Lincoln's damp hair, dragging him closer. Their bodies collided, lips desperate and hungry.

Xavier ran his fingers down Lincoln's chest, stopping at his waistband. Lincoln groaned and pulled him even closer.

Then he lifted Xavier easily, setting him on the mossy edge of the spring. Xavier's legs wrapped tightly around his waist. Water lapped at their skin, tension building in every breath, every shiver.

Xavier bit Lincoln's bottom lip gently, and Lincoln moaned, his hands roaming over Xavier's hips.

When his fingers hooked into the waistband of Xavier's boxers, he paused.

Xavier placed his hands on Lincoln's forearms.

"Link… I'm still confused," he whispered.

Lincoln didn't flinch.

"If having you means I have to share you," he said, voice hoarse, "then I will."

He kissed Xavier again—slow and deep—and Xavier kissed him back, just as hungry.

Then Lincoln slid Xavier's boxers down.

Xavier helped strip away the last barrier between them.

Nothing separated them now. Nothing but air and aching need.

They moved together on instinct and urgency. The kisses turned rougher, hands bolder. Every brush of skin made Xavier burn hotter. Lincoln kissed down his chest, over his ribs, his tongue dragging slow over his skin.

Xavier gasped, arching into him.

Lincoln gripped his thighs and pressed their foreheads together.

"Tell me you want this," he whispered.

"I want this," Xavier breathed. "I want *you*, Lincoln."

Lincoln lined himself up, then hesitated—just for a second.

Xavier nodded.

And Lincoln pushed inside.

Xavier cried out, clutching Lincoln's back. The sting was sharp, real—but so was the want.

They hadn't prepared.

But he didn't care.

All he cared about in that moment was Lincoln.

The two of them sharing something impossible.

"Are you okay?" Lincoln asked, freezing.

"Don't stop," Xavier whispered.

Lincoln held him close as he began to move—slow, careful. Every shift brought new sensation. Every gasp pulled them deeper. Xavier kissed his shoulder, his jaw, anything he could reach.

They found their rhythm, the spring water swaying with them. Moans filled the clearing, raw and real, muffled by breathless kisses and trembling limbs.

Xavier gripped Lincoln like they might fly apart.

Lincoln drove into him harder now, sweat mixing with water, bodies colliding.

When Xavier came, he cried out Lincoln's name, voice ragged and high. Lincoln followed seconds later, burying his face in Xavier's neck with a strangled moan.

They collapsed into each other, slick and panting, wrapped in arms and moss and steam.

The world around them was silent, save for the trickle of spring water and their gasping breaths.

Lincoln held him.

And Xavier didn't want to move.

Not yet.

Not ever.

As the sun disappeared behind the canyon walls, casting the clearing in gold, Xavier let himself believe—for the first time in a long time—that maybe, just maybe, he *could* be loved.

∞

Aubrey appeared at the overgrown pathway just as the final light faded from the sky. The forest had turned dim, shadowed, and peaceful—until she came crashing through it.

"There you are!" she called out, breathless and frantic. "I was so worried… Five minutes into my vow and I lost you. I'm *so* sorry!"

She rushed straight to Xavier, scanning him like she expected to find him missing a limb.

Lincoln raised an eyebrow, glancing toward Xavier. "Her vow?"

"I'll tell you about it later," Xavier said as he stood, stretching slightly before grabbing his clothes. "No, Aubrey. *I'm* sorry. I should've waited for you. Lincoln wanted to show me this beautiful spring you told him about."

Aubrey flushed, her cheeks going pink. "I'm so glad you like it," she said. "And I'm sorry to interrupt, but… The Council is asking for you."

She bowed slightly, hands clasped in front of her. "I'll wait for you at the tunnel entry, my Lord."

Lincoln burst out laughing. "'*My Lord*?' What's that about?"

"Aubrey wants to be like… my protector or something," Xavier said with a shrug as he stepped out of the water.

"Your *protector?* Well… that's strange."

"Everything that's happened is strange. I figure the best thing I can do is go with it." Xavier pulled his shirt over his damp shoulders. "Not like I really have a choice, anyway."

Lincoln's smile faded into something more serious. "So… you're going to say yes? To The Council?"

Xavier hesitated, then nodded. "I'm going to say yes."

He smirked nervously as he finished dressing. "I guess I'd better go give them my answer. Are you coming?"

Lincoln nodded. Xavier waited while he got dressed, and then they made their way toward the tunnel where Aubrey stood waiting.

"Are you ready?" Lincoln asked, reaching for Xavier's hand.

Xavier laced their fingers together. "As ready as I'll ever be," he murmured.

Lincoln squeezed his hand gently. "You're going to do great," he said. "I think you're going to be an amazing Shepherd."

Xavier didn't answer. He couldn't.

His heart was pounding too fast.

As they walked into the tunnel, the narrow walls seemed to close in tighter with each step. The flickering torchlight made shadows dance along the stone, and Xavier's palms began to sweat.

Lincoln glanced at him.

"You okay?"

Xavier looked up, his face pale. "I don't think I can do this, Link," he whispered.

Lincoln stopped and turned to him fully. "You're stronger than you think," he said softly.

"No… Link," Xavier said again, his breath quickening. "I don't think I…"

He trailed off.

His head spun.

The tunnel tilted.

And then everything went dark.

Xavier collapsed.

∞

Lincoln

"XAV!" Lincoln yelled, lunging forward just in time to catch Xavier before his head hit the tunnel floor.

A fresh stream of blood trickled from Xavier's hairline, soaking into Lincoln's shirt. His stomach twisted.

He's bleeding again.

Lincoln didn't hesitate. He gathered Xavier into his arms and followed Aubrey as she sprinted ahead through the tunnels.

"I'm sorry, Xav," Lincoln whispered, tears threatening. "We should've gone to Jessica when you asked… I should've listened. But don't worry—I'm taking you to her now. I've got you."

"Just up here!" Aubrey called, rounding a bend and gesturing frantically.

They burst into the infirmary.

Inside, Izzy, Genevieve, and Nick looked up in shock as Lincoln rushed through the door with Xavier limp in his arms.

"Where's Jessica?" Lincoln demanded, panic lacing his voice.

"Nick!" Izzy gasped. "Go get Jessica—now!"

Nick darted from the room as Lincoln laid Xavier on the bed opposite Izzy. His hands trembled as he brushed damp hair away from Xavier's pale face.

"Hold on, Xav," he whispered. "Jessica will be here soon."

"What happened?" Izzy asked gently, coming over to his side.

"It's my fault," Lincoln said, his voice breaking. "I should've—"

"I'm sure that's not true." Izzy touched his shoulder with quiet reassurance. "Don't worry, Jessica will fix him up."

She slid off her bed and sat beside Xavier, reaching to comfort both him and Lincoln.

"Xavier's always been a bit clumsy," she added, trying to lighten the tension.

Before Lincoln could respond, the infirmary door burst open.

"WHAT DID YOU DO TO HIM?!" DJ bellowed.

Lincoln stood and turned sharply. He grabbed DJ by the collar, rage flaring to the surface.

"Stop that right now!" Jessica's voice cut through the room like a blade as she entered with Nick at her heels.

Lincoln released DJ and stepped aside to let her through.

"He passed out," Lincoln said quickly. "I brought him straight here."

Jessica examined Xavier's head, frowning. "He's reopened his stitches."

"How?" DJ asked.

"When did he get stitches?" Lincoln added, his brow furrowed.

"Last night," DJ replied smugly. "We had to wake Jessica at two a.m. to do them."

Lincoln clenched his fists.

So that's where he was. With DJ. All night.

DJ turned on him. "What did you do to Xavier?" he growled. "He was fine when I saw him—then he ran after you… Aubrey?"

He whipped toward her.

"I… I don't know," Aubrey stammered. "When I found Xavier, they were in the…" She trailed off, eyes darting to Lincoln.

"In the what?" DJ pressed.

"In the private spring," Lincoln said coolly. "We were spending some time… alone."

The temperature in the room dropped as DJ and Lincoln stared each other down.

"That's just about enough, you two!" Izzy snapped. "Xavier doesn't need this. Either play nice or *get out*."

Both men backed off but didn't stop glaring.

"Will he be okay?" they asked in unison.

Jessica smiled kindly. "He'll be just fine. I'll redo the stitches and clean up the wound. Then he just needs to rest."

As Jessica finished up and left the infirmary, Lincoln sat on one side of the bed, DJ on the other. Both held one of Xavier's hands.

"What did you do?" DJ hissed.

Lincoln lowered his head, guilt burning his throat.

"It's my fault," Xavier croaked suddenly, his voice hoarse. "I tripped and hit my head. When I felt the stitches had opened… I ignored it."

DJ looked between them, suspicion still heavy in his eyes—but he didn't argue.

"How—"

"How are you feeling?" Lincoln interrupted quickly.

"I'm fine," Xavier said with a weak smile. "But I would *really* like my hands back."

DJ and Lincoln both let go instantly.

"Sorry," they muttered in unison.

From across the room, Nick leaned toward Izzy. "Does it sound that weird when DJ and I talk like that?"

"Oh yeah," Izzy whispered back with a grin. "It creeps the hell out of me."

She nudged him playfully.

Nick stood. "It's getting crowded in here. Let's leave these three to… whatever this is. Genevieve could use the rest."

He offered Izzy his hand. "C'mon. I'll give you the tour."

Once they left, the tension snapped right back into place.

DJ turned to Xavier.

"What *really* happened?" he asked. "Please, Xavier… don't lie to me."

Xavier glanced at Lincoln. "Link, would you mind getting me some water? My mouth's dry."

Lincoln hesitated, then nodded. "I won't be long."

He leaned down, kissed Xavier on the forehead, and whispered, "This evening was amazing."

Then he cast one last glare at DJ and left.

Now alone with Xavier, DJ leaned closer and took his hand again.

"What happened?" he asked. "Did that oaf hurt you?"

Xavier smiled. "It was an accident. Lincoln knocked me over earlier, and I ignored it when I felt the bleeding. That's all."

"So, it *was* him," DJ growled.

Xavier blinked. "Why are you acting like this?"

DJ looked down at their entwined hands. "I just… I worry about you. I want to protect you."

"Well, that's what I have Aubrey for now," Xavier said with a grin.

From nearby, Aubrey sighed. "And I'm not doing an excellent job at all."

"That's my fault," Xavier said gently. "Next time, I'll wait for you."

DJ still didn't meet his eyes. "You spent the evening with him?"

"I…" Xavier faltered. "I don't know what to say."

DJ stood. "I need a moment. I'm glad you're okay."

As he turned to go, Xavier squeezed his hand tighter.

"DJ…" he whispered. "Please…"

DJ turned slowly.

Their eyes locked.

Xavier pulled him closer.

"Please," he said again.

DJ kissed him—hard, aching—and then left the infirmary.

Xavier stared at the ceiling, his heart racing.

What the fuck are you doing? You need to decide, or this is going to end badly.

"You have a lot of big decisions to make," Aubrey said softly.

"A lot," Xavier echoed, chewing the skin around his fingernail. "A lot."

∞

DJ

491

DJ walked the dim corridor, his mind still racing. That kiss in the infirmary—brief, heated, unresolved—wasn't just confusing. It was electrifying.

But Xavier had also spent the entire evening with Lincoln.

His stomach churned.

What did they do?

As he turned the corner back toward the infirmary, DJ collided hard with someone coming from the opposite direction.

Lincoln.

Of course.

Lincoln's eyes narrowed. The tension between them surged instantly, hot and bitter.

"It looks like Xavier's made his choice," Lincoln said flatly, voice low and tight.

DJ tilted his head, feigning calm. "Oh, really?"

Lincoln stepped in closer. "So back off."

DJ gave a slow, dangerous smirk. "And why would I do that?" he asked casually. Then, deliberately, "Xavier *just* kissed me."

Lincoln's pupil blew wide. He looked like he'd been slapped.

His jaw clenched, and his grip on the water bottle tightened.

Too tight.

The plastic buckled with a sharp *pop*, and water exploded across DJ's shirt.

DJ jerked back, startled. Cold water soaked through his chest, but he didn't step away. He didn't blink. He just stared.

Lincoln dropped the mangled bottle at DJ's feet and turned without a word, storming back the way he'd come.

His footsteps echoed hard down the tunnel, fast and furious.

DJ stared after him, breath caught somewhere between adrenaline and amusement.

He looked down at the crumpled bottle, then picked it up and chuckled softly to himself.

"Whoops," he said, crouching to pick it up. His smirk returned, sharper this time. "Guess I'll have to get Xavier a new one."

But even as he turned to leave, DJ's fingers clenched around the plastic.

He couldn't shake the image of Lincoln's eye—furious, wounded, possessive.

And that scared him more than he cared to admit.

∞

"You're back!" Xavier said excitedly as DJ stepped through the infirmary doors. His face lit up—until he noticed who wasn't with him. "Where's Link?"

DJ handed him the water bottle with a shrug. "Dunno. I saw him storming off and figured he wasn't coming back. So… figured *I'd* bring you your water."

Xavier took it with a quiet, "Thanks," but his tone dipped, his smile fading slightly.

DJ sat on the edge of the bed, hesitating before speaking. "I'm sorry," he said softly. "I shouldn't have walked out before. I was just… I was jealous." He reached for Xavier's hand. "And I didn't want you to see me like that."

Before Xavier could respond, the infirmary door opened again.

Lincoln entered, a half-empty bottle of vodka in hand.

"I thought you might prefer this," he said, offering it to Xavier with a crooked grin. "Considering the conversation you're about to have."

His eyes flicked to DJ with the faintest smirk.

Xavier smiled as he accepted the bottle. "Thanks, Link."

DJ's jaw tensed. "What conversation?"

Xavier looked between them, trying to summon the right words. "Well… I've made my decision."

DJ's heart stuttered. *He's about to tell me he's choosing Lincoln.*

"I… I'm going to overthrow my brother," Xavier said. "And take his place as The Shepherd."

Relief and pride crossed DJ's face. He reached for Xavier's hand again. "I'm glad I could help."

"I think *I* was the one who helped," Lincoln snapped, stepping closer.

"You *both* helped, okay?" Xavier said quickly, his voice tight. "Please. I'm so sorry I'm doing this to both of you."

His voice cracked.

"I think… I think we need to slow things down. So I can figure this out. So I don't hurt either of you more than I already have."

Neither DJ nor Lincoln had the chance to reply.

The infirmary door swung open again—and The Council filed in.

"Xavier," Nora said warmly. "How are you, my dear?"

Xavier sat up straighter, shoulders stiff. "I'm all right," he said, though it didn't sound convincing to anyone.

"You've got this," DJ whispered, squeezing his hand again.

"Yeah," said Lincoln, taking the other. "You're going to do great."

Xavier looked between them, heart pounding. Then he looked up at Nora.

"Dinner is being served now," she said gently to Lincoln and DJ. "Why don't you two go get something to eat? I'll have something brought up for Xavier."

Both men hesitated.

Then Lincoln leaned in and kissed Xavier's cheek. "I'll wait in the main hall."

DJ kissed the other. "So will I."

Without another word, they slipped past The Council and exited the infirmary.

∞

Xavier

Xavier exhaled shakily as the door closed behind them.

"It seems like you're in a bit of a pickle with those two," Nora said gently, a glimmer of sympathy in her voice.

Xavier gave a half-hearted smile. "Yeah… a pickle."

He shifted on the bed, pulling the blanket higher around his waist. "I'm sorry I didn't make it to you earlier. Is everything okay?"

"Don't even worry about it," Nora said, waving it off with a soft smile. "We were hoping to speak with you about what happened during the escape… with Vince and Fred."

Xavier's breath caught.

The Enforcers who tried to kill me.

"Oh," he said, trying to mask the sudden tightness in his chest.

"As you know, we have Fred in custody," Nora continued calmly. "We've already taken a statement from Marcus. Now we need to hear yours—then Lincoln's."

Xavier sat up straighter, nodding. "I… I don't remember much," he admitted. "It all happened so fast."

"That's okay," Nora said gently. "Just tell us what you do remember."

Xavier took a deep breath, then began to speak—walking The Council through that night in careful detail.

He gave them everything he could recall. Every heartbeat, every shiver.

When he finished, silence lingered.

"Thank you, Xavier," Nora said at last. "You've helped a lot. We'll have your dinner brought in shortly."

She rose, and the other Council members began turning toward the door.

"Wait," Xavier said suddenly, his voice catching.

They stopped.

He sat a little taller, shoulders tense. "I… I've made my decision."

Nora turned back, eyes steady.

The others followed suit, expectant.

Xavier looked at each of them, and then down at his hands.

He inhaled.

Exhaled.

"I'll do it," he said, his voice trembling but sure. "I'll overthrow my brother… and take his place."

The silence that followed was heavy—but filled with quiet understanding.

Xavier had crossed a line.

There was no going back now.

CHAPTER

TWELVE

Pandora's Gift

Nick

The tunnels were warm and winding, the walls close but not claustrophobic. Izzy walked beside Nick, their footsteps soft against the packed dirt floor. Every now and then, their shoulders bumped, but neither of them seemed to mind.

They weren't headed anywhere in particular. Just walking. Just talking.

"You're a great tour guide," Izzy said, flashing him a dry grin.

Nick rubbed the back of his neck, already turning pink. "Uh… sorry. You distracted me."

She gave him a look. "With what? My charming personality?"

He chuckled awkwardly, then slowed in front of a narrow door. "This… is my room."

Izzy arched a brow. "Yeah. *Not* happening."

"What? No—I didn't mean it like that!" Nick's hands went up in alarm. "I swear, I wasn't—"

She burst out laughing. "Relax. I'm fucking with you."

Nick let out a breath, chuckling a little.

"Come on," he said, giving her a light nudge. "I'm starving."

∞

The main hall was already buzzing. The air was thick with the scent of something starchy and comforting. People sat in loose clusters at long tables, hunched over steaming bowls. At the far end, an old man stirred a massive pot, ladling out slow, steady portions like he had nowhere else to be.

"Over here," Nick said, weaving through the crowd. "Victor's potato and leek soup. Good for nausea."

Izzy gave him a side glance.

"Leeks are packed with B6," Nick said as he grabbed two bowls. "It helps with morning sickness. Plus, its packed with calcium."

She raised an eyebrow. "Okay, science boy. How do you know that?"

Nick hesitated, then looked at the ground. "My mum was four months pregnant when she died. She got sick a lot, and this soup helped her."

Izzy blinked. "Shit. I'm sorry."

He shrugged. "It's fine. Just something I remembered."

She reached out, giving his shoulder a quick squeeze.

Before she could say anything, a familiar voice cut through the crowd. "Izzy!"

She turned with a groan. "I was hungry," she called, arms crossed before he could even start.

Jaysen was already stalking toward them. "I would've brought you something."

"Yeah, well, you didn't. We were just getting soup."

He shot a look at Nick. "We don't know him."

Izzy rolled her eyes. "Xavier doesn't know DJ, and they're all over each other. Maybe go wreck that instead of interrogating my friend."

She grabbed a bowl from Nick and stomped off to an empty spot at the nearest table. Nick followed, quiet, and took the seat beside her.

"Sorry about my brother," she muttered, blowing on her spoon. "He thinks he's being protective. He's just being a dick."

Nick gave a crooked smile. "It's alright. I get it."

He handed her a spoon. "You forgot this."

"Thanks," she said, offering a quick nod.

When he returned to the soup table and grabbed another spoon, Jaysen came back up to him. "What are you doing with my sister?"

Nick stiffened. "Oh—Jaysen. I was just… giving her a spoon."

Jaysen stared at him. "A what?"

Nick held up the second one like evidence. "A spoon. Just a spoon."

Jaysen stepped closer. "If you lay a finger on her, I'll take that spoon and—"

"Hurry up, Jaysen," Connor cut in, grabbing him by the elbow. "Your soup's going cold." He shot Nick a look and winked before dragging Jaysen away.

Nick let out a breath and went back to his seat.

Izzy looked at him. "What was that about?"

Nick cleared his throat. "He, uh… wanted to apologize?"

She stared at him for a beat. "Are you asking me that. Or telling me?" She had a mouthful of soup, and moaned. "This soup's amazing. Victor really knows what he's doing."

Nick grinned. "He really does."

∞

Lincoln

Lincoln carried the soup bowl with a focused scowl. DJ peeled off to sit with Izzy and Nick, grinning like nothing in the world could go wrong. Lincoln didn't follow. Instead, he made his way over to where Jaysen and Connor were seated, dropping down beside them without a word.

"What's your sister doing with those two?" he muttered, nodding toward the table where DJ was now laughing with Izzy and Nick.

"I don't know," Jaysen growled. His jaw was tight, eyes locked like a laser on the back of Nick's head.

"They're not that bad," Connor offered. "You two seemed to like them before they started getting close to Izzy and Xav."

Lincoln and Jaysen both turned to stare at him.

"I mean," Connor added quickly, "it's not like you and Xavier had anything going on before, Link. And Jaysen... Izzy's a grown woman. She can choose who she eats soup with."

Lincoln gave a noncommittal grunt and jabbed his spoon into his bowl. Jaysen did the same. Neither of them said another word.

Connor sighed, then looked toward Lincoln. "How's Xavier?"

Lincoln shrugged. "He's okay. Talking to The Council right now."

That got both their attention.

"About what?" Jaysen asked, brow furrowed.

Another shrug. "Probably about the fact that he's going to overthrow his brother and take his place."

Both Jaysen and Connor froze, spoons halfway to their mouths.

"WHAT?" they blurted in unison.

Heads turned. Soup paused mid-sip. Conversations around the table quieted.

Jaysen leaned in, lowering his voice. "He is?"

Lincoln nodded and kept eating like he hadn't just dropped a bomb.

When he finished, he stood abruptly and set his empty bowl down. "I need to go."

Neither of them tried to stop him.

He headed into the tunnels, letting the buzz of the hall fade behind him. The quiet out here was better. Cooler. He followed the winding path, trying to remember the turnoff that led to the spring.

"Hi!"

Lincoln jumped. The voice came out of nowhere.

He turned to find a small woman standing behind him, smiling apologetically. Her voice was soft, almost mouse-like, but her eyes were sharp.

"Oh gosh, I'm so sorry," she said, stepping back slightly. "I didn't mean to scare you. Are you lost?"

"I'm not lost, and you didn't scare me." Lincoln grunted, already half-turned to keep walking.

She tilted her head. "Well, where are you going?"

"The canyon floor."

"Oh! That's where I'm going too," she said brightly. "I'll walk with you."

Before he could say anything, she reached out and looped her arm through his.

"I'm Pandora," she added with a cheerful tug. "It's this way."

Lincoln stared at her in disbelief as she pulled him forward like he weighed nothing.

Shit. This little woman is fucking strong, he thought, stumbling a half-step before keeping pace beside her.

∞

It was raining when Lincoln and Pandora reached the canyon floor.

Pandora let go of his arm and skipped ahead into a small clearing, spinning with her arms outstretched like a child who didn't know better—or didn't care.

"It's raining!" she called out, laughing. "Perfect!"

This chick is weird, Lincoln thought, watching her twirl. *Where did she even come from?*

He cleared his throat. "What are you doing?"

Pandora ran back and grabbed his hands. "I'm enjoying the rain. Join me."

Before he could protest, she pulled him out from under the overhang and into the open. Rain splattered against his face, soaking his clothes instantly.

"The rain cleanses us," Pandora said, still holding his hands. "It washes away all the hurt and pain… It feeds the earth, then everything is new again. Rain is mother nature's finest creation."

Lincoln just stood there, stiff and uncomfortable. The cold crept into his bones, but he didn't pull away.

"Take off your shoes," she said gently, "and feel the grass beneath your feet. Close your eye. You can feel it."

If I don't, she'll probably do it for me, Lincoln thought as he bent down and pulled off his shoes. The wet grass squished between his toes. Reluctantly, he closed his eye.

"Imagine tiny little tree roots growing out of your feet," Pandora whispered. "Making their way deep down into the earth."

Lincoln cracked his eye open and looked at her sideways.

"Trust me," she said with a soft smile.

Something about that smile made him pause. It was genuine. Warm. Like she saw something in him no one else ever had. Slowly, he let his eye fall shut again and tried to picture the roots.

This is weird.

"All the drops of rain," Pandora continued, her voice just above the sound of the storm, "feel them running down your body and into the earth, feeding it. And all that hurt… all that anger you've been holding onto… find it. It's little balls of light in your veins."

Okay, this chick is nuts.

"I can feel your apprehension," she said quietly. "Please. Trust me."

Lincoln didn't respond, but something in him softened. He did as she said. He looked for the lights. The rain traced cold lines down his skin. His feet began to feel heavy. Grounded. Rooted.

Then, he thought of his father.

Of the shouting. The fists. The shame. His hands twitched, and he nearly clenched them—forgotten that Pandora was still holding them. She squeezed his hands in return.

"That's good," she said, almost inaudible.

"Now find where it is, and help your blood move it through your body… feel it… and then help it leave. Push it through the roots, and into the earth."

He searched.

And then—he found it.

The pain glowed. Dim at first. Then brighter. Brighter still.

Tears slid down his cheek without him realizing. One by one, silent and clean.

YOU'RE PATHETIC!… YOU FUCKING FAG!… YOU'RE NOT MY SON!

His father's voice boomed inside him, echoing like it had been waiting just behind his ribs this whole time.

Lincoln's knees trembled. His chest heaved. He felt like he might shatter into a thousand pieces.

Pandora didn't let go.

"It's okay," she breathed. "You can do this."

The light pulsed inside him. He helped it move. Down through his chest. His legs. Toward his feet.

And as it left him, images of his father flashed—shards of memory— flaring in the dark. Lincoln's mind slipped somewhere deeper, and he fell into a trance.

The rain fell away. The sound of it dulled into silence.

Lincoln was no longer in the canyon.

∞

He was back in his childhood bedroom.

The walls were covered in peeling posters—fighters, engines, things he used to think would make him tougher. A faint hum came from the old overhead fan, its blades ticking with every slow turn.

The boy from his dream was there—Xander.

Lying on Lincoln's bed, a gentle smile on his face. His dark curls were damp, like he'd just come in from the rain, and his eyes searched Lincoln's face with a kind of reverence.

Lincoln was on top of him, their lips pressed together in a kiss that felt desperate and holy all at once. Fingers tangled in fabric as they undressed each other, piece by piece. Breathless. Unafraid.

"I love you, Link," Xander whispered into the space between their mouths.

"I love you too, Xander," Lincoln said, voice thick with emotion.

But the moment shattered.

The door slammed open with a deafening crack.

His father stood in the doorway, face twisted with fury. Without a word, he stormed over, grabbing Lincoln by the collar and throwing him aside like trash. Lincoln slammed into the wall, crumpled in the corner.

"No—NO!" he cried out, already knowing what was coming.

His father turned to Xander. The boy hadn't even gotten off the bed before the first punch landed. Then another. Then another.

"STOP!" Lincoln screamed, crawling forward on hands and knees. "Please! STOP!"

His father didn't hear him—or chose not to. He climbed over Xander and kept punching, over and over, until the sound of cracking ribs filled the room. It echoed off the walls. Off the inside of Lincoln's skull.

"CRACK."

"CRACK."

"CRACK."

By the time the blows stopped, Xander's face was still, his chest unmoving.

Lincoln crawled onto the bed and pulled him into his arms, blood soaking through his shirt.

"XANDER... NO!" he sobbed, over and over, rocking him gently. "Please—please, no…"

His father's voice thundered behind him.

"THIS IS ALL YOUR FAULT!"

Lincoln didn't look at him.

*"YOU KILLED THIS FAGGOT WHEN HE CAME ON TO YOU...
GOT IT?!"*

Lincoln looked up then, horror and disbelief twisting his features.

*His father pulled a cloth from his pocket—calm now—and began
wiping the blood from his knuckles. As if this was normal. As if this was
nothing.*

*Then he turned toward the door and shouted, "Get the Midnight
Enforcers. Now."*

*Lincoln remained on the bed, clutching Xander's lifeless body as the
tears poured silently down his face.*

*Lincoln didn't know how much time had passed, but his father had
boarded up all the windows.*

*The room had gone quiet. Still. The fan above him ticked on, its
rhythm like a clock counting down.*

*He stayed there, arms wrapped around Xander's broken body,
rocking slightly, the blood drying against his skin. The warmth had left
Xander long ago, but Lincoln couldn't let go. Wouldn't.*

*A sound broke the silence—a mechanical clink, followed by the heavy
drag of boots on tile.*

Then the door opened.

*Two Midnight Enforcers stepped into the room, their armor
gleaming, featureless. Cold.*

*Lincoln looked up, dazed. One of them spoke, voice modulated and
emotionless.*

"On your feet."

He didn't respond. Couldn't.

The Enforcers didn't wait.

*One reached down and wrenched him away from the bed. Lincoln's
hands clung to Xander until they were forced apart, his fingers scraping
along bloodstained sheets. He screamed, kicked, tried to twist free—but
they were too strong.*

"Let me go!" he shouted. "He needs help—please, HELP HIM!"

But Xander didn't move.

The Enforcers didn't speak again.

They dragged Lincoln out of the room, down the hall, through the house, while his father stood by the front door, arms crossed, silent. Watching.

The rain had stopped outside. The world smelled like damp earth and endings.

Lincoln screamed until his voice broke. Until there was nothing left but breath.

The last thing he saw before the black van door slammed shut was the memory of Xander, lying on his bed, still and forgotten.

And then—darkness.

∞

Lincoln came out of his trance slowly, like surfacing from deep water.

The air felt different. Cooler. Quieter.

The remaining lights that had gathered in his feet—bright and trembling—flowed out through the imaginary roots and into the earth. It wasn't forced. It wasn't painful. It was like a river returning to the ocean, like something finally finding its place.

Lincoln kept his eye closed for a moment longer, letting the last remnants of grief bleed from his chest.

His breath came easier now. The tension in his shoulders had melted away. His fists were unclenched. His heartbeat no longer thundered in his ears.

When he opened his eye, the world was still soaked with rain, but it no longer felt heavy. It felt… quiet.

Pandora stood in front of him, both hands still wrapped around his. She looked up at him, her wet hair clinging to her cheeks, her smile soft and patient.

"Don't you feel better now?" she asked.

Lincoln stared at her for a long beat. The words wouldn't come.

His throat was tight, but not with fear. With awe. With confusion. With something he couldn't name.

"How did you do that?" he finally asked.

Pandora stepped forward and wrapped her arms around him. The hug was warm, grounding, and totally uninvited—yet somehow not unwelcome.

"I didn't do it," she whispered against his shoulder. "*You* did."

Lincoln didn't move right away. He just stood there in the rain, letting her hold him, unsure what to do with the space she had cracked open inside him.

∞

Nick

Nick, Izzy, and DJ sat together in the main hall, their empty bowls pushed to one side as conversation filled the space between them.

"So, when do I get my room?" Izzy asked, stretching out her legs. "A woman needs her privacy, after all."

Nick and DJ laughed.

"Pandora's sorting out the rooms," Nick said.

"She'll want to make it homely for you first," DJ added with a grin.

"Don't worry. It shouldn't be much longer," they said together, exchanging a quick look before chuckling.

"Until then, you can have my room," Nick offered. "I'll bunk with DJ. It'll be just like when we were kids."

DJ rolled his eyes. "Lucky me."

Izzy smirked. "Don't worry," she said, mimicking their earlier words with mock drama. "It shouldn't be much longer."

They all laughed and stood, the conversation drifting with them as they made their way toward the tunnels.

"Do you remember where my room is?" Nick asked as they moved down the corridor.

"Uh… no," Izzy admitted.

"That's okay," Nick said with a smile. "I'll take you there. I need a few things anyway. See you later, DJ."

"There's a map of the hideout in my room," he added as he walked beside Izzy. "You can have it."

"Thanks," she said. "I'm going to need it."

When they arrived, Nick stopped her at the door.

"It's not fancy," he said, pushing it open. "But it's home."

The room mirrored DJ's in size and layout—just arranged differently. The same kind of plain furniture, only placed with a bit more care. Crystals sat on nearly every surface, catching the soft light.

"Still better than an infirmary bed," Izzy said as she stepped inside. She sat on his bed, bounced lightly on the mattress, then looked around. "Comfy."

She reached for a large crystal on the bedside table, holding it up. "What's this?" Her eyes flicked to the others scattered around.

"That's Pandora's decorating," Nick said, rubbing the back of his neck. "She's… eccentric."

Izzy smiled and set the crystal back down. "So I can expect something like this for my room?"

"Definitely," he laughed.

Nick crossed the room to a small desk in the corner and sifted through the neatly stacked papers. He pulled out a folded map and handed it to her.

"Here. You can keep it. I know every inch of this place now."

He moved to the wardrobe and grabbed a change of clothes, tucking them under his arm.

"I'll let you rest," he said, heading for the door.

"Nick, wait…"

Izzy stood, stepping closer. Her voice softened. "Thank you," she said. "For everything."

Nick stopped. He turned, and she met him halfway.

"You've been such a great friend," she added.

He smiled, the kind that almost didn't reach his eyes. "Of course. You've been through a lot. I want to help."

He held her hand for a brief moment—warm, steady—then let go.

"I'll see you at breakfast," he said as he stepped through the doorway. "Sweet dreams."

The door closed behind him.

Nick made his way toward DJ's room, the halls quiet around him.

He kicked at the dust beneath his feet.

When Nick arrived at DJ's room, DJ was already inside, sitting cross-legged on his bed. A thin mattress on the floor beside him.

"I'm not sharing a bed with you," DJ smirked. "You can sleep there."

Nick snorted, strode over to DJ's bed, and without hesitation flopped down between him and the wall, shoving DJ sideways onto the mattress.

"Now, where are your manners?" he said, grinning. "You know guests always get the best bed."

DJ sat up, brushing himself off. "Fuck you," he laughed. "Where are *your* manners? Guests are supposed to bring a gift."

Nick pulled a joint from his pocket and waved it in front of DJ's face. "Who says I didn't?"

DJ snatched it before he could finish the sentence. "That's more like it."

They lit it up, laughing as the familiar burn filled the space between them. DJ took a few slow drags, then passed it over.

"Izzy seems nice," he said.

"She is," Nick replied, smiling faintly.

"What's going on with you two?"

"We're just friends."

DJ raised an eyebrow. "Yeah, okay… friends."

Nick rolled his eyes. "Well, I like her," he admitted after a moment. "But she doesn't see me that way. I can't blame her. We hardly know each other."

DJ's teasing softened into something gentler. "She's also been through a lot. Don't push her, yeah?"

"I know," Nick said with a nod. "I won't."

"You'll just have to admire her from afar," DJ said, passing the joint back. "Anyway, could you imagine how her brother would react if you two were together? Jaysen would probably kill us both."

"He's just being protective," Nick replied. "His talk with me may have been a bit more aggressive than mine with Xavier, but his intentions were good."

DJ stiffened. "What?"

Nick said innocently. "I just told him that if he hurts you, I'd hurt him. Forgot to mention that after I found out who he was."

DJ stared. "Nick…"

Nick held up a hand. "Hey, I didn't actually threaten him. Just brotherly warning vibes."

DJ groaned. "You can't go around threatening people. Xavier's not his father."

Nick gave him a pointed look. "But you're my little brother."

"Only by like two minutes!"

"And yet I'm still the older, wiser one," Nick smirked.

DJ folded his arms. "Nick, I appreciate your concern, but I don't need you babying me. And Xavier shouldn't be held accountable for his father's actions. He's a good man… You must see that after reading his file."

"I did read the file," Nick said, getting more serious now. "And that's why I'm worried. This is your first real crush, DJ. I'm scared it's gonna hurt you if Xavier chooses Lincoln. And I'm scared Lincoln's gonna hurt you if Xavier doesn't. That guy's unstable. He gives me a bad feeling."

DJ opened his mouth, but Nick cut in.

"I'm also worried Xavier turns out to be just like his father. You must remember the old nurse—on his first day in the infirmary!"

DJ winced. "I told you, Nick. It's more than a crush… I love him. And I want to see him happy. If that means he chooses Lincoln, then yeah, it'll hurt—but he'll be happy. And that's enough for me."

Nick stared at him. "You also know he didn't mean for it to go that far with the nurse," DJ added quickly. "It's not like he killed her."

Nick didn't answer right away. He just sighed and moved closer, settling next to DJ and wrapping an arm around his shoulders.

"I know you say that you'd be okay if he chose Lincoln," he said quietly, "but look at you. Just thinking about it hurts you."

He felt DJ's breath catch. Saw the way his eyes shimmered.

"I know you, little brother. It's going to hurt you so much more than you realize."

∞

Jaysen

Jaysen clenched his fists as he watched Izzy walk away with Nick, the laughter echoing behind them like a challenge.

"Calm down, mate," said Connor, placing a hand on Jaysen's shoulder. "You'll only push her away if you go all overprotective brother on her."

Jaysen grunted. "I'm not being overprotective. I'm being a normal level of protective, given *everything* that's happened."

"I know," Connor said gently. "But Izzy clearly doesn't see it that way... Now let's figure out our sleeping arrangements. I don't want to crash on that infirmary couch again. It's worse than the beds in our cage."

Jaysen nodded toward the center of the hall. "Let's ask Marcus. He'll know."

∞

"Pandora's sorting out the rooms," Marcus said when they approached. "She always insists on doing something with feng shit. Just keep the crystals in place, or she'll cry."

Marcus laughed, but Jaysen frowned slightly.

"Feng what?" Connor asked.

"Feng shit," Marcus repeated with a shrug. "Something about crystals and energies, I don't know. I just keep 'em where she puts 'em. Trust me—you don't want to deal with a hysterical Pandora. No one does."

"You mean Feng Shui?" Jaysen asked, raising an eyebrow.

Marcus just shrugged again.

"Where can we find her?" Connor asked.

"She's probably off frolicking in the rain," Marcus said. "She's strange, that girl. Spends most of her time on the canyon floor. You know where that is?"

"The rain… It's raining?" Connor asked, eyes lighting up.

"Yeah," Marcus scoffed, eyeing him from head to toe.

"We know where it is," Jaysen said sharply. "Let's go, Connor."

As they left, Connor muttered, "Well, he seems…"

"Arrogant," Jaysen finished, pulling out the map of the hideout. He traced the tunnel to the left. "This way."

Connor followed, hands in his pockets, quieter now.

"Who'd have thought all this would happen when we met?" he said eventually. "I honestly thought we were both gonna die in that prison."

Jaysen gave a small smile. "Same here, mate."

∞

They stepped onto the canyon floor—and stopped.

Lincoln was hugging someone.

Not just hugging—clinging to her.

"Is Lincoln… crying?" Connor asked.

"I think so," Jaysen murmured.

They started to turn back, unsure if they were intruding, when a voice rang out behind them.

"Don't leave!"

They spun around.

Pandora skipped toward them, drenched and glowing with joy. She threw her arms around both of them, soaking them instantly. Jaysen stood stiff, stunned.

"Come join us! The rain is beautiful!"

She's beautiful, Jaysen thought, staring. The way her hair clung to her cheeks, the way her smile didn't seem to belong to this place. *Say something, you idiot.*

Before he could, Pandora grabbed their hands and tugged them into the open.

Connor burst out laughing and spread his arms wide. "I haven't felt the rain in twenty years!" Then, without warning, he scooped Jaysen up. "IT'S THE RAIN, JAYSEN!"

"Connor, don't you dare—"

Too late. He dropped Jaysen straight into a muddy puddle and flopped down beside him, cackling like a kid.

Jaysen stood, flicking off the mud, and leaving Connor to enjoy himself, he got as far from his reach as he could. Pandora giggled from next to Jaysen, her laugh light and unbothered. Even her giggle… it was different. Not like the others here. Unfiltered. Free.

Who is she?

"He loves the rain just as much as I do," she said brightly. "Hi, I'm Pandora."

Jaysen opened his mouth. "Hi… I'm, uh—" He froze.

Brilliant. Real smooth.

"This is Jaysen," Lincoln said as he joined them. "And that's Connor."

"Hi, Jaysen," Pandora said, her voice lilting. She hugged him without hesitation. "Isn't tonight just beautiful?"

She lay back on the wet grass, looking up through the canopy as rain danced over her face.

"All our troubles seem so far away when you're down here," she whispered. "Don't they?"

She patted the ground beside her, beckoning Jaysen and Lincoln to lie down. Jaysen glanced at Lincoln.

"She may be quirky," Lincoln whispered. "But she's amazing."

He lay back, and Jaysen followed, his soaked clothes forgotten.

Connor's laughter echoed in the background as they stared up into the shifting branches above.

"It is beautiful," Jaysen said quietly.

"It is," Lincoln agreed.

Pandora took their hands, linking her fingers between theirs. Jaysen glanced down at their hands, then up at her. She gave his fingers a small squeeze.

"A moment to think is what everyone needs," she said. "And this is the best place. A calm place in the storm… And yes, I know that sounds stupid because we're literally laying in the rain."

"I don't think it sounds stupid," Jaysen said, his voice softer than before. He looked at her. "Sometimes the storm *is* the calm."

Pandora smiled at him, then looked back up at the sky.

"I should go," Lincoln said after a while, sitting up. "I need to see Xavier before he goes to sleep."

Pandora sat up with him. "Oh! Please tell him I said hi, and I hope he's feeling better soon."

"You've met Xavier?" Jaysen asked, surprised.

"Yes, briefly. But I was in such a rush preparing your rooms that I couldn't chat for long." She suddenly gasped. "That's right—your rooms!"

She sprang to her feet. "Your rooms are ready!"

∞

"I'm so sorry," Pandora said as she led Jaysen and Connor through the tunnels. Her soaked dress clung to her ankles as she walked, but she didn't seem to notice. "The rain distracted me."

"That's okay," Jaysen said quickly, almost too quickly. "We weren't even worried about it."

Connor gave him a sideways glance and smirked. "Yeah," he said, voice dripping with sarcasm. "We didn't mind sleeping on the infirmary couch, did we, Jayse?"

Jaysen flushed. "It was fine," he muttered.

Connor kept teasing. "It was quite comfortable. I think I cracked my spine in three places."

Jaysen elbowed him hard in the side. "Cut it out."

Connor grinned and nudged him back.

Pandora glanced between them with a soft smile, then stopped at a worn wooden door with a vine-shaped carving etched faintly across its surface. "This is your room, Connor," she said, pushing it open. "There's not much to work with, but I do hope you like it."

She stepped aside and gestured warmly inside. "There's a double bed too, so your wife can join you when she's ready."

Connor took a step in and paused. His face softened. The room was small, but it was his. A double bed rested against the far wall, its wooden frame sturdy and simple. A small desk sat beneath a wall sconce, next to a modest wardrobe. Black candles flickered gently on the shelves, casting a warm glow against the stone. Crystals had been placed in delicate, thoughtful spots—on the bedside table, along the windowsill, even tucked between the desk drawers.

"Thanks," he said, almost reverently. "It's perfect."

Pandora's eyes lit up. "I'm so glad you like it." She turned to Jaysen. "Your room is just up ahead." Then to Connor: "Oh—and there's a map on your desk."

She closed Connor's door softly behind them, then slipped her arm through Jaysen's without asking.

Jaysen tensed.

Her sun-kissed skin was warm despite the rain.

"This way," she said cheerfully, pulling him along as if they'd known each other for years. "I made sure to keep all the boys close together.

That one's Xavier's." She pointed to a narrow door they passed. "And that one up ahead is Lincoln's. Your room is just there."

Jaysen barely heard her. Her voice was airy, musical—like the wind that moved through the upper trees back home. He glanced down at their linked arms, then up at her face. She walked as if the world never hurt her, as if none of this had touched her, and somehow—he believed it. Believed that wherever she came from, it wasn't a place that had cages or bloodied fists or bruised hope.

She doesn't belong here, he thought. *And yet... she does.*

They reached his door. She pushed it open and stepped inside.

The room was similar to Connor's—same layout, same furniture—but it felt different. Maybe it was the way the crystals glimmered under the flickering candlelight, or the way the bed was made with care, not just utility. There was a small stone on the bedside table—different from the ones in Connor's room. This one shimmered faintly, almost pulsing.

"I placed your crystals in the same spots," Pandora said, stepping back so he could look. "But I gave you a different bedside stone. This one's for clarity."

Jaysen didn't know what to say.

"There's a map on the desk," she added.

"I have one." He reached for his pocket, tugged out his old map—but it came out in pieces, soaked through and ripped from the rain.

"Maybe not," he muttered, cheeks burning.

Pandora giggled. "There's also a towel and a change of clothes in the wardrobe. I marked the bathhouse on the map for you. I think Connor's going to need one."

Jaysen crossed to the wardrobe and pulled it open. Inside was a folded towel and a clean set of clothes—his size, or close enough.

"I hope they fit," she added. "But if not, my room is just next door. Let me know, and I'll run and grab you something else."

Jaysen held up the shirt. "They'll fit. I'm sure."

She beamed. The kind of smile that made your chest go still for a second.

"I'd better go find your sister," Pandora said. "Her room's also finished."
She pointed to a note tucked into the corner of his map. "I've marked
everyone's rooms for you, too."

Jaysen hesitated. "Thank you. Really. It was great meeting you."

He meant it. More than he could say.

Pandora gave him one last smile and slipped away down the tunnel, her
wet dress trailing behind her like a whisper.

Jaysen stood there for a long moment, alone in the quiet hum of the
crystals and candlelight.

Where did she come from? he thought. *And why does she feel like
something I never knew I needed?*

When Pandora left the room, Jaysen stood in the stillness she left
behind.

He found himself staring at the closed door, as if it might open again.
It didn't.

He turned slowly toward the wardrobe, pulling it open. A mirror was
built into the inside of the door. Jaysen caught sight of his reflection and
winced.

He was filthy.

His hair was a matted mess, clumped from rain and sweat and
whatever else had dried into it since the escape. His beard had grown in
patches—wild, uneven, and definitely not intentional. There were
shadows under his eyes, and grime along his collar. He didn't recognize
himself, not fully. Not like this.

He sighed and ran a hand through his knots. "Bloody hell," he
muttered. "Great first impression."

He rummaged through the wardrobe again—towel, shirt, pants—but
no grooming kit. He tried the bedside table next. A few crystals. A folded
note from Pandora with bathhouse directions. And tucked beneath it
all—a razor.

He held it up with a small grin. "Thank Fuck."

Just then, a knock sounded at the door.

"Jaysen?" Connor's voice came through.

"Yeah, mate, come in," he called, slipping the razor into his pocket.

Connor entered, shirtless, towel slung over one shoulder, fresh clothes in his arms. "Looks like we both had the same idea."

Jaysen smiled. "No razor?"

"Nah mate, I've got my grooming kit." Connor pulled a small tin from his pocket, popped it open, and revealed a comb, a pair of scissors, and a tiny jar of balm. "You'll never see me without this baby."

He stroked his own beard proudly. "You've got to look after the assets."

Jaysen chuckled and shook his head. "Let's go check out this bathhouse."

"Definitely."

Jaysen grabbed his towel and clothes, and together they slipped through the tunnels toward the bathhouse.

∞

When they entered, the scent of warm water and herbal soap filled the air. The room was dimly lit with hanging lanterns, steam curling up to the ceiling beams. Several people were already there—bathing in quiet pairs or washing their hair in carved stone basins.

As they walked in, heads turned.

Jaysen slowed. "Everyone's staring at us," he whispered.

"Well, yeah," Connor replied, unfazed. "It's like our first day in The Aviary. We're fresh meat again." He grinned. "Give it a day or two. They'll find something new to gawk at."

They found an empty pool tucked in the far corner and stepped inside. The water was deep enough to sink into and hot enough to melt the tension right out of his shoulders. Jaysen let out a quiet sigh as he eased in.

"It's great to sit in warm water instead of having it blasted at you," Connor said, dragging his hands across the surface.

"You got that right," Jaysen mumbled, letting his head tip back against the stone edge.

Connor dipped under to rinse off the dried mud. When he came up, he pushed his hair back, wiped his face, and glanced over with a smirk.

"So… Pandora," he said.

Jaysen blinked. "What about her?"

"She seems nice," Connor said, all innocence—except for the wink.

Jaysen groaned softly and covered his face with both hands. "I don't know what came over me," he muttered through his fingers. "I could barely speak. I just stood there like a complete idiot."

"She does that to people?" Connor offered.

Jaysen dropped his hands and looked over at him. "She's… beautiful. Like, in every way. I don't just mean her face or her hair. It's the way she moves. The way she talks. Like she's not part of any of this—but she still belongs here."

Connor gave him a look—half-teasing, half-concerned. "You barely know her."

"I know," Jaysen said, cheeks warming. "I'm not saying I'm in love or anything. Just…" He trailed off, eyes drifting toward the steam rising off the water. "She caught me off guard."

Connor didn't poke further.

Jaysen turned quiet for a moment, then added, "Maybe I've been overcompensating lately. Pushing too hard. Getting all protective with Izzy… I need to talk to her. Tomorrow."

Connor gave a small nod. "She'd probably appreciate that."

Jaysen leaned back again, soaking in the quiet. The heat. The calm after the storm.

But even with the steam swirling around them, and the water easing every sore muscle… he couldn't stop thinking about the girl with the soaked dress and the smile like sunlight.

∞

Connor

"We should go check on Xavier," Jaysen said as they returned from the bathhouse, their skin still warm from the steam and their clothes clinging slightly from the humidity of the tunnels.

"Yeah," Connor nodded. "I wanna know what happened with The Council."

"I wonder if we have to call him *your grace* now that he's going to be The Shepherd."

Connor snorted, and both of them laughed.

"I'm not doing that uncomfortable bow every time he walks in the room, that's for sure," Connor added as they turned the final corner and reached the infirmary.

When they stepped inside, the light was low. Lincoln was curled up on Xavier's bed, fast asleep. Xavier was lying beside him with his head resting on Lincoln's chest, Lincoln's arm protectively wrapped around him.

Connor blinked. The sight was... unexpected. Intimate. Gentle.

"Uh..." Jaysen whispered, shifting awkwardly. "We should see him tomorrow."

"Yeah," Connor said, just as quietly.

Jessica was nearby, kneeling beside Genevieve and gently removing the drip from her arm.

"Connor." Genevieve said brightly, her eyes lighting up the moment she saw him. "Once one of the builders fixes me a wheelchair, I'll be able to go out!"

Connor made his way to her, heart squeezing at the sight of her sitting up, her smile tired but bright. He knelt beside her.

"She can leave now?" he asked, glancing at Jessica.

"Well, I suppose she could leave now," Jessica said kindly. "But we don't have the chair yet."

"That's okay. We don't need the chair right now."

He looked over at Jaysen. "I'll see you later."

Jaysen gave him a knowing smile and nodded before stepping out of the infirmary.

Connor pulled the map from his pocket and folded it open. Then he scooped Genevieve into his arms with care, her weight fragile against his chest.

"Let's go for a walk," he said, offering her a soft smile.

"That would be lovely," Genevieve replied, wrapping an arm around his neck and resting her head against his heart. "Where are we going?"

"We're going for a swim."

He walked slowly, carefully, eyes flicking between the map and the tunnel ahead. His steps were cautious but confident. He'd already memorized half of it by now.

Connor chuckled softly. "You're going to love this."

They exited the tunnel and stepped into the poolroom. The scent of wet stone filled the space, and the soft trickle of water echoed through the cavern. Lanterns lined the walls, casting a golden glow across the surface of the bay.

Genevieve gasped. "It's beautiful… but I don't have anything to wear in the water… or a towel."

Connor glanced at her body, so thin beneath the oversized medical gown. *Shit. Of course she wouldn't want to be naked. This isn't Augmentation Bay. She has a choice here.* "Fuck. There's some in the room. We can go back and get it."

Genevieve laughed, a sound like light. "You can't carry all that and me," she teased. "I'll wait here."

Connor hesitated. The idea of leaving her alone in here even for a moment twisted something tight in his chest.

"I'll be okay," she said, sensing it. "No one is going to hurt me in here."

"I'll be as quick as I can," he promised. "Where would you like to sit?"

"By the water."

He helped her sit against the wall beside the bay, kissed her forehead gently, then turned and rushed out of the room.

When Connor returned, arms full, he paused in the doorway.

Genevieve was tracing her fingers through the water, her face peaceful, content.

"I got you a towel," he said, stepping closer. "A change of clothes… and a sports bra and underwear. I'm sorry—there weren't any bathing suits. I guess they don't get access to everything out here."

Genevieve giggled. "That's perfectly fine. Although I'm going to need your help."

A lump formed in Connor's throat. He knelt in front of her, hands shaking as he helped her out of the old gown and into the clean clothes. The underwear fit loosely on her thin frame, and the sports bra was a little snug—but it worked.

He couldn't stop looking at her.

Be gentle, he reminded himself. *It's been twenty-one years.*

She was still Genevieve.

Still his wife.

He lifted her into his arms once more and stepped into the bay. The water welcomed them, cool and slow-moving. Connor walked them deeper, holding her close, the river cradling them both.

Genevieve sighed as the warmth wrapped around her. She rested her cheek against his shoulder.

Connor spun her gently in the water. Just once. Just enough for her to laugh.

"Thank you," she whispered. "This is exactly what I needed… Can we sit somewhere? I feel like I haven't sat up in years." She giggled softly.

"Did you just try to make a joke?" he teased, smiling down at her.

She blushed. "Maybe."

"You still have the same terrible sense of humor, I see."

He carried her back to the bay and sat down in the shallow edge, settling her beside him. The water lapped softly at their waists. He put his arm around her and pulled her close.

Tears welled in his eyes before he could stop them. They spilled silently down his cheeks.

"I've missed you so much," he whispered.

Genevieve reached up and cupped his face. She brushed a tear away and traced his jawline with her fingertips.

"I missed you too," she said. "I'm so sorry you spent so long locked away… That you thought I was dead."

Connor closed his eyes and leaned into her touch. "I'm sorry I stopped looking for you."

She kissed him—soft, slow, full of forgiveness. Her lips trembled against his.

"It's all behind us now," she murmured. "You found me… just like I knew you would."

Connor wrapped his arms around her waist and held her tightly, as if the world might try to steal her away again.

"Genevieve," he whispered, voice breaking. "Genevieve."

She wrapped her arms around his shoulders and stroked his hair. "Shush, baby. It's okay," she whispered. "We're together now. And nothing will tear us apart again."

∞

Jaysen

Jaysen wandered through the tunnels of The Renegade hideout, his mind foggy with thoughts he didn't want to name. The air was cooler here—thicker somehow. It smelled of old earth and something softer, something lived in. He didn't know where he was going. He just moved. Step after step. Head down. Kicking up small clouds of dust with the worn tips of his shoes.

He rounded a corner and bumped into someone soft—warm.

Pandora.

"I can't find your sister," she said, brushing her hair out of her face. "Have you seen her?"

Jaysen blinked. "No… but I can help you look."

She smiled, looping her arm through his like it was the most natural thing in the world. "Okay," she said brightly, already tugging him forward. "I thought I'd ask DJ. He'll know where Nick is, and I saw her last with him."

Jaysen let himself be led, still trying to catch up with her pace. Her skin was warm against his, her movements effortless.

Then he looked down.

"Why aren't you wearing shoes?" he asked, his brow furrowing.

"It's better for your feet," Pandora said. "It also keeps me close to nature… You should try it."

Before he could argue, she stopped outside his room. "Your room is right here. We'll leave your shoes at the door."

"Wait, I don't—"

But she was already crouched, gently untying his laces. He stood frozen as she slid his shoes off and placed them neatly beside the wall.

"See?" she said, stepping back with a grin. "Doesn't it feel nice?"

"Uh… I guess," he muttered, shifting awkwardly on the stone floor.

"Trust me," Pandora said, linking her arm through his again. "Give it some time. You won't go back."

They moved quietly through the tunnels, bare feet brushing over cool rock and packed earth. Somehow, it didn't feel strange. Not with her beside him.

When they reached DJ's door, Pandora knocked gently.

"DJ, are you in there?" she called.

The door cracked open, and Nick appeared, looking groggy but alert.

"He's asleep," Nick said, keeping his voice low. "What's up?"

"We're looking for Izzy," Jaysen grunted before Pandora could answer.

"Oh—she's in my room… sleeping."

Jaysen's glare hit him like a thrown blade.

Nick threw his hands up. "Not—Not like that," he stammered. "I'm sleeping here. She's in my bed. I just—she needed somewhere quiet."

Jaysen stepped forward.

Pandora took his hand and gave it a soft squeeze.

"Thanks, Nick," she said gently, defusing the tension with a hug. "See you later."

Nick nodded, closing the door, and they turned to walk away.

"He's not a bad guy," Pandora said after a moment. "You should give him a chance."

Jaysen didn't answer at first. His jaw was tight. His fingers curled unconsciously around the edge of his shirt.

"I just don't want Izzy to get hurt," he said. "She's already pregnant with that monster's child. I don't want her suffering anymore."

"What monster?" came a sharp voice ahead of them.

Jaysen looked up—and froze.

Izzy stood in the hallway. Pale. Her arms crossed. Her expression unreadable.

"Izzy… I… Uh—"

"What monster, Jayse?" Her voice trembled.

He opened his mouth—but nothing came out.

"What monster, Jaysen!" she snapped, louder this time. Her voice cracked, but she stood firm.

Pandora, still holding his hand, squeezed it gently again.

"Feel the earth," she whispered. "Let it ground you… You'll find your words."

Jaysen took a shaky breath. The ground beneath his feet suddenly felt very real. Cool. Solid.

"Izzy…" he started. "There were medical files. At the end of your bed."

Pandora didn't let go of his hand.

"I looked through them," Jaysen continued. "I found out who the biological father of your baby is."

He stared at the floor.

"Izzy… It's Kaylus."

The silence that followed felt like a wall collapsing inside her.

Izzy's face turned ghostly white.

Pandora let go of Jaysen's hand and moved to her in an instant, wrapping her arms around her.

"I'm so sorry," she whispered.

Izzy broke.

Her body shuddered with sobs as she clung to Pandora. She buried her face into Pandora's shoulder, trembling, and finally hugged her back.

"Would you like me to take you to your room?" Pandora asked softly.

Izzy nodded.

When they arrived at her door, Izzy wiped her face with the sleeve of her shirt and turned to Pandora. "Will you ask Nick to come and see me… if you see him?"

Pandora nodded.

Jaysen's jaw tightened, and he clenched his fists.

What is it about him? he thought bitterly. *I want to be okay with him, but I just can't help it.*

"Izzy," he said quietly as she reached for the door.

She paused.

"I'm sorry," Jaysen said. "I'll try to be nicer to Nick."

Izzy gave him a weak smile. "Thanks, Jayse."

"Goodnight, Izzy. Get some rest. I'll see you in the morning."

She nodded and slipped inside, closing the door behind her.

Jaysen stood there a moment longer, the silence wrapping around him like a fog.

Barefoot.

Still trying to understand what Pandora was doing to him.

Pandora gently linked her arm through Jaysen's again.

"Let's go and let Nick know his room is free," she said. "Then I want to show you something."

Jaysen nodded wordlessly, still shaken by what had happened with Izzy. They walked in silence for a few moments, Pandora's presence grounding him in ways he didn't understand.

"That was a good thing you just did," she said quietly. "I know Izzy is hurting, but she deserved to know. And I think it's great that you're going to try harder with Nick."

Jaysen let out a soft exhale. He wasn't sure if he deserved the praise, but it helped to hear it.

Pandora knocked gently on DJ's door. "Maybe you can tell him that Izzy is looking for him?" she whispered.

Nick opened the door again, eyes alert. "What's up? Is Izzy okay?"

"Yeah," said Jaysen.

Pandora reached for his hand and gave it a gentle squeeze.

"She's asking for you," Jaysen said, voice a little tight, but honest.

Nick blinked. "She is?"

"Yeah. She has her own room now."

"Two doors down and across from you!" Pandora chimed in. "That's where you can find her… We need to go now."

She hugged Nick before he could say more, then eagerly linked her arm through Jaysen's and pulled him down the tunnel before he could think too much about how annoyed—or relieved—he felt.

When they entered the main hall, most of The Renegades had already cleared out. Only a few lingered. Marcus was one of them—still perched in the same spot Jaysen had seen him in before, like a fixture.

As soon as he spotted them, Marcus stood and strode over.

"I see you found her… Good luck getting rid of her now," he said mockingly. "And would you look at that! She already has you barefoot!" He laughed as he passed.

Pandora's smile faltered. Her gaze dropped to the floor. She didn't say anything.

527

Jaysen let go of her arm and slipped his own around her shoulders instead.

"Hey…" he said softly. "Don't listen to him."

She looked up at him, blinking quickly.

"I think you're wonderful."

A small smile found its way back to her face. She wiped her eyes with the back of her hand.

I'll make him pay for that, Jaysen thought as he held her close, feeling a heat rise in his chest.

He cleared his throat, nudging her playfully. "So… what did you want to show me?"

Pandora's smile returned fully now, and she wrapped her arms around Jaysen's waist in a sudden, warm hug.

"Thank you," she whispered.

Then, without giving him time to respond, she took his hand and led him down a tunnel he hadn't seen before—one that twisted away from the main hub, its walls darker, quieter.

"This is my favorite part of The Burrow," she said.

"The Burrow?" Jaysen asked.

"Oh, that's just my name for the hideout," she replied, her voice dreamy. "It's much nicer… Don't you think?"

Jaysen chuckled. "It is."

They walked for a long time. Time enough for his feet to adjust to the stone beneath them. For the silence to become something soothing rather than awkward. The tunnel slowly widened. The air changed—crisper, with a faint smell of water.

Jaysen heard it then.

Running water.

It grew louder as they moved forward.

"Not many people come here because it's so far away," Pandora said. "But I think it's worth every step."

When they stepped out of the tunnel, the sight took Jaysen's breath away.

The rain had stopped.

Moonlight poured through a break in the stone ceiling, illuminating a lagoon fed by a stunning waterfall that spilled down the side of the mountain. The water was impossibly clear—glassy and calm, lit silver by the stars above. The bottom shimmered with white and golden sand. A small river branched away into the trees, swallowed by thick foliage. It looked like something out of a dream.

Jaysen was silent.

Pandora saw the awe in his eyes and smiled. She gently released his hand and walked to the edge of the water.

Then, without a word, she slipped off her dress and stepped into the lagoon.

Jaysen's breath caught.

"Come join me," she called as she swam gracefully toward the center. "The water's always perfect!"

Still stunned, Jaysen walked to the edge, stripped off his shirt and trousers, and stepped in.

She was right.

The water was warm and soft. It embraced him. Wrapped around his body like silk.

The water is perfect, he thought. *So is she... Don't fuck this up, Jaysen.*

He swam out to meet her. The water reached his chest, it reached Pandora's collarbone, the moonlight gilding the curve of her shoulders.

"It is worth every step," he said.

Pandora smiled, her eyes reflecting starlight.

"Lay on your back," she said gently. "Trust me."

Before he could hesitate, she placed her hand on the small of his back and pushed him upward. Jaysen found himself floating, limbs loose in the water, the sky stretching out endlessly above him.

"Look at the stars," she whispered. "They're so far away from one another... Yet they come together to form the night sky."

Her hand moved slowly, up his back, to his shoulders, lifting them gently from the water.

How is she so strong? he wondered, still looking skyward.

"Breathe in the night air and remember," she said softly. "We need to let others make their own decisions. Their own mistakes. Their own triumphs. In the end… it all comes together."

Jaysen closed his eyes.

He thought of Izzy. Of Connor. Of Xavier and Lincoln. Of everything they'd been through. Everything still ahead. He thought of Charlie…

"They make their own decisions," he breathed. "In the end, we all come together."

A single tear slid from the corner of his eye.

And as it did, the world around him faded.

The stars blurred.

And Jaysen slipped into a trance.

∞

Jaysen opened his eyes—only he hadn't.

He was somewhere else now.

The air was colder. Heavy. His breath puffed out in clouds, but there was no wind. No sound. Just silence.

He was in Feltwood Mountains. He knew them immediately—the skeletal branches, the twisted trunks, the strange way the moonlight cut through the trees like knives. He was inside the dead tree. The one from his dreams. Its hollow trunk was wide enough to hold him, and he lay curled in its center like a child hiding from a storm.

Then he saw him.

The faceless man crouched nearby, half in shadow.

Jaysen's heart kicked against his ribs. He tried to move, to scream—but nothing came. Panic spread through him like ice.

The faceless man tilted his head slowly, as if sensing Jaysen's fear.

"It's okay," he said, voice low but steady. Gentle, almost. "You're safe now... Just don't look."

Jaysen trembled.

The man reached out and scooped him into his arms—effortlessly, like he weighed nothing.

"I'll take you home," the man whispered.

The forest shifted around them as they moved. The trees bent and breathed. Roots coiled and uncoiled like snakes beneath the dirt. Jaysen's limbs hung heavy, limp, his cheek resting against the faceless man's shoulder as he was carried forward.

They passed the barn.

The barn from his dreams.

The one he always ran from.

And now—it was burning.

The crackle of flames broke the silence. Smoke curled around them, thick and choking. Jaysen turned his head, eyes wide.

"Don't look," the man said again—but it was too late.

Jaysen saw.

The roof had collapsed. Fire licked through the rafters like hungry tongues. The wooden walls groaned and split, collapsing inward. The heat singed his skin, even from here.

And the smell—Zoti, the smell. Smoke and scorched hay. Charred timber.

And burning flesh.

Jaysen buried his face in the man's shoulder and sobbed.

The faceless man kept walking.

Crack. Crack. Crack.

The barn was gone.

The fire kept burning.

The man held him tighter.

Jaysen couldn't answer. His voice was gone. His tears soaked into the man's coat, and still, he carried him. Through the smoke. Through the ash.

Back into the dark.

∞

Jaysen opened his eyes.

The stars above him blurred back into focus, and the water beneath him stilled.

He blinked.

What did she just do to me?

He felt as though he'd been pulled out of something vast and wordless—a dream that had reached into his core. His chest still ached from the weight of it. From the once lost memory. From the warmth of being carried.

Jaysen lay there a while longer, the gentle current lapping against his sides, his arms drifting beside him. The sky above looked endless, untouched.

Then a white streak ripped across the darkness.

A shooting star.

Pandora's laugh echoed softly across the lagoon. "A shooting star!" she said, her voice full of awe. "Make a wish… Just don't tell me what it is, or it won't come true."

Jaysen closed his eyes.

I wish… I hope… that it will all come together in the end.

When he opened them again, the sky was quiet, but something inside him had shifted.

He stood, the water dripping from his skin as he moved toward her. Pandora stood in the shallows now, her body glowing in the moonlight, still and waiting.

"Pandora," he said, voice barely above a whisper.

She turned to him.

He stepped closer, slow, deliberate, and placed his arm gently around her waist. She didn't flinch. Didn't step away. Instead, she leaned into his touch, her hands resting lightly at his sides.

"You're the most amazing woman I've ever met," he said. "You have this way about you that draws me in. It's like… like you belong to the world, but you still found your way to me."

She tilted her head slightly, searching his face with eyes that shimmered like the stars above them.

"You're magical, Pandora… And you're kind. The moment I met you… I think I started falling in love with you."

The words escaped before he could stop them.

His cheeks flushed, and he looked down, heat crawling across his skin. "I'm sorry… I didn't mean to say it like that. I just—"

Pandora stepped closer, her hands now resting on his waist. She didn't say anything.

She didn't need to.

She looked at him as if she already knew. As if she'd been waiting for him to say it.

"Can I… kiss you?" Jaysen asked shyly, barely meeting her gaze.

Pandora didn't answer with words.

Instead, she rose onto her toes and kissed him—without hesitation.

Her lips met his with a heat that stole his breath. Her fingers curled gently around the back of his neck, and his hands found her hips, pulling her closer until there was no space left between them.

The world faded around them—just water, moonlight, and the steady rhythm of two people who had found each other in the most impossible of ways.

∞

"I have something for you," Pandora said softly, her head resting on Jaysen's chest as they lay on the cool grass near the water's edge.

She sat up slowly, kissed his shoulder, then stood and walked toward a clearing just beyond the trees. Jaysen rose and followed, curious, the breeze drying the droplets clinging to his skin.

In the clearing, she knelt beside a small mound of carefully arranged stones. He hadn't seen it before—hadn't even noticed it. It was like the space had been waiting to be revealed.

She reached into the center of the pile and pulled out a small, glistening stone—clear as glass.

"Here she is," she said.

She stood and returned to him, placing the crystal in his palm with reverence. "Quartz," she said. "I think you need her."

Jaysen turned the stone slowly in his hand. It caught the moonlight and shimmered.

"She'll always remind you to cleanse your thoughts," Pandora continued. "Be positive, and you'll make the right decision."

Jaysen pocketed the crystal and reached for her hands. "You really are wonderful," he whispered, pulling her close. "Where have you been all my life?"

Pandora's smile faded into something quieter. "I've been here… mostly," she said. "In The Burrow. But I came here as a child… from The Farm."

Jaysen's heart cracked.

He reached up and cupped her face as tears formed in her eyes, sliding down her cheeks.

"I'm so sorry," he said. "You're so much better than that place. You've given so much to my friends and me since we arrived."

He wiped a tear from her cheek with his thumb.

"But what you're failing to see… is that you're the best gift of all."

He kissed her softly, and she melted into him—arms wrapping around his shoulders, breath catching between them.

They stayed there for hours, wrapped in each other, until sleep found them beneath the stars, curled together in the grass on the forest floor.

∞

When the sun began to rise, Jaysen stirred.

Golden light spilled through the trees, catching on dewdrops and setting the world aglow. The spot where Pandora had been lying beside him was now only a warm imprint in the grass. Her dress was folded beside him.

Jaysen sat up and looked toward the water.

She was there—naked, swimming through the lagoon like she was made of the morning itself. Her skin glistened, the sun gilding every curve, every motion. The waterfall behind her thundered softly, alive with light.

He stood and walked to the water's edge, then pulled off his boxers and stepped into the lagoon.

The water welcomed him. Warm. Gentle. Familiar.

He swam toward her.

Pandora reached the side of the waterfall and began to climb. Her bare feet gripped mossy stone, her body rising with every deliberate pull. She turned once at the flat stone base and flashed him a smile.

"Come find me!" she called, giggling as she vanished behind the falls.

Jaysen swam faster, heart racing. He gripped the rocks, pulling himself up. It was slick, but he didn't slip.

He pushed through the curtain of falling water and stepped into a hidden alcove behind the veil.

The world was muted here.

Pandora stood beneath a slender stream that flowed down from above, her arms raised, fingers combing through her soaked hair.

"There are no showers in The Burrow," she said, turning to look at him. "Not that I mind... Mother Nature *always* provides."

Jaysen stared.

The water flowed down her bare body, each droplet tracing a new path. Her eyes held his, steady, unblinking.

He didn't move.

"Well," she said, tilting her head, "you can't have a shower from over there, can you?"

She stretched out her hand.

He took it.

And she pulled him into her.

Their mouths met slowly, tenderly. It wasn't rushed. It wasn't wild. It was reverent.

Jaysen cupped her face, brushing his thumbs across her cheeks, as she pressed her body into his. The water ran between them in warm rivulets, but it couldn't cool the heat building beneath their skin.

Her hands slid to his chest, down his sides, memorizing him.

He kissed her again—longer this time—his hands slipping to her breast. She moaned softly into his mouth, and he felt her smile.

She wrapped her arms around his neck and pressed her lips to his throat, his shoulder, the space just beneath his jaw.

"Jaysen," she whispered.

He met her eyes—searching, asking.

And in them, he found his answer.

He lifted her easily, cradling her as she wrapped her legs around his waist. Her breath hitched as she clung to him, and he carried her to the flattest stretch of stone beneath the fall.

He knelt, then gently laid her down, water cascading over them in a silver curtain.

She opened to him without fear.

Their bodies came together slowly, a soft gasp escaping her lips as he entered her.

Their foreheads pressed together.

Their hands clutched and curled.

Each movement was slow, intentional, electric.

She moved with him, hips rising to meet his, her fingers tangled in his hair, her mouth trailing kisses across his collarbone, his jaw, his lips, every scar that lined his face. Learning him.

Loving him.

The rhythm built—long and deep and aching with emotion. They whispered to each other without words. Cried out in breathless gasps.

Water splashed softly around them, a second heartbeat beneath their own.

She moaned his name like a prayer.

And when their bodies finally trembled together, when their mouths parted in silent release, Jaysen clung to her, arms locked tight around her frame, heart pounding against her chest.

They didn't move.

They didn't speak.

They simply held each other.

Water fell around them.

And the world, for a while, was still.

∞

Nick

When Izzy opened the door, Nick was already standing there, smiling softly.

"You wanted to see me?" he asked, voice low and kind.

She didn't answer with words—just stepped back and let him in. He entered quietly, standing in the middle of her dimly lit room, unsure of what to say.

Izzy walked past him and sat on the edge of her bed.

Then she started crying.

Nick's heart dropped.

"Hey, hey, hey…" he rushed to her, dropping to his knees beside the bed. "What's going on?"

She couldn't speak. Her sobs came hard, fast, and loud, shaking her whole body. Nick didn't hesitate—he wrapped his arms around her and held her tight.

"It's okay," he whispered. "I've got you."

Her tears soaked through his shirt, and still she cried.

He didn't let go.

Time passed slowly. Her sobs turned to sniffles. Her breathing evened out, little by little. Nick stayed there, grounded and calm, letting her fall apart in his arms.

Finally, she spoke—just a whisper.

"It's my baby…" She paused, trembling. "His father… it's… it's Kaylus."

Nick went still.

Then, without hesitation, he pulled her tighter.

"I'm so sorry," he whispered, and she buried her head deeper into his shoulder.

"I heard what happened… why Jaysen went to Augmentation Bay."

He pulled back just enough to take her hands, then placed them gently on her stomach.

"Just remember what you said," he told her. "He is *your* baby. Let's not call that pathetic excuse for a human being a father."

He reached up and wiped away a tear with his thumb.

"All Kaylus is… is a donor."

Izzy looked at him, tears still falling.

"He… You think my baby is a boy?"

Nick smiled gently. "Well, you're the one who said it. All I did was listen."

A small sound broke in her throat—half a laugh, half a sob.

Nick kissed the backs of her hands, cradling them in his.

"You can do this," he said. "You will be amazing at it."

Izzy's tears came again—softer this time, but steady.

Nick stood and carefully climbed into bed beside her, his movements slow, respectful. He pulled her gently into his arms.

"I'll be here to help you," he whispered into her ear, his breath warm against her skin.

Izzy rolled over and pressed her face into his chest. Her fingers curled into his shirt as he wrapped her in a protective embrace. She cried softly as he held her close, and eventually, her tears gave way to silence.

Her breathing slowed.

Sleep found her.

Nick lay there, awake, staring at the ceiling as the weight of her body rested against him.

I wish I could hold her like this every night, he thought. *Just one won't hurt.*

He leaned down and kissed her forehead gently.

"I'll *always* be here to help you, Isabelle," he whispered.

And as the quiet settled over the room, Nick's eyes finally closed. He drifted off to sleep with her in his arms—holding her like something fragile, something precious.

Something worth everything.

"And I invited Pandora to sit with us," Jaysen added, draping an arm around her shoulders and kissing her temple.

Everyone turned to look at the two of them.

"When… No, wait… How did this happen?" DJ asked, gesturing between them in disbelief.

Pandora blushed and shrugged. "It just happened," she said with a smile up at Jaysen.

"Oh, but Jayse, you barely know her," Izzy said mockingly.

Jaysen shot her a glare, then softened. "I'm sorry, Nick," he said, looking at him and Izzy. "I *may* have been *slightly* overprotective."

Nick chuckled. "Don't stress, mate. I'd have done the same thing for my little brother." He slung an arm around DJ and ruffled his hair.

"We're twins, Nick! I'm not your little brother!"

"I was born first. You *are* my little brother."

"So what, we're all friends now?" Lincoln muttered, skeptical.

DJ met his eyes, his voice softer. "I'm sorry, Link. All I want is for Xavier to be happy. And that's not gonna happen with us at each other's throats." He reached across the table and held out a hand. "Truce? For Xavier's sake."

Lincoln paused, eyeing DJ's hand. Then he reached out and shook it—gripping just a touch harder than necessary. "Truce," he said gruffly. "For Xavier's sake."

Pandora stood and raised her glass of orange juice. "To new friends," she said brightly.

"To new friends," the others echoed, some more enthusiastic than others. But Pandora smiled as she looked around at them all.

"This is just perfect," she said. "After breakfast, we should go see Xavier. I'll get him a plate right now." She skipped toward the breakfast counter—and as Jaysen spotted Marcus heading her way, he stood quickly and followed.

Izzy watched as Jaysen followed Pandora toward the breakfast table. "This is so weird," she murmured, a hint of concern in her voice. "I've never seen him like this… He's never been interested in anyone. Like, ever. And now he's following Pandora around like a lost puppy."

Nick smiled. "Pandora's a sweetheart. She'll look after him."

"The purest person I've ever met," DJ added. "People are drawn to her."

"Unfortunately, that includes people like Marcus," said Nick, nodding toward him.

Marcus was already on his way over to Pandora and Jaysen.

"Well, well, well," Marcus drawled in that arrogant tone that always set Jaysen's teeth on edge. "What did I tell you? You won't get rid of her now. Wait until she starts talking to her rocks. You can hide in my room if you need to escape."

"What's your problem?" Jaysen snapped, his voice low and dangerous.

"Hey now, I'm just trying to look out for you," Marcus said, grinning like it was all a joke. "This one here is fucking crazy. Best get away from her as soon as you can, mate."

"I think you'd best get away from me as soon as you can… mate," Jaysen growled, fists clenching at his sides.

Lincoln saw the tension from across the hall. The way Jaysen's fists trembled was enough—he stood abruptly and stormed over.

Nick, DJ, and Izzy shared a look of unease.

"I have a bad feeling about this," DJ muttered.

"Me too," said Nick, already rising to his feet. The three of them hurried over.

Marcus laughed, not noticing—or not caring—what was heading his way. "Well, you've got your panties in a twist. Or are you just stressed from trying to ditch this slut?"

Jaysen's jaw tightened. Every insult was a spark, and when he saw tears streaking Pandora's cheeks, he ignited.

He lunged forward, slamming his fist into Marcus's face. There was a sickening crack as Marcus's nose broke, and blood poured down over his lips. He stumbled back, reeling.

Lincoln caught up just as Marcus tried to regain his footing. Without a word, he grabbed him by the collar and hauled him clean off the floor.

"Is there a problem here, Jaysen?" Lincoln asked through clenched teeth, not looking away from Marcus's paling face.

Jaysen grinned. He'd seen it—Lincoln hadn't.

"I think Marcus has learned his lesson, Link," he said, his voice low with satisfaction. "Let him go clean up… He's pissed himself."

Lincoln looked down. A dark patch had spread across Marcus's crotch, urine dripping steadily from his shoes into the puddle beneath him.

"FUCK!" Lincoln yelled, throwing Marcus down into the mess and stepping back. "For someone who acts so tough, you sure have a weak fucking bladder."

DJ, Nick, and Izzy arrived just as Marcus scrambled in the muck, trying to get up. Around them, the main hall had fallen silent, all eyes locked on the scene.

Whispers spread quickly as Marcus staggered away, soaked in piss, blood, and grime. He looked around, and saw them all watching. Saw them whispering.

Izzy hugged Pandora. She was still crying.

"Are you okay?" Izzy asked softly.

Pandora hugged her back and shook her head.

"Let's talk about it, hey?" Izzy offered kindly. "Alone."

She shot Jaysen a sharp glare. Pandora nodded again.

"Pandora… I—" Jaysen started, but Izzy shook her head and led Pandora away into the tunnels leading to their rooms.

Nick placed a hand on Jaysen's shoulder as he watched them go. "Don't worry, mate… Pandora's sensitive," he said. "But she's wicked strong—physically and mentally. She'll be okay. Just don't hurt her. She's like a sister to me. And I really don't want to revisit that spoon conversation."

He gave a half-smile. "Now, how about we see Xavier?"

"Mind if I go to our room, darling?" Genevieve asked Connor as they joined the group.

"Of course, my love," Connor replied gently. "I'll catch up with you boys soon."

Jaysen, Lincoln, DJ, and Nick turned toward the infirmary while Connor and Genevieve disappeared into one of the tunnels.

"I've never seen anyone stand up to Marcus like that," Nick said as they walked.

"Yeah, it was epic," DJ grinned.

"Is he always such a cunt?" asked Lincoln.

"Pretty much," DJ shrugged. "But maybe he'll think twice now."

"Or maybe he'll become an even bigger cunt," said Nick.

"Either way, it was fucking great," the twins said in unison.

∞

Xavier was sitting up in bed when the group arrived at the infirmary.

"Finally!" he said, beaming. "Some company!"

He looked between Lincoln and DJ.

"You should have seen it, Xavier," DJ said excitedly, hopping onto the edge of the bed. "Jaysen and Lincoln made Marcus piss himself in the middle of the food hall!"

Lincoln took a seat on the other side. "It was pretty funny," he said with a grin. "He ran away in piss-covered pants."

"What happened?" Xavier asked, laughing despite his confusion.

"Well, get this," Connor said as he walked into the room. "Jaysen's in *love*." He chuckled.

"So Jaysen and Lincoln made Marcus piss himself… because Jaysen's in love?" Xavier blinked, trying to follow.

"Marcus is a cunt," said Nick. "He was being cruel to Pandora, and Jaysen made sure he paid for it."

"Wait… you're in love with Panda?" Xavier asked, his eyes lighting up.

"Panda?" Jaysen asked.

"Yeah, I… uh, accidentally called her Panda. It kinda stuck," Xavier said sheepishly.

"She's so kind," Lincoln said. "I can see why you'd fall for her."

Jaysen rolled his eyes. "Can we please stop talking about my personal life?"

Xavier smiled at him, then looked around. "Where is she?"

"She and Izzy are hanging out," Nick said. "Probably talking about us." He smirked at Jaysen.

Jaysen looked down at the floor. "She's so gentle," he said. "And I'm… not. I hope I didn't scare her off. Marcus just… he just…"

"He deserved it," said Nick. "He doesn't treat many people kindly, but the women here all seem to swoon over him. Pandora turned him down, and he's been cruel to her ever since. He's hurt her before… and if you ask me, he's got a thing for her and can't handle that she doesn't want him."

Jaysen's fists clenched. "Marcus has done this before?… Maybe I should go finish him off."

He glared toward the door.

"Chill out, Jaysen," said Xavier. "If you act this pigheaded around her, you *will* scare her off."

"He just makes me want to explode," Jaysen muttered. "And how he hurt Pandora…"

"It's sweet that you're so protective of her," Nick said. "She deserves someone who'll treat her well. Just try to work on that temper. Like you said—Pandora is gentle. Even if you're standing up for her, aggression makes her shut down."

Jaysen dropped his head. "She's perfect," he said. "And… well… look at me."

"You're great, Jaysen," said Xavier.

"I'm sure she sees that," Nick added. "Just let her spend some time with Izzy. She'll be back to her usual happy self in no time."

"So what happened with The Council?" Jaysen asked.

Xavier smiled nervously. "Well... they wanted to know what happened during the escape. You know... with the guys who tried to kill me. So I told them what happened. Then I told them I would be their Shepherd."

"So you're going to do it, then?" asked Jaysen.

Xavier nodded. "I don't think I have a choice." He shrugged. "So I might as well lean into it."

DJ reached for his hand. "You always have a choice."

Lincoln took the other. "DJ's right... Always."

Xavier looked from Lincoln to DJ, then back to Lincoln. "What's going on here?" he asked. "You two were at each other's throats yesterday... now you're agreeing?"

DJ squeezed his hand. "A truce."

"We don't want you having more worries than you already do," Lincoln added.

"Uh... thanks," Xavier said with a laugh. "I've had just about enough of this room, though. I think it's about time I went for a walk."

"Our rooms are ready," said Connor. "We'll show you to yours after you eat."

Xavier grinned. "I'm starving. Let's eat."

∞

Xavier

"Well... we already ate," said Jaysen.

"But breakfast should still be served. We've got about fifteen minutes left," DJ added.

"Well, we'd better hurry then," Xavier said, his stomach rumbling quietly in agreement.

They made their way through the tunnel, the familiar cold stone pressing in around them. As they neared the food hall, Xavier slowed. He could hear the low murmur of voices inside—casual conversation, clinking cutlery, the scrape of trays—but as they stepped through the archway and into the light, the atmosphere shifted.

The people still lingering over their meals looked up. Forks paused mid-air. Conversations died midsentence. All eyes turned to the group.

Xavier felt it instantly—that shift in energy. The way the air thickened around him. Something unspoken had changed. He stepped closer to Lincoln, instinctively seeking the comfort of numbers, but he was still just barely behind them. For now.

A blur of Auburn darted through the crowd. Aubrey rushed toward them, her eyes wide with excitement.

"Did you make Marcus pee his pants?" she asked Jaysen breathlessly. "I wish I'd seen it. It's all anyone's talking about! That—and the fact we finally have our Shepherd!"

She hadn't noticed Xavier until he stepped out from behind Lincoln's shoulder.

"Hey, Aubrey," Xavier said quietly.

She gasped.

Then came the whispers.

"There he is…"

"That's him…"

"It's The Hidden Heir."

The change was instant. Aubrey's body dropped in a graceful motion, down onto one knee. Her head bowed, fist pressed to her chest. "Sorry— I didn't see you there," she murmured.

The whispers stopped.

And then, as if a silent command had been given, chairs scraped back. One by one, every person in the hall rose to their feet. Xavier could feel their eyes on him, hundreds of them. Waiting. Watching.

Then, just as slowly, they all dropped to one knee.

A sea of bodies bowed before him—rows of fists pressed over hearts, heads lowered, reverent silence filling the space where laughter and noise had been just seconds before.

Xavier froze.

The weight of it hit him all at once. Not just the silence or the sight of so many kneeling bodies—but the meaning behind it. The surrender. The expectation. The responsibility.

"What the fuck is happening?" Lincoln whispered, tension edging his voice.

Xavier looked to DJ, searching for explanation, but DJ only gave a helpless shrug.

Then Aubrey whispered, just loud enough for Xavier to hear. "Don't worry, my lord… I told everyone you hated that old bow. We hope you're okay with this one."

Xavier blinked at her.

My lord.

He let out a sharp breath and stepped forward, placing a hand gently on her shoulder.

"Thank you, Aubrey," he said softly. "But please—will you stop calling me *lord*?"

A faint chuckle rippled through the room, tentative but warm.

"This is… this is going to take a lot of getting used to," Xavier continued. "But I do prefer this bow. It doesn't look so… uncomfortable."

He looked around the room, meeting the eyes of a few brave enough to glance up.

"Now, please… stand up. Go back to your food." he said. Kind, yet commanding.

Chairs shuffled again. People rose slowly, cautiously, but with faint smiles. The tension broke, if only slightly, and the food hall started to breathe again.

Aubrey stood and smiled. "I hope you're well rested?"

"I am—and now I need breakfast," said Xavier.

Aubrey beamed. "I can get that for you. And don't worry, I also told everyone not to bow longer than sixty seconds."

"Don't expect *us* to bow for you," Connor said with a laugh.

"I don't want anyone bowing for me," Xavier replied. "But apparently, I don't have a choice in that either."

DJ placed a hand on Xavier's shoulder. "You're a beacon of hope for so many of these people. I know it's hard, but everyone here… they look up to you now. They see a way to be free. A way to be who they were born to be—following a Shepherd who truly cares for them."

Xavier looked around at the faces watching him. Some whispered behind their hands. Some just smiled whenever he caught their gaze.

"I didn't think of it like that," he said quietly.

"They adore you," DJ said. "We all do."

Lincoln stepped up and placed his hand on Xavier's other shoulder. "Yeah," he said to DJ. "We *all* do."

Xavier shifted slightly between them, caught in their closeness.

I'm not sure if this makes me more or less comfortable than before.

DJ noticed and pulled his hand back. Lincoln didn't.

Aubrey returned, crestfallen. "I'm so sorry. There's nothing left." Her voice cracked under the weight of disappointment. "I let you down."

"That's okay, Aubrey. I can wait," Xavier said with a warm smile, trying to ease her guilt.

But before anyone could respond, a small voice piped up from behind him.

"You can have mine, sir."

Xavier turned.

A young boy stood there, maybe ten years old, with tousled red hair and wide, eager eyes. He held out his plate with both hands.

"I couldn't do that," Xavier said gently. "You need your strength to grow big and strong. But I do appreciate your kindness."

He knelt down and placed a hand on the boy's shoulder. "What's your name?"

"I'm Beau," the boy said proudly.

"It's an honor to meet you, Beau."

Beau's smile grew. "It's an honor to meet you too, sir."

"Please, call me Xav. *Sir* is too formal for me."

Beau looked down at his plate and carefully lifted one of his boiled eggs. "Please take one," he said. "It would mean so much to me."

Xavier reached out. "Thank you, Beau. I'm sure it's going to be the best egg I've ever tasted."

Beau suddenly wrapped his arms around Xavier in a hug.

"Thank you, Xav," he whispered. "I can't wait for you to be The Shepherd!"

Then he ran off toward a nearby table, where a group of children waited, grinning and bouncing in their seats.

"Looks like you've got yourself a fan," Jaysen laughed.

"And it looks like there's going to be a few more," DJ added, nodding toward the kids' table.

Sure enough, one by one, each child picked an egg off their plate and brought it over to Xavier—offering it with a proud smile and a warm hug.

Xavier sat with his friends on a nearby bench, holding a growing pile of boiled eggs and holding down the lump forming in his throat.

"They look up to you," DJ said softly.

Xavier nodded, watching the children as they giggled and waved.

"Where are their parents?" he asked.

"Their mothers are probably still in The Cell," said Nick. "We rescued them from The Farm, same as Pandora. Some of the kids here came from there too. They were getting too old, and no one wanted them anymore. So Nora spent everything she had to buy them and bring them here."

He paused.

"She couldn't get everyone though… It almost broke her."

Xavier's chest ached. "That's horrible," he said, eyes drifting back to the children.

"They grew up here, listening to stories of you," DJ added. "Stories of how one day… The Hidden Heir would come and save us from hiding. From war. So they're probably a bit star-struck."

Xavier looked at DJ, emotion catching in his throat. "I can't let them down," he said, voice trembling. A tear slipped down his cheek.

"You won't," DJ said simply.

Xavier finished the last bite of his breakfast as the men talked around him. The pile of eggs from the children had been overwhelming at first—but somehow, each one had gone down easier than the last.

"So," Connor asked with a grin, "are we like your guild now?"

"Or your royal party?" Jaysen added, nudging Xavier with a smirk.

Lincoln, DJ, and Nick all burst out laughing.

"Right now…" Xavier said, shooting a look at both of them, "you're just being a royal pain in my ass."

He nudged Connor in return.

"Yeah, Jaysen, cut it out," Connor echoed, smirking as he shoved Jaysen lightly.

"What about Pandora?" Jaysen asked, shifting focus. "Did she come with the kids too?"

Nick smiled faintly and shook his head. "She's been here as long as we have."

"Pandora's like our sister," DJ added. "Nora introduced us."

"She left this place to get her," Nick continued. "Went and bought her herself. Pandora still calls her mother. It's sweet."

"Nora's… Pandora's mother?" Jaysen asked, blinking.

"So you're in love with Charlie's granddaughter," Connor said with a chuckle. "I wonder what he would've said about that."

Jaysen rolled his eyes, but there was a flicker of a smile underneath.

"I wish I could've met Charlie," said Nick quietly.

"Me too," DJ agreed. "He's kind of a legend around here."

"A legend?" Connor asked, raising an eyebrow. "What do you mean?"

"Man, Charlie was one of the founders of The Renegades," Nick said.

"He helped build this place," DJ added.

Jaysen, Connor, Lincoln, and Xavier looked around the food hall. It was large—practical—but there was something deeply comforting about the stonework, the carved beams, the handmade tables that had clearly weathered time and use.

"Charlie built this?" Connor asked, tears beginning to well in his eyes.

Jaysen placed a hand gently on his shoulder. "Charlie was a great man."

They were silent for a moment—each letting that truth settle.

Then, a deliberate cough broke through the moment. Thomas approached with his usual quiet weight, hands clasped behind his back, expression unreadable.

"I believe we need to have a few words," he said, looking between Jaysen and Lincoln. "I've just had quite an interesting conversation with Marcus... he has a broken nose."

His tone was firm. Jaysen seemed to brace himself, expecting the lecture. But then—

Thomas sat down at the table, leaned in slightly, and smiled.

"Did it feel as good as his face looked?"

DJ and Nick both snorted, barely stifling their laughter.

Jaysen blinked. "Uh... does no one like this guy or something?"

"No... not really," DJ replied, still grinning. "I mean, put a gun in his hand—he's a killing machine. But that's all he's good for."

"He's a dickhead, but good for the cause," Thomas agreed. "Now—did it feel good?"

"It felt great," Jaysen said, laughing now.

"I'm going to get back to Genevieve," Connor said as he stood. "I'll see you all later."

"Well, actually," Thomas interrupted. "The Council needs to see you all. Midday."

He gave them a nod, then stood and walked off without another word.

"I wonder what it's about," said Nick.

"Probably me," Xavier said, rubbing the back of his neck. "Sorry you guys got dragged into this."

"Don't be," said Jaysen. "I always wanted to be a Renegade when I was a kid."

"I always hoped they'd come and rescue me from my father," Lincoln added quietly.

DJ tilted his head and glanced at Lincoln, his expression softening.

Connor looked at Xavier and smiled. "I've been reunited with my dear Genevieve. Don't you ever be sorry for that."

"I'll see you guys at midday," Connor added, then turned and disappeared down one of the tunnels.

The others lingered, talking in low voices, seated on the benches while the noise of the hall slowly returned around them.

A little while later, Connor returned, looking amused.

"Well," he announced, "the girls are in my room. Said they're having *girl talk*."

Nick chuckled. "Of course they are."

"I suppose they all have that connection with Augmentation Bay… with The Cell," Jaysen said after a pause. "If Pandora came from The Farm, then that's where she was born. Izzy is right… We need to make them pay."

The group all nodded.

"We will," Nick said, his voice low and firm.

Xavier looked between them—at how naturally they fell into sync. Not soldiers. Not rebels. Just people who had found each other in the ashes.

"I need to think," Jaysen said, rising from the bench. "I'll catch up with you all later."

Without waiting for a response, he turned and walked toward the tunnel that led to the waterfall—his steps steady, but heavy.

"Well, I'm full," said Xavier, stretching slightly. "I think I'd like to see my room now."

"I can take you," came a voice from behind.

Xavier jumped.

It was Aubrey.

"Sorry!" she blurted, hands up.

"No, that's okay, Aubrey," Xavier said quickly, feeling the heat rise in his cheeks. "I just forgot you were there."

She smiled, already stepping ahead. "Sure—let's go."

She led the men through a curved tunnel that gradually opened into a quieter corridor, the walls smoothed from years of wear. Lanterns flickered along the stone, casting warm, dancing shadows as they moved. Aubrey stopped in front of one of the heavy timber doors and gestured.

"Here it is," she said, then nodded further down. "And just down there is Lincoln's room."

Lincoln stepped closer. "Right next door to each other," he said with a grin, shooting a quick look at DJ.

"I'm only a few doors down," DJ added. "Remember?"

Then his smile softened. "Anyway, there's something I need to do quickly." He reached out and gently squeezed Xavier's forearm. "I'll see you later… I promise."

Xavier nodded, watching DJ head off down the tunnel alone.

Turning back to the door, Xavier placed a hand on the carved handle and pushed it open.

"Wow," said Connor behind him. "Classy digs… I thought I was special getting a double bed—but look at *that!*"

The room was far more spacious than Xavier expected. A thick, round beige rug held a sturdy wooden table in the center of the space, with five chairs spaced neatly around it. Soft yellow light spilled across the polished stone floor from wall sconces made of curved metal and frosted glass.

But the bed… the bed was something else.

It was enormous. Crafted from thick tree trunks that looked like they'd grown directly out of the floor, their branches curled upward to form a canopy over the mattress. Mossy-green drapes hung loosely from the limbs, and leaves—real or sculpted, Xavier couldn't tell—shimmered gently under the light.

The wardrobe stood tall and wide along the far wall, almost twice the size of the others Xavier had seen. And just beside it, an ornate mirror framed in twisting timber sat mounted on a heavy swivel frame, its surface perfectly clear.

And, of course… the crystals. Pandora's crystals. They were tucked into the corners and nestled along the ledges, just like in every other room.

Xavier stepped inside slowly. "It's way too much," he murmured.

"You deserve the best," Lincoln said quietly as he followed him in.

"Mind if I chill out here for a while?" Connor asked. Before Xavier could answer, he flopped onto the bed and spun so he landed on his back with a soft *thump.*

"By all means," Xavier said with a smirk. "Make yourself at home."

$$\infty$$

Isabelle

"Jaysen isn't a bad guy," Izzy said gently. "He just gets protective of the people he cares about."

"By the sound of it, this Marcus guy deserved it," Genevieve added, shaking her head.

Pandora smiled faintly. "I know. Marcus has always been horrible. It was just so unexpected, and… well…" Her voice faltered. "When I was in The Farm, I saw so much aggression. Every day. It just… it takes me back there."

The tears came again. She didn't try to stop them this time.

Izzy moved closer, instinctively taking her hand.

"You were from The Farm?" she asked softly.

Pandora nodded.

"That means you were born in The Cell," Genevieve murmured, her voice heavy with understanding. She reached out and took Pandora's other hand. Izzy placed her own gently over her stomach, her thumb tracing slow circles over the fabric of her shirt.

The room quieted. No one needed to fill the silence. It was sacred.

"Give Jaysen another chance," Izzy said after a moment. "He's not always like that."

Pandora wiped her eyes and gave a small, fragile smile. "I know he's a good guy. I can see it. It's just that I needed some time to… to center myself. I might go for a walk. I need to be in the forest again. I think Connor wants to come back soon anyway. He seemed like he wanted to be alone with you."

She winked at Genevieve, who laughed softly.

"I don't think I'm ready for that yet," Genevieve said with a smirk. "I'd like to walk again first."

Pandora stood and reached for both of their hands again, squeezing them gently. "You're both stronger than you know," she said. "Don't let anyone make you feel like you aren't."

"We won't," Izzy promised, and Genevieve nodded beside her.

Pandora smiled—genuine, calm—and slipped out the door, her presence leaving a quiet warmth in the room.

Izzy laid back beside Genevieve, resting her head on the pillow. The silence between them wasn't awkward—it was easy now, familiar. Like they'd known each other far longer than they had.

"I'm keeping the baby," Izzy said softly, staring up at the ceiling. "I… I just…"

She trailed off, words too heavy to finish.

Genevieve reached out and took her hand without hesitation. "You don't have to explain anything," she said gently. "After all, look how lovely Pandora is. She came from there. And I think your little one will be just as lovely."

Izzy turned her head, her throat tight. "You really think so?"

Genevieve nodded. "I know so."

Izzy rolled onto her side and hugged her. "Thank you," she whispered. "I didn't know how much I needed this."

"Neither did I," Genevieve replied, brushing a strand of hair behind Izzy's ear. "But I'm glad we have each other."

For a long moment, they just lay there—two women who had been through shared horrors but found comfort in one another. Their connection felt like something unspoken but certain, a quiet thread binding them across trauma and survival.

Eventually, Izzy sat up. "I should get going. If I see Connor, I'll let him know the room's free."

Genevieve smiled sleepily. "Tell him to bring me a cookie if he wants a kiss."

Izzy laughed, the sound genuine and full.

She stood and left the room, her footsteps soft in the corridor. Behind her, Genevieve shifted under the blankets, tucked herself into the warm silence, and smiled to herself before finally drifting off to sleep—no longer alone.

∞

Pandora

Pandora moved quietly through the long tunnel, her fingertips grazing the cool stone walls as the echo of her footsteps faded behind her. Light filtered in ahead—soft, golden, and warm. When she emerged into the clearing, the sound of the waterfall greeted her like a familiar song, steady and calm.

She saw him there.

Jaysen was sitting at the edge of the water, half-dressed and soaked through, his back to her, head tilted slightly as he stared out across the cascading falls. He didn't turn when she approached.

Pandora stepped onto the smooth rock beside him and slowly sat down. They didn't speak. Not at first. The silence wasn't tense. It was gentle. Healing. The rhythm of the water filled the space between them, steady and grounding.

After a while, Jaysen spoke.

"I'm sorry," he said quietly. "I shouldn't have lost control like that." He turned to her then, his eyes soft, searching. "I never wanted to scare you."

He reached out and brushed a strand of her hair away, tucking it carefully behind her ear.

"I only ever want to protect you… to make you happy."

Pandora smiled faintly and placed her hand over his, guiding it to her cheek. She closed her eyes, resting her face in his palm.

"I know," she whispered. "I'm sorry I'm so… sensitive."

A single tear slid down her cheek. Jaysen caught it with his thumb.

"Now you listen to me," he said, his voice firmer but no less kind. His other hand cradled her face, holding her like something precious. "*Never* apologize for being you… because who you are is everything that makes you amazing."

And then he leaned in.

The kiss began as a question—tentative, soft, a breath between them. Pandora tilted her head, her lips meeting his with a vulnerability that made her chest ache. It wasn't hurried. It wasn't about heat or passion.

It was about connection.

His lips moved slowly against hers, reverent, like he didn't want to scare her but couldn't stop needing to be near her. She let out a shaky breath as her fingers curled into his shirt. He smelled like river water and sun. His hand stayed at her jaw, steady and warm, his thumb still pressed gently beneath her cheekbone.

When they finally pulled apart, neither of them spoke.

Pandora leaned into him, letting her head rest against his shoulder. His arm wrapped around her, and she curled into the curve of his chest, her body relaxing fully for the first time that morning.

They stayed like that for a long time. The world slipped away. The breeze danced through the trees, birds called in the distance, and the sun climbed higher into the sky.

Eventually, wrapped in each other, they drifted into sleep—curled beneath the soft light, safe for the first time in what felt like forever.

Jaysen

A shadow moved across Jaysen's face, breaking the warmth of the sun. His eyes opened slowly, still hazy from sleep, and found a figure standing over him.

Evie.

She stood with her hands on her hips, lips pressed into a thin line.

"So *this* is why we had to come find you?" she asked, her tone biting. "Because you decided to have a romantic nap by the waterfall?"

Jaysen sat up, blinking against the light as he rubbed the sleep from his eyes. Beside him, Pandora stirred, lifting herself up with a startled gasp.

"Sorry!" she blurted. "It's my fault."

"Not now, Pandora," Evie snapped, cutting her off without a glance. "We don't have time for this. Xavier's agreed to be our Shepherd. We need to train—to plan."

Pandora flinched. Jaysen's jaw tensed.

"Calm down, Evie," came a voice from behind her. Ethan. "As *you* said—we don't have time for this."

Pandora shrank beneath the weight of Evie's voice. Jaysen instinctively moved closer and wrapped an arm around her shoulders, trying to shield her from the blow of it. She leaned into him without a word.

"I'm sorry," Jaysen muttered, though every syllable was forced through clenched teeth. "Let's just get this over and done with."

Evie scoffed, casting him a glare. "If only it were as easy as getting it over and done with."

"I'm sure you've heard *that* from a lot of men, Evie," Ethan said, grinning as he sidestepped her with ease. "Now, come on—let's get to it already."

Jaysen stood and reached down, helping Pandora to her feet. Her hand lingered in his as she brushed herself off, eyes still lowered.

At the edge of the clearing, three figures appeared—Xavier, Lincoln, and Connor stepping into the light.

"It's beautiful out here," Xavier said, his gaze sweeping over the sunlit clearing and shimmering cascade of the falls.

"Yes. It's great," Evie said flatly. "Now, let's go to the chambers."

But Xavier didn't move. He stepped forward instead, walked to the center of the clearing, and dropped down cross-legged on the grass.

"I think I'd rather stay out here," he said. "No point wasting another hour walking back."

"I think that's a lovely idea," Nora said softly as she followed, taking a seat beside him.

Evie looked like she might argue—but then thought better of it. Her lips pressed tighter, and she stayed silent.

"I should go," Pandora whispered beside Jaysen.

He turned to her quickly, tightening his grip around her fingers.

"Please… stay," he said. "I need you here."

She hesitated only a moment longer—then sat beside him again.

Their fingers remained laced together, anchored in the grass, as the group began to gather around them in the clearing.

Nora smiled gently at them, and both Jaysen and Pandora flushed with color.

"Now," she said, her voice shifting into something more formal, "we have two crucial matters to discuss here."

She turned to Xavier. "The first is our new Shepherd. I can't tell you how grateful and proud I am of your decision."

Xavier gave a small nod.

"We begin training at first light tomorrow. Right here should work perfectly." She looked around the clearing. "Ethan will meet you at sunrise for weapons training. Then it's on to Thomas for hand-to-hand combat. After that, Zara will take you for foraging. The following day, you'll hunt with Lance. Then camouflage techniques with Evie, followed by strategy and leadership planning with me."

She looked to the others. Every one of them nodded without hesitation. It wasn't even a decision. It was instinct. Muscle memory. Like soldiers responding to a command.

Then Nora's voice shifted—gentler now, more cautious.

"As you all know," she said, her gaze sweeping across the circle, "we extracted Jaysen and Connor under the information that The Architect wanted them. What we didn't know—was *why*."

"The voice!" Lincoln blurted out suddenly. All eyes turned to him. "I heard someone. Inside the roof, during the raid. They said The Architect had information about Connor's brother."

"My brother is dead," Connor said sharply. The words dropped like steel.

Nora's voice softened. "Well… actually." She looked directly at him. "Connor… that's what we need to talk to you about. We've discovered why The Architect wanted you."

Connor's hands curled into fists. His jaw tightened.

"Cypher Industries has made advances in the medical field—quiet ones. Ones the public never knew about. Ones *we* never knew about."

"No…" Connor whispered, already shaking his head.

Nora's eyes filled with something deep—regret, maybe. "When you were sent to Augmentation Bay… the Emerald Enforcers took Sammy to Donovan."

Connor's breath hitched. "What did the CEO of Cypher want with my little brother?"

"They wanted to test a cure for his condition," Nora said softly. "And it worked."

The world seemed to stop.

Connor's jaw dropped. His entire body tensed as tears began to swell in his eyes. "My little brother's alive?" His voice cracked. "No… he can't be… That's not possible. Sammy *couldn't* be cured."

"He could," said Nora. "And he was. But… that's not all they tested on him."

Connor's voice was a growl now. "What did they do to Sammy?" he asked through clenched teeth. "Where is he?"

"I'll explain," Nora said quickly. "But there's a lot to explain. Please—just listen."

Connor gave a single, broken nod.

"When our people are taken to Cypher Industries," Nora continued, "they aren't the same when they come back. Their memories—who they were, the people they loved—are overwritten. Replaced with synthetic ones. At first, they were randomized. Just fragments—details stitched together from a small database."

Jaysen felt the ground shift beneath him.

"No…" Connor murmured again. "This can't be happening."

"But over time," Nora said, her voice dipping lower, "we started noticing patterns. Recurring memories. Memories like a day going fishing with their dad at sunset on the beach, and getting ice cream after because…"

Jaysen's voice rose before he could stop it. "A hook got stuck in my foot, and Father had to cut it out…"

Nora's eyes met his.

"And the ice cream after," she said gently.

"With rainbow sprinkles on top," Jaysen whispered. "Down at the park by the duck pond."

Connor was staring at him now.

"The rowboat in the river," Nora said next.

"That I fell out of," Jaysen said quietly. "And Mother had to pull me back in."

Nora nodded slowly, her eyes moving between the two of them.

"Sammy was the first," she said. "The first person they used the technology on. Jaysen…" Her voice trembled. "You're him. You're Sammy."

Silence.

Jaysen turned to Connor. Their eyes locked, and everything inside him reeled—like he was falling, fast.

"No…" Connor gasped. "No, it can't be. S—Sammy? Is it really you?"

Jaysen's voice was barely more than breath. "I… I don't remember."

"Can we get his memories back?" Connor turned to Nora desperately, tears now flowing freely. "Please—tell me we can bring them back."

"I'm sorry," Nora said, her own voice breaking as a single tear slipped down her cheek. "We haven't figured out how. But we're not giving up."

Jaysen couldn't speak. That same bitter cold he'd felt his first day in Augmentation Bay crawled back through his chest—paralyzing and hollow.

Pandora pulled him into her arms. He hadn't realized how badly he needed to be held until he was there, surrounded by her warmth, her strength.

"I think we should give you all some time," Nora said gently. "If you need anything, please—don't hesitate."

The Council began to move, quiet and respectful, their footfalls retreating into the tunnel.

Jaysen, Connor, Xavier, Lincoln, and Pandora remained behind—stunned into stillness.

Xavier was the first to rise. He crossed the clearing and placed a steady hand on Jaysen's shoulder.

"If you ever need to talk to someone who understands," he said, voice low, "I'm here."

Jaysen nodded faintly.

"I'm sure you need time. Lincoln and I will give you that… but we won't go far."

He leaned down and wrapped them both in a hug—Jaysen and Pandora, who still hadn't let go.

"Look after him for me, will you?" Xavier whispered to her.

Pandora nodded.

Lincoln followed Xavier toward the tunnel and back into the burrow.

Connor sat beside Jaysen, eyes glassy and fists clenched in his lap.

"I'll give you two some privacy," Pandora said softly, easing her arms away from Jaysen. He caught her hand.

"I'll just go for a swim," she whispered, kissing his cheek. "I won't go far."

Jaysen let go slowly, his hand lingering in the air after she turned away.

She dove into the water, disappearing beneath the surface.

The silence that remained was thicker than before. And in it, Jaysen and Connor sat—brothers, strangers, tethered by something neither of them could fully understand.

∞

Connor

Jaysen looked up at him, lips parting like he wanted to speak—but no sound came out.

And Connor couldn't take it.

"Sammy."

The name left his mouth like a prayer, broken and breathless. His chest seized, and in the next instant, he was on his knees in front of Jaysen, arms wrapped tightly around him.

The dam inside him burst.

He held his brother like he might vanish again, sobs tearing through him with years of grief, guilt, and hope he never let himself feel until now. His tears soaked into Jaysen's shirt. His fingers clutched at him like he was a lifeline.

"How… how couldn't I have recognized you?" Connor choked out through the storm of it. "Fuck, I'm so sorry."

Jaysen returned the hug, slower, more cautious, like he was still trying to understand what was happening. "I just… it's hard to believe," he murmured.

Connor tried to pull himself together, wiping his nose with the sleeve of his shirt. He sat back just enough to look into Jaysen's face—those eyes, that crooked smile. Familiar. And not. "You heard Nora," he said, voice still thick. "They're going to find a way to get your memories back."

"They're going to *try*," Jaysen said quietly. "But if they can't… I'll never really be Sammy. I'll always be…" His voice caught. "Well. Jaysen."

Connor stared at him. At the boy—no, the man—who had walked beside him through everything, and somehow, been his brother all along.

Then he smiled. Tear-streaked and shaking, but genuine.

"You're alive," he whispered. "Whether you're Jaysen or Sammy… that's enough for me."

He reached for him again, holding him tight, not out of desperation this time, but from something deeper.

Love.

"This must be so hard for you," Connor said as he held him. "You're still my best mate, Jaysen… but now you're this whole other person. My little brother. Someone you don't even know."

He paused, then pulled back just enough to look him in the eyes.

"But know this—" his voice steadied. "I'll always be here for you, little brother. And I'll protect you this time. I promise."

They sat together in silence for a while. The kind of silence that said more than words could. The kind that came when something broken had finally begun to mend.

Connor looked out over the lagoon.

Pandora was gliding through the water, her movements graceful and serene. Light danced across the surface around her. Jaysen followed his gaze.

"You should join her," Connor said, nudging him gently in the ribs. "She's a great person."

Jaysen gave a quiet smile and rose to his feet. Without a word, he walked to the edge and slipped into the water to meet her.

Connor watched him—one of the two people he cared about more than anything in this world. He watched as Jaysen laughed, watched as Pandora reached for him in the water.

My little brother, he thought, as his chest swelled and a lump rose in his throat. *He's been right under my nose this whole time… Just like Genevieve.*

He closed his eyes for a long moment.

I can't lose them again. I won't. Not ever.

∞

The sun had dipped beneath the trees, casting long shadows across the clearing when Lincoln and Xavier emerged from the tunnel. Lincoln carried Genevieve in his arms, and Izzy followed close behind, her arms crossed tightly over her chest.

"Lincoln says you and Jaysen have something to tell us," Genevieve said as he gently set her down beside Connor.

"Sorry," Xavier added with a small shrug. "They overheard us talking… and we thought it was better to bring them here."

"What's going on?" Izzy asked, arms still folded. Her foot tapped the ground in a rapid rhythm, her brows knit with frustration.

Connor shifted uncomfortably. "Jaysen's coming in now," he said, stalling. "Let's wait until he's here."

Jaysen stepped into the clearing. His hair was damp, his shirt clinging slightly to his skin from the swim. His expression changed the moment his eyes locked with Izzy's.

"What are you doing here? You should be resting."

"Why don't you tell me?" she snapped. "We heard Lincoln say something about Sammy… and then we were walking in silence for an hour to find you two. I have no fucking clue why I'm here, and no one will tell me anything."

Her voice rose, tight with emotion, and her foot stomped against the earth.

"Let's all sit down," Pandora said softly, reaching for Izzy's hand. "The grass is so soft here."

She knelt, gently guiding Izzy with her. "See?" she said, placing Izzy's hand on the ground.

Izzy's tension wavered. She looked at Pandora, then up at Jaysen, her voice quieter now. "Please, Jayse. Tell me what's going on."

Jaysen sank down slowly onto the grass. He looked to Connor first, then back to Izzy and Genevieve.

"It's a long story," he said. "Just… please don't say anything until we've finished."

So they told them.

He and Connor shared everything—the experiments at Cypher Industries, the memory replacement, the truth about Sammy being alive. About how Jaysen wasn't just a friend or a survivor. He was something else entirely.

Jaysen leaned forward and took her hands in his.

"Izzy…" He took a breath. "I… I'm Sammy."

Silence fell like a stone.

Genevieve gasped softly. Her eyes darted to Connor, who nodded with tear-filled eyes. "He is," he said. "He's my little brother."

Genevieve wrapped her arms around Connor. holding him tightly. Then she looked back at Izzy and Jaysen.

But Izzy didn't move. She didn't blink. She just stared at Jaysen like she'd never seen him before.

Then, without a word, she stood and turned.

"Izzy—" Jaysen started, rising to follow her.

But Pandora gently reached for his hand, stopping him.

"She's going to need some time," she said, her voice soft but certain.

Jaysen hesitated, eyes fixed on the tunnel where Izzy had vanished—then he slowly sat back down.

The clearing felt quieter now. Heavier.

And they all sat in it—silent, hurting, hopeful.

∞

Isabelle

Run.

That was all Izzy could think as she sprinted through the tunnel, her breath ragged, her chest tight, her legs aching with every step.

Run.

The walls seemed to close in around her, the sound of her own footfalls thundering in her ears. She didn't know where she was going—she just knew she had to get away.

Away from Jaysen.

From Sammy.

From whoever he was.

She barely registered when she reached Nick's door. Her knuckles hit it before she could think. When it opened, everything broke.

"Whoa, whoa, whoa—what's going on?" Nick asked as he caught sight of her. Tears streaked down her face. Her hair was damp with sweat. Her chest heaved as if she hadn't stopped running since the moment the truth hit her.

Nick didn't hesitate. He put his arm around her and gently pulled her inside, guiding her to the edge of his bed like she might fall apart if he let go.

"Here, sit down."

She collapsed onto the mattress, her hands trembling.

Nick grabbed a bottle of water from his bedside table, unscrewed the cap, and handed it to her. She took it with shaking fingers, nodding in silent thanks, though it took her a few moments before she even remembered how to drink.

He sat beside her, close but not crowding. Letting her breathe. Letting her cry.

And she did.

For a long time, she cried into her hands while Nick rubbed her back in slow, steady circles.

Finally, her breathing calmed enough for her to speak.

"It's my brother," she whispered, her voice hoarse. "He's… He's not my brother."

Nick's brow furrowed. "What do you mean?"

She looked at him, eyes red and raw. "He's not Jaysen. He's Sammy. Connor's brother. Not mine."

She told him everything.

About the experiments. About Cypher Industries. About the fake memories, and the fishing trips, and the rowboats, and the rainbow sprinkles. How it all unraveled in the clearing like someone had pulled a single thread, and now her whole world was coming undone.

And Nick listened. He didn't interrupt. Not once.

When she finished, her voice barely more than a whisper, he wrapped his arms around her and held her tight.

"I'm so sorry," he said. "But just because he's Sammy, it doesn't mean he's not your brother anymore."

Izzy pressed her face into his shoulder.

"You grew up together," Nick continued. "That's real, Izzy. No matter what some company did to his brain, no one can take those years from you. And I'm sure—*so sure*—he still loves you."

Izzy clung to him, tears pouring freely again now. Not the sharp kind she'd shed in the tunnel, but the slow, quiet kind that came from somewhere deeper.

Nick didn't say anything else. He just held her.

Eventually, her body grew heavier in his arms. Her breathing slowed. And then she was asleep—exhausted from the shock, the crying, the grief.

He shifted carefully, lifting her into his arms with surprising ease. He laid her down on the bed, covering her gently with his blanket. She stirred slightly, then settled into the warmth.

Nick pulled a thin foam mattress out from beneath the bed, unrolled it on the floor, and lay down beside her. He stared at the ceiling for a long time, listening to the soft sound of her breathing.

And when he finally closed his eyes, he prayed to Zoti—for the first time in years—that somehow, this wouldn't break her.

∞

Jaysen

Genevieve stared at him, her eyes wide with wonder and disbelief. "I can't believe it," she said, her voice barely above a whisper as tears welled in her eyes. "Sammy…"

Jaysen froze.

There was something in the way she said his name—like it had been waiting in her throat for years, afraid to come out until now.

She reached out her hand to him. Hesitant. Trembling.

He paused, unsure if he could take another emotional wave crashing over him.

But then he moved. Slowly, he crossed the space between them and placed his hand in hers.

She pulled him in gently and wrapped her arms around him. Her warmth, her familiarity, unsettled something deep inside him—something that both comforted and hurt.

"I should have known as soon as I saw you," she said as she cupped his face in her palms. Her eyes searched his with such intensity, he had to look away for a second—but she held him there.

"Your eyes are still the same," she whispered, her thumbs brushing over his cheeks. "Just like your mother's."

She swept a few strands of hair from his forehead, the gesture slow and tender.

"You'd always be arguing with her about growing your hair," she added, letting out a soft laugh through the tears that now rolled down her cheeks. "Of course she never let you. And you'd come crying to me every time."

She ran her fingers through the longer wisps framing his face.

"I'd tell you, 'Wait until you're all grown up. Then you can have it as long as you want.'"

Her voice broke.

Genevieve pulled him into a tight hug, her body trembling against his. Jaysen let her, still unsure if it was okay to feel anything at all.

"I know you don't remember me," she whispered into his ear. "But I can't forget you. So I'll remember enough for the both of us, Sammy."

Jaysen pulled back just slightly, offering a soft smile. But it felt fragile—like it would fall apart if anyone touched it.

"Sweetie," Connor said gently. "Because he can't remember being Sammy…" He looked at Jaysen with a gentle, steady smile. "We should still call him Jaysen."

Genevieve's face turned red. "I'm sorry," she said, quickly wiping her tears. "I should have known that."

Jaysen leaned in and hugged her again.

"It's okay," he murmured, a tear escaping his own eye. "This is going to be hard for all of us."

And it was.

But it was also something else.

Through the rest of the evening, they stayed by the water. Genevieve and Connor shared stories—fragmented memories of a little boy with scraped knees and big dreams. Of arguments about bedtime. Of bad hiding spots and laughter that echoed through narrow hallways. They spoke about Sammy like he was still there. Like he hadn't been erased and reprogrammed into someone new.

Jaysen listened.

And he laughed with them sometimes. He cried, too. But through it all, he felt like a guest at his own funeral—hearing about a life he should have lived, one he'd never gotten the chance to know.

The moon rose high above them, casting silver across the still water. The breeze was cool now, brushing through the grass like a whispered memory.

Jaysen stared at his reflection in the rippling surface—this person who was somehow both Jaysen and Sammy, and neither at all.

"I want my memories," he said suddenly. His voice cracked, but he didn't care. "My real ones."

He blinked, and more tears came—tears he hadn't even known were waiting.

"They stole my childhood," he whispered. "And I want it back."

Pandora moved closer, her hand slipping into his. She didn't say anything.

She didn't have to.

∞

One Month Later

"You've become quite the hunter," said Thomas, arms crossed, a rare glint of approval in his eyes as Lincoln and Jaysen hauled the mountain boar through the narrow corridor leading back into the burrow.

Jaysen's hands were bloodstained, the weight of the kill dragging heavily between them. But he was grinning.

"Lance is a brilliant teacher," he replied.

"He's being modest," Lincoln added, nodding toward Jaysen. "You should've seen it—one shot, straight through the eye."

Thomas gave a low whistle. "Looks like it's mountain boar stew tonight."

At that, Victor appeared, already rolling up his sleeves. "The kids and I will get onto it now."

He whistled, and almost instantly, a gaggle of children came running out of one of the side tunnels—wide-eyed and barefoot, all of them chattering at once.

"Whoa!" they gasped in unison when they saw the massive boar.

"You're the best, Jaysen!" Beau shouted, practically vibrating with excitement. "Uncle Victor's finally gonna teach us how to make the stew!"

Jaysen laughed as the kids swarmed around Victor like little ducklings, each trying to help in their own enthusiastic, mostly unhelpful way. One tried to lift the leg. Two others grabbed a hoof and promptly lost control of it, tumbling into each other and giggling.

He shook his head, smiling.

They were safe. Fed. Happy.

That alone made everything worth it.

"There's no training today," Thomas said suddenly, his tone shifting. "The Council has an urgent matter to attend to. Use this day to rest. You've all been doing well."

Jaysen's smile faltered. He exchanged a glance with Lincoln.

"What matter?" Lincoln asked.

"That's confidential," Thomas said simply. "Now, if you'll excuse me, I'm needed in The Council Chambers."

He turned and walked away.

Jaysen watched him go, unease already crawling up his spine.

"We've never been given a day off," he muttered to Lincoln. "Not even when we got that stomach bug…"

"Something big is happening," Lincoln agreed.

They didn't waste time. Together, they headed down toward the pool chamber to find Connor.

He was in the water with Genevieve, gently supporting her as she glided through the shallow end. Her new wheelchair rested neatly against the stone wall nearby.

"Sorry to interrupt physio," Jaysen called out as he approached the edge. "Do you have a minute?"

Connor swam with her to the side. "That's okay," he said, helping her balance as she reached for the edge.

"How's it going?" Lincoln asked, crouching nearby.

"Really well," Genevieve said, her voice breathless but proud. She pushed away from the wall for a few strokes, then floated back to Connor.

"She's amazing," Connor said, beaming. His eyes didn't leave her.

"That's great, Genevieve," said Jaysen.

She smiled. "Thank you."

"What's up?" Connor asked, lifting her from the water and carrying her easily back to the chair.

Jaysen lowered his voice. "Something's going on. And The Council won't tell us anything."

Connor's brow arched. "What makes you think something's going on?"

"They canceled training," Lincoln said. "Told us to get some rest."

Connor's smirk disappeared instantly. "They never cancel training. Not even when we got—"

"Got that stomach bug, yes," Lincoln cut in, his voice quick. "Now let's find Xavier and figure out what the hell's happening."

Connor turned to Genevieve. "Where would you like to go, darling?"

"They'll be serving breakfast soon," she said. "I'll just wait in the hall for the others."

Connor kissed her forehead before joining the others.

When they arrived at the food hall, it was already filling with the smell of porridge and spice. Xavier was finishing his plate at a corner table, surrounded by a half-dozen kids who were peppering him with questions between bites of food.

"Sorry, kids," Jaysen said, approaching. "I need Xavier's help with something."

"Aww," they chorused with theatrical disappointment, but they obeyed and shuffled back to their table.

Xavier looked up, mouth full of oats. "Why aren't you at training?" he asked, eyes wide. "We're going to be so late!"

"Training's canceled," Jaysen said flatly.

Xavier froze. Then he choked.

"What?" he coughed, thumping his chest. "They never cancel—not even when we—"

"When we got that stomach bug," Lincoln said again, this time even faster. "Yeah. We know."

Xavier wiped his mouth and stood. "Something's off."

Connor leaned down to Genevieve again. "Are you okay here?"

"Yes, sweetie," she said, giving him a soft kiss on the cheek. "Now go."

Jaysen paused for just a moment, scanning the room before following the others. The food hall was loud, filled with laughter and chatter—but under that, something was shifting.

The Council was hiding something.

And whatever it was, they wanted to find out.

∞

It was quiet when Jaysen, Connor, Lincoln, and Xavier reached The Council Chambers.

Too quiet.

They crept down the dim corridor, their footsteps barely making a sound against the stone floor. Jaysen's heart thudded in his chest—not from fear, exactly, but from something close. Something colder. Like they were about to discover something they shouldn't.

They reached the door and paused.

Still nothing.

No voices. No movement. No light from within.

Lincoln stepped forward, glancing back at the others before pushing the door open.

He stepped inside, scanned the room, then let out a quiet grunt. "No one's here. We took too long."

"Well, they can't be far," Xavier said, frowning. "Can they?"

"Thomas only said they had an urgent matter to attend to," Jaysen replied. "That's all. For all we know, they've left the burrow completely."

Xavier sighed and rubbed his temple. "Well… I say we go relax. We have the day off. I'm sure everything is fine."

But Jaysen didn't feel fine.

Still, they left the empty chamber behind and returned to the food hall, the silence following them like a shadow.

When they sat down, Genevieve looked up from her tea. "What happened?"

"Nothing," Connor said, shaking his head. "No one was there."

Izzy, Pandora, Aubrey, Nick, and DJ sat nearby, all looking confused.

"Why aren't you at training?" DJ asked. "Ethan is gonna be so pissed."

"It's canceled," Xavier replied. "The Council said they had an urgent matter to attend to… and now they're just gone."

Nick and DJ exchanged a look—one of those twin-glances that held entire conversations.

Everyone at the table quieted.

"For The Council to not tell *anyone*…" the twins said together, their eyes scanning the group.

"Something's happening," Nick said slowly.

"Something big," DJ added.

"Why didn't they say anything to me?" Aubrey asked, her voice barely audible. She looked more hurt than suspicious, her gaze cast toward the now-empty corridor.

After breakfast, Xavier, Lincoln, and DJ left for the lookout point, with Aubrey trailing behind them, trying to keep pace but remaining a few steps back.

Jaysen watched them go, then turned to Nick.

"What's going on with them?" he asked quietly.

Nick rubbed the back of his neck. "I'm still trying to figure it out myself," he admitted. "I think DJ and Lincoln are both… seeing Xavier. But not each other. Nothing official. It's messy."

Jaysen raised an eyebrow. "And they're just okay with that?"

Nick sighed. "They're *trying* to be. But it's not going well. Every time I see them together, they're sizing each other up. Always trying to one-up the other. I just… I don't want my brother getting hurt. Xavier needs to decide already."

"I'm sure they'll figure it out," Pandora said calmly. "How they share their love is none of our business."

Jaysen smiled at her. "You're right."

"I know," Pandora said with a wink.

Nick looked like he was about to argue, but Izzy stood abruptly and turned to him.

"Let's go for a walk, hey, Nick?" she said. "I was thinking we could go for a swim."

She didn't wait for a reply, just started toward the tunnel that led to the pool.

Nick glanced at Jaysen, offering a small, understanding smile. "Give her a bit more time," he said quietly, then followed after her.

Pandora squeezed Jaysen's hand. "Don't worry," she said sweetly. "I'm sure she'll be ready to talk about it soon."

Jaysen nodded, though his chest still felt tight.

"Let's go to the waterfall," she continued, her smile gentle. "A swim sounds perfect for your day off."

"Mind if we come too?" Genevieve asked. She leaned into Connor. "There's something I want to show you."

Pandora grinned and nodded. "Of course."

As they rose from the table and made their way toward the tunnel, Jaysen glanced back toward the corridor that led to The Council Chambers.

He couldn't shake the feeling.

Something big was happening.

And it was only a matter of time before they found out what.

∞

Connor

When Jaysen, Pandora, Connor, and Genevieve reached the falls, the morning light had just begun to break over the mountains. Sunlight streamed down in warm beams, catching the mist and throwing silver across the surface of the lagoon. The water shimmered like liquid glass, and the sound of the cascading falls filled the air with a peaceful, familiar rhythm.

"It's always so beautiful here," Genevieve said, her voice soft with awe.

"Only when we're not dragging ourselves here for training," Connor replied with a laugh.

They stripped down to their underwear, the air still carrying a faint chill from the night. Connor rolled Genevieve's chair to the edge of the water, as he'd done so many times before.

Instinctively, he moved to lift her.

But her hand stopped him.

"No," she breathed, smiling up at him. There was something in her expression—something determined and gentle and quietly radiant. "This is what I wanted to show you."

Connor blinked.

Genevieve gripped his hand. She didn't let go.

And then, slowly, she rose from her chair.

Connor reached for her waist, startled, ready to catch her.

But she shook her head. "I only need your hand," she whispered, steady and sure.

He stilled.

And held on.

One step. Then another. And another.

Before he even realized what was happening, they were waist-deep in the water, standing together. The sunlight wrapped around her like a second skin. She was trembling, yes—but she was standing. Walking.

Free.

Overcome, Connor laughed—half in disbelief, half in joy—and lifted her by the waist, spinning her gently through the water. She let out a small squeal, laughing with him, her arms around his neck.

"You're absolutely amazing," he said, grinning through the tears already welling in his eyes. "When did you—how—I mean, I'm so happy, but… how did you come so far without me knowing?"

Genevieve giggled, breathless. "Pandora, Izzy, Nick, and DJ have been helping me while you've been off training," she said just as Jaysen and Pandora came wading out to meet them.

"You did so well, Genevieve!" Pandora beamed, her voice filled with pride.

"Thank you, Pandora," Connor said, still holding Genevieve close.

"Don't forget to thank the others," Pandora added with a knowing smile. "They helped too… but Genevieve did all the hard work. She's so strong."

Connor looked down at the woman in his arms and hugged her tighter. "You don't have to tell me that."

"I still need the chair most of the time," Genevieve said, her breath catching slightly. "But hopefully not for much longer."

Connor laughed, the sound breaking as tears ran freely down his cheeks. "I don't think it will be," he said. "Soon you'll be running laps around us all."

He kissed her—gently, gratefully—and Jaysen pulled Pandora into a hug nearby.

"Thank you," Jaysen whispered. "You've made them both so happy."

Pandora smiled and rested her head on his shoulder. "So have you."

The group spent the rest of the day in the lagoon, swimming beneath the falls and laughing until their cheeks hurt. The tension that had hovered over the morning was gone—washed away, for now, by sunlight and water and the sound of joy echoing through the trees.

∞

Jaysen

"You two go on without us," Jaysen said as the sun reached the peak of the sky, casting diamonds across the lagoon's surface.

"Yeah," Pandora added quickly, grinning. "We're still full from breakfast."

Connor raised an eyebrow as he helped Genevieve into her chair. "Full from breakfast… right. Enjoy your alone time!"

He smirked as he and Genevieve disappeared into the tunnel.

Jaysen turned toward the water—just in time to catch Pandora wrapping herself around him. Arms behind his neck, legs coiled around his waist, her weight suspended in the lagoon. Then her lips found his, sudden and demanding. It wasn't just a kiss. It was a promise.

A tease. A challenge.

She tasted like sunlight and morning and something more.

When she pulled away, her lips swollen and parted, he could barely breathe.

"You really are wonderful," he whispered, heart pounding against her chest.

Pandora smiled mischievously, nuzzling his nose. "Come find me," she whispered, then splashed him and vanished beneath the surface in a swirl of bubbles.

Dazed, he turned, searching.

She reappeared far across the lagoon, standing on the rocks near the waterfall. And then she was gone again, slipping behind the curtain of water like a memory.

He swam after her, heart racing. He pulled himself onto the rocks, water streaming from his skin, and stepped into the roar of the falls.

But she wasn't there.

"Pandora?" he called, his voice almost lost in the sound.

Then—her voice. "I found something. Come see."

She peeked out from behind a cluster of rocks, her eyes glowing. Then disappeared again.

Jaysen followed.

The narrow gap in the cliffside opened into a cavern glowing with the delicate shimmer of fireflies. Thousands of them. Their golden lights hovered midair like dust suspended in time.

Pandora stood barefoot at the center, her skin glowing in the soft light, her finger to her lips.

"If we're too loud, their lights will go out," she whispered.

Jaysen stepped inside slowly, reverently.

"I've never seen anything like this," he whispered back.

A soft blanket was spread out on the cave floor, with a small bottle of lavender oil and two wildflower sprigs placed with delicate intention.

"When did you do this?"

"Yesterday," she whispered. "I wanted to surprise you."

She spun slowly, arms stretched wide, fireflies dancing around her like she was part of the air itself. They clung to her hair, glided across her skin, gathered at her fingertips like they belonged to her.

She doesn't look like she belongs in this world, Jaysen thought. *She looks like she made it.*

"I can't believe I've been outside so many times," she whispered as she slowed, "and never found this place until then."

She lay on the blanket, the fireflies hovering above her like stars drawn to her warmth.

Jaysen joined her, lying beside her in silence. Their shoulders touched. Their breathing synced. Time stopped.

"They're like tiny stars in the night sky," he murmured. "I'm glad we can share it. It's magical… Just like you."

He leaned in and kissed her cheek.

Pandora turned, meeting him in a kiss that was slower this time. Deeper.

Her hand traced the line of his jaw, then slid down his chest. Jaysen's fingers grazed her ribs, her waist, her hip—memorizing every line, every curve. She shifted closer, her body molding against his like she had always belonged there.

He kissed her again—her mouth, her neck, the hollow beneath her collarbone. Her breath caught in her throat as his lips found the edge of her shoulder. Her hands were in his hair, pulling him closer, grounding him.

They undressed slowly, stripping away more than fabric.

Stripping away fear. Stripping away what the world had done to them.

When Pandora pressed her chest to his, skin against skin, he let out a slow breath.

There was no rush.

No need to impress. No need to prove anything.

Just presence.

Every touch was careful. Every sigh was answered. His fingers moved across her like poetry—like he was trying to learn a language only she could speak. Her hips responded in time with his, her breath becoming his rhythm.

She gasped when he kissed the inside of her thigh.

He stilled when she whispered his name.

It was soft, sacred.

And when they came together, the fireflies didn't vanish—they pulsed brighter, like they were alive with the energy between them. The cave glowed like a cathedral, and for a moment, Jaysen didn't feel broken. Didn't feel like a ghost of someone else's life.

He felt like a man who was *wanted*.

Like he *belonged*.

Afterward, they stayed wrapped in each other's arms. No words. Just touch. Just heartbeats.

Jaysen brushed his fingers over her spine, slow and reverent, as her head rested against his chest.

"I've never felt more at home," he whispered.

Pandora smiled against his skin and pulled the blanket tighter around them both.

And above them, the fireflies shimmered on—unflickering and golden—like stars that had decided to stay a little longer.

∞

Nick

"You should talk to Jaysen soon," Nick said quietly as he and Izzy sat at the edge of the pool, their legs drifting in the still water.

The stone around them was cool and damp, lit only by the soft flicker of lanterns mounted along the wall. Their reflections rippled faintly in the dark water. The air smelled of minerals and something earthy—old, familiar.

"I will," Izzy murmured. "Soon… I just don't know how to start. Or what to say."

Nick glanced at her. She gripped her knees tightly, her voice smaller than usual.

"I know it's hard," he said. "But imagine how hard it is for him."

Izzy didn't respond right away. Her gaze stayed fixed on the water.

"I'm horrible, aren't I?" she whispered.

Nick shook his head. "No, you're not. You've got a lot going on yourself. Stuff like this… it's hard for everyone involved."

She nodded slowly, her lips pressed together. The silence stretched for a beat, broken only by the soft echo of dripping water from the far side of the cave.

"I'll talk to him tomorrow," she said. "After his training. He deserves a day off… from everything."

Nick hesitated. The moment hung there, fragile and uncertain. He wasn't sure if this was the right time—but he also knew he couldn't keep holding it in.

"Izzy…" he started, his voice a little rough. "I need to tell you something."

She turned slightly toward him, brow furrowing. "What's up? Is everything okay?"

Nick offered a nervous smile, rubbing the back of his neck. "Yeah. It's just that—"

He trailed off. *Come on. Just say it.*

Izzy tilted her head, waiting patiently. "Whatever it is," she said softly, "you can tell me, Nick. You're one of my best friends."

That made it harder.

He looked down at the rippling water, then back up at her.

"That's the thing," he said. "I don't want to be friends."

She blinked.

Nick reached out and took her hands in his.

"I want to be *more*."

Izzy's breath caught. Her face tightened.

"Nick…" she said carefully. "I'm having a baby."

"I know."

He released one of her hands and gently placed his palm on the small rise of her belly.

"And I want to be there with you through it all," he said. "I'll help you raise him. Just like he was my own. I don't care who the father is. I want to be with you, Isabelle. I want to be yours."

The lanternlight danced faintly in her eyes as she stared at him.

Then she stood abruptly, stepping back from the pool's edge.

"I… I need some time," she said, her voice shaky.

She didn't wait for a reply. She grabbed her towel and wrapped it tightly around herself, then scooped up her clothes from the stone floor. Without looking back, she hurried toward the tunnel.

Nick didn't move.

He watched her go, her retreating footsteps echoing off the walls.

Then he looked back at the water—still and dark—and let the silence settle around him, swallowing the words he could no longer take back.

∞

Isabelle

When she got back to her room, all she wanted to do was sleep.

When Izzy woke, her stomach ached with hunger.

She blinked at the dark ceiling above her, still groggy, her body sore from restless dreams. The cave was quiet—eerily so. Everyone else was sleeping, or gone. She reached for her dressing gown, pulled it around her, and padded barefoot down the winding corridor.

The soft glow of lanterns lit the way, casting her shadow against the rough stone walls. The further she walked, the louder the quiet became.

When she reached the food hall, it was empty.

Except for one figure.

An old man sat alone on a bench in the center of the room, his back straight, his hands resting on the table. He was staring up at the roof like it was speaking to him—like something lived in the silence above.

Izzy hesitated at the entrance.

There was something familiar in his stillness. Something that tugged gently at her chest.

She made her way over.

"Excuse me, sir… you don't know what time it is, do you?"

The man chuckled softly. His voice was warm and dry, like earth in the sun.

"Sir… I like you already," he said, smiling. "I'd say it's about three."

He nodded toward the seat across from him. "What brings you out here at such a late hour, little lady?"

Izzy sighed and lowered herself onto the bench, folding her arms on the table and resting her chin on her hands.

"I slept through dinner," she said. "I was hungry, but I didn't realize it was so late."

The man tilted his head slightly, watching her. "You seem troubled," he said gently. "What's on your mind?"

Izzy hesitated. Then smiled faintly. "I wouldn't even know where to begin."

He reached out and placed his hand on hers. His skin was warm, his touch light but steady.

"Why don't you start with how you're feeling?"

She blinked at him—something about the way he said it made her chest tighten. She took a breath.

"I just..." Her voice wavered. "I feel like everyone around me is destined for all these great things. And I'm just… here. Stuck. I'm only nineteen, and… I'm having a baby."

A tear slipped down her cheek before she could stop it.

The old man didn't flinch. He simply gave her hand a gentle squeeze.

"You're destined for great things too," he said. "We all are. Everyone here has a greater role to play than they know—even your baby."

Izzy's shoulders trembled. "But what if we fail?" she whispered. "What if it's too hard?"

"Destiny isn't always easy," he said, his voice soft but steady. "But it isn't always hard, either. Surround yourself with the right people, and you'll always find your way."

Izzy stared at him, her heart slowing. The ache inside her eased—just slightly—but enough.

"Thank you," she whispered.

She heard voices behind her—echoes from one of the tunnels. She turned.

Jaysen and Pandora were entering the hall, hands linked, hair still wet from the waterfall.

They spotted her instantly.

Jaysen's smile faltered when he saw she wasn't alone.

And then the old man turned.

Jaysen stopped. His face went white.

He dropped to his knees.

"Charlie," he gasped, his voice barely more than breath.

The old man—Charlie—stood slowly from the bench, his eyes never leaving Jaysen.

"Hi, son."

He crossed the space between them and crouched beside Jaysen, placing a hand gently on his shoulder.

"Sorry I'm late," he said with a quiet smile. "I got a bit of a bump on the head."

Izzy watched as Jaysen trembled beneath Charlie's touch, his hand covering his mouth, his eyes filled with disbelief—and something deeper.

Hope.

The moment stretched out, tender and impossible and completely real.

And in that moment, Isabelle understood something she hadn't before.

No one was ever truly lost here.

Not forever.

To be continued…

Epilogue

∞

Donovan Blakewell

Donovan Blakewell's office was silent—thick with the kind of quiet that came with absolute control. Not the absence of sound, but the presence of expectation.

Outside the towering windows, the city of Dennison shimmered beneath a sheen of rain. Neon lights flickered off the glass, casting his reflection across the room—sharp suit, steel-gray eyes, and a jaw clenched so tight it could've cracked bone.

He didn't look like a man with patience.

Because he wasn't.

He leaned back in his chair, one hand gripping the polished armrest while the other held a slim black phone to his ear. On the desk before him—a slab of obsidian imported from the old world—his other hand twisted a gleaming pocketknife, the tip digging into the grain like it belonged there.

"Tell me everything, Zygote," he snarled into the phone. "And you'd better not hold anything back…"

His voice dropped to a hiss.

"I will find out."

The moment he stopped speaking, he pressed the knife deeper into the surface—an old habit. He liked leaving scars. Even on his furniture.

Zygote's voice buzzed in his ear—nervous, fidgeting, deflecting. Typical. Always hiding behind technicalities and jargon, hoping data sheets and protocols could excuse failure.

Donovan wasn't interested in excuses.

He ground his teeth as he listened, jaw tightening with each sentence.

"You incompetent little freak," he muttered under his breath. "You never deserved that lab."

The knife made a slow, deliberate circle into the obsidian.

"I can't believe you were so stupid," he snapped suddenly. "All of you."

He stood now, voice rising as he moved to the edge of the desk, looming over it like a predator about to strike.

"That Renegade was our last chance at getting the incubators back. And you fucked it up!"

He slammed the base of the phone against the table—once. Hard. Not enough to break it, just enough to make a point.

The line went quiet for a moment on Zygote's end. Blakewell could almost smell the panic bleeding through.

They're losing control at that prison. Maybe I need to step in…

Control was the only thing Donovan had ever cared about.

He stopped pacing, turned back toward the desk, and leaned in.

"I don't care how you fix it," he growled. "I want those incubators recovered. And I want the fugitives neutralized."

A pause.

His lip curled.

"And if you fail again… I'll pull your eyes out and give them to someone who knows how to use them."

He ended the call.

The silence returned.

But this time, it was heavy with the promise of consequence.

Donovan glanced at the knife and exhaled slowly, his pulse steady, his fury measured. His eyes then flicked to that *disgusting extra digit*— a side effect from a test gone wrong. One performed on his mother when she was pregnant.

Maybe I should just cut it off already.

Cypher Industries wasn't built on mercy.

It was built on the bones of those who thought they could disappoint him.

∞

Charlie

The silence was the worst part.

It followed him through The Light Mile like a ghost—quiet, sterile, patient. As if even the walls were waiting to see him finally break.

But Charlie didn't give them that.

He wouldn't.

Dr. Zygote's words rang in his head as the Enforcer led him away. "This moon, you're going to die." Spoken like a promise. Or a sentence. Charlie wasn't sure which.

And maybe it was true.

Maybe this was the end.

But he'd walked through worse already. Bled through worse. And he hadn't done all that—hadn't kept Connor alive, hadn't helped Jaysen learn the ropes, hadn't survived the Harvest platform and the slicing hands of the organ market—just to let The Pits have him.

The white of the first room was blinding. A mockery of cleanliness. Another illusion of order in a place built on blood and flesh.

Then came the stairs.

He didn't need to be told to go down.

The stench hit first—rot, shit, damp earth. The smell of death trying to climb its way out of the floor. His stomach churned, but he kept moving.

Don't give them the satisfaction.

When the final door opened, Charlie stepped into a stone basin of nightmares.

Thirty-foot walls. Grandstands above, ringed with fences and shadows. Spotlights overhead, waiting to turn men into meat.

He was led into the men's cage.

It was crowded, but quiet.

Not the kind of quiet you could mistake for peace.

No—this quiet was full of knowing. Of resignation. Of fear too old to shake.

As Charlie made his way to the back, a hand grabbed his shoulder.

He turned. For a second, his heart jumped.

"Barry," he breathed.

"What are you doing here, Charlie?" the man whispered. "We all thought you were dead."

Charlie shook his hand. "Nah, mate. It'll take more than a riot to kill me. I was just in a little coma." He shrugged, trying to downplay it.

He tried to smile. It felt hollow.

"What is this place?"

Barry looked around, jaw tight. "The fighting pits. They make us fight to the death. The rich fucks bet on us like dogs."

"You're kidding."

"I wish I were." Barry nodded toward the women's cage across the way. "They've got their own matches too. No one's safe down here."

Charlie's gut clenched.

"And why are you here?"

Barry gave him a look. "This is where they dump the cageys who didn't sell. Or the ones whose organs are going bad. Old ones. Sick ones." His voice dropped. "Ones like me."

Charlie scanned the cage again. He saw the pattern now—gray in the hair, tremble in the hands, sunken cheeks, scars.

And then he saw the others.

Younger. Healthier. Hungry.

"They're the ones we'll have to watch," Barry said grimly, nodding toward a tall, broad-shouldered man sitting alone.

Before Charlie could answer, the lights blazed to life.

The pit lit up in stages—harsh beams slicing down like judgment.

Voices erupted from the stands.

Eager. Cruel.

Charlie felt the heat from them. The thirst.

Then The Warden appeared.

He walked the perimeter like a man choosing pigs for slaughter. And when he left, the Enforcers moved in.

"The Warden has chosen the second round of champions!" a voice boomed through the speakers. The crowd roared.

An Enforcer pointed to Charlie and Barry. "You two. Out."

They stepped forward.

In the center of the pit, they were handed blood-stained vests.

"Five," Charlie read aloud.

Barry unfolded his. "Two."

They both turned to find the others who wore the matching numbers.

Charlie found his across the pit—a man built like a freight train, all shoulders and sneer. Their eyes met. The man smirked.

Charlie looked away.

Barry was staring at a kid.

Strawberry-haired. Pale. Couldn't have been older than thirteen. Maybe younger.

"Look how scared he looks…" Barry whispered. "I can't kill a kid, Charlie."

Charlie placed a hand on his shoulder.

"I don't think we'll get a choice."

He turned back to the crowd—saw the twisted hunger in the way they watched.

"They came here for blood. They're going to get it."

The Enforcers shoved the first pair forward—both young, both strong. Swords and shields were handed to them. The crowd began to cheer.

"At least *they've* got a fair fight," Barry murmured.

Charlie's jaw tightened.

"None of this is fair."

And somewhere inside him, a small fire started to burn.

This wasn't the end.

It wasn't going to be.

He had one more fight left.

And if he could help it—he'd make sure someone else walked out alive.

"Thirty seconds left to make your bets!" the voice boomed from above.

The chatter in the grandstands grew louder, more manic, filled with laughter, whistles, and the clink of glasses. Charlie could barely hear himself think over the pounding in his chest.

Barry stood beside him, silent, watching the two men now pacing in the center of the pit—each gripping a shield in one hand, a dulled sword in the other.

Then the bell rang.

It echoed like a gunshot.

The two men charged, shields raised, swords aimed.

But there was no grace in it. No skill. Just desperation.

They clashed in the dirt, blades clanging, shoulders slamming. Within seconds, both men dropped their shields—too heavy, too cumbersome in this frantic mess—and swung wildly, yelling as their swords met flesh.

Blood spattered across the pit floor.

The crowd roared.

One man screamed as the other hacked into his thigh. He stumbled, and the second fighter pounced—slicing across his chest, then ramming his shoulder into him to knock him down.

But it wasn't enough.

The man on the ground grabbed a rock—something jagged and sharp—and smashed it into the other's face. Teeth flew. A scream tore through the air.

The crowd howled with delight.

The standing man recovered first. He kicked the other aside, then drove his blade into the downed man's stomach and tore it sideways.

A sickening *rip* echoed.

And then came the sound of wet slaps as he pulled out coils of intestine with his bare hands.

The bloodied man howled triumphantly as he held the slick, steaming organs to the crowd like a prize.

Charlie turned his head. He couldn't watch.

Barry didn't look away.

A tear slipped down his cheek.

He grabbed Charlie's arms with shaking hands.

"How am I supposed to do this?" he asked, voice cracking.

Charlie pulled him into a hug, holding him tight.

"I don't know," he whispered. "I'm sorry."

Another tear rolled down Charlie's cheek.

"You're a good man, Barry. And you've been a great friend."

Before either of them could say more, two Enforcers stepped forward and seized them both.

Barry was yanked toward the boy.

The red-haired kid—maybe thirteen—was trembling, his knuckles white on the handle of the sword he'd just been handed.

Charlie watched as they were positioned twenty feet apart in the center of the pit. The kid's shield shook in his hands. His mouth was twitching, trying not to cry.

Barry turned back, locking eyes with Charlie one last time.

Charlie gave him a nod, then placed a fist over his heart.

Barry nodded back, eyes glassy.

The loudspeaker crackled.

"Thirty seconds left to make your bets!" it announced again, almost cheerful. "A classic underdog match—one old, one young. Place your wagers!"

The crowd erupted into laughter and applause.

Charlie stood motionless in the cage, clutching the bars, throat clenched tight.

The bell rang.

Barry didn't move.

The crowd booed.

"It seems our champions need a bit of… motivation," the voice boomed.

Above, Enforcers raised their guns—real ones—aiming straight at both of them.

Barry turned, offering Charlie a weak smile—small, sad, but full of peace.

Then he stepped forward.

The boy flinched.

Barry dropped his sword.

Then his shield.

Gasps spread through the grandstands.

"It's okay, kid," Barry said softly, loud enough for only those nearby to hear. "It's my time. Just… make it quick."

He dropped to his knees.

The boy's eyes flooded with tears. His sword shook violently in his hand.

"I'm so sorry," he whispered.

Then, with both hands, he drove the blade into Barry's chest.

It pierced his heart.

Barry exhaled sharply—but didn't cry out.

His eyes locked with Charlie's one last time.

Then he fell.

The boy stumbled back, yanked the sword free, and dropped it with a clatter.

Silence.

Then, from above:

"Well, *that* was anti-climactic," the announcer spat. "Have a drink, on the house! And let it be known—if something like *that* happens again…"

His voice turned cold.

"…we *will* hang them."

The crowd roared.

Charlie couldn't move.

He watched as the boy was dragged away, tears streaming down his face, blood drying on his hands.

Another tear slipped down Charlie's cheek.

He didn't wipe it away.

Charlie shuddered as Barry's body was dragged from the pit, limp and heavy, leaving a slick trail of blood in the dirt behind him.

A good man until the end.

The boy who had killed him stood frozen at the cage entrance, wide-eyed, blood still dripping from his shaking hands. His skin had gone pale beneath the grime.

The Enforcers shoved him back into the cage.

He stumbled forward, dazed, and the others looked away.

Charlie didn't.

"Come here, kid," he said softly.

He reached out, pulled the boy in, and draped an arm around his trembling shoulders.

The boy didn't resist.

Charlie guided him to the back of the cage and sat down against the cold stone wall. The boy sank down beside him without a word.

The fighting continued. Somewhere in the pit, more blood was being spilled for sport. The crowd was cheering again. Spotlights cut across the dirt floor, but none of it reached this corner.

Still, the voice echoed through the speakers.

"Thirty seconds left to make your bets…"

Charlie shut his eyes. *Ignore it all. Just for a moment.*

He looked at the boy. His whole body was shaking, his chest jerking with shallow breaths. His face was wet—tears, sweat, blood. All of it.

"What's your name?" Charlie asked gently.

The boy shrugged.

"I don't have one," he said. "I was in The Farm. They just called me GM-7."

Charlie's stomach turned.

"No one wanted me," the boy went on, voice flat. "Then I found our mothers… our *real* mothers."

Charlie blinked.

He sat up straighter. "What do you mean?"

GM-7 hugged his knees to his chest, still not meeting Charlie's gaze.

"They're all sleeping. But they won't wake up. There's… there's so many of them in this big room called *The Cell.*"

He paused. Swallowed hard.

"They're having babies. Over and over. And then this place—" he gestured vaguely toward the pit. *To Augmentation Bay.* "—they take us away. Sell us to rich people. That's when we get names. Until then, it's just letters and numbers."

Charlie felt the breath catch in his throat.

"I tried to escape when I found out," the boy said. "But I got caught. And now I know too much. So… here I am."

Charlie stared at him, jaw slowly lowering.

That's what they're doing in there.

The words clung to the inside of his skull like oil.

He looked at the boy again—so small, so broken—and he felt something in his chest twist tight.

No one had protected this kid.

Nobody had even given him a name.

Charlie reached out and ran a hand over the boy's matted hair.

"You're not just a number," he said quietly. "Not to me."

GM-7 looked up at him, startled.

"You need a name," Charlie said. "So you're not just someone they made."

The boy blinked. His lips parted.

Charlie's eyes misted.

"I'm gonna call you Red," he said, nodding toward the boy's hair. "Something real. Something yours."

Red nodded slowly. A whisper of something passed across his face— maybe the beginning of a smile. Maybe disbelief.

Charlie pulled him in closer.

"You're not alone anymore," he said.

The crowd roared again in the distance.

But here, in the corner of the cage, there was a quiet too deep for any of it to reach.

Charlie didn't flinch when the figure emerged from the shadows near the cage wall—he recognized the posture before the face. Thomas.

He moved fast and low, eyes sharp, lips tight.

"Charlie," he whispered, gripping the bars. "We don't have much time."

Charlie looked at Red, curled against his side, still trembling.

"Get up," Charlie whispered, helping him to his feet. "It's okay, kid."

He placed a hand on the boy's shoulder, steadying him.

"We're getting out of here."

Thomas's eyes flicked to Red.

"We don't have time for—"

"He's coming with us," Charlie snapped. "Or I don't go."

Thomas stared for a moment, then gave a sharp nod. "Fine. But move."

He slid aside a loose panel near the edge of the cage, revealing a narrow, shadowed gap behind the wall. One by one, they slipped through.

The air changed instantly—cooler, stale. Stone pressed in on all sides. The roar of the pit faded behind them, the cheering crowd replaced by the scuffle of feet and the distant groan of old pipes.

They kept moving, twisting through the forgotten veins of Augmentation Bay, where secrets were kept in silence and stone.

When they reached a dead end, Thomas pressed his ear to the wall, listening. After a breath, he tugged on a rusted pipe.

The wall creaked open.

They stepped through into a cold, lightless chamber—and the stench struck like a punch.

Charlie gagged.

It wasn't rot alone. It was something older. Something butchered and forgotten.

When his eyes adjusted, he stopped breathing altogether.

Bodies. Hanging from hooks overhead. Limbs missing. Faces covered in dried blood and surgical mesh. Torso after torso, strung up like meat slabs.

Red gasped beside him.

Charlie grabbed his hand.

"Close your eyes, kid," he whispered. "I'll lead you through."

The boy obeyed, squeezing his eyes shut as Charlie shielded him with one arm and guided him carefully around the lifeless forms.

Charlie recognized them.

Not all, but enough.

Men he'd shared meals with. Slept beside. Cageys who'd vanished after The Harvest, assumed to be long dead—or long sold.

They never left.

They'd been brought here.

For this.

At the far end, Thomas opened another hidden door.

They slipped through into another tunnel—this one tighter, colder. The walls were wet to the touch, streaked with black mold and old blood.

No one spoke.

They walked in single file, Charlie pressing Red close as they wound deeper into the underbelly of the bay. The ceiling dropped low. At times, they had to duck beneath beams and crawl.

The smell shifted again—less death, more rot. Sewage. Old waste.

Eventually, the passage opened near a crumbling stairwell.

A narrow, ancient stone spiral led downward into total darkness.

Charlie paused at the edge, coughing as the air hit his throat.

"Smells like an old camp toilet," he muttered, covering his nose with his sleeve.

Before Thomas could respond, a shriek pierced the dark.

"RACHEL!"

They froze.

Red clutched Charlie's arm tighter. "What was that?"

Charlie raised a finger to his lips.

They moved slowly now—each step deliberate, breath held tight.

The next voice was broken. Wild.

"The Architect… I can't stop him… I can't do it…"

They reached the bottom of the stairs.

Torchlight flickered from the next corridor.

And then, in that swaying glow, a face emerged from the dark.

Sunken eyes. Blood-crusted cheeks. A mouth moving with words too shattered to hold meaning.

Thank you to everyone who helped turn this dream into a reality…

∞

Imogen, Elwood, Thomas, Charlotte, Matthew, Josh, Archer, Hunter, Joan, Glen, Steve, Tracey, Rebecca, Niki, Tahnia, Telique, Gabbie, Jason, Nivvie, Ash

A very special thank you to G.R. Thomas—author of Child of Fear & Fire. You inspired me to follow my dreams of becoming an author and helped me find my path. I will be forever grateful.
~ Sarah Scream.

A very special thank you to directors, Wes Craven & John Carpenter. I grew up watching your movies. They have given me a love for the horror genre and inspired my thoughts while writing this book.
~ Sherree Scream.